PANIC

THE ULTIMATE EDITION

JEFF ABBOTT

www.atombooks.net

ATOM

First published in Great Britain in 2011 by Atom

Copyright © 2011 by Jeff Abbott

A CIP catalogue record for this book
is available from the British Library.

ISBN 978-1-907410-98-7

Typeset in Melior by M Rules
Printed and bound in Great Britain by
Clays Ltd, St Ives plc

Atom
An imprint of
Little, Brown Book Group
100 Victoria Embankment
London EC4Y 0DY

An Hachette UK Company
www.hachette.co.uk

www.atombooks.net

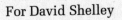
For David Shelley

FRIDAY MARCH 11

1

'Evan, what are you working on?' Mrs Crabtree's voice jerked Evan Casher out of his long stare at the computer screen. His fingers went to the keys on the school computer that would make his Internet browser vanish, but it was too late. Mrs Crabtree was leaning over his shoulder, and he could feel the gaze of the rest of study hall falling on him.

'Um, homework.'

She looked at the website, which read, 'FilmzKool,' in bold red letters at the top, and said, 'This doesn't appear to be your history paper.'

'No, ma'am.'

'What is that?' She pointed at the film running on his screen, its sound muted.

'A short movie a kid wants to post on my site. He's from Japan. It's about his dad being a professional skydiver. He jumped out a plane with his dad and filmed it.'

She watched the images unfold, a boy and father plummeting through the sky, their mouths working silent words. 'How can you understand what's being said? It's not subtitled.'

'The pictures should be enough to tell me if the story's good.'

Mrs Crabtree sighed. 'Evan. Study hall, weirdly enough, is actually for studying. Get back to your assignment.'

'Yes, ma'am,' Evan said. 'Sorry.'

Mrs Crabtree gave him a stern stare to show she meant business and walked back to her desk.

'Busted,' Carrie said, sitting across from him, working

through her math homework, trying hard not to smile, and failing.

'Yes. For the moment.'

'Running that film in class – not clever. And you're normally all about the clever.'

'I thought I would just see if some of the movies I'm expecting have been uploaded yet.' Evan smiled back at her as she made her face very serious and zoomed through a trigonometry problem. He opened up the computer's word processor, plugged in his homework flash drive, and opened his history-paper file: 'In 1969, something happened. Blah, blah, blah.'

Not really a great start.

'Kids,' Mrs Crabtree said, 'I've got to run up to the principal's office for a few. Keep doing your work.' The study hall, about fifteen kids in total, glanced up at her. 'Evan' – she pointed a finger – 'stay off your website.'

'Yes, ma'am.'

At another table, Evan saw Dezz Germaine smiling at him. He was a new kid, sixteen like Evan and Carrie, with hair dyed snow-white and cut into a rough buzz cut. He had a vaguely European accent; Evan had heard rumors that he'd moved to Austin from Germany, or France, or Sweden. The best gossip was, he'd been kicked out of every creatively oriented school in Western Europe and his father had shipped him off to relatives here in Austin. Dezz smiled a lot at Evan, and Evan couldn't decide if he was being friendly or mocking. Carrie said the guy probably just wanted a friend; Evan thought Dezz was odd. He put his fingers back on the keyboard and started typing out his paper, just trying to outline it at first, get every idea down, the way he did his short films.

Thirty seconds later, everything changed.

The phone's ringtone startled Evan; he wasn't supposed to have his cell on in study hall, but he'd forgotten to turn it off. Carrie, sitting across from him, racing through her math homework, laughed. 'Web-surfing and a phone. You're lucky Crabtree's not here.'

He fumbled for the phone, was about to power it off when he saw it was his mom calling. It couldn't be against the rules to talk to his own mom, right?

Carrie pointed at the vibrating cellphone. 'You better answer it before Crabtree comes back.'

Evan answered. 'Hello.'

His mother said, 'Evan, I need you to come home. Right now.' She spoke in a low whisper.

'What's the matter?'

'Not over the phone. I'll explain when you get here.'

'Uh, okay, but you're not supposed to call me, phone the school office and they get—'

'Evan, I don't want to talk to the school office.' Her voice went tight, like wire. 'Don't tell anyone you're leaving. Just come home.'

Evan thought he must be dreaming. He turned away from the other tables and whispered into the phone, 'You want me to *cut school*?'

'It's your study-hall hour, right?'

'Yeah.'

'Just get up and walk out. Don't tell anyone you're leaving school. Just leave. If anyone tries to stop you' – and here she took a breath – 'then I want you to run. Get home. Don't let anyone see you.'

This did not sound like his mother. 'Are you serious?'

'Yes!' She lowered her voice. 'Do as I say, Evan. No

argument. Don't even tell Carrie.' A weird kink in his
mother's voice. Something so not right.

'Is this like one of those *Punk'd*-style shows? Is this a joke
for TV?' he whispered.

'No, Evan, this is life. Not everything is filmed.' She
sounded odd, like she might be about to … cry.

He got up and went to the corner of the study hall, away
from the other students. 'Is Dad all right?' he asked softly.
His father, a computer consultant, had left Austin three days
ago for a job in Australia. He designed databases for big companies and governments. Australia. Long flights. Evan had a
sudden vision of a plane scattered across Sydney Harbour,
ripped metal, smoke rising, and fear clutched his throat.
'What's happened?'

'I just need you here now, okay?' Calm but insistent.
'Evan' – he heard his mother take another steadying breath –
'please.'

The naked, almost frightening neediness – a tone he had
never heard in his mother's voice – made her sound like a
stranger to him. 'Um, okay.'

'Hurry, Evan. As fast as you can.'

'Okay.' He fought down a rising panic.

'Thank you for not asking questions right now,' she
said. 'I love you and I'll see you soon and explain everything.'

He turned off the phone and glanced at the clock. Twenty
more minutes of study hall and then five minutes to get to
trigonometry. Mrs Crabtree was still gone at the principal's
office. He could be home before he was missed, and then
Mom could call the school so he didn't get into trouble. But
this wasn't like her. Not at all.

He felt a tightness in his chest. What was wrong?

Carrie moved a lock of her honey-blonde hair out of her eye as he sat back down. Evan was about to pick up his backpack and pull his flash drive from the school computer when he remembered his mother's words: *Just get up and walk out.*

Carrie was staring at him. 'Is something wrong?'

'No, of course not. My mom's clueless, you know that. She got confused about if I was working at the film lab today.' Evan stood.

'Where are you going?' she asked.

'Bathroom. My stomach hurts.' Better for Carrie to think that he wasn't feeling well if he didn't return in a few minutes. 'Will you tell Mrs Crabtree I'll be right back?'

'Evan' – Carrie leaned forward and he felt his heart shift in his chest – 'are you okay?'

Don't tell anyone. Why would his mom say something like that? It made no sense. 'I'll be back in a minute.'

He left his books and his backpack on the table and the flash drive in the computer. He glanced over at Dezz, who was watching him, tapping a pencil against his cheek, then glancing at Carrie, now sitting alone. Dezz liked Carrie; Evan was sure of it. He kept looking at her all the time.

Evan walked down the empty hallway to the boys' room. He passed hallways, heard the teachers lecturing about Jane Austen and calculus and cellular division. Penrod was a small school, but a good one, strong in the arts, and he liked it here. He didn't want to get kicked out.

The bathroom was deserted. He hesitated for a moment. He had never cut school before, ever, but the tone in his mom's voice urged him onward. Her orders had been so unexpected, so unlike her, that there must be a good reason for it.

He hoped she was being honest about his dad. What if something *had* happened to him? Maybe if Dad was ... dead ... his mom couldn't bear coming to the school and telling him in front of all his friends. Because he would lose it, totally, if his dad was ... Don't think that, Evan told himself.

The windows were above the stalls. He took two steps toward them and the door behind him opened.

He turned and saw Dezz Germaine walking into the boys' room. Dezz didn't exactly walk; it was more of a loping strut. He was taller and thicker-built than Evan, his short hair white as sugar, spiked.

'Hey, Evan,' he said.

'Hey.'

'You all right?'

Okay, this was weird. 'No, not feeling well.'

'You sure that's all there is, Evan?'

'Excuse me?'

'You're just not setting a good example to all of us in study hall. Getting caught working on your little film projects. Taking phone calls. Leaving without permission.'

'I don't need a pass to go to the bathroom. I mean, I guess you would know that if you'd been a student here longer than a week.'

Dezz gave an icy smile. 'Sure. Fine. Just wanted to be sure you were all right.'

Evan fake-swallowed hard. 'Now, if you'll excuse me, I think I'm gonna go barf.'

He went inside the stall and shut the door, then leaned over the toilet like he thought he might be sick into it.

Hurry and leave, he thought. What is your problem, weird kid?

The door to the boys' room opened and closed and he heard the sound of Dezz's footsteps walking down the hallway.

Evan climbed onto the toilet and opened the window. He was a tall, wiry kid and it was easy to wriggle through the window feet first; he then kept his grip and dropped to the grass. Penrod's bike rack stood at the side of the school. He unlocked his bike, jumped on, and pedaled fast for home.

The morning sky hung gray like a faraway mist and promised rain; springtime in Austin often meant storms. He got round the corner of the street, then stopped and tried his father's cellphone. No answer, not even voicemail picking up. But his dad's phone might not connect in Australia. He jumped on his iPhone to a news site: no disasters reported in Australia. He put the plane-crash scenario out of his mind.

He clicked on his email, shot off a message to his dad saying, *Call me ASAP*, then downloaded his awaiting emails, in case his father had sent him a note. His inbox held only an email from an old friend in Los Angeles and a pile of music files along with a couple of his mother's latest digital photos, all sent by her late last night. Mom, whose musical tastes were a lot younger than her years, thrived on obscure bands and tunes, and she'd found three great songs for his film projects from unknown bands that might not charge him a fee, though he couldn't tell his friends that his mother found songs for the movies he wanted to make, even if she had great musical taste.

He bore down and pedaled hard.

Ten minutes later, he jumped off his bike, leaving it on the grass of the front yard, and raced to the door.

8   JEFF ABBOTT

2

The front door was locked.

He opened it with his key and stepped inside the tiled entryway. 'Mom?' he called out.

No answer. That was weird. He had expected her to meet him at the front door, given her tone.

He walked toward the back of the house, toward the kitchen. 'Mom, if I get in trouble for this, you got to tell the school that you told me to—'

Evan turned the corner and saw his mother lying dead on the kitchen floor.

He froze. He opened his mouth but did not scream. The world around him went thick with the sound of his blood pounding in his throat, in his temples.

He took two stumbling steps toward her. Her face was purpled, her tongue distended, and the kitchen air held the unmistakable stink of death. He saw a silver gleam of wire wrapped around her throat. An empty kitchen-table chair stood next to her, as though she might have been sitting on it before she died.

Evan made a low moan in his throat, knelt by his mother, brushed a tangle of her blonde hair from her face. Her eyes were wide open and swollen, unseeing.

'Oh, Mom.' He put his fingers over her lips: stillness. Her skin was still warm.

'Mom! Mom!' His voice shattered in grief and horror. It wasn't happening; it couldn't be happening; he'd *just* talked to her . . .

Evan stood. A wave of dizziness buckled his legs. The

police. He had to call the police. He staggered round her body to the kitchen counter, where the remains of her breakfast still sat: a coffee cup with a lipsticked rim, a plate dotted with plum-jelly drips and a scattering of muffin crumbs. Evan reached for the phone with a shaking hand.

Metal hammered the back of his head. He dropped to his knees, his teeth biting into his tongue, the tang of blood a bright taste in his mouth. The world started to crumple into darkness.

A gun pressed against the back of his head; the perfect circle of the barrel was cool in his hair. He tried to jerk away, but the gun cracked hard against his temple.

'Be still, boy,' a voice said, 'or you're dead.' A man's voice, raspy and cold. A foot pressed against his throat, pushing his cheek to the floor. His mother's dead face stared into his eyes, half a meter away.

'I have a question for you, Evan, and I want you to be a good boy and answer it.'

'You killed my mom!' The foot on his throat stamped down hard and Evan couldn't speak, couldn't breathe.

'I don't want to hear anything else from you except answers to my questions.'

He heard another set of footsteps on the stairs, coming from his room. Someone else was entering the kitchen. Two killers. How could he get away from two of them? He wasn't going to get away. They were going to kill him, same as his mom. He was going to die, right here in the kitchen where he ate breakfast and he and his parents made cookies and he'd messed up the last Christmas turkey trying to carve it just like Dad did. Right here. Die. Now.

Then his laptop's powering-up chime sounded, louder than his own ragged breathing. Then long seconds of

silence, fingers tapping on the keyboard, then the grind of
the hard drive.

The foot eased slightly on his throat. 'Your computer. Do
you back it up other than on to your extra hard drive?'

His computer? His mother lay dead and they were asking
him about his computer? This just could not be happening
to him.

'No, just to the hard drive.' He closed his eyes; he
couldn't bear to look into Mom's face any longer.

'Already erased, boss, and the woman's computer, too,' he
heard the other voice say. Another man, with a slightly
European accent.

'Please . . . why? Why?' Evan heard himself ask.

No answer, but the foot lifted off his throat, and a strong
hand grasped his hair, the gun hard against the back of his
head. Now his face was above his mother's and a hard cry
broke out from his chest.

'My mom, you killed my mom—'

'Hush now. It'll all be over soon.' The raspy voice of the
boss sounded almost soothing.

Evan wanted to twist round, see the man's face, but he
couldn't. The man released Evan's hair. Then a loop of rope
went over his head.

A noose. It tightened, digging savagely into Evan's
throat.

'Got it,' the European voice said. Then the whisper of
fingers on the keyboard. 'All gone off the laptop.'

'You do it, please,' the boss's voice said. 'I can't bear to
kill him. I can't bear to watch. I'll finish searching
upstairs.'

He heard footsteps on the stairs. Then steel cracked
against Evan's head. Black circles exploded before his eyes,

edging out his mother's blank, dead stare. He fell into darkness.

Then Evan awoke. Dying.

He couldn't breathe because the rope scorched his throat and his feet danced in empty space. A plastic trash bag covered his head, making the world milky-gray and indistinct. He grabbed at the rope, choked out a cry as the noose strangled him.

'You took breathing for granted, didn't you, now, sunshine?' The European voice, cold and mocking.

Evan kicked his feet. The countertop *had* to be there to take his weight, to save him. He scissored his legs with what strength he had left because there was nothing else he could do.

'Kick twice if it hurts bad, little boy,' the European voice said. 'I'm curious.'

A blast filled his world. Shattering glass. Gunfire. A second of silence. Then the European man screaming in pain.

The rope swung. Evan attempted to inch his fingers under the choking, killing cord. Then another rattle of gunfire boomed huge in his ears and he fell, hit the floor, plaster and splintered wood dusting him. The loose length of the gunshot-torn rope landed across his face.

Evan tried to breathe. Nothing. Nothing. Breathing was a forgotten skill, a trick that he no longer knew. Then his chest hitched with sweet air. Drinking in oxygen, drinking in life. His throat hurt as if it had been skinned from the inside.

Evan heard another eruption of shots, the sound of weight crashing into shrubbery outside the window, feet running, the back fence door creaking open. He lay on the cold tiled floor.

Then an awful silence.

Evan tore the plastic trash bag from his face. He blinked,

spat blood and bile. He heard someone coming back into the kitchen. A hand touched his shoulder; fingers prodded him.

'Evan?'

He looked up. A man stared down at him. Pale, bald, tall, maybe in his fifties, but trim and strong.

'They're gone, Evan,' Bald said. 'Let's go.'

'Ca-call ... ' Every breath was fire in his mouth. 'Call ... police. My ... mother. He—'

'You've got to come with me,' Bald said. 'You can't stay here. They'll be hunting you now.'

Evan shook his head, kicked away from the man.

Bald reached down, worked the broken rope off Evan's neck, hauled him to his feet, herded him away from his mother's body.

'I'm a friend of your mom's.' Bald held a wicked-looking shotgun. 'Gonna get you out of here.'

Evan had never seen him before, and most of his mother's acquaintances did not walk around with shotguns. 'My mom!' His voice, barely above a whisper, broke.

'Look at me, Evan.' Bald shook Evan's shoulders, forced Evan's gaze to his eyes. 'Your mother is gone. Gone. There is nothing you can do to help her, except listen to me. And live. That's what she wanted. You, safe. We have to go. We have to run. Now.'

Evan shook his head. 'The police. Call the police. There were two men ... '

'They've run. We'll call the police,' Bald said, 'just not here.' He propelled Evan fast toward the back door with a shove.

'Who are you?' Evan said, fighting the panic rising in his chest. A man he didn't know, with a gun, who didn't want him to call the police. No. *No.*

'We'll talk later. Can't stay. I need your—' But he didn't finish. He had hold of the collar of Evan's jacket and Evan shrugged free of the jacket, running.

Evan ran out the front door he'd left unlocked.

'Evan, no! I'm trying to save you! Come here!' Bald yelled.

Evan bolted into the damp spring air. The pounding of his sneakered feet against the asphalt was the only sound in the quiet of the oak-shaded neighborhood. He glanced behind him. Bald sprinted from the house. Shotgun in one hand, Evan's jacket in the other, jumping into a weathered blue Ford sedan parked on the street.

Evan tore across the manicured yards. He saw an open garage door and veered into the yard. Please be home. He jumped onto the front porch, leaned against the bell, pounded the door, shouting to call 911.

An elderly man with a military buzz cut opened the door, cordless phone already in hand.

The blue Ford sped past him.

Evan ran back into the yard, yelling at the neighbor to call the police, trying to catch the number on the Ford's license plate.

But the car was gone.

3

'Walk me through this morning one more time,' the homicide detective said. His name was Durless. He had a kind, thin face, with the gaunt healthiness of a long-distance runner. 'If you can, son.'

The investigators had kept Evan away from the kitchen, but had brought him back into the house so he could identify anything that was out of place or missing. He stood now in his parents' bedroom. It was a wreck. Four suitcases lay thrown against the wall, all open, their contents spilled across the floor. They didn't belong here. But his mother's favorite photos, which did belong on the walls, lay ruined and trampled on the carpet. He stared at the pictures behind the spider webs of smashed glass: the Gulf of Mexico orange with sunrise, the solitude of a gnarled oak on an empty expanse of prairie, London's Trafalgar Square, lights shaded by falling snow. Her work. Broken. Her life. Gone. It could not be, yet it was; the absence of her seemed to settle into the house, into the air, into his bones.

You cannot afford shock right now. You have to help the police catch these guys. So have shock later. Snap out of it, he told himself. He wanted to curl up into a ball and cry. But he couldn't. He was sixteen; he had to be a man now, he told himself. That's what his father would tell him to do if he were here.

'Evan? Did you hear me?' Durless said.

'Yes. I will do whatever you need me to do.' Evan steadied himself. Sitting out on the driveway, crumpled with grief, he'd given the responding officer a description of Bald and his car. More officers had arrived and secured the house with practiced efficiency, strung crime-scene tape over the front door and the driveway, across the shattered kitchen window where Bald had fired his shotgun.

His cellphone was gone, in the pocket of the jacket that Bald had grabbed off his shoulders and taken with him.

Durless had arrived, first interviewing the patrol officer and the ambulance crew who had responded to the neighbor's call. He'd introduced himself to Evan and taken his initial statement, then asked him to come back into the house, escorting him to his parents' bedroom.

'Anything missing?' Durless asked.

'No.' Through the haze of shock Evan knelt by one opened suitcase; it lay choked with men's pressed khakis, button-downs, new leather loafers with tassels. Yuck. All the kinds of clothes he hated, all in his size. Why would Mom want him to dress so differently than he normally did?

'Don't touch anything,' Durless reminded him, and Evan yanked his hand back.

'I've never seen these suitcases or clothes before,' he said, 'but this one looks like she packed it for me.'

'Where was she going?'

'Nowhere. She was waiting for me here.' His voice shook and he thought, What if I hadn't argued with her? What if I'd ridden my bike faster? What if I hadn't stopped to call Dad? A shiver ran along his skin.

'But she had four packed suitcases, with clothes for you, and a gun in her bag.' He pointed at a gun, tossed atop one of the clothes piles spilling from a suitcase.

'I can't explain it. Well, the gun looks like my dad's Glock. He uses it in target shootings. It's his hobby.' Evan wiped his face. 'I used to shoot with him, but I'm not very good.' He realized he was rambling and he shut up. 'Mom ... must have not had a chance to get to the gun when the men came.'

'She must have been afraid if she was packing your dad's gun.'

'I just don't know.' Evan shook his head.

'So, let's go through it again. She called you at school and told you to come here, without telling anyone.'

Evan could hear the slight rise at the end of the sentence, like it was a question, like it was doubt.

'Yes.' Evan again walked Durless through his mother's frantic phone call insisting he come home, his sneaking out of Penrod and grabbing his bike, the men attacking him. Trying to dredge up any detail that he'd forgotten to give in his initial account.

'That's very unusual, for a parent to want their kid to get into trouble for ditching school.'

'Yes.'

Durless went quiet, as though waiting for Evan to say something more, to say something that made sense.

'I can't explain it.'

'But you obeyed your mom.'

'Yeah.'

'And she had these bags packed, ready to go. She was ready to leave with you, and didn't want your school to know you were leaving, is that it?'

'I guess. I don't understand it.'

'We found an unopened bottle of hair dye in the bathroom, Evan. Black hair dye. Did your mom dye her hair?'

'No, never.'

Durless glanced at the luggage and shifted subjects. 'These men who grabbed you in the kitchen, you're sure there were two?'

'I heard two voices. I'm sure.'

'But you never saw their faces?'

'No.'

Durless frowned. 'And then another man came, shot at them, blasted the ceiling, cut you down from the rope. You saw his face.'

'Yes.' Evan rubbed a hand across his forehead. In his

initial statement, still trembling with shock, he had said it was a bald man, but now he could do better. 'Older than my dad – in his fifties. Thin mouth, very straight teeth. Mole on his' – Evan closed his eyes for a minute, picturing – 'left cheek. Brown eyes, strong build, ex-military possibly, about six feet. He looked like he might be Latino. No accent in his voice. He wore black trousers, a dark green T-shirt. No wedding ring. A steel watch. I can't tell you anything more about his car except it was a blue Ford sedan.'

Durless wrote down the additional details, handed them to another officer. 'Get the revised description on the wire,' he said. The officer left. Durless raised an eyebrow. 'You have an exceptional eye for detail under stress.'

'I'm better with pictures than words.'

Evan heard the low voices of the crime-scene team as they analyzed the carnage in the kitchen. He wondered if his mother's body was still in the house. It felt strange to stand in her room, see her clothes, her pictures, know she was dead now. Shouldn't he be crying? He should be crying, but he just felt numb and cold, like ice had formed under his skin. In his heart, his chest, where the rope had burned his throat. He felt like he was trapped in sleep, cocooned in the most awful dream. Surely he would wake up in a minute. Maybe back at his desk at study hall, where Mom's phone call interrupted his work on his history assignment.

'Evan, let's talk about who would have wanted to hurt your mom,' Durless said.

'No one. She was the nicest person you could imagine. Gentle. Funny.' He put his face into his hands and he was afraid he would cry. No. He fought the tears back down.

He felt Durless put a hand on his shoulder. 'Had she mentioned being afraid or threatened by anyone? Think. Take your time.'

'No. We're the most normal people in the world. Nobody hates us.'

'Anyone with a grudge against your family?'

The idea seemed ridiculous, but Evan took a deep breath, thought about his parents' friends and associates, about his own. 'I can't think of anyone who wants to hurt us. This has to be random.' As soon as he said it he knew it couldn't be true. What had the boss said to the European man? *You do it, please. I can't bear to kill him.* Like Evan could ... matter to him. That made no sense.

'But the bald man saved you,' Durless said. 'He, according to you, chased the killers off, called you by name, claimed he was a friend of your mom's, and tried to get you to leave with him. That's not random.'

Evan shook his head.

'I didn't get your dad's name,' Durless said.

'Mitchell Eugene Casher. My mother is Donna Jane Casher. Did I tell you that already? Her name?'

'You did, Evan, you did. Tell me about the relationship between your parents.'

'They've always been happy. They love each other. They don't fight, hardly at all.'

Durless stayed quiet. Evan couldn't stand the silence. The accusing silence.

'My dad had nothing to do with this. Nothing.'

'Okay.'

'My dad would never hurt his family, no way.'

'Okay,' Durless said again. 'But you see, I have to ask, because she wanted you here, without the school knowing, and she had all these bags. Sometimes when a marriage ends ...'

'My dad is in Australia, on a business trip, for the next several days. If she wanted to leave him, there was no rush to do it today. But she wouldn't. They loved each other.'

'Yeah.' Durless sounded like a guy with no reason to believe in true love.

'Even if you think my parents were having problems,' Evan said, 'my dad would never hurt me.'

'How d'you get along with your folks?'

'Fine. Great. We're all close.'

'You said you were having trouble reaching your dad?'

'He's not answering his cellphone.'

'You got his itinerary in Australia?'

Now he remembered. 'Mom usually keeps his travel schedule on the refrigerator.'

'That's great, Evan. That's a help.'

'I just want to help you get whoever did this. You have to get them. You have to.' His voice started to shake and he steadied himself. He rubbed at the raw rope burn on his neck.

Durless said, 'When you talked to your mom, did she sound afraid? Like these guys were already here in the house?'

'No. She didn't sound panicked. Just emotional. Like she just wanted me to get home as fast as I could.'

'You talk to her this morning before you went to school? Tell me about her mental state then.'

'Everything seemed fine. She mentioned she might take an assignment in France when my dad got back. She's a freelance travel photographer. Her studio's above the garage.' He pointed at the cracked frames, the photos distorted under the broken glass. 'That's some of her work. Her favorites.'

Durless cast his gaze over London, the coast, the prairie. 'Places. Not people,' he said.

'She likes places better than faces.' It had been his mother's joke about her work. Tears crept to the corners of Evan's eyes and he blinked. Willed them to vanish. He did not want to cry in front of this man. He dug his fingernails into his palms. He listened to the snap of cameras in the kitchen, the soft murmurs of the crime-scene team working the room, breaking down the worst nightmare for his family into jotted statistics and chemical tests.

'You have brothers or sisters?'

'No. No other family at all.'

'What time did you get here? Tell me again.'

He looked at his watch. The face was broken, hands frozen at ten thirty-four. It must have happened when he fell as the rope broke. He showed the stopped watch to Durless. 'I didn't really notice the time. I was worried about my mom.'

Durless spoke in a whisper to a police officer who stood in the doorway, then left. He gestured at the luggage. 'Let's talk about these suitcases she had packed, for both of you.'

'I don't know. Maybe she was going to Australia, to see my dad.'

'So she begs you to come home, but she's getting ready to leave. With a suitcase for you, and a gun.'

'I ... I can't explain it.' Evan wiped his arm across his nose.

'Maybe this crisis was all a ruse to get you home for a surprise trip.'

'She wouldn't scare me for no good reason.'

Durless tapped his pen against his chin. 'Evan. Help me get a clear picture. Two men grab you, hold you at gunpoint, but then don't shoot you. Instead, they try and hang you, and another man saves you, but then tries to kidnap you and takes off when you run.' Durless spoke with the air of a math teacher walking a student through a thorny problem. He leaned forward. 'Help me find a line of thought to follow.'

'I'm telling you the truth.'

'I don't doubt you. But why not just shoot you? Why not shoot your mother, if they had guns?'

'I don't know.'

'You and your mother were targeted and I really need your help to understand why.'

A memory crowded back into his head. 'When they had me on the floor ... they talked about our computers – my laptop, and my mom's upstairs computer.'

Durless called in another officer. 'Would you go find Evan's laptop and Mrs Casher's computer, please?'

'Why would they want anything on my laptop?' Evan heard the hysteria rising in his voice and fought it back down.

'You tell me. What's on it?'

'Film footage, mostly. Video-editing programs.'

'Footage?'

'I want to be a filmmaker,' Evan said. 'I've already made a couple of short documentaries.'

'On what?'

Like that could matter now. His mother was *dead*. But he forced himself to answer the question. 'I made one about skateboarding clubs around the world, with footage the clubs sent me. And I did one on a summer camp for kids who have gotten into trouble. I called it *Juvie Camp*. They're just projects I post on my website.'

'You're young to be making movies.'

'My mom's a photographer – it's in me.' Evan shrugged. 'Movies are the new diaries for kids my age. My mom says that if I keep at it . . . ' He stopped, because those were words about a future, one his mom would never see.

. 'I'm very sorry about your mom, Evan,' Durless said. 'I need you to come downtown with us to make a more detailed statement, and to talk to a sketch artist about this bald man.'

The officer dispatched to retrieve the laptop stuck his head back round the door. 'There's no laptop out here.'

Evan blinked. 'Those men might have taken it, or the bald guy.' His voice started to rise. 'I don't understand any of this! Why would they care about anything on my laptop?'

'We're going to find out,' said Durless. 'Let's go downtown and talk, get you to work with an artist. I want a sketch of the bald man out on the news fast.'

'Okay.'

'We'll go in a minute, all right. I want to make a couple of quick calls.'

'All right.'

Evan went back to the kitchen. His mom's . . . body was already gone. The local TV stations had arrived. Cameras focused on him as he glanced through the parted curtain. Evan stepped back. More police.

He turned his back on the chaos. His mom was dead, and nothing made sense.

4

Evan had never felt so alone. A shiver took hold of him and he willed himself to calm down. He had to find his father. An itinerary, penned in his father's tight, precise handwriting, wasn't on the refrigerator in its usual spot, but he found it folded underneath the phone. The itinerary listed a number for the Blaisdell Hotel in Sydney. Durless came back into the kitchen and Evan pointed at the itinerary.

Durless dialed the Blaisdell's number. 'Mitchell Casher's room, please,' Durless said to the clerk.

Evan waited.

'Please check again. C-A-S-H-E-R. Maybe they registered him wrong. Put "Mitchell" as the last name.'

Evan and Durless waited. In just a minute, Durless would hand Evan the phone and he'd hear his father's voice . . .

'Thank you.' Durless clicked off the cell. 'Your father's not a registered guest, Evan.'

Evan could feel the shift in the room. Mom dead, Dad not where he was supposed to be. Most murders weren't difficult to solve.

Evan shook his head. 'I don't understand this at all.'

Durless took the itinerary. 'We'll find your dad, Evan. Let's get a statement and a description while your mind's fresh.'

Fresh. It's not likely I could ever forget, he thought.

Durless hurried him past the press, guarding his face with the back of a heavy hand. The cameras swung toward him; he heard the bleat of a shouted question. Evan glanced past the fence of Durless's fingers and saw a few of the neighborhood work-at-home moms and dads watching from their yards, curious, horrified.

'Evan do you need anything, honey?' one of the moms yelled, and he couldn't answer her, his throat felt so tight. I need my family, he thought.

Durless sat him in the back of a cruiser, then put himself in the front passenger seat. A young uniformed officer got behind the wheel.

Evan leaned back, staring up at the smoke-colored clouds through the rear windshield of the police cruiser as it drove away from his house. His mind whirled in a strange, panicked dance of logic and emotion. He wondered where he would spend the night. Would he be put with Child Protective Services, handed over to some foster family? He would have to call his family's friends; but both his parents, though successful, tended to keep their circle of acquaintances small. Surely one of them, or the neighbors, would give him a place to stay. He would have to make funeral arrangements. He wondered how long it would take for the police to do an autopsy. He wondered at which church he should have his mother's funeral. She didn't go to church. He wondered how it had been for his mother. If she had known. If she had suffered. If she had been afraid. That was the worst. Maybe the killers had come up behind her, the way that they had on Evan. He hoped she never knew, never suffered a pitch-black terror overpowering her heart.

He closed his eyes. Tried to reason past the shock and grief. Otherwise he thought he might just break down. He needed a plan of attack. First, find his dad. Contact his dad's local clients, see if they knew whom exactly Dad worked for in Australia. Second, maybe the police would let him talk to Carrie. Third ... make sense of the horror of who wanted his mother dead.

But the killers looked on your laptop. What if this isn't about her? What if it's about *you*? The thought chilled him, broke his heart in one swoop.

There is nothing there that they could want from him. Nothing.

The police car, driven by a patrol officer who had been a responder to the initial 911 call, with Durless sitting in the front seat, turned out of the Cashers' quiet, bungalow-remodeled neighborhood onto Shoal Creek Boulevard, a long thoroughfare that snaked through central and north Austin.

He sat up suddenly. A mother, strangled to death, a son, apparently having hung himself in remorse. No suicide note, just a scene of mindless violence. No explanation. He thought of how it would have looked to the police entering the house, his body dangling from the rafters, his mother dead and helpless on the floor below him. He saw the scene with a filmmaker's eyes, thinking of the immediate impression of the visuals: the light gleaming through the kitchen window, where any neighbor would have spotted his body with ease within a few hours. His mother, bags packed – the police might wonder, Had she feared her son? Wanted to flee while he was at school? He knew that wasn't so, but perhaps the killers had taken in his mother's packing; maybe they'd forced her to tell them he was on his way home and decided to use the situation to their advantage.

'They staged the scene,' Evan said, half to himself. His voice shook.

'What's that?' Durless asked, turning to look at him.

'Staged. I mean, the killers murdered my mother, then were hanging me to fake a suicide. It wasn't just to kill me. It was so the police would think that I killed her and then killed myself.'

Durless said, 'We would always look deeper than the surface.'

'But it would be the first and most obvious theory.'

Durless's cellphone rang in his pocket. He answered it. He listened. He jerked round and stared at Evan. 'Who is this?'

'What's the matter?' Evan said.

'No, you tell me who this is!' Durless said into the phone.

Evan watched Durless staring at him. Durless, after a moment, slid the phone through a slot in the mesh to Evan. 'It's for you. Someone knows you're with me and is desperate to reach you.'

Evan took the phone. 'Hello?' He thought, It must be my dad, right. The hotel made a mistake and Dad's called home and the police told him to call Durless . . .

'Evan?' It was . . . Carrie, his girlfriend.

'Uh, how did you get this number?'

'Listen. You're in danger. Serious danger.'

'My mother's dead. She's dead.' He didn't want to cry in front of his girlfriend, but suddenly, hearing her voice, saying those words, Evan's face turned hot. Then he thought about what she was saying. 'What danger?' Her first words rang in his head. 'What the hell do you know about this?'

How could Carrie know anything about what had happened to him?

'Listen to me,' she said. Her voice was barely a whisper now. 'A man will come to see you at the police station. He'll say he's a friend of your parents, and even though you've never seen him before, you say he is a friend and that you want to go with him.'

'Why would I do that?'

'Because he can protect you.'

'Protect me?'

'From the people who killed your mom.'

Evan's voice rose to a yell. 'What do you know about my mom?' It wasn't possible. Carrie was his girlfriend. She couldn't be involved.

But then how had she known he was with this specific police detective?

Suddenly a car passed them, cut them off hard, forcing the cruiser into a manicured front lawn, a blue Ford sedan skidding to a stop, Durless yelling as the brakes threw him forward into the windshield. Evan wasn't buckled in and the brake-jam slammed him into the back of the front seatwire mesh.

Evan heard Durless saying, 'What on earth is that lunatic doing?' He heard the click of the patrol cop opening the driver's door.

On the other side of the windshield, the bald-headed man got out of the blue Ford. Raised a shotgun. Aimed it right at Evan.

5

Panicking, Evan fumbled for the door handle, dropping Durless's cellphone. But he couldn't get out of the car: the locks were controlled from the driver's seat. The metal mesh dividing him from the front seats trapped him.

The young officer hit the pavement, crouching down as he swung open the door. Bald jumped onto the police car's hood, then roof, pivoted the shotgun in a blur, felled the policeman with two precise blows to the side of the head with the shotgun's butt stock. The officer crumpled. Bald jumped down from the hood and leveled the shotgun through the driver's door at Durless.

'That's him!' Evan yelled. 'The guy from my house!' He heard Carrie's voice screaming his name, sounding tinny on the dropped phone.

'Hands where I can see them,' Bald ordered in a voice of total calm. 'Don't be an idiot.'

Durless raised his hands.

'Unlock Evan from the back.'

'Durless, he's the guy!' Evan yelled.

Durless threw himself out his door and Bald vaulted over the cruiser, skidding across the hood. Durless landed on his back on the grass, freeing his service revolver in a smooth yank, firing. He missed. Bald slammed both feet onto Durless's chest, a brutally efficient blow that purpled Durless's face. Bald kicked the service revolver onto the well-cut green of the yard.

Bald leaned down, nailed Durless with two sharp blows in to the jaw. Durless went down, consciousness fading from his eyes as his gaze met Evan's.

It had taken all of ten seconds.

Evan pivoted onto his back, kicked at the window with his sneakers. The reinforced glass held.

'No need for that,' Bald said.

Evan scrambled off the seat onto the floor.

Bald leaned in the driver's side, studied the controls, and popped the rear door locks.

Evan leaned forward and pushed the passenger-side door open. But Bald already had the driver's-side door open, his hands grabbing the back of Evan's neck. Evan froze.

'You're coming with me,' Bald said.

'Please, what do you want?' Evan yelled. Carrie might hear this conversation on the dropped phone. He had to give her information to help him. 'What do you want with me?'

'It's for your own safety. Come on.'

Evan was suddenly full of determination not to go with this man. Bald had dispatched a much younger cop and Durless with ease. The police might have heard the attack over the radio, or a busybody on this street might be peeking out his window, dialing for help. The cops might arrive at any second. 'No, I'm not going anywhere.'

'I didn't kill these cops when I could've – you think I'm gonna kill you? You're dead in a day unless you come with me. I'll tell you everything, I promise. But you've got to come with me.'

'No! Tell me what this is about.'

'Later.' Bald seized Evan by the hair and hauled him from the back of the car. Then Bald closed his fingers round Evan's throat with a practiced hand, squeezing on the rope burn. Black circles widened in the air before Evan's eyes.

Bald jammed the shotgun's barrel up under Evan's jaw. 'Listen, little boy. This has all gone bad, and I don't have time to coddle you.'

The barrel was cold against his throat and Evan nodded.

Bald lowered the shotgun, frowned. 'I don't mean to scare you, but we gotta go now.' He shoved Evan toward his Ford. 'You know how to drive?'

'Yes.' Evan had gotten his license two months ago, right after his sixteenth birthday.

A passing car slowed – a Lexus SUV, a woman driving, an old lady in the passenger seat, staring at the police car in the yard. Bald raised his hand – the one not holding the shotgun – in a friendly wave. The Lexus zoomed away.

'She'll call the cops. We got seconds,' Bald said.

Evan got in the driver's seat, his hands shaking. Bald slid in next to him. He rested the shotgun so that it wasn't aimed at Evan but it sure wasn't far off.

Evan glimpsed the unconscious officers in the rearview. 'They're hurt.'

'They're lucky they're breathing,' Bald said.

'Let me check them, be sure they're all right. Please.'

'No way. Go,' Bald said, jabbing Evan with the shotgun. Evan drove the Ford off the curb, roared down Shoal Creek Boulevard.

'Turn west onto FM 2222,' Bald said. FM 2222 was a winding, curving farm-to-market road that led out of Austin, into the hill country west of town.

Evan obeyed. 'What do you want with me?' He tried to focus on the road.

'Listen carefully. I'm an old friend of your mom's and she asked me for help.'

'I've never seen you before.'

'You don't know me, but you also don't know anything true about your parents.'

That couldn't be right. 'You know so much, tell me who killed my mother.'

'A man named Jargo.'

'Why?' Evan shouted.

'I can explain everything, once we're settled. We're going to a safe house. Turn right here.'

Evan veered south onto another major thoroughfare, Burnet Road. *Safe house.* A place where hit men couldn't find you. Evan thought he'd stepped into a mobster movie. His guts clenched; his chest ached as if it were being wrung from muscle into string.

'Did you see their faces? Can you identify them?' he asked.

'I saw them,' Bald said, 'both of them. I don't know if one is Jargo or if they just work for him.' Bald glanced through the back window.

'Why would this Jargo kill my mother? Who is he?'

'The worst man you can imagine. At least, the worst I can imagine, and my imagination is pretty twisted-sick.'

'Who are you?'

'My name is Gabriel.' Bald softened his tone. 'If I wanted you dead, I would have shot you back at your house. I'm on your side. I'm the good guy. But you must do what I say. Exactly. Trust me.'

Evan nodded but thought, I don't know you and I don't trust you.

'Do you know where your father is?' Gabriel asked.

'Sydney.'

'No, where he really is.'

Evan shook his head. 'He's not in Sydney?'

'Jargo may already have grabbed your father. Where are the files?'

'Files? What are you talking about?' Evan's voice broke in fury and frustration. He pounded the steering wheel. 'I don't have any stupid files! What do you mean, grabbed my dad? You mean he's been kidnapped?'

'Think, Evan. Calm down. Your mother had a set of electronic files that are very important. I need them.' Gabriel cleared his throat. 'We need them, you and I. To stop Jargo. To get your dad back safe and sound.'

'I don't know anything. I don't understand.'

'Here's where you start trusting me. We need new wheels. That lady in the Lexus is calling the cops, no doubt. Turn here.'

Evan drove into a shopping plaza that had been caught in the last economic downturn, half the storefronts empty, the others held by a church thrift shop, a used-book store, a *taqueria*, and a mom-and-pop office-supplies store. A center on its last legs.

People are here, Evan thought. He could get away, yell for help. The parking lot wasn't too crowded, but if Gabriel let him park close to a store, he could run inside.

'Show me you're smart.' Gabriel gave Evan a cool stare. 'No running, no yelling for help, because if you force my hand, someone gets hurt. I don't want it to be you.'

'You said you're the good guy, but you keep threatening me.'

Gabriel glanced at Evan, as though surprised by the spark of fire in his voice. 'I'm good until you make me be bad, Evan. Be still, shut up, and you'll be fine. Don't forget if it wasn't for me, you'd be hanging at the end of a noose right now.'

Evan surveyed the parking lot. Two women, laughing, getting into a station wagon, carrying grease-spotted bags from the *taqueria*. An elderly woman with a cane hobbled toward the office-supplies shop. Two black-clad twenty-year-olds window-shopped at the resale store.

'Don't test me, Evan,' Gabriel said. 'None of these good folks need trouble today, do they?'

Evan shook his head.

'Park next to this beauty.'

Evan stopped the Ford next to an old, gray Chevrolet Malibu. A sticker on the back window announced that a child was an honor student at a local high school.

'I didn't plan on your mother getting killed and rescuing you from the police in a car that could be identified. Pop the hood, like we're jumping the battery.' Gabriel stepped out of the Ford, fiddled at the Malibu's lock with a slim finger of metal, opened it, and dove under the steering column for a fast hot-wiring.

Open the door, Evan thought. Get out and run. He's bluffing.

He opened the door and Gabriel was back in the car, gun at Evan's ribs. 'What part of "don't" do you not get? I told you not to force my hand. Shut the door.'

Evan closed the door.

Gabriel ducked back into the Malibu and once again put his head under the wheel.

Evan thought, This is my chance. Figure out what you're going to do and do it.

6

Carrie closed the phone. She had heard Evan's scream – *The guy from my house!* – and then the brutal sounds of fighting, a man's voice she didn't know ordering Evan out of the car, the squeal of tires against pavement, and then just the low moan of the wind brushing the trees.

He had been taken.

She stood alone in the music room at Penrod, panic fierce

in her chest. She was too late. Whoever else was after Evan had found him. She would be missed in her own class by now, but that didn't matter. She had to get out of here. She would never step foot in Penrod's classrooms again. She'd been lucky that the small glee club hadn't had this as their practice hour. She'd needed absolute privacy to make that first phone call, and then a second warning call to Evan.

She crushed the phone's identifying SIM card under her heel. Then she dismantled the rest of the phone, tossed the bits into the garbage.

She opened the door and that new guy Dezz stood there, smiling at her.

'Hello, Carrie,' he said.

'Hi. Excuse me, I'm late to class.'

'No need to go to class now.'

She tried to move past him. 'I have to go.'

Dezz shoved her back. 'We need to talk.'

It was a struggle to keep her emotions under control. All she could think of was that Evan was in danger right now, and she could do nothing to help him, and this loser jerk wanted to pretend like they needed to have a conversation. Her face felt hot, and she put her stare right on him. 'Don't you ever lay your hand on me again,' she said.

'What are you doing in here, Carrie?'

'I . . .' She'd needed a moment's privacy and she'd known she wouldn't get it in the girls' room. 'That is none of your business. Get out of my way.'

'You are my business, and we're going the same way.' Then he grabbed her arm.

She reared back and leveled a hard punch at his jaw. He staggered against the closed rehearsal-hall door. He lunged at her and she ran, grabbing one of the heavy, black metal music stands. She whirled and slammed the stand hard into his ribs.

'Wait . . . ' he said. Then he smiled, like the pain felt good.

'Who are you?' she said.

He grabbed a music stand, same as hers, balanced the heft of the weight in his hand. 'The question is, Carrie, who are you?' Then he swung the base of the stand hard at her; she blocked it with her own. A giant clang sounded in the acoustics of the room. She hammered a kick into his gut and he staggered back. He laughed at her. He started to slowly twirl the heavy music stand. She stood her ground, watching, waiting.

Then he swung at her. She parried the blow. He thrust the base of the stand toward her again, caught her in the chest. She gasped and fell back.

'You're not just some high-school student, are you, Carrie?'

Fear bolted along her skin. 'Neither are you.'

'Neither am I.' Then he swung again, chasing her up the risers, as she blocked the vicious swings of his improvised weapon with her own. The *clang, clang* of the metal became its own beat. Finally he caught her by surprise, knocking the stand from her hands, hitting the base of it against her throat, pinning her to the wall. She stared back at him and for a moment she thought, He's going to kill me.

'Very good,' he said. 'My father trained you well. Shall we go find him now?' He dropped the stand and the pressure on her throat eased. She clutched at her neck, gasping.

'What?' she said.

Dezz gave her his crooked smile. 'Jargo's my dad. He just called me. He wants us to come meet him. Time for you and me to drop out of school, love.'

7

Leave a sign, Evan thought. He stared down at the wheel. His fingers. He pressed his fingertips against the steering wheel, then his forefinger and middle finger against the ashtray and the face of the radio. He didn't know what else to do; a fingerprint was the only trace of himself he could think to leave.

Gabriel gestured him over with the gun. Evan got into the Malibu, behind the steering wheel. The car smelled of stale hamburgers and French fries.

Gabriel returned to the Ford and quickly wiped it down. Evan's heart sank. He watched Gabriel smear a cloth along the steering wheel, the doorknobs, the windows. He was fast and efficient.

But not the radio, not where Evan had pressed his fingertips.

Gabriel left the Ford's keys in the ignition.

Gabriel slid into the Malibu's passenger seat next to Evan, tossed out the smelly McDonald's bag of trash. Evan drove out of the lot, slow and casual, and merged into a steady stream of Burnet Road traffic.

Gabriel fished a baseball cap from where it rested on the back seat. He shoved it down hard on Evan's head. He stuck a pair of wire-framed sunglasses that had rested on the middle seat onto Evan's nose.

'Your face will be all over the news tonight.' Gabriel's lips were a thin, pale line. 'I'd prefer no one be able to recognize you.'

'Please listen to me, really listen to me. My mom doesn't

have your files, whatever it is you or this Jargo guy want. This is a huge mistake.'

'Evan, in your life, nothing is as it seems,' Gabriel said softly. 'Everything in your life is a lie.'

The statement made no sense, but then it did. His mother packing up bags for an extended secret trip. Her demand he ditch school secretly and immediately, without explanation. His father, the best man he had ever known, lying about his Australian hotel. Carrie calling him on a phone she should know nothing about and warning him, telling him about a mysterious stranger he was supposed to pretend was a friend. *You're in danger. Serious danger.* Carrie. How would she know his life had crumbled into dust in the past hour?

The question burned like a match struck and held too close to his face.

'Get onto the highway here,' Gabriel ordered. 'Head south to Highway 71 West. Keep going until I tell you different.'

Evan eased onto MoPac, the major north–south highway on Austin's west side, pushed the speed up to sixty. After fifteen minutes, MoPac ended, merging onto Highway 71, which fed into the rolling Hill Country west of Austin. The city traffic faded as they moved past the outlying housing developments on the edge of Austin.

Evan found his voice. 'You said you'd explain the situation to me.'

Gabriel watched the hills. He didn't answer.

'You promised me.' Evan pushed the accelerator up to seventy. He was sick of being pushed around; a sudden awful rage burned into his skin.

'When we get settled. Slow down.'

'No. You tell me now. Or I crash this car.' And suddenly

he knew he would do it. At least take the car off the road, let Gabriel's side be torn up by the wire fencing marking property lines, render the Malibu into junk you couldn't drive. The thought that he would do this surprised him, but after this morning, nothing was normal.

Gabriel frowned, as though deciding whether to play along. 'Well, you might.'

'I will.'

'Listen. Your life as you knew it is over. If that life was sunshine, now you got to stay in shadows. You have to hide. It may be for a very long time. You got to be a boy of shadows, Evan. If you want to live.'

'What you're saying doesn't make sense to me. Tell me what this is about!'

'Your mother has certain files that would be devastating to some very powerful people. Your mom wanted my help in getting out of the country in exchange for those files.'

'Who? What people?'

'It's best you not know specifics.'

'I don't have these files.' Evan rocketed past a pickup truck. Here he was speeding like a maniac and he couldn't get a police officer's attention. Traffic was light, and the few cars he raced behind politely inched over to the right lane.

'I think you do,' Gabriel said, 'but you don't know it. Slow it down and drive steady if you want to know more.' Gabriel nudged the shotgun into Evan's kidney.

'Tell me everything you know about my mom. Now.' Evan floored the accelerator. 'Tell me!'

The last thing Evan he saw was the speedometer inching past ninety as Gabriel slammed his fist into Evan's head, sending it smashing into the driver's window, and the world went black.

8

Steven Jargo was killing mad. He hated failure. It was a rare occurrence, but it haunted him longer than most men, and he despised the sensation of panic that gripped him. Panic was weakness, a lack of preparation and resolve, a poison for his heart. The last time he had been afraid was when he'd committed his first murder, but that terror had soon dissipated, like smoke caught in a breeze.

Now, though, he was scared and running, his hands scraped raw from sliding down the rooftop of the Casher house when gunfire had blasted in the kitchen while he was upstairs. He hadn't wanted to watch Evan Casher die, even though the boy's death was necessary. He had dropped down to the cool of the yard, still clutching Evan's laptop, crashing into Donna Casher's rosebushes, thorns ripping at his hands, heard the shriek of the bullets, and seen Frank staggering, wounded, out the back door. They had both retreated to their car, parked one street away. The noise meant police would soon be arriving; this was a nice, quiet neighborhood.

Frank was hit, and bleeding.

'Who shot you?' Jargo asked him.

'Bald guy. Don't know him,' Frank wheezed.

'Did you kill the boy?'

'I ... I think so. I hung him up. His neck might have snapped.'

'Yes or no. Is Evan dead?'

'I don't know. I don't know.'

Jargo had rented a vacant apartment in Austin yesterday,

40 — JEFF ABBOTT

under a different name and for cash, and perhaps it wasn't safe, but they had no other place to go.

'Shaved head, the guy had.' Frank breathed hard as Jargo drove 20 miles over the limit to a quiet, faded neighborhood on the southeast side of town. 'Hispanic, maybe. That's all I saw.' Frank gasped in pain. He bled all over the seat of the car. 'Didn't recognize him. I saw a blue Ford on the street. License plate XXC. Didn't see the rest. Texas plates.'

'Did Evan take a bullet?'

'Unknown. But the attacker fired in his direction.'

'Why would he do that?'

'I . . . I don't know.'

'You idiot. He shot the rope. He shot Evan down from the rope.' Jargo slammed a hand on the steering wheel.

Frank wheezed. 'Evan was almost dead from the rope. It doesn't matter. We erased the files on her system.'

'But he had the files on his laptop,' Jargo said. 'He knows.'

Frank leaned against the car window. 'I need a doctor.'

Jargo thought, Well, this will be awkward. 'You know I can't take you to a hospital, Frank.'

'But . . . but I need a doctor. Take me to hospital, please, man, please.' Frank's plea turned into a slurring moan.

Jargo, as he drove, inspected Frank's wound. It was very serious. Frank wouldn't make it without medical attention. Jargo turned, heading away from the apartment. Out past the edge of town.

'Where are we going?' Frank's eyes were half open, trying to focus.

'To get you a doctor,' Jargo lied.

Frank died ten minutes past the Austin city line, and Jargo found an empty lot on a rural road. He pushed Frank out of the car, watched him bounce into the high grass.

Frank hated the outdoors. Oh well. Jargo turned the car round and headed back to the apartment.

It had all gone very, very wrong.

Jargo hurried upstairs and made two phone calls. In the first, he gave no greeting, just brief directions on how to drive to the new apartment, heard a confirmation, then hung up. Next he called a woman who used the code name Arwen. He employed a group of computer experts on his payroll and he called them his 'elves', for the magic they could work on servers and databases and codes. Arwen – the name came from Tolkien's elvish heroine – was an ex-CIA computer expert. Jargo paid her ten times what the government had.

He fed Arwen Frank's description of the attacker and the blue Ford's plates, asked her to find a match in their databases. She said she'd call him back.

Jargo put antibacterial lotion on his scored hands and stood at the window, watching two young mothers walk in the sun, carrying their babies, indulging in idle gossip. Austin embraced this beautiful spring day, a day for watching pretty moms lift their faces to the sun, not a day for death and pain and everything in his world unraveling. He studied the street. No cars parked with occupants. Foot traffic heading to a small local grocery. He wanted to see if anyone watched him.

What he needed, what had been stolen from him, Evan Casher had it on his laptop. And if it was on the laptop, it could have been copied to his phone, or his flash drive, or another computer. Which meant they had to find him, and Evan had to die.

Twenty minutes later, he heard a knock at the door. He opened it.

'Hello, Dezz. Hello, Carrie.'

The two teenagers came inside. Dezz was how he always was, wearing a smile that was half a snarl. Carrie seemed quiet and withdrawn.

'Any trouble ditching class?'

'No,' Dezz said. 'I shot our way out of the office and hijacked a school bus for our escape. It was very cinematic, Dad.'

'He's lying,' Carrie said. 'We snuck out. No one noticed.' She folded her arms across her chest, as if cold.

Dezz gave her a disappointed frown. 'Don't spoil my fun.'

'Why didn't you tell me this guy was working the same as me?' Carrie said.

'Because I wasn't sure I could trust you,' Jargo said. 'And if Evan's parents figured out who you were, I wanted you to have backup. Dezz has been watching over you, too.'

Dezz gave her a wicked smile.

Carrie was silent.

'Obviously, neither of you will be returning to that school,' Jargo said. 'It will be suspicious, you two vanishing at the same time Evan does, but it can't be helped. We knew it might unfold that way anyhow.'

'If we had to kidnap him,' Carrie said.

'Yes.'

'But I wanted to go out for debate, and American football, and glee club.' Dezz made a frown on his face, collapsed on the sofa. 'So can we go now? Is the little geek dead?'

'No. Frank is dead. And Evan's mom is dead. I don't know if Evan is or not.' Jargo told them what had happened.

Carrie went pale; Dezz shrugged.

'If I'd known ... Mrs Casher was planning to run, I would

have had you two kill him at the school' – Jargo glared at Carrie – 'but no one told me.'

'He got up and went to the bathroom,' Carrie said. 'He said he had a stomach ache. I didn't know he was running.'

'You should have been paying the right kind of attention to him,' Dezz said, 'not the starry-eyed sort.'

Carrie said, 'You followed him to the bathroom. You couldn't tell he was going to bolt? Jerk.'

'He said he was sick. I didn't get suspicious until he didn't come back to study hall and Crabtree sent me to look for him.' Dezz crossed his arms. 'He took a phone call before he left. What did he talk about?'

'He stepped away; I couldn't hear it.'

'Children, please.' Jargo knew how much they both hated being called children. 'The files were on Evan's laptop. I must assume he's seen them. We erased them with a reformat and I brought the laptop here.'

'He saw them and learned the truth and just went ahead and came to school this morning?' Carrie said. 'That doesn't sound likely.'

'He and his mother would have wanted to keep up appearances. He probably suspected the two of you were watching him.'

'I don't think he suspected anything,' Carrie said quietly.

'Whatever, Dad. The files are gone,' Dezz said. 'Even if Evan's alive, he can't hurt us.'

'If Evan had them on his laptop, I assume he saw them,' Jargo said. 'He can name names. It's not a risk I'm willing to take.'

Dezz sat on the couch in the condo, turning over his PSP in his hands, not playing it. He wadded a caramel into his cheek. Jargo saw Dezz was angry and nervous. Dezz would vent all that pent-up fury on the next weak person he encountered.

Carrie sat next to Dezz.

'I'm wondering who let Mr Shotgun know Dad and Frank were there.' Dezz slid the blob of caramel from one side of his mouth to the other.

'Are you serious?' she asked. 'I told you I didn't know he was running.' She bit on her lower lip.

'Did you know,' Dezz said, 'you do that when you're nervous? Just a little habit I've noticed in you, love.'

'Don't call me that,' she said.

'Your amateur spy here was in the music room instead of class.'

'I was trying to call Evan,' she said. 'I was trying to find him for you when he didn't show up at study hall again.'

'Really?'

'Yes.'

'I'm just saying maybe someone *else* was watching Evan and his mom,' Dezz said.

Jargo went to the kitchen bar, poured himself a glass of water. Evan resembled his mother, and that had made trying to kill him harder. Jargo thought about Donna Casher's once-lovely face, how he had said, 'I'm sorry,' to her after she was dead.

'The suitcases make me believe his mother told Evan they had to run. The files being on his laptop explain why they had to run. She had to get him home fast.'

Dezz powered on the PSP, twiddled the controls. Jargo let him, although he found the *ping, ping* noise of the game annoying. The electronic opiate, the cheek full of candy, calmed the young man. 'It doesn't matter – the files are gone.'

'Evan talks to the police,' Jargo said, 'and we're dead.'

'He doesn't have proof. He didn't see you, right? Maybe they'll think it's a robbery interrupted,' Carrie said.

Jargo turned on the television, found a twenty-four-hour local news channel. After a commercial, the station began a story about two police officers attacked and a witness in a morning homicide abducted from their custody. Dezz turned off the game player. The reporter said two officers were injured and gave a description of Evan Casher and a bald-headed assailant.

Carrie sat very still and listened.

Jargo drummed a finger against his glass. 'Evan's alive and our bald friend let him speak to the police before snatching him back. I wonder why.'

Dezz unwrapped another caramel.

Jargo slapped the candy from his hand. 'My theory is Donna knew she was in danger and she hired protection in the form of this bald guy.'

'But if this dude's just hired muscle, why does he grab Evan back? The job's dead. No need for him to risk his neck.'

Jargo frowned. 'That's a very good and a rather unsettling question, Dezz. Clearly he thinks Evan has something he wants.'

Dezz blinked. 'So what do we tell Mitchell about his wife? Or do you just kill him and not bother with explanations?'

Jargo looked at him as though he smelled something bad. 'We tell him that we were too late to save her, that a hired gun killed her, kidnapped his son. Mitchell will be devastated – easy to manipulate. Don't you agree, Carrie? You spent the most time around the family.'

She nodded, wordlessly. Jargo watched her.

Dezz shrugged. 'Fine. Next step?'

'Consider who Donna might have asked for help. Find the bald guy, we find Evan, tell him we can take him straight to his father. That's the shortest distance between two points.'

Jargo looked hard at Carrie. She stared at the floor, but she felt the weight of his glare and met his gaze. 'You recognize the rescuer?'

'No. Evan doesn't know anyone who fits that description. I know everyone he knows.'

Jargo gave her a hard stare. 'Carrie, you were supposed to find those files if Evan had them. They were on his laptop. I saw them myself. You didn't do your job.'

'I swear . . . they weren't there.'

He studied the shock and fear in her eyes. 'When did you last look for them?'

'Last night. I went to his house. He helped me with my math homework. I asked him if I could check my email. He said yes and he went downstairs to get us apple pie. I looked while he was gone. There were no new files on his system, I swear.'

'Did you kiss him good night?' Dezz asked, amusement in his voice. 'Maybe he hid the files under his tongue.'

'Shut up, Dezz,' she said.

'The files I found were placed on Evan's system early this morning, according to the timestamp,' Jargo said, 'so I believe you, Carrie. Lucky for you.'

'You're losing your perspective, Carrie,' Dezz said. 'Pretending to be his girlfriend wasn't a good idea.'

'Don't be a jerk.' She crossed her arms. 'Who would have taken Evan?'

'Anyone who knew his mother had the files. She must have tried to cut a deal for them with the wrong people.'

'Evan doesn't know anything,' she said. 'He's clueless.'

'Perhaps, Carrie, or maybe he figured out you and Dezz were spying on him and he was watching the two of you like you were watching him.'

She opened her mouth, as if to speak, then closed it.

'Carrie, one chance. Are you telling me everything you know?' Jargo asked.

'Yes. Do we go looking for him or not?'

Jargo watched her, decided what to say. 'Yes. Because the other possibility is that it's the CIA who grabbed Evan. They have the most to lose. They had every reason to kill his mom.' He let the words sink in. 'Just like they killed your parents, Carrie.'

Carrie's poker face didn't change. 'We have to get Evan back.'

'Tall order,' Dezz said. 'If the CIA has him, we'll never find him.'

'The more worrisome angle is the Agency killed Donna,' Jargo said, 'and then the gentleman who grabbed Evan has another agenda entirely. Then we're fighting on two fronts.'

Carrie opened her mouth, then shut it.

'You're worried about him,' Dezz said.

'In the way you worry about a dog that's gotten lost,' Carrie said. 'A neighbor's dog, not yours,' but her voice wavered, very slightly, perhaps too little for a man to notice. Jargo didn't glance at her, but Dezz stared and she felt a hot flush creep up her neck.

'We'll see if Arwen can get a trace on the bald man or Evan, see if they surface anywhere.'

'If the CIA has the files, then we need to run,' she said.

Dezz grabbed her by the throat, gave a cruel squeeze with his fingers that worked the flesh around the carotid and the jugular arteries like dough. 'If you'd done your job and gotten those files from him, girl, this wouldn't have happened.'

'Let her go, Dezz,' Jargo said.

Dezz licked her cheek and she wrenched free from him, her fist drawn, ready to punch him.

'Stop it, son.'

Dezz licked his lips. 'Don't worry, Carrie – all is forgiven.'

Carrie stumbled back against the door, not looking at Dezz or his father.

Jargo's cellphone rang. He went into his room to answer it, shut the door behind him.

Carrie sat huddled on the couch.

Dezz leaned down and massaged the feeling back into Carrie's neck. 'I'm watching you, sunshine. You messed up.'

She slapped his hand away. 'Don't touch me, Dezz. Don't.'

'Evan got under your skin, didn't he?' Dezz said. 'I don't get it. He's not better-looking than I am. He's kind of skinny. He's not nearly as cool as me, myself, and I.'

'He was an assignment.' Carrie stood and walked to the kitchen bar and poured herself a glass of water.

'You enjoyed playing high-school romance,' Dezz said, 'but playtime's over. If Evan's seen those files, then he's a dead man, and you and I both know it.'

'Not if he's made to understand.'

'You mean if you can lie to him well enough that you had nothing to do with his mother's death.'

'We didn't know your dad and Frank would kill her.' She nearly spat the words at him.

'You didn't. I did. I know my father. Evan's a dead man.'

'Not if I can talk to him. I can turn him to work with us. I can.'

'I hope so,' Dezz said, 'because if you don't, I'll kill him.'

9

Carrie thought, My short, sweet life as Carrie Lindstrom is over. She left Dezz playing his PSP and glanced into Jargo's bedroom. He was on the phone, talking to his 'elves', the technical experts who worked for him. They were masters at locating information, rooting into private databases, uncovering crucial nuggets to help Jargo find who and what he wanted.

But she knew more than they did.

Jargo looked at her. 'The elves found the Ford's plates. Dead end. Stolen last night from a car in Dallas.'

She nodded. She knew now the elves would begin to tiptoe into the Casher phone records, credit-card accounts, and more, searching for a pointer to Evan Casher's savior.

She went down the hall into the bathroom and closed the door. Carrie washed and then studied her dripping face in the mirror. No pictures of her as Carrie Lindstrom existed, except for her forged passport and Penrod Academy ID, and a photo that Evan had snapped before she could stop him when they'd gone on a date and stopped at a Starbucks before he dropped her off at the apartment. That girl with the latte in her hand would soon be dead. When the elves found Evan, their next job would be to create a new persona for her. She liked the name Carrie – it was her own – but since she had used it recently, Jargo would make her use another one.

It had been twenty-nine days since she had walked into an early-morning trig class at Penrod and begun worming her way into Evan's life. Jargo's instructions were simple and clear: *Go. Be this boy's girlfriend, win him over with that pretty smile, show an interest in him, find out about any film projects he's doing.*

Why are you interested in a teenager's film project? she had wondered. Kids put videos up all the time on YouTube. Millions of them. Zombie satires, confessionals, pretend wars with toy guns, spoofs of movie trailers, clips of skate-boarding. They were harmless fun. But Evan had started a website specifically aimed at kids who were making serious, more ambitious short films, called FilmzKool. She liked the name. 'Film's cool' and 'film school', all wrapped up in one term. He'd created a very cool YouTube-style site for teens to post their most accomplished work. He'd gotten some press coverage, with some of the best videos from young film-makers around the world receiving review attention.

Couldn't I just break in and search through his files, his computer?

No. Get close to him. If it takes a while, it takes a while. I have my reasons.

Who is he, Jargo?

He's just a project, Carrie.

So Frank had created a false history for her, transferred her from a Chicago-area private school that she had never actually attended, posed as her guardian, paid a full year's tuition to make sure that she was admitted to Penrod, and manipulated the computer system to give her four of her classes with Evan Casher.

It was no fun being the new kid at school. She smiled and stayed quiet. A couple of girls approached her the first day, the kind of girls who shouldered the social duty of welcoming new kids, one girl eyeing Carrie's face, expecting snobbery behind the beauty. Carrie found it best to come across as an introvert; fewer questions to answer that way. She dressed stylishly but not in flashy or overpowering colors. She didn't volunteer more information than she needed. She could be honest about which TV shows and bands and books she liked: she *was* a teenage girl and she was playing a teenage girl. Evan noticed her the first day – their eyes met as she was introduced to their second-period class – but he didn't talk to her, didn't approach her in any of the other three classes they shared. Penrod was a school geared to the creative kids and it wasn't considered too weird to be quiet or thoughtful. Introverts were on equal footing with extroverts. Evan was one of the quiet ones. He was friends with a motley group of three boys and two girls, and they sat together at lunch. Carrie sat with her new friends three tables away, and while she tried not to be obvious, one of her new friends, Julia, saw her glancing at Evan.

'That's Evan Casher,' Julia said, before Carrie could ask his name.

'He's in, like, four of my classes,' Carrie said by way of explanation. 'If I miss school, he'll be my notes lifeline.'

'Like he takes notes. I think he doodles through class,' Julia sniffed. Like all people who feared snobbery, she was a terrible snob. 'He wants to be a filmmaker, which I think sounds like a one-way ticket to obscurity.'

'That's not quite fair,' the other girl said. 'He got written up in the Austin paper earlier this year.'

'Oh, that,' Julia said. 'Well, anyone can have a website.'

'Website?' Carrie pretended like she didn't know about FilmzKool.com.

Julia made the website sound much less impressive than it was.

'Really. Sounds cool.' She glanced again and Evan was laughing at one of his friends' jokes. He had a nice smile. He wasn't looking at her; he was smiling at one of the girls at his table. Her assignment would be easier if there was no romantic competition. 'Who's his girlfriend?'

'Oh, she's not a girlfriend. They're just friends. What, do you like Evan?' Julia managed to sound surprised. 'He's not, like, good at sports.' She cocked her head, as if seeing Evan for the first time. 'Sort of nice eyes, but he's too skinny.'

Carrie decided she didn't much like Julia, but she smiled and said, 'I don't even know him. I think that girl's in one of my classes, too.' Carrie decided to change the subject and asked Julia where she'd bought her purse.

The fourth day, Carrie followed Evan, at a safe distance, after school; he didn't go home. He went to a coffee shop called Joe's Java a few blocks away from Penrod, in a quiet, upscale residential neighborhood. There he opened up his laptop and sat at a back table, earplugs plugged into the laptop. She arrived ten minutes after he did, sitting at the opposite end of the café, opening her own laptop, baiting her trap for him. He preferred to sit close to the electrical outlets where he could plug in his laptop. She never saw him with a camera, only frowning over the laptop, listening to headphones; she assumed he was editing a film and having problems.

Carrie watched him. His hair was blondish-brown, a bit too long and shaggy for its cut, and he had the unconscious habit of dragging a hand through it when he was deep in thought. He wore a small silver bracelet, hipsterish, but no other jewelry. He had a nice face. Penrod was too artsy to require uniforms and his wardrobe seemed to consist of worn jeans, funky old shirts, and high-top sneakers or sandals.

She was careful to spend most of her time tapping at her computer, not watching him, not being too obvious. It would work better, much better, if he made the first move.

She kept her gaze locked on her own laptop, but out of the corner of her eye she saw him lumber up from the chair and head to the barista's stand. She deepened her frown the closer he got to her laptop, tapping at a key.

For a moment she thought he wasn't going to talk to her, that he would just snag his coffee and go back to his seat.

'Hey. You go to Penrod, right?'

She glanced up at him. 'Yeah, I do. I'm new. I think you're in a couple of my classes.'

'Four out of seven,' he said. So he had noticed her. She bit her lip. 'I'm Evan Casher,' he said.

'I'm Carrie Lindstrom, and this is my stupid laptop, Eunice, who is not working right.'

He gave her a blank look. 'You named your computer?'

She shrugged as if to say, *Well, I'm a dork.*

A very slight smile from him. 'What's the matter with Eunice?'

'I'm trying to edit some video ...'

She saw the shift in his eyes then – Julia was right: he had nice blue eyes, the color of bright winter sky – and felt the line tighten as he bit on her hook. He came round to her screen.

'Oh, I use FinalEdit Pro, too,' he said.

She knew this already.

When he'd gone out for a Tex-Mex dinner with his
parents two nights ago, she'd disarmed the Cashers' electronic alarm system with a code-breaker program on her
iPhone, eased open the lock of the back door with a lock-
pick that had been her father's. It was a nice house, lots of
family pictures. She had stopped at one in the living room,
the three Cashers sitting in a field of Texas bluebonnets.

Her throat had felt tight. She'd thought of a picture of her
with her mom and dad, when she was a kid, in a park. She
didn't have a copy of it; Jargo didn't let her keep anything
from her old life.

She had hurried upstairs to Evan's room. If you wanted a
teenager's secrets, then go to his room. She had cataloged
what DVDs he owned, surveyed his computer, hunted for
his weaknesses. In his room she found no pot, no alcohol,
no prescription pills. He didn't have serious vices that she
could exploit. Pretty much everything in his room related
back to his interest in filmmaking: books, magazines, downloads on his computer. He was currently working on a film
project about the history of extreme sports. Why would Jargo
care about this, or this kid, she wondered? She hadn't
copied any of the data; she didn't want to leave an electronic
trail.

She had locked the door, reset the alarm, and left, feeling
dirty, feeling like a thief even though she'd taken nothing.
She'd stolen his privacy, and she was probably going to do
much worse.

'So what are you trying to do?'

'I wanted to add a custom transition effect,' she said, 'but
it's locked up.' She had written a small automated script that
would lock up the application; she'd needed to look like she
needed his help.

'Here,' he said. His long fingers tapped on the keys. He hit on the right combination on the third try and her fake lockup script switched off and the program's video began to run again. It was footage of her in a forest, glancing over her shoulder.

'Thanks,' she said.

Then the images cut to shoreline, to beach.

'Is this a vacation video?'

'Oh, no,' she said. 'I'll sound stupid if I tell you what I've got on Eunice.'

'No, you won't,' he said.

'Well, I have ideas for a short movie, and I'm trying to put them together.'

'What's it about?'

'I don't know. I just had ideas for scenes, but I don't have a script. I don't know how to tie it together into a story.'

He was next up to place his coffee order and he did, turning his back on her, and she thought, That didn't work.

But he gave the barista his order and returned the five steps back to her table. 'I make movies.'

'Really?' She gave a smile of polite interest.

'Yeah. I did one about kids at a reform-school camp I got to meet. Twenty minutes.'

'That's pretty long.'

'I started up a website last year, like YouTube for film students. I have kids from all over the world submitting films to put on it. It's called FilmzKool.'

'Oh, I get it. "Film school" and "film's cool".'

'Yeah!' He smiled and nodded, pleased she'd caught the double meaning. She felt a pang of guilt. He was a nice kid, and he was in Jargo's sights.

'So, did you write a script for your movie?'

'Sure.'

'See, that seems to be where I failed,' she laughed. 'I just had images in my head and no real story.'

'Well, not every image is right. Not every picture fits together.'

'I know. I was trying to be artsy, like a music video, but I think it would be cooler to tell an actual story. I know I sound dumb.'

'No, you don't. You learn by doing.'

'So would you tell me how to start on a movie? Any advice?'

The barista called, 'Mocha latte for Evan,' and he stepped away for a minute to snag his drink. He came back holding his cup, but he didn't sit down.

He's shy, she thought. She wondered how much of life he'd seen by only looking at it through a lens, or on a screen, rather than with his own eyes.

'Well, I can only tell you what works for me, but if my movies aren't what you like, then my process might not work for you.'

'Show me,' she said. 'Show me one of your movies.'

Evan's mouth crinkled. 'Uh, I don't usually sit there while someone watches it. That's why I put it on the web.'

'I'm not a harsh critic,' she said. 'I'm the girl without a script.'

He sat down, blushing slightly, and she knew that even if Jargo hadn't aimed her at him, she would have noticed him, at a coffee shop, at a mall, walking across campus.

'Um, okay.' So he typed on her system, brought up his FilmzKool site. It was organized by filmmaker, by nation, by age range. 'They're not all good,' he said.

He's nervous, she thought. He cares what I think.

He'd done dozens of short films: mock interviews with fifteen-minute celebrities, a pretend documentary on the perils of too much social networking, a monologue and mashup making fun of the worst of reality television. The clips were funny and imaginative, even the silly ones. Then he showed her the one he'd made with the reform-school kids and she was silent. This was good work, the kind you'd expect from an adult.

She glanced at him when she was done. 'You have talent.'

He blushed bright red. 'Um, not really. I just work at it a lot. I finish what I start. Lots of kids don't ever finish their movies. Sometimes they email me to ask for help ...' He stopped.

He needed a shot of confidence. 'Learn to take a compliment, Evan.'

'Okay. Thank you, Carrie.'

A few moments of awkward silence ticked by, until she broke it. 'So, I better write a script, now that you've inspired me.'

He blushed again.

'Will you help me, Evan? I don't want to take away time from your extreme-sports project.'

He blinked. 'How did you know what I was working on?'

Slip-up. She'd spied on his laptop. That's how she knew; she'd read a detailed outline that he'd written. This film was going to be closer to an hour, a major project for a teenager. 'You mentioned it.'

'I did?' He looked very uncertain for a moment, nearly suspicious.

She held her breath.

Then he smiled. 'Huh, I don't usually ever talk about my work in progress.'

'Mmm. I must be a bad influence, then.' Carrie gave him her most winning smile, thinking, Please believe me. Please believe me. Please believe me.

'Sure I'll help you with your script.'

And so it had begun, the best twenty-nine days of her life since her parents died. They ate lunch together, his friends accepting her, Julia looking at her from a neighboring table with wry disdain for abandoning her; they met after school and he helped her flesh out a ten-minute script that had nothing to do with her old footage; it was about a girl leaving home for a year and saying goodbye to the people she loved.

When she'd suggested the plot, she'd nearly slapped her hand over her mouth. Too close. But Evan had liked the idea. 'What she doesn't say is part of the story, then,' he'd said, and helped her brainstorm about the girl's character.

Just don't make anything real, she told herself. She spied on him. She peeked on his computer, watching for any files that could interest Jargo. His work on the extreme-sports film slowed because he was busy helping her.

The fourth time they worked together on her film script, in the media lab, he kissed her. He leaned in close and their lips brushed and then she kissed him back.

Because she wanted to, and because Jargo had ordered her to. *Get closer. Find out what he knows about his parents. Does he know the truth?*

It'll be all right, she told herself. He's nice and good-looking and you like him. It would be easier, though, if she hated him, because kissing would only make her hate him more. She realized that with a shock as their lips met, his kiss tender and slow. She pulled away.

'What's wrong?' he said.

'Nothing.'

He leaned back. 'Oh. You didn't want me to kiss you.'

'You're such a dumb boy,' she said.

'Am I? Something's wrong.'

'You think too much.' She kissed him hard again, willing him to just not care, willing herself not to respond to his touch, the warm wonderful of his mouth. He's just a project.

He kissed her again, but then broke it off. His forehead rested against hers. 'Tell me what's wrong.'

Oh God, if I could, Carrie thought, but I never, never will. 'Nothing's wrong, except I'm taking all the time away from your project.'

'I don't really care about the project right now.' He smiled, but then Ms Torrance, the visual-arts teacher, came back into the media lab and they moved away from each other.

The kiss with Evan broke her heart.

He's just a project, Carrie.

The next morning, she called Jargo. 'He kissed me. He likes me.'

'Is he talking about his films?'

'No. He says if he talks too much about a movie, he's told the story and then he loses the passion for making it. He's working on a movie about skateboarding and sports like that. Why do you care? How can this matter to you?'

Jargo's voice sounded like the scraping of ice. 'Keep searching his computer, his notebooks.'

'He's not much of a note-taker.' She paused. 'It would be helpful to know what exactly I'm looking for.'

'Just find out what film projects he's considering. Kiss him enough and he'll tell you.'

'Why won't you tell me more about your next project?' she'd asked Evan one afternoon after pulling him away from his video-editing. They were sitting at his kitchen table, eating chips and drinking Coke. 'Extreme sports is kind of vague.'

'Because it's too much to do. I need the whole summer to work on it, and maybe you'll laugh at me. My mom told me I couldn't do it.'

She kept her face close to his. 'Tell me.'

'Well, I got the idea after doing the skateboarding-club film.' He had knitted together footage sent to him from skateboarding clubs around the world into a pounding montage of styles and jumps that showed how clever and new and boundary-pushing the clubs were, and how they reinforced the idea that through sport we had more in common than differences. It had been the most popular short film on FilmzKool.

'Okay.'

'About doing a history on extreme sports in general. How they got popular, how they took off, and not just in California or New York, but a more global picture. Highlighting the people who helped the sports get their starts. Who gets pulled toward extreme sports to a level that they turn an obsession into a business.'

'Sounds interesting.'

'Well, this girl I met at a film camp in New York, she told me about a guy who popularized boarding in London, who got murdered like twenty-five years ago. She thought he might make a good subject for part of the film.'

Carrie felt a little sting in her heart. This must be tied to what Jargo wanted to know: a crime. 'Whose murder?'

'The guy was named Alexander Bast. He was a crazy skater, lived large. Then someone put two bullets in him for no reason.'

An old murder. That sounded exactly like what Jargo

would be interested in. She would not be surprised if Jargo killed this Bast guy and didn't want the case reopened. She could tell Jargo, and then what? What would he order her to do to Evan? Maybe hurt him?

So she made no mention to Jargo, in the days ahead, of Evan's new interest in Alexander Bast.

'He's focused entirely on helping me and school,' she said the next day when she talked to Jargo. She had a cellphone that Evan didn't know about; she kept it hidden in a pocket under the driver's seat. She sat on the curb in the parking lot of a Krispy Kreme.

'I wonder,' Jargo said, 'if you think Evan might ever consider working for me.'

The thought made her throat thicken – Evan, trapped in the same nightmare she was. 'No, he wouldn't. He wouldn't be good at it.'

'It's an unbeatable cover for the years to come, a rising-star documentary filmmaker. International contacts. He can go anywhere, film about anything, and no one would doubt his credentials or his intentions.'

She was afraid to argue further, afraid of what would happen if Jargo thought Evan was a danger to him. 'I don't think you'd like him or he'd like you. He won't work for you.'

'Then I want you to be prepared,' Jargo said, 'because you may have to kill him.'

Carrie watched the line of cars slowly move through the doughnut-store drive-through. The back of her eyes hurt; her stomach felt like a stone. The silence began to get dangerously long. She knew he would get suspicious. 'If you say so,' she said. There was nothing else to say. 'Then I should get distance. I don't want to be a suspect.'

'No, you stay close. If it has to happen, you and he both

vanish. Evan goes missing and will never be seen again. You don't stay around. You're both gone, and we build you a new legend. I can probably use you more in Europe anyway.'

'Very well,' she said.

He told her to have a good day and then he hung up. He left her alone until two days ago, when he rung and said, 'I want to know if Evan has any files on his computer that shouldn't be there.'

'What kind of files?'

'A list of names.'

'I'll see what I can find.'

An hour later, she searched Evan's computer. She called Jargo. 'I found no files like that.' Evan had scant data on his computer other than scripts, video footage, schoolwork, and basic programs.

'Check every twelve hours, if possible. If you find the files, delete them and destroy his hard drive, then report back to me.'

'What are these files?'

'That you don't need to know. Don't memorize the information or copy the files. Just delete them and make sure that hard drive can't be recovered.'

'I understand.' And she did. The files were what Jargo was truly worried about. She wondered what the names on the list meant: who they were, why they mattered so much, how they tied back to this sports film that Evan was making.

But if Evan's hard drive was to be destroyed, she had a sinking, awful feeling that Evan was to be destroyed as well.

'Anything about us, about me?' Jargo would ask her on the phone. She sat alone in the apartment that Frank had rented for her. She lived alone right now; Frank had gone back to England, after renting the apartment and posing as her dad when he enrolled her at Penrod. She never let Evan come back to her apartment; it was too dangerous. She'd made vague noises about her father being home a lot, and difficult.

'No, Jargo,' she said.

But he didn't believe her. So, without her knowing, he sent Dezz.

They had worked on their homework together last night, Mrs Casher pottering about in the kitchen. They were in the family room, where the Cashers kept their computer, and were nearly done analyzing a poem by Emily Dickinson for English class.

'Poetry makes me hungry,' Evan said. 'And crazy.'

'Everything makes you hungry,' she said. 'No comment on the crazy.' She smiled at him. It was too easy to smile at him.

'We've got apple pie. You want some?'

'Sure.'

He went down to get the pie for them and she stuck the flash drive Jargo sent her into his laptop. It was coded to copy over any new files. Nothing. Nothing new that looked suspicious.

No list of names.

She unplugged the drive, put it back in her jeans pocket. Sweat coated her hand. As soon as she sat down, Mrs Casher and Evan came back upstairs with the slices of pie, laughing while they talked. Suddenly she missed her own mom with a force that felt like a punch in the heart.

'Thank you,' Carrie said as Mrs Casher handed her the plate.

'You remind me of someone, Carrie,' Mrs Casher said, 'and it's driving me nuts trying to decide who it is.'

'Really?' Carrie tried to keep the nervousness out of her voice. She kept her gaze on the pie, as though her face could be a traitor. Mrs Casher couldn't know who she was. 'I think I just look like me.'

'No, someone else. Can't place it.' And Mrs Casher gave her a long, studying look. Carrie gave her a smile.

Mrs Casher went back downstairs and Evan grinned at her. 'Mom. Apple pie. I don't know how I got all wholesome at once.'

Carrie rolled her eyes and dug into the delicious pie. 'Your mom's a really good cook.'

'Both my parents are.' He cleared his throat. 'You never mention your mom.'

'She died when I was very young,' Carrie lied. It was easier this way.

'I'm really sorry.'

'I kind of don't want to talk about it,' Carrie said, because she had a million memories of her mom and if he started in asking questions, she wasn't sure she could keep control. Her mother had never imagined or wanted this life of lies and death for Carrie; her mother had loved her fiercely.

'All right.'

'So, this poem.' She glanced back at her paper. 'It's all about love but not admitting that you love someone.'

'That's the case I make. Am I gonna get an A?'

'B,' she said. 'Not convincing enough.'

'Convincing is my problem?'

'You could make your argument with a little more force.'

'I hate this poem.'

'All boys hate love poems,' she said.

'Generalizing.'

'Totally.'

'But true. I don't need a poem.' He leaned in and kissed her, his fingertips soft against her cheek. 'I love you.'

She knew in the moment he'd said it that he hadn't thought about it. He'd just said it, the shape of the words against her mouth. It was an accident.

She smothered his mouth with another quick kiss before he could say anything else and then she stood. 'I have to get home.'

'Carrie . . . ' He looked stricken.

'I know. Okay, I'll see you in class tomorrow, all right?' She went to the stairs and he followed her, as though trying to stop both her and the words.

'Carrie, I'm sorry. I didn't mean to freak you out.'

'I'm not. I'm not freaked out. Thank you. For what you said. I just . . . I just need to get home right now.'

'I'll drive you.'

'No. I've got my bike. I'll see you tomorrow.'

She didn't look back at him standing beneath the front-door light until she was a block away, and she couldn't see him, the tears smearing the street, the lights, the stars.

Frank arrived late last night, frightening her when the door opened. She slept with a gun under her pillow. He stood inside, dropping off duffel bags, and she stood blinking at them, the gun cold in her hand.

'Hello, Carrie,' Frank said. 'Nice gun.' He kicked his duffel toward the couch. 'Shoot me now – I won't feel it. Damned jet lag.'

'What . . . what are you doing here?'

'Escalations,' Frank said.

'What kind?' Panic ran its bony finger down her spine.

'Just keep an eye on Evan.'

'I can handle Evan Casher.'

'But you're not finding out what we need to know about

him. His mother has been making some rather troubling investigations on her work assignments. She acts like a woman ready to run. What's changed? Why would she want to vanish with her son?'

Carrie said nothing.

'Some girlfriend you are,' Frank said. 'Fix me something to eat.' And she saw Frank pull out a case from under the couch and open it. Inside was a loop of silver wire, a gun, a knife.

'I told you, go cook me something,' Frank said, not looking over his shoulder at her. 'Then go back to bed. It's a school night.'

That had been last night, the end of her twenty-nine days.

Carrie washed her face again. Evan was gone, stolen by a man who might be very, very bad, and soon Jargo's technical elves would find a trace of him and they would go get Evan from the man who had taken him. The files had been sitting on his system this morning.

If Jargo doubted her word, he would kill her. She had to win back Jargo's trust. Now.

Last night, Evan telling her that he loved her, seemed like a moment from a world that no longer existed, a pocket of time where there was no Jargo and no Dezz and no files and no fear or pretending. She wished he hadn't said it. She wanted to hit him, to push him away, to tell him, 'Don't, don't, don't. You don't know anything. I'm not a girl you can love. I can't be normal ever again. It can't ever be, so just don't.'

She had to harden her heart now. She had to catch Evan. Before Jargo and Dezz did.

SATURDAY MARCH 12

10

Evan opened his eyes. He was lying on a bed. The cream-white sheets had been folded back; a heavy cotton towel was spread behind his head. One of his arms was raised, bound to the bed's iron-railing headboard with a handcuff. The bedroom was high-end: hardwood floors, an expensive-looking reddish paint on the walls, abstract art hung to precision above a stone fireplace. A sliver of soft sunlight pierced a crack in the silk drapes. The door was closed.

He had been seconds from wrecking the car when Gabriel had hammered him. His tongue wormed in his dry mouth. A throbbing ache settled in along his jaw and neck for permanent residence. He smelled his own sour sweat.

Mom, I failed you. I'm so sorry.

He swallowed down the panic and the grief, because they weren't doing him any good.

He had to be calm. Think.

Because everything had changed.

What had Gabriel said? *Everything in your life is a lie.*

Well, one thing was true: he was in nearly unimaginable trouble.

Evan tested the handcuff. Locked. He sat up, pushing with his feet, wriggling his back against the headboard. A side table held a thick book, a lamp, no phone. A baby monitor stood on the far table.

He stared at the monitor. He couldn't act afraid with Gabriel. He had to show strength.

For his mom, because Gabriel knew the meat of the story as to why his mom had died. For his dad, wherever he was.

For Carrie, however she was mixed up in this nightmare. She *knew* he was in danger – how? He had no idea.

So, what do you do now?

He needed a weapon. Imagine the guy who killed Mom is here. What do you hurt him with? Look at everything with new eyes. New eyes. It was advice he gave himself when he was setting up scenes to shoot. He'd read it in a book about film.

Evan could barely reach the side table. He managed to fingertip the knob and open the drawer. His hand searched the drawer as far as he could reach: empty. The book on the table wasn't heavy enough. The lamp. He couldn't reach it, but he could reach the cord, where it snaked to a plug behind the bed. As silently as he could, keeping an eye on the baby monitor, trying to quiet the handcuff from rattling against the metal headboard, he tugged the lamp closer to him; the base was heavy, ornate, wrought-iron, but at the angle he was bound, he wouldn't be able to swing it with enough force to cause serious hurt. He unplugged the cord, looped it neatly behind the table so it wouldn't catch or snag. Just in case he got a chance. Lamps could be thrown. He peered down the back of the bed, to the floor. Nothing else but miniature tumbleweeds of dust.

'Hello,' he called to the monitor.

A minute later, he heard the tread of feet on stairs, then the rasp of a key in a lock. The bedroom door opened; Gabriel stood in the doorway, a sleek black pistol holstered at his side.

'Hello, boy of shadows,' Gabriel said.

'You're not funny.'

'I'm trying to make you understand you can't be who you were.'

Evan stared at him.

'You okay?' Gabriel said.

'Yeah.'

'Thanks for putting our lives at risk with your stupid stunt.'

'Did we crash?'

'No, Evan. I know how to drive a car to a stop while seated in the passenger side. Standard training.' Gabriel cleared his throat. 'How you feeling now?'

'I'm okay.' Evan tried to imagine the skill required to drive from the passenger side to avoid a high-speed crash. He wondered where you learned a skill like that. 'So where did you learn that driving trick?'

'A very special school,' Gabriel said. 'It's early Saturday morning. You slept through the night.' A coldness frosted his gaze. 'You and I can be of great help to each other, Evan.'

'Really. Now you want to help me.'

'I saved you, didn't I? If you had stayed out in the open, well, you'd be dead now. I don't believe even the police could protect you from Mr Jargo.' Gabriel leaned against the wall. 'So, let's start afresh. I need you to tell me exactly what happened yesterday when you got to your house.'

'Why? You're not the police.'

'No, I'm not, but I did save your life. I could have let you hang. I didn't.'

'True,' Evan said. He watched Gabriel. The man looked as if he hadn't slept at all. Jumpy. Nervous. But there was nothing to be gained by silence, at least not now.

So Evan told him about his mother's urgent phone call begging him to ditch school, trying to reach his father, the attack in the kitchen. Gabriel asked no questions. When Evan was done, Gabriel brought a chair to the foot of the bed and sat down. Frowning, as if he were considering a plan of action and not caring for his options.

'I want to know who exactly you are,' Evan said.

'I'll tell you who I am. And then I'll tell you who you are.'

'I know who I am.'

'Do you? I don't think so, Evan.' Gabriel shook his head. 'I'd call your childhood sheltered, but that would be a sick joke.'

'I kept my promise to you. You keep yours.'

Gabriel shrugged. 'I own a private security firm. Your mother hired me to get you and her safely out of Austin, get you to your father. Clearly she slipped up and tipped her hand to the wrong people. I'm sorry I couldn't save her.'

So he knows where Dad is, Evan thought.

'Go back to the attack. You were unconscious,' Gabriel said. 'For a few minutes, at least, between when they hit you and they strung you up.'

'I don't know how long. Why does it matter?'

'Because the killers could have gotten the files I mentioned, found them on your or your mother's computer.'

'They wouldn't have been on my computer.' But one of the men had accessed his laptop. He remembered now through the pounding of his headache, the start-up chime, the sound of typing, telling Durless about it. 'The killers, they typed on my laptop. Said something about ...' He struggled to remember past the haze of trauma. '... about "All gone".' He waited to see what else Gabriel would say. 'They erased my laptop, they said.'

'Your mother emailed you the files.'

'No,' Evan said. Emailed. His mother had sent him those music files early yesterday morning, but they were just music files, nothing unusual. She hadn't put anything weird in her email to him. He hadn't mentioned the emails to Gabriel in relating yesterday morning's events; it hadn't seemed important compared to the horrors of the day. 'My mom didn't email me anything weird, and even if she did, the killers couldn't have gotten past the password.'

So what did 'All gone' mean?

'You saw the files, Evan, if they were on your laptop.'

'No, I don't have these files.'

'But your mother told me yesterday morning that you did, Evan. She hired me a week ago, to leave today. I was heading to take you and her out of the country, at her request, when Jargo and his thug beat me to the house.'

Evan shook his head. 'These files you want ... what are they?'

'The less you know, the better. That way, I can let you go and you can forget you ever saw me and you can go have a nice new life.' Gabriel crossed his arms. 'I'm an extremely reasonable man. I want to give you a fair deal. You give me the files; I get you out of the country, provide you a new identity and access to a bank account in the Caymans, which your mother had me arrange. If you're careful, no one will ever find you.'

'Live overseas? Hide in a foreign country?' Evan yelled. 'I'm a kid!'

'Your childhood just ended, Evan. You're the boy of shadows now.' Gabriel leaned back in his chair and it was clear to Evan, with a deep shock, that he was entirely straight-faced serious. 'Boys your age went to sea, went to war in centuries past. Grow up. You have no choice.'

'You're ... you're crazy.' Evan tried to keep the shock out of his voice.

'You want to go back home, go ahead, but if I were you, I wouldn't. Home is death.'

Evan chewed his lip. 'I help you, then what about my dad?'

'If your father contacts me, I'll tell him where you are, and then finding you is his problem. My responsibility to your mother ends once you get on a plane.'

'Please tell me where my dad is.'

'I've no idea. Your mother knew how to get in touch with him, but I don't.'

Evan let a beat pass. 'I could give you what you want and you'd just kill me.'

Gabriel reached in his pocket and tossed a passport on the bedspread. It bore the seal of South Africa. With his free hand, Evan opened it. A picture of him was inside – his original passport photo, the same as he had in his American passport. The name on the passport was Erik Thomas Petersen. Stamps colored the pages: entry into Great Britain a month ago, then entry into the United States two weeks ago.

Evan shut the passport, dropped it back on the bed. 'Very legitimate-looking.'

'You need to slip into being young Master Petersen very carefully. If I wanted you dead, you'd be dead. I'm giving you an escape hatch.'

'I still don't understand how my mother could have gotten any dangerous computer files.' And then he got it. Not his mother. His father. The computer consultant. His father must have found files, in working for a client, that were dangerous.

'All you have to do is tell me where the files are.' That was why Gabriel had taken the enormous risk of returning for Evan, ambushing the police car, kidnapping him. He had to have those files.

'But I don't ...' Suddenly Evan saw it. My phone, he thought. Gabriel took my jacket when I shrugged out of it; he held onto it. My phone is in my jacket pocket. The files must be hidden in that music Mom sent me. It was the only explanation he could think of. And his phone would have synced, automatically, with his laptop early yesterday morning. He had it set up that way, to keep his calendar and mail up to date.

No one – not Gabriel, Jargo, his thug – had realized the files might be on Evan's phone as well. They were all focused on the family's computers. Old guys, he thought.

Gabriel leaned closer to him. 'Tell me, Evan, where else would she have hidden the files?'

Evan stared at him. His childhood was over. He couldn't be scared, or he couldn't show that he was scared, so he forced his voice to be steady, like he was pressing down with a rock. 'You're supposed to get me out of the country, so your job, technically, isn't done until you deliver. I'll tell you where the files are when you get me to my father.'

'No, tell me now.'

Evan shook his head. 'Contact my dad. If you were supposed to get me and my mom to safety, that means getting us to where my dad could find us. You must have a way to reach him.'

'Your mother knew. I didn't.'

'I don't believe you, Mr Gabriel.'

'You don't give me those files, you spend the rest of your brief life handcuffed to that bed. Dying of thirst. Of starvation.'

Evan realized something, with a sting of shock: when

your mom died, one of the worst things in the world you could imagine happened, so things could not get much worse. He stared at Gabriel; he waited; he let the silence grow heavy. 'You know who killed her, this Jargo guy, who he is.'

'Yes.'

'Tell me about him and I'll help you. You're asking me to run away from my life. Do nothing about my mother's murder. Simply hope I can ever find my father again. I can't just walk away not knowing the truth.'

'You're safer not knowing. A kid with a ton of money can live anywhere.'

'I can hardly run, though, and be successful at it if I don't know who's after me. So I'll trade you the files for information on Jargo. Deal?'

After ten long seconds, Gabriel nodded. 'All right.'

'Tell me about Jargo.'

'He's . . . an information broker. A freelance spy.'

'A spy. You're telling me my mother was killed by a spy.'

'A freelance spy,' Gabriel corrected.

'Spies work for governments.'

'Not Jargo. He buys and sells data to whoever pays – companies, governments, other spies. Highly dangerous.' Gabriel bit his lip. 'I suspect it's CIA data that Jargo wants.'

Evan shook his head. 'You're suggesting, with a straight face, that my mom stole files from the CIA. That's impossible.'

'Or your father stole the files and he gave them to your mother, and I didn't say the files belonged to the CIA. The CIA simply might want the information, the same as Jargo does.' Gabriel looked as if admitting this possibility was causing him a heart attack. His face reddened with anger.

'The CIA.' It was insane. 'How would my mother be involved with this Jargo?'

'I believe she worked for Jargo.'

'My mother worked for a freelance spy,' Evan repeated. 'It can't be. You're mistaken.'

'A travel photographer. She can go anywhere, with her camera, and not raise suspicion. You live in a nice house, Evan. You attend an expensive private school. Your parents are well-to-do. You think freelance shutterbugs make that much money?'

'This can't be true.'

'She's dead and you're shackled to a bed and I'm discussing with you how to live under a false name in a foreign country as a minor. How wrong am I?'

Evan decided to play along with the man's fantasy. 'So did my mother steal these files from Jargo or from someone else?'

'Listen. You wanted to know about Jargo, I told you. He's a freelancer. People need information stolen and the job needs to be off the books, he's the man. The files are about Jargo's business, so he wants them back. So do the CIA, I imagine, because they'd like to know what he knows. There. You know more about Jargo than any person currently alive. Tell me where the files are.'

'Can't unless you unlock me.' He rattled the handcuff.

'No. Talk.'

'Where am I gonna go, Gabriel? I'm a kid. You're a big, tough guy. You've got a gun on me. You have to unlock me sooner or later, if you're taking me out of the country. Handcuffs set off metal detectors.'

He jabbed the gun into Evan's cheek. 'I've waited years for this, Evan. I'm not waiting one more second.'

Evan whispered, 'Okay, I'll tell you where the files are. They're on my phone, in my pocket.'

11

Gabriel grabbed at Evan's pocket, trying to find the phone.

Evan squirmed away from him, toward the lamp. He may not get this close to you again, he thought.

'The phone's not in your pocket. Where is it?' Gabriel kept the gun at his side, loosely aimed toward the bed. Evan crouched against the headboard, his left hand still hand-cuffed. The lamp was close to his right, the unplugged cord in a neat loop on the floor.

Evan snatched the wrought-iron lamp with his free hand. It was a heavy monster, but he lifted and swung it in one awkward sweep.

The lamp's base smashed into Gabriel's arm. He fell forward and Evan pinned him with a leg over his waist. Evan brought the lamp down into Gabriel's face. Blood welled, the base's edge cutting Gabriel in the mouth, the chin. He howled in fury.

Evan aimed the lamp downward again, but Gabriel deflected it with his arm, threw a fist, barely connected with Evan's jaw. It hurt, but the adrenaline was pumping now. He had to escape. Evan dropped the lamp, snaked his arm round Gabriel's neck, wrapped both legs round Gabriel's waist. His left arm, shackled to the bed, twisted as if it would break as Gabriel struggled.

The gun, Gabriel had the gun. Where was it?

'Let me go, you stupid brat,' Gabriel said.

'I'll bite it off if you're not still.' Evan closed his mouth around Gabriel's left ear, bit down. Gabriel screamed.

'Don't,' Gabriel gasped. Evan bit down again, let his teeth grind. Blood seeped into his mouth.

'Stop!' Gabriel yelled, and went still.

Evan saw the gun, just beyond the reach of both of them, twisted in the white sheets where they had rucked the bed-covers in their fight. He couldn't reach it. Gabriel saw it, too; his muscles strained with sudden resolve, trying to break free.

Desperation fueled Evan. He bit down on the ear again and jabbed his fingers into Gabriel's eyes. Gabriel howled in pain. He twisted to fend off Evan, but Evan's legs kept him locked in place. Every muscle in Evan's body screamed.

Gabriel squirmed toward the gun, pulling Evan's body with him. Evan's wrist wrenched in the cuff.

He'll sacrifice his ear to get that gun, Evan thought. Bite it off. He couldn't.

Instead Gabriel grabbed the lamp's cord, dragged the lamp to him. He seized the lamp's body, swung it backward at Evan. The base struck him on the top of his head and Evan, dizzy with pain, let go of the ear. A sliver of skin stayed behind in his mouth.

Gabriel released the lamp and lurched forward, caught the gun's barrel with his fingertips. Evan kept Gabriel's other arm pinned with his leg, pivoted – his arm twisting as if it were a centimeter away from breaking – and clutched the gun's grip as Gabriel pulled it forward. Evan wrenched the gun free and jabbed the barrel against Gabriel's throat.

Gabriel froze.

'Where's the key?' Evan screamed.

'Downstairs, in the kitchen. You brat, you tore my ear off.'

'No, you still got an ear.'

'Listen, new deal,' Gabriel said. 'We'll work together to get Jargo. We'll—'

'No.' Evan clubbed the gun into Gabriel's temple. Once. Twice. Three times, four. The fifth time, Gabriel went limp, his temple cut and bruised. Evan jabbed the gun against Gabriel's head and waited. Please don't make me shoot you. Please. He counted to one hundred.

Gabriel was out.

Holding his breath, his hand shaking, Evan put down the gun. Gabriel didn't move. He jabbed his hand into Gabriel's left trouser pocket, fumbled across coins, fingered the shape of keys.

'Liar,' he said to the unconscious Gabriel. He pulled out a ring that held a small key and a larger key for the bedroom door. Evan kicked the man away from him, worked the small key into the handcuff lock.

The cuff sprang open. Evan rolled off the bed, his arm on fire with pain. He held it close to him, unsure if it was broken or dislocated. No. Broken would be serious agony. He was sore but unhurt. He dragged Gabriel to the headboard, snicked the cuff over his wrist, checked Gabriel's pulse in his throat. A steady beat ticked beneath his fingertips.

Evan trained the gun, with shaking hands, on the door. Waited. Steadied himself to shoot if anyone charged to Gabriel's rescue. Told himself he could do it; he had to do it. He knew how to shoot – his father had taught him when he turned fourteen – but he had not fired a gun in five months.

And never at a living human being.

A minute passed. Another. No sound in the house.

He noticed a small card on the bed, next to the South African passport, forced out from Gabriel's shirt or trousers in the fight. It was an ID card, government issue, worn with age and fingering. Gabriel looked fifteen years younger.

Joaquin Montoya Gabriel, Central Intelligence Agency.

Gabriel was telling the truth, or a partial truth. But if he was CIA, why was he operating alone?

Deep breath. He slipped the South African passport and Gabriel's ID into his back pocket. Evan went out the bedroom door, then stopped in the darkened hallway. *Be a boy of shadows.* What a joke that was, Gabriel's little nickname for him. His arm and hand ached, his head hurt like hell, and now, the fighting done for the moment, in the darkened house, the fear rushed back into his chest.

A dim light shone from the open area downstairs; Evan was on the second floor of what appeared to be a spacious house. Thick pile carpet covered the hallway, more high-end art on the walls. The air-conditioner purred a blanket of noise. From below, he heard the thin whisper of the television, its volume inched low.

He crouched, the gun out in front of him, listening.

He fortified himself with two deep breaths and crept down the stairs. What do you do next? Keep fighting. That's the choice you made.

Evan reached the last stair when he thought, You idiot, you should have gagged Gabriel. He'll wake up and shout for help while you're sneaking up on any buddies downstairs.

He had gone too far to turn back. He knew in his heart that he wouldn't hesitate now, that he would shoot anyone who tried to stop him. He just hoped he could remember to aim at their legs, unless the other guy had a gun, and then he would aim for their chest. Chests were big; he could hit a chest. Remember to take a second to aim, squeeze, prepare for the kick ... if he had a second. No practice target had ever shot back at him.

He tried not to laugh, his nervousness bubbling up through his chest. He was just a kid. But what had Gabriel said? *Boys your age went to sea, went to war in centuries past.* Okay, he'd just gone to war. Boy of shadows. He could do this.

Evan entered the den. A widescreen TV stood in the corner next to an ornate stone fireplace. A commercial announced the latest pharmaceutical that you couldn't live without, as long as you risked at least ten side effects. Then the CNN theme played and the anchor started a story about a bombing in Israel.

He moved along the wall, peered into a top-of-the-range kitchen. Empty. A lunch sat on the counter: a ham sandwich, a glass of ice water, a pile of potato chips, a chocolate bar. Lunch for himself, probably, if he'd cooperated with Gabriel.

He checked the back of the house, stopping at a marble-topped bureau with a smattering of family photos. Gabriel posed with two girls young enough to be his grandkids.

No one around. The only sounds were the air-conditioner and CNN beginning a story about a bizarre homicide and kidnapping in Texas.

Evan ran back to the den and saw his face was on the TV. It was his Penrod ID photo: shaggy brownish-blond hair, high cheekbones, blue eyes, thin mouth, the single small hoop of earring. The crawl under his face read MISSING STUDENT. The news announcer said, 'Police investigators are still searching for Evan Casher, a sixteen-year-old student, after his mother was strangled to death in her Austin, Texas, home, and an armed gunman kidnapped Casher from a police cruiser, assaulting two officers.

'Joining me is FBI special agent Roberto Sanchez.'

Roberto Sanchez looked like a politician: perfect haircut, immaculate suit, an expression that said, *I am the most competent person on earth.*

The newscaster went for the bone: 'Agent Sanchez, is it possible that whoever kidnapped Evan Casher was responsible for Donna Casher's death? I mean, Evan was the only witness and then he's grabbed right from the police.'

'We're not prepared to speculate as to motives, but we are concerned about the boy's safety.'

'Is the boy a suspect in his mother's murder?' the anchor pressed.

No, Evan thought. They couldn't think that. No. It was inconceivable.

'No, he's not a suspect. Obviously, he's a person of interest to us because he found his mother's body, and we have not had a chance to fully talk with him, but we have no reason to believe that he was involved. We would like to talk to Evan's father, Mitchell Casher, but we have not been able to locate him. We believe he was in Australia this week, but I can't share further details.'

A picture of Mitchell appeared next to Evan's on the split screen. His father, missing.

'Could the father be involved?' the anchor pressed.

No way, Evan thought.

'We really cannot speculate,' Sanchez said.

'Why has the FBI taken over the investigation?' the anchor asked.

'We have resources not available to the Austin police,' Sanchez said. 'They asked for our assistance.'

'Any idea of a motive as to the murder?'

'None at this time.'

'We have also police sketches of the man who allegedly assaulted the two Austin officers and took Evan Casher,' the newscaster said, and the display shifted from Evan and Mitchell Casher to a penciled drawing of Gabriel.

'Any leads on this man?' the anchor asked.

'No, none yet.'

'But the Austin police found the car he used to kidnap Evan Casher, correct? A report leaked from the Austin police that the blue Ford sedan matching the description of the kidnapper's car was found in a nearby parking lot where another car had been stolen. Evan Casher's fingerprints are reportedly on the radio in the kidnapper's car. If he's selecting music, he hasn't been kidnapped, has he?' Now the anchor was trying to rewrite the news, spice it with rumor to make Evan look bad and, Evan thought, boost the interest in his story and boost the ratings.

Evan thought he might throw up on the floor.

Sanchez shook his head. 'We cannot comment on leaks. Of course, if anyone has details on this case, we'd like for them to contact the FBI.' The license plate of the stolen car and an FBI phone number popped up on the feed below the photo of Evan.

'In case Evan Casher has been kidnapped, what would you say to the kidnappers?' the newscaster asked.

'Well, as we would in any situation, we'd ask the kidnappers to release Evan unharmed and to contact us with any demands, or if Evan is able to contact us directly, all we want to do is to help him.'

'Thank you, FBI Special Agent Roberto Sanchez,' the newscaster said. 'Evan Casher gained notoriety at his arts-centered private school, Penrod, for launching a YouTube-like website geared specifically to young filmmakers. He has posted nearly two thousand clips from teenage filmmakers from four dozen countries. He's also known for his own film work, which received interest from cable companies. One of his subjects was the kids at a summer camp for teen offenders. Our correspondent Amelia Crosby spoke with the one camper who knew Evan Casher through his film projects.'

The camera shifted to a young African-American man, around eighteen, looking uncomfortable in a tie. The subtitle read JAMES 'SHADEY' SHORES.

'Mr Shores, you've known Evan Casher since he featured an interview with you in one of his student-project films. What do you think could be behind Evan Casher's bizarre disappearance?'

'Oh, this will be epic,' Evan said.

'Listen, first of all, that other guy – your anchor, with that freeze-dried hair – suggesting that Evan Casher could be involved in his mama's death, that is straight-out *nonsense*.'

'Do you know of any motive anyone could have to hurt Evan or his family?' the reporter's voice asked.

'Hurting Evan's like kicking a puppy, ma'am. My worry is that the Austin police have let Evan down, allowing him to get kidnapped. I think they ought to be looking hard at those officers and how they let some loser kidnap Evan out of one of their own police cars. You need to be doing a report on what kind of police can't keep their witnesses safe ...' Shadey's voice rose, like an engine's roar.

The reporter started trying to talk over Shadey, to no avail.

' ... All I'm saying is, the police got to show they're serious about finding Evan. How do you misplace a kid if

you are the police? Why are you asking the wrong
questions?'

'But do you know of any reason anyone would target the
Casher family?'

'No, none, but my rap group, Shadey D, we're gonna put
on a benefit concert for Evan, raise money for a reward, get
him home.'

Evan couldn't decide if he was grateful for Shadey's help
or annoyed that Shadey was promoting his rap group (He
has a rap group now? Evan wondered) on national TV. He'd
help me, Evan thought. Shadey is in Houston; it's a few
hours away; he'd help me. Wouldn't he?

The reporter briskly thanked Shadey and shifted to
another satellite feed to introduce Kathleen Torrance, the
visual-arts teacher at Penrod.

'Ms Torrance, you know Evan Casher well,' the reporter
began.

'Yes.' The teacher nodded. 'He's an excellent student, a
great kid.' Ms Torrance looked like she might have been
crying.

'What do you think has happened?'

'Well, I have no idea. The Cashers are a lovely family. I
just hope that if whoever has taken Evan can hear me, they
will let him go. I can't imagine him being involved with anything that is illicit or harmful to anyone.'

The reporter asked Ms Torrance more questions about
Evan and he listened to his favorite teacher say nice things
about him. Pictures of his mom, of Evan, of his dad, played
on the TV while Ms Torrance talked. Images and clips from
the FilmzKool site. The reporter then thanked Kathleen and
went back to the anchor, and the coverage shifted to a bank
robbery in New Hampshire.

Evan stared at the screen. His life was being dissected on national television. His father was missing. The FBI wanted to talk to him. He hurried to the phone, picked it up, started to dial.

Then put it back down on the cradle.

Gabriel was a CIA operative, and he had put two cops in hospital and kidnapped Evan. If he was working on the CIA's orders, and Evan went to the police ... what happened next? The CIA wasn't supposed to beat up cops or chain citizens to beds, so whatever had befallen his family wasn't a story that the CIA wanted in the public eye.

He needed to know more. He had a sudden terror of making a wrong move, stepping out of one prison into a far worse one.

Quickly he checked the rest of the house. A dining room and living room, a media room with a massive TV, a laundry area. Back upstairs were four more bedrooms, one occupied by two duffel bags. No sign anyone other than Gabriel was here.

He went downstairs again. He found a garage that held a motorcycle, a gleaming Ducati. His dad had a motorcycle he'd nicknamed Mid-Life Crisis and only rode on weekends; he'd let Evan ride it a few times, much to his mom's annoyance. Next to it was an old Suburban. No sign of the stolen Malibu.

Evan found the keys for the Suburban, dangling from a key-holder in the kitchen. He pocketed them and went back upstairs.

Gabriel was awake, one eye swelling with a purple blossom of bruise, his jaw red and scraped. He stared at Evan and tried to laugh.

'Very good. I underestimated you.'

'Are you working alone?' Evan said.

Gabriel let five seconds pass. 'Yes, and I'm prepared to have an honest discussion with you now about our situation.'

Evan waggled the ID in front of Gabriel. 'You said you owned a security firm. This says you're CIA. Which is it?'

'I own a firm. I used to be CIA. There. Honesty.'

'Thank you.'

'Here's more honesty, boy. You're in a great deal of trouble.'

'You have information on who killed my mother, Mr Gabriel. I have a gun. Do you see how this equation works out?'

Gabriel shook his head.

Evan leveled the pistol at Gabriel's stomach. 'Answer my questions. First, where are we?'

'You won't hurt me. I know it; you know it.' He put his gaze to the wall, as though bored.

Evan fired.

12

Arwen, Jargo's computer goddess, spent the night trying to track Evan and his kidnapper. She broke into national databases. She wormed her way into the Austin Police Department's computer system, searching for traces, for reports, for the barest sign of Evan Casher. She moved through a jungle of information as patiently and efficiently as a hunter bringing down prey.

She called at dawn on Saturday with her first report.

Jargo woke Carrie from a restless sleep in her bedroom and Dezz from the other bedroom. Jargo spoke at length with Arwen, then put Carrie on the phone while he tended to private business on his phone in his own room.

'Evan hasn't used his credit cards or accessed his bank account. No one has. Do me a favor, hon – look at the file I just sent you.' Arwen was a former librarian, a heavyset woman who spent her hours away from the computer refining gourmet recipes and watching 1950s movies, when she believed the world had been a kinder place. She had a warm, Southern accent and sounded as if she ought to be a friend's brownie-baking mother. 'See if you see what I see.'

Carrie opened the email attachment and a list of messages appeared, lifted from the Cashers' email accounts: a private account for Donna, one for Mitchell Casher's personal emails, and another for his work as a computer-security consultant.

'I just tiptoed into their ISP's database and copied their messages, since the guys didn't have time at the Casher house to go through their emails,' Arwen said.

Carrie scanned through the messages on Mitchell Casher's account. Mitchell had sent a few emails to his son, nothing of great interest. One update on how his golf game was progressing, a mention of a couple of vintage jazz recordings he liked and thought Evan would enjoy, along with the songs in digital format, a request that Evan remember to set the digital video recorder for a Houston Rockets game, a few Christmas photos done by his mother. No message appeared encoded or encrypted in any way. There were no suspicious attachments.

Donna Casher had a separate email account through the same provider. More messages to and from Evan. The rest of her emails were mostly chatty exchanges with fellow free-lance photographers. Except for Friday morning.

'She sent him four digital songs, two photos,' Arwen said, 'but note the size of the photos. They're larger than they should be.'

'They had the files hidden in them,' Carrie said.

'I suspect one photo contained a decryption program. The other photo contained the files. So when he downloads the photos, the decryption software launches secretly and decodes the files hidden in the second photo. Buries them in a new folder deep on his computer's hard drive, where he wouldn't look normally. He never sees or knows that they're present.'

'Please tell that to Jargo, that she could have snuck the files to Evan without him seeing them.'

'But he could have seen them, hon, if he knew they were coming,' Arwen said. 'You know Jargo isn't going to take the risk that he saw them.'

And you, Carrie thought, you act like you're sweet as sugar, but you won't be stupid and help me when I really need it. She wasn't fooled by Arwen's honeyed voice. A steel-spined woman was at the other end of the line. 'Are there copies on the servers that delivered the mail?'

'Cleaned off. I assume by Donna. Smart cookie,' Arwen said.

'Was Donna your friend?'

'I don't have friends in the network, honey, even you. Friendships are dangerous.'

'So we have nothing to go on.'

'Actually, we do. Donna had been on email discussion lists for opera and books, and a group on tracing genealogies in Texas.'

'Genealogy,' Carrie said. 'Researching ancestors and family trees?'

'Yes. Odd that Donna Casher would be interested in genealogy.'

'Right. No point in tracing a family tree when you're living under a false name.' Carrie jumped to the genealogy group's website and found a message index. The emails to the group were mostly requests from people looking for connections to particular surnames in particular counties in Texas. Every message went to every member through the genealogy list's email address, which meant that every message to that address reached all subscribers. It was not the forum for a private dialogue.

'I just did a cross-check on who sent Donna emails within the subscriber list,' Arwen said. 'Go to message number forty-one.'

Carrie did. An email from a Paul Granger read:

I'm very much interested in Samuel Otis Steiner family history you mentioned on genealogy forum. My grandmother was Ruth Margaret Steiner, born in Dallas, died Tulsa, daughter of an immigrant family from Pennsylvania. I can supply records you requested for the Talbott family that originated in North Carolina, moved to TN, appeared again in Florida. Please indicate whether you have appropriate records or access to them.

My daughter and I are visiting Galveston soon and are interested in tracing our history back to 1849. I can be reached at 972.555.3478.

Regards,
Paul Granger

Carrie jumped back to the genealogy discussion list. At the bottom of each email was a link to the list's online archive. She entered it and did a search on Samuel Otis Steiner.

She found a single posting about Steiner, from Donna Casher, approximately two days ago. She did a search on Donna Casher's name; that single posting was the only time Donna had ever contributed to the group discussion. She'd simply requested information on anyone with knowledge of the Samuel Otis Steiner family.

'This isn't about tracing roots, clearly,' Arwen said. 'It's a contact.'

'An innocent-looking way to communicate without arousing suspicion.' Carrie studied the awkwardly worded message. No obvious code, but the numbers might be a key. 'That number, what is it?'

'One sec.' Arwen put her on hold, jumped back on twenty seconds later. 'Hon, it's a Dallas, Texas, metro code. Got a voicemail system. No identifier as to who it belongs to. I'll have to see if I can find it in the phone-company database.'

Carrie studied the email again. 'Eighteen forty-nine. Doesn't an end date seem odd in this context? You only want to go back so far and no further? Genealogists wouldn't stop at a particular date. Don't they keep going until they run out of records?'

'I'm playing with the numbers, sugar. I suspect it's a code.'

'One we've used?'

'I can't tell you that, honey, but I'll check.'

Carrie clicked her tongue. 'Eighteen forty-nine might be the key to the rest of the message. Taking the first letter, the eighth, the fourth, and the ninth, then repeat. Or the same pattern, with words.'

'Too obvious an approach, dear,' Arwen said. 'I'm looking at the server log for Donna Casher's email account. No messages again from Paul Granger or anyone else.'

'So this voicemail account in Dallas, it's all we've got.'

'Eighteen forty-nine,' Arwen said, 'could be a code word itself, a warning, an instruction, and everything else in the message, other than the phone number, is camouflage. Like 1849 means "Run right now" or "We've been caught" or "Go to Plan B."'

'Does Granger's name ring a bell?'

'No. I've checked – he's not in any of our databases. I'll search national driver's license records, but most likely it's an alias. I've checked the message logs. No messages from Granger to Evan or Mitchell Casher.'

Carrie said, 'Please trace the email.'

'Already did. Sent from a public library in Dallas.'

'So what next?'

'We have a convergence of data in Dallas. I'll see if we can connect any of our known enemies to the Dallas area.' Arwen paused. 'You working this with Dezz?'

'Yes.'

Arwen made a noise in her throat. 'Good luck on that, sugar.'

'Thanks, Arwen.' Carrie hung up and knocked on Dezz's door. He was sitting on the edge of his bed, staring off into space. She wondered what he was thinking and decided she didn't really want to know.

She told him about the leads. 'What are we supposed to do if we find this Granger and find the whole US government right behind him?'

'Run,' Dezz said. 'Fast and far.'

'They'll kill Evan. He doesn't deserve to die.'

'What Evan Casher deserves could change from second to second. He goes public with what he knows, we're finished. Maybe he lives; maybe he dies. Depends on what he does and what he says.'

'It must be nice to have so little morality you can just tuck it in your pocket.'

Dezz smiled. 'This from the lying fake girlfriend. Do you need me to loan you some conscience? I've got conscience to burn.'

'Evan doesn't have to die if he can help us. He'd listen to me.'

'So you think.'

'So I think.'

'You think a lot,' Dezz said. 'Every brain cell firing all the time.'

'Newsflash: most people do.'

'Most people don't, including you. You messed up, not finding those files.'

She ignored him.

'Tell me true, sunshine, does he know about the Deeps?'

'No,' she said. 'No, he doesn't know. I'm sure of it.'

She could see he didn't believe her. She went back into the kitchen; Dezz followed her. She poured coffee. Jargo came out of his room, pale.

'The bald man,' Jargo said. 'We got a positive ID from the elves, off the phone records for the voicemail and from the ID. His name is Joaquin Gabriel. He's ex-CIA. The elves are tracking back every connection in Gabriel's life to see where he might stash Evan Casher.'

'Why would Gabriel want Evan? What did he do at the

CIA?' Carrie asked. A slow curl of horror rose up her spine.

'CIA. Our worst nightmare,' Dezz said.

'He got kicked out years ago,' Jargo said.

'Maybe he got kicked back in,' Dezz said.

'Gabriel cleaned up internal spills and messes,' Jargo said. 'He's what folks call a traitor-baiter, finds the people on the inside who can bring the CIA down.'

A hush filled the room. This was a dangerous enemy. 'Our worst nightmare is a man like Gabriel. If he gets those files ...' Jargo said, nodding at Dezz, using his son's words.

'So what do we do, Dad?' Dezz said.

Jargo's phone rang again. He listened, nodded, clicked off the phone. 'Gabriel's son-in-law has a weekend house near Austin, in a town called Bandera. Gabriel might run there. It's just an hour or so away.'

'Good,' Dezz said. 'I'm getting bored,' and he made a gun out of his hands, fired it between Carrie's eyes.

13

The bullet smacked into the wall 6 inches above the headboard. Gabriel jerked and flinched; his eyes widened.

'Mister, my mother is dead. My dad is missing. Do you understand how upset I am?' Evan said.

Slowly Gabriel nodded.

'Where are we?'

'Near Bandera.'

Evan knew it was a small town in the Texas Hill Country.

'It's my son-in-law's vacation house. My daughter married well.' Gabriel watched the gun, not Evan.

'Tell me how to reach my father.'

'I don't have a way.'

Gabriel was sticking to his story. Evan decided to turn the question the other way. 'Does my dad know how to get in touch with you?'

'No. This was your mom's arrangement. I had no contact with him.'

'You're lying.'

'I'm not. Your mom didn't think I needed to know.' Gabriel gave Evan a crooked, slightly crazy grin. 'Your mother stole Jargo's files. Jargo has access to your dad because your dad works for Jargo, too. Your dad is missing. Do the math.'

Evan had not thought clearly, given the chaos of the past twenty-four hours. 'Jargo has my dad.'

'Quite likely. I suspect he was on an assignment for Jargo when your mom decided to run. Jargo found out, grabbed your dad.'

'So I need those files, to ransom my dad from Jargo.'

'All they'll care about now is being sure you don't know what was in the files, and that you have no copies of them.' Gabriel closed his eyes. 'Clearly I used the wrong approach in dealing with you, Evan. I should have trusted you.'

'You think?'

'Congratulations, you've proven yourself to me, but you don't understand what's at stake. These files your mother stole, they could take down Jargo, and he's a very bad guy. I've got to have those files. They're the evidence I need.'

'Against Jargo?'

'Yes. To prove I shouldn't have lost my career, all those years ago, that Jargo has traitors inside the CIA working for him.' Gabriel coughed. 'The CIA, overall, is an organization with great, hardworking, honest people. But a few bad apples rot in every barrel, and Jargo knows the bad apples. Your mom came to me because she knew I wasn't a bad apple, Evan. She was afraid to go straight to the Agency, because she didn't want to give this information and warn Jargo. He's got people in the Agency on his payroll, people in the FBI, too. They get wind of these files, or where you're at, and they've got the same motive to get rid of you that Jargo does. They don't want to be exposed.' Gabriel licked his lips. 'Evan, the files are on your phone, right?'

'The emails that held the files are.'

'Give me your phone, then.'

Evan shook his head. 'Or we can just call the CIA.'

'Evan, do you think the CIA wants this news going public, that a freelance spy ring operates under their nose, inside their own walls?' Gabriel licked his lips again. 'The CIA drove me out of work years ago just for suggesting the possibility. Certain people in the CIA would rather kill you than let you harm the Agency's credibility. You go to them or go public with this, you're a dead kid. They're hunting you as much as Jargo is.'

'So they and Jargo both want the files. Are the files lists of traitors inside the CIA who help Jargo, or agents, or names, or operations that are underway?'

'Names. See me trusting you now?'

'Of agents?'

Gabriel hesitated for a moment. 'I think so.'

'It either is or isn't names of agents.'

Gabriel shrugged.

'What were you going to do when Mom gave you these names?' Evan steadied the gun at him. 'I don't have a single reason to believe a word you've said. You could have been lying to me from minute one, and I don't think you saved me out of any debt to my mom or out of the milk of human kindness. You want those files as bad as Jargo. You could lie about what's in them and why you need them.'

Gabriel kept his mouth shut.

'Fine. Play silent treatment. You can tell me about it on the way.'

'Way where?'

Evan left the room. Gabriel didn't deserve an answer. Evan sat down in the darkened hall, put his head in his hands, weighed his options. Gabriel knew the complete truth, but wasn't talking. He could stick a gun up to Gabriel's head and threaten to kill him if he didn't talk, but he and Gabriel both knew that Evan wouldn't murder him in cold blood. Gabriel saw it in his eyes.

So another tactic, a better one, something that would give Evan his dad and stop Jargo. The man behind his mother's death, if Gabriel wasn't lying.

But Evan had a call to make. He went and found his jacket, which Gabriel had fled the house carrying in his rush to escape. His cellphone was still inside the pocket. He checked the emails he'd downloaded when he turned on his phone as he snuck out of school. The emails were still there, music and photo files, but nothing more.

The secret files must still be locked inside those songs, or those pictures, and he didn't have a way to decode them or get to them.

He turned on the phone and dialed Carrie's number.

14

They had rocketed south on I-35 from Austin, veering west onto Highway 46, through the old German town of Boerne. Live oaks and twists of cedar covered the hills. The sky began to cloud.

Carrie sat in the front, Jargo in the back; Dezz drove. The highway sign read BANDERA 10 MILES.

Carrie's phone hummed in the silence. She had set it to vibrate, not ring, and she thought, Oh, no.

'I hear a phone,' Jargo said.

'Mine.' Carrie's palms went damp with sweat.

'Evan, calling his new true love,' Dezz said.

'Answer it, but hold the phone so I can hear.' Jargo leaned backward, put his chin over the seat, his head close to hers.

Carrie dug the phone from her purse, flipped it open. 'Hello?'

'Carrie?' It was Evan. 'Are you all right?'

'I'm fine. Where are you?'

'Why did you call me? Who did you say would protect me?'

Jargo twisted, trying to hear. Carrie's finger slid to the off button and pressed it.

'Evan, where are you?' she said into the silence. 'Evan?' She lowered the phone. 'He hung up.'

Jargo shoved her hard against the window. The barrel of his Glock pushed against her throat. She trembled.

'Should I pull over?' Dezz asked.

Jargo stared at Carrie. 'You spoke to him? After his mother was dead?'

She watched Jargo's gun, wondered if he would really shoot her. She was sick with fear.

'I told you I tried to call him; that's what I was doing when Dezz found me in the music room at school.'

He remembered and his grip softened, very slightly. Carrie took a breath. 'I left him a voicemail. Trying to let him know that I knew people who could protect him. You see it worked, he called me.'

'You failed to mention that little detail.' His voice went cold.

'Did I? I thought I told you.'

He lowered the gun. 'This is really not the time for me to worry about your loyalty. We clear?'

'Crystal clear.' She gripped his arm. 'The CIA killed my parents – you think I want them killing Evan? If he's with Gabriel, and we can get Evan back, let me talk to him. It'll be much easier if you let me handle it. Please.'

Jargo watched her, with a calculating look. 'You think you can recruit him.'

'I think I can start the process. He's lost everything, except me. He's vulnerable. I can win him over, I know I can.'

'Has he told you he loves you?' Jargo said.

'Yes. He told me the night before last.' She faced the front of the car. 'But boys say stupid things.'

'So you're his weakness,' Jargo said with a laugh.

'Apparently.'

'Him loving you should make things easier,' Dezz said, with iron in his tone. 'Give him what he wants and we're set.'

'Shut your stinking mouth,' she said. She wanted to smash Dezz's nose in, break the teeth in his smirk.

Jargo's cellphone beeped. He answered, 'Arwen, don't disappoint me.' He listened, nodded. 'Thank you.' He clicked off. 'The phone call came from a residence outside of Bandera.' He gave Dezz an address.

Carrie held her breath for a moment. 'How far away are we?'

Dezz studied the car's GPS readout. 'It should be just further up here off the highway. Five minutes away.'

15

Carrie hung up on him.

Evan stared at the phone. She had broken the connection, not him.

Why?

Maybe she's in trouble. He started to redial; then he stopped. There had to be a reason she had hung up on him.

He went back to the bedroom where Gabriel was chained. Now Gabriel was sitting close to the headboard.

'Do you know Carrie Lindstrom?'

'Never heard of her. Sorry.' Gabriel rattled the chain. 'Are you leaving me here?'

'I don't know yet.' Evan locked Gabriel in the bedroom. He hurried down the hall into Gabriel's room, opened the first duffel bag. A few clothes. A small wad of cash. No ID in the bag, but the luggage tag read J. GABRIEL and an address in McKinney, a suburb of Dallas.

He searched Gabriel's other duffel. A few clothes. In one pouch, he spotted a small metal box.

He tried opening it. Locked. Locked meant important. He needed tools and time to crack it open. He put the locked box in the first duffel, put it on his shoulder, and ran downstairs to the garage. He stuck the duffel in the passenger seat.

He went back upstairs. Getting Gabriel downstairs in the handcuffs would not be easy, but it was a risk he had to take. He would stick Gabriel in the back of the SUV, hit the road, and call Durless. He thought Durless would listen to him; he thought Durless was a man he could trust. He was probably mortified and furious at losing Evan, and then losing the case to the FBI. Evan would give him a chance to save face.

He unlocked the door and walked into the bedroom.

The bed was empty. The handcuff dangled from the metal headboard. The drapes danced in the breeze allowed by the open window.

Evan ran downstairs. His own breathing, panicked, filled his ears. CNN warbled in the den. He opened the door leading to the garage, ducked inside. No sign of Gabriel. He edged in the dimly lit garage over to the Suburban.

Where was Gabriel?

He's somewhere in the house, hunting you now.

The garage door powered upward in sudden motion.

16

Evan knew he would be seen in a matter of seconds. The Suburban was parked farthest from the house. As the garage door motored up, Evan slid over the hood of the SUV, putting the Suburban between him and the rest of the garage. He huddled down close to the front right wheel. He pulled the gun he'd taken from Gabriel from the back of his jeans.

Gabriel ran into the garage.

I have his keys. He went out the window. This must be his only way back in the house, Evan thought.

Either Gabriel had seen him or he hadn't and Evan would know in a moment.

Footsteps, heading toward the door that led to the kitchen. Evan heard that door open, then the garage door powering downward along its tracks. Gabriel was cutting off his escape. He believed Evan was still inside the house.

Evan risked a peek above the Suburban's hood. He's probably got more guns in the house and he's heading for one, because he knows I've got one and now I might have heard the garage door, wherever I am in the house.

Evan eased inside the Suburban from the passenger side, slid into the driver's seat, inserted the key in the ignition. He found the garage door-opener clipped to the sun visor and hit the button. The garage door stopped.

He hit the button instantly again and the door crept up as he started the Suburban. Evan thought, Please let him have run upstairs already.

The door to the house flew open; Gabriel stood in the doorway, gun in hand. The garage door still motored upward.

Gabriel slammed his fist on the door control; it stopped. He ran past the motorcycle, heading right for the driver's door.

Evan shifted into reverse and hit the accelerator. The Suburban roared backward, metal screeching as it scraped the lowered garage door.

Gabriel fired. The bullet pinged off the roof, his aim too

high. Evan spun the wheel, slamming backward into metal in the wide stretch of driveway, trying not to think that Gabriel had finally lost his mind, shooting at him. In the rearview mirror he saw the stolen Malibu.

Gabriel sprinted toward the car's front, aiming at the tires, bellowing, 'Stop! Evan! Give it up!'

Evan wrenched the car into drive. The Suburban rocketed forward; Gabriel screamed as he went over the hood and off the side of the car.

I hit you, Evan thought, his mind fuzzed with shock. How do you like the boy of shadows now, jerkwad?

He aimed the Suburban down the driveway, which cut down a sizable hill studded with cedars and live oaks. It looked like the Hill Country. Gabriel had mentioned Bandera. For once he'd told the truth.

The driveway snaked down to a closed metal gate that fenced the property off from a small country road. Evan pressed the other button on the garage door-opener, hoping that the gate was electronic. The gate didn't budge. Then he spotted a loop of chain locking the gate shut.

He searched in the dividing console of the Suburban, then hunted on the car keyring. No extra key.

Evan grabbed the gun from the passenger seat, got out of the Suburban, left the engine running. He aimed at the hefty lock on the chain, took two steps back, and fired.

The gunshot thundered across the silence of the hills. The lock rocked, a hole blasted in its edge. He tested the lock. It held.

He heard the whine of a motorcycle. The Ducati, revving down the driveway.

Evan steadied his aim and fired again. The bullet chocked through the lock dead center. The lock fell open under his hands and he unwound the chain, dropping the links to the gravel at the road's edge. His breath grew heavy and loud in his ears. He shoved the gate open.

The whine crescendoed. He saw the Ducati arrowing down the driveway through a break in the trees, then roaring toward him. Gabriel raised his pistol. The warning shot kicked up dust near Evan's feet.

No place to hide. Evan, the chain in one hand, the gun in the other, slid under the Suburban at the passenger side, into the grit and gravel.

He had taken cover in panic. Stupid, stupid, stupid.

The Ducati stopped ten feet away. Limestone dust from the gravel coated the bottom of its wheels.

'Evan.' Gabriel sounded as if he were talking around broken teeth. 'Be a good boy. Toss the gun out. Now.'

'No,' Evan said.

'Listen to me. Don't be an idiot. Don't run. You're basically a helpless kid and they'll kill you.'

'Back off or I'll shoot you.'

Gabriel's voice lowered. 'You shoot me, you're completely alone in this world. No money. No place to go. The cops hand you right over to the FBI and then you know what happens.'

'No, I don't.'

'FBI comes and collects you on behalf of the CIA. Takes you into federal custody. And then they lose you, Evan, because the government wants you and your family dead.'

'You're lying.'

'I'm your only hope. Now come on out.'

'I'm not talking to you. I'm counting. When I hit the magic number, I'm shooting you in the foot.' He wanted out from under the hot, dusty car, the heat of the engine pressing against his back.

Gabriel kept his voice calm, as though trolling his options and seeing which one would lure Evan into sunlight. 'Evan, I know what it's like to have no place to go.'

Evan waited.

'I know how these people work, Evan, how they'll hunt you. I can hide you from them, or get you to a place where you could work out a deal with them.' Slowly moving, slowly circling the Suburban. 'Best of all, I have a plan to get your dad back.' Gabriel's voice had softened, turned to a gentler tone.

Evan aimed at Gabriel's feet. His heart hammered against the gravel.

'Your mother trusted me, and I failed her. I feel responsible, but remember, I shot through the rope; I saved your life.' Gabriel's voice dropped lower. 'I'm talking with you. I'm not dragging you out by your heels to fight you.'

Because I hit you with a car and because I have a gun, and you know it: You heard me shoot the lock. And you're hurt, bad hurt from being hit by the car, but you still chased me down here. You need me. Because you want Jargo so bad, and I'm the bait.

'We need to go to Florida,' Gabriel said. 'That's where I was taking your mother. That's where she expected to find your dad.' Tossing Evan a bone.

'Where in Florida?'

'We can talk about details when you come out. I've got a great idea on how to get your dad back for you.'

'So let's hear your plan,' Evan said. Keep Gabriel talking. Let his voice give away any sudden effort, like rushing toward the Suburban.

'Jargo wants your dad, to ensure you can't hurt him with the files. The CIA wants your dad or those files, to nab Jargo

and whoever's in the CIA who works with him. I suggest
you offer deals to both sides, get them face to face. Then you
threaten to expose both sides – Jargo as a freelance spy, the
CIA for dealing with him, which is an embarrassment to
them – and play them against each other. Come out and let's
talk.'

And what does that plan buy you? Evan wondered. He
could not figure out what Gabriel wanted – revenge, but
against both Jargo and the CIA? It made no sense. Unless he
really was ex-CIA and the disgruntled employee of the
century.

'All right,' Evan said. 'I'm coming out. Don't shoot me.'

'Toss the gun out, Evan. Flick on the safety and toss the
gun out.'

Evan, lying flat, aimed with care at Gabriel's foot. His
hand trembled and he willed it still. *Make it count.* But
the surface of the road, all rough edges of gravel, made
him worry the bullet might not fly straight into Gabriel's
leg. He knew back when he fired the gun at the handcuffed
Gabriel that he wasn't going to hit him. He didn't hesitate
then, but now ... Hurt him just bad enough so you can get
away.

The thought that he was going to shoot another person
made his arms shiver.

'I'm coming out!' he yelled.

He aimed. But before he squeezed the trigger, a single shot
rang out. A smack of bullet slammed into flesh and Gabriel
screamed and fell to the dirt.

17

'Find a back way,' Jargo said. 'Pull up the GPS map for me. Just because Evan called Carrie doesn't mean he's free of Gabriel. This could be a trap, Gabriel or the CIA pulling us in.'

A trap, with Evan as bait. Carrie didn't want to think about that. 'Evan . . . '

'Carrie, I know. You don't want him hurt. We don't, either. I have my own reasons for wanting to be sure Evan is safe.' The lie – she was sure it was a lie – sounded smooth on Jargo's lips.

Dezz pointed at the GPS screen. 'There's an access road a half-mile from the front entrance of the ranch. We'll go in that way.'

Get to Evan first, Carrie told herself. Find him and get him out of there before Dezz and Jargo kill him.

The hill rose from the back ranch road in a sharp incline, limestone breaking through the thin soil in heaves and cracks, thirsty cedars and small oaks competing on the scrubby land. Dezz took the lead, Carrie the middle; Jargo brought up the rear.

Dezz stopped so suddenly Carrie nearly walked into his back.

'What's wrong?'

'I heard a hiss.' For the first time Carrie heard a tremble in Dezz's voice.

'Snakes are still hibernating,' Jargo said. 'No need to be afraid, little boy.' Annoyance and arrogance blended in his tone.

'Are you all right?' Carrie asked. She put her hand on the back of Dezz's shoulder.

'I truly dislike snakes,' Dezz said. He took a tentative step forward.

Carrie went round him to take the lead. Dezz walked as if he were navigating a minefield, one cautious step after another.

'Dezz, I think you heard the wind in the branches.'

He didn't move.

'Dezz hates snakes, reptiles, anything that lives belly on the ground,' Jargo said. 'I should get him a cobra as a pet, help him overcome his weakness.'

Dezz moaned in his throat.

'Now you know how to punish him when he won't listen to you,' Carrie said to Jargo. 'Put a copperhead in his bed.'

'He did that once, but it was an adder,' Dezz said.

Carrie was speechless, thinking he must be joking. Jargo didn't smile or laugh.

They heard a crash of metal, then another crash, a gunshot, a scream, the roar of an engine moving away from them.

Jargo grabbed Dezz's arm and the three hurried down an incline, then climbed up another small hill. They ran past a stable and a limestone pool, heard the rev of a second engine, the distant crack of another gunshot, saw a bald man racing a motorcycle down the driveway.

'Gabriel,' Jargo said.

Dezz bolted, hurtling down the driveway, Jargo following. He called back over his shoulder, 'Carrie, see if he's in the house.'

She didn't stop and Jargo raised a gun toward her and said, 'Do what you're told.'

Evan wasn't on the motorcycle; he might be in the house.

This is my chance, she thought, so she nodded and ran back toward the house.

Seeing Gabriel talking to a parked Suburban, Dezz hunkered down among the cedars. Jargo knelt next to him.

Evan, Dezz mouthed. *He's in the car.*

Jargo nodded. They waited through two minutes of talking.

Dezz couldn't see where in the Suburban Evan was, but then he heard, from under the car, a clear yell – 'I'm coming out' – and saw Gabriel training his pistol at the SUV's underside.

Jargo stood, aimed, and fired.

The bald man jerked, blood popped from his back, and he fell with a choked cry of agony.

'I winged him for you,' Jargo said. 'Show me what you can do, or you and I will have a problem. I need to see how tough you are.'

Dezz gave a soft swallow. 'Dad ...'

'Do it. Show me the man I've made you into.'

'All right.'

'Don't kill Evan,' Jargo whispered. 'Wound if you must. I prefer him alive to answer my questions.' He gripped Dezz's arm. 'Clear?'

'Totally.' Then Dezz yelled, 'Freeze!' and started down the hill. Jargo stood, glancing back at the house where Carrie had vanished. Silence. He hoped Gabriel worked alone. Traitor-baiters often did; they trusted no one. It was, Jargo knew, a sad and smart way to live. He drew back into the trees to watch, in case Evan came out shooting.

Gabriel crawled for his gun, face contorted in pain. Another bullet kicked up the limestone crush by his head and he stopped.

'I told you to freeze,' Evan heard a voice say. Euro accent. He knew the voice: Dezz, the weird new kid at school. 'It wasn't a suggestion; it was a strongly worded suggestion.

'Evan? You're safe now. The cavalry's arrived,' Dezz called. 'You all right, Evan?'

'Run, Evan—' Gabriel gasped, and a second bullet hit him, this time in the shoulder. Gabriel shrieked, twisted in the dirt with a stunned look on his face. Evan could see blue-jeaned legs walking toward him. He could hear nervous laughter on the gust of the breeze.

Dezz? Here? Shooting a man and laughing? Evan fought down the sudden surge of terror in his chest, his guts.

The voice called, 'Be still now, Mr Gabriel. You keep moving, you make me very nervous. I don't like being nervous.' Then the voice brightened. 'Evan? You under the car or in it?'

Evan gave no answer.

'Hey, Evan, the good guys are here. I'm here to help you.'

Evan didn't trust anyone who shot a wounded man.

'All's well, Evan. It's safe now. If you've got a gun, toss it out. We don't want any accidents.'

Gabriel groaned and sobbed.

'Evan, I don't know what this crazy old freak told you, but you're perfectly safe. Look, I was assigned to go undercover and protect you at the school. I'm a good guy. I was trying to watch out for you yesterday. I know your dad. He's sick with worry about you. We tracked Mr Gabriel here. I need you to come out. We're gonna take you to your dad.'

'Dezz, stay back,' Evan yelled.

'Well, there you are,' Dezz called kindly.

'He's a liar,' Gabriel yelled, and the walking legs delivered a sudden kick, then another, to Gabriel's ribs. Gabriel groaned, curled up into a ball. He went very still. Evan couldn't tell if he was still breathing.

'Evan, come out now, please,' Dezz said, 'for your own safety.'

'I don't believe you,' Evan said.

'I understand what a confusing couple of days you've had, but you just need to come on out.'

'You could have told me at school you were supposed to protect me.'

'I had to keep it secret.'

'Well, you did a very bad job of protecting me.'

'I did, until now. Mr Gabriel here isn't going to bother you anymore.'

'Who do you work for?'

'I work for my dad, Evan. He's friends with your dad, all right? Come out from there and let's talk.'

'Who?'

A moment's hesitation. 'His name is Jargo.'

Evan fired at Dezz's feet.

18

Carrie moved from the garage to the kitchen. Silence, except for the television in the den, tuned to CNN.

'Evan?' she called. 'Evan, it's me, Carrie. Come on out.'

Silence. A shiver took hold of her chest as she went into each room. Afraid she would find him dead.

Unless it was a trap, and as soon as Evan called her, Gabriel killed him. She tried to think. Gabriel was ex-CIA.

These files – she wasn't sure what they contained that made Jargo sweat – were of interest to Gabriel because he'd gone freelance, or he'd turned traitor, or he'd gone back to work for the Agency. Smoke and mirrors, this world was nothing but smoke and mirrors, and she could not see the truth of anything except Evan saying, 'I love you.'

She moved through the downstairs rooms quickly, efficiently. She hurried upstairs. He had endured a horrible two days. His mother dead, and she had been powerless to stop it or protect Donna or him.

His mother strangled. Hers had been shot.

Please, Evan, be here, not down there with Dezz. Or be gone, gone far away where we can't find you.

She ran through each room.

Dezz howled and jumped at the missed shot, but only retreated halfway up the hill. He gave a twisted laugh. 'Oh, think we're bad now that we've got a squirt gun. Funny way of saying thanks for the save,' he called. 'Gabriel was aiming for you when he was telling you to come out. We shot him to protect you, you idiot.'

We? Evan waited. He thought Dezz would run for deeper cover. It was sensible. Dezz didn't, but he didn't come any closer.

'Your father,' Dezz said, 'his name is Mitchell Eugene Casher, born in Denver. He's been a computer consultant for nearly twenty years.'

'So?'

'So, his favorite ice-cream flavor is butter pecan. He likes his steak medium. His favorite television show of all time is *Miami Vice* and he often bores people with plot summaries. Sound familiar?'

It did. 'How do you know all that?'

'Evan, your family and my family work together. We do good work, but your family has been targeted by very bad people, including Mr Gabriel here, who was kicked to the curb by the CIA.'

Evan waited. A caramel wrapper dropped by Dezz's feet.

'Your parents didn't want you to know. We had to respect their wishes.'

Silence for a minute.

'Got a friend at the house who's worried about you,' Dezz said. 'Carrie's here with me.'

Evan thought he had heard wrong. 'What?' His chest tightened.

Ten seconds of silence and Dezz said, 'Sorry, Evan, stay still. I just need to take a simple precaution,' and he shot out the right front tire of the Suburban. The heavy SUV sank and settled down where the tire blew. 'I can't risk you driving off,' Dezz said. 'I want to take you to Carrie, and to your father. Come out, hands up, we call him. Get everyone back together. Nice family reunion.'

Evan gritted his teeth. No. Dezz was a liar; it was a trick; it had to be a trick, to lure him out. He had to get out of here, but he couldn't drive the Suburban, not with a shredded tire.

The Ducati. It stood near the front of the Suburban, where Gabriel had parked it. The Suburban faced the gate. The bike was to his right, and Dezz stood over to the left and halfway up the hill. No way Gabriel pocketed the keys when he got off the bike, ready to shoot Evan. He wouldn't have taken the time, right?

Gabriel gave out what sounded to Evan like a long, dying

sigh. Maybe the bullet had hit him in a major organ, Evan couldn't see, but he couldn't do anything for him. He couldn't decide whether or not he'd feel guilty; Gabriel had saved him from hanging, but Gabriel had only done it for his own agenda.

In his pocket he had his iPhone, Gabriel's CIA ID, and the South African passport that Gabriel had shown him. Gabriel's duffel bag was in the car, too, but, he remembered, on the passenger side. He played the sequence of escape in his mind. Roll out on the passenger side of the Suburban, ease the door open, grab the duffel – it held cash he would need and the small locked box he'd taken from Gabriel. Shoot at Dezz to chase him back up the hill, jump on the bike, go through the gate. It was probably suicide, but at least he was going down trying.

'Bring Carrie down here. Let me talk to her and I'll come out,' he called.

Silence for a second, and Dezz said, 'You come out and I'll bring her to you.'

Dezz paced about twenty feet away, close into the trees.

He's waiting for you to go for the motorcycle. No, Evan decided. He was just waiting. He could see Dezz's face now: that snow-pale hair, thin features, a patient smile on his face. He's sixteen and he may have killed Gabriel and it didn't make him blink.

Dezz had a European accent. One of the men who killed his mother had a European accent. Were they connected?

Stay focused. Keep your hand steady when you fire. His father's voice in his ear, although he'd never been very good at target practice when his father had dragged him to the range, bored and indifferent to shooting, and he hadn't been in months. Evan wriggled out from under the car on the passenger side, the Suburban's chassis between him and Dezz. He opened the door. He grabbed the duffel, put the strap over his shoulder.

Dezz ran straight for him, aiming, yelling, 'Evan, great. Arms up, please, where I can see them, okay?'

Evan fired over the hood and Dezz's jacket sleeve jerked as if tugged from behind. Dezz dropped to the ground and Evan kept firing over Dezz's head until the gun emptied as he ran. He reached the motorcycle and shoved the gun into the back of his jeans.

The keys gleamed in the ignition. He cranked the engine, squeezed into gear, spinning gravel, and shot through the narrow opening of the gate. The bike wobbled, but he kept it steady. He did not look back, because he did not want to see the bullet coming for him. So he did not see Jargo step from the oaks, shoot at his shoulder, and miss, did not see Dezz stand, take careful aim, and a running Carrie shove Dezz as he fired. Evan heard the crack of the two pistols, their echoes bouncing around the mesquite-studded hills, but nothing hit him. He bent over the motorcycle, low, the duffel killing his balance, his chin close to the handlebars, and all he saw was the road leading away from death.

19

Evan needed a car. Fast. Dezz could come after him at any moment, thundering down and running him off the road, smearing him into jelly. A sign down the road indicated he was 2 miles from Bandera.

He drove into town, stopping only to tuck the emptied gun into the duffel so he wasn't flashing around weaponry. A scrawny sixteen-year-old on a luxury motorcycle was probably going to be noticed anyway, he thought. Lots of shops, a barbecue restaurant, signs for festivals happening every month. He peeled off the main road and wondered how he would go about borrowing – no, taking – no, let's be totally honest, he told himself, *stealing* a car.

It was a strange decision. He wasn't part of the normal world anymore; he had stepped over into a shadowland where he had no map, no compass, no North Star to guide him. He had seen his face on the national news, seen himself discussed as a victim of crime. He had run over Gabriel and kept driving. He had seen Gabriel shot twice but was not heading to the police. He had escaped from a violent boy who had pretended to be his friend.

The rulebook of his life was in the gutter.

What would the boy of shadows do? he asked himself. Think like Gabriel. Think like a boy who must hide until he can fight back.

He drove until the houses were smaller, the edges of the lawns less precise.

Small towns. Unlocked doors, keys in cars, right? He hoped. He parked the Ducati, pocketed the keys, slung his dusty duffel over his shoulder. A slow rain began; the sky rumbled. Most of the homes had driveways with carports instead of garages. Good. That made spotting a target car easier, and he wondered if this was how thieves approached their work. The rain chased everyone inside. He hoped no one watched him as he ambled from driveway to driveway, peering into cars, testing the doors. Everything was locked. So much for small-town trust.

He was on his eighth driveway, soaked now, approaching a pickup when the front door opened and a tough, thick-necked guy stepped out on the home's small porch.

'Help you, son?' he called, in a tone not exactly a threat. 'What you doing?'

The lie came to Evan's mouth so easily it astonished him. 'Flyers.' He pointed at the duffel bag. 'Supposed to leave flyers on windshields, but it's too wet, so I was gonna stick 'em in the driver's seats.'

'Flyers for what?' The giant stepped forward, giving Evan a doubting eye: his shaggy hair, the now filthy shirt, grimy with wet dirt.

'New church in town,' Evan said, 'the Holy Temple of Tested Faith. We use rattlesnakes in our services and—'

The giant said, 'Thanks, I'm good,' stepped back inside, and closed the door.

Evan headed down the street. Fast now, running in the rain. The giant either bought it or he didn't and was calling the cops.

Two more doors down, he found an unlocked truck with the keys in the ignition. It was a Ford F-150, red, an interior clean except for a Styrofoam coffee cup in the holder, a cell-phone wedged in the seat divider, a pair of sunglasses, a baseball cap, and a *Dora the Explorer* doll, worn out with affection. The lights were off in the house; the mailbox read EVANS. There you go, Evan thought, it's a good sign. He took a gas receipt from the floor and wrote, 'Sir/Ma'am, I am very sorry about taking the truck. The Ducati parked down the street is yours to keep. I'll call and tell you where I've left your truck so you can get it back.' He put the note and the *Dora the Explorer* doll and the Ducati keys on the porch in plain sight, got in, started the truck, backed up. He thought the phone might be useful before the angry owner deactivated its service.

No one came out of the house.

He drove out of Bandera at modest speed, checking the gas gauge. Almost full. Finally a break he hadn't had to fight for.

Now you're a real criminal. What would his mom say?

She'd say, 'Go get the bad guys who killed me.'

No, she wouldn't. She'd say, 'Run, Evan. Run and hide, and never let them find you.' Revenge didn't matter – saving his father did.

Florida, Gabriel had claimed, was the rendezvous point for Evan's dad. His father might already be there, if he wasn't being held by Dezz Jargo's group. Evan would drive to San Antonio – it was almost noon now – and head east. He cranked on the radio as he hit the highway. Mostly his driving consisted of back and forth between house and school; he'd never driven to another city before. The highway made him nervous. Bad country music blared and he punched the preset buttons, found a rock station. The storm blossomed into full fury, and he pointed the truck southeast. He knew the signs would guide him into the sprawl of San Antonio. Then he could take Interstate 10 in a straight shot to Houston and beyond, across the Louisiana flatlands and bayous, across the toes of Mississippi and Alabama, and into the westward finger of Florida.

Then he could find his father. In a big, crowded state, where he had no idea where to start looking. But he couldn't stay still.

He thought about the files. The files were the center of the whole nightmare, the negotiating point, the key to rescuing his father. If Dezz, Jargo, and company believed he possessed another copy of the files and would eventually exchange them for his dad, then the files shielded his father. Kill his father and Evan had no reason to keep the files secret.

His whole body hurt; his whole body said, *Enough.* Concentrate on the road. Don't think about Mom, about Carrie. Just drive. *Every mile gets you closer.* That's what his dad had said on the long family drives. They never had other family to visit; these were always trips to the Grand Canyon, to New Orleans, where his parents had lived when he was born, to Santa Fe, to Disney World once when he was twelve, too cool for Disney and carefully camouflaging his excitement. Whenever he asked the inevitable childish question of 'How much farther?' Dad would say, 'Every mile gets you closer.'

'That's no answer,' Evan would complain, and his father would just repeat the answer: 'Every mile gets you closer,' smiling at Evan in the rearview mirror.

Finally Mom would say, 'Just enjoy the journey.' She'd lean back from the passenger seat, squeeze his hand, which embarrassed him but now seemed like heaven's touch made real. Typical motherly, zippy optimism. He missed her as he would an arm suddenly gone.

Gabriel had said Jargo was like a spy. Dezz said Jargo and Evan's dad worked together. So your parents are spies. Even if Dezz was a liar, this had a ring of truth, given the events of the past two days. The concept was hazy, foggy. He didn't know what a spy looked like, but he didn't picture his father, who was just like all the other neighborhood dads.

But that wasn't his father. His father read Graham Greene and John Grisham, loved baseball, hated fishing, wrote computer code, and adored his family. Evan had never known a lack of love.

So did your dad tell you he loved you, go get on a plane, and then go steal secrets? Or maybe even *kill people*? Did blood money pay for fancy Penrod Academy, put food in your belly, fund chewing gum and comic books and your camera equipment to make your stupid little films and host your stupid FilmzKool website?

The miles of Texas unfurled, long and rainy. 'Every mile gets you closer,' he said under his shallow breath. Again and again, a mantra to keep away the pain and to harden his heart.

He would find out the truth. He would find his father. And he would make the people who had killed his mother pay with everything they held dear.

20

'I could kill you!' Dezz screamed at Carrie. 'I had him!'

She crossed her arms. 'Jargo wanted him alive. You were aiming for his head.'

'I was aiming for the bike. The bike!'

'If you were aiming for the bike,' Jargo said, stepping between them, 'you could have shot it out when you shot the Suburban's tire, son.'

Dezz's red face frowned. 'What?'

'You hoped Evan would run,' Jargo said. 'Give you a reason to shoot him dead. Get over this jealousy regarding Carrie. Now.'

Dezz blinked at him, his face reddening. 'What? Are you serious? Are you *serious*?'

Jargo leaned forward and slapped his son. Dezz

stumbled backwards. Then he slapped him again, on the other cheek.

'Stop!' Carrie said, and Jargo shot her a look of such venom that the rest of her words tangled in her brain. For the first time, she felt sorry for Dezz. Having this man as a father ...

'Dad,' Dezz said, 'I ... I'm sorry.'

'You like this girl and it's distracting you,' Jargo said.

This is humiliating, Carrie thought. Why does he do this to his own son?

'That's not true.' Dezz shook his head, fished in his pocket for candy. He jabbed a caramel in his mouth. 'I don't care about her or what she does.'

'Why didn't you take out the bike, then?' Jargo said. He went over, prodded Gabriel with his shoe.

'I didn't think he'd try for the bike. Who knew the little moppet would fight back!' Dezz spat. He whirled on Carrie. 'He knew how to shoot. Why didn't you warn me?'

'I didn't know he could shoot. He never mentioned it.'

'Dezz,' Jargo said in a cold voice, 'please. Evan's father is a crack shot, so was his mother. It's not unreasonable that they might have taught Evan about guns.'

Dezz jerked off his jacket, pointed at the scorch on his skin where Evan's bullet had passed. 'He nearly shot me and you want to give me a lecture.'

'My lecture is done. Now you can have a bandage,' Jargo said.

Carrie kept her voice cool. 'If you want to know with certainty what Evan knows, and how big a threat he is, you need him alive. I can find him. He has few friends, few places to hide.'

'Where will he go, Carrie?' Jargo asked. He was calm, unruffled, kneeling to check Gabriel's pulse.

'Think about it from Gabriel's perspective. He is ex-CIA. He not only has a bone with you, but with the Agency. If we assume he's operating alone, he'll have wanted to maintain total control over Evan. He stole him from the cops, for God's sake. That means he would have warned Evan off the cops, off the authorities.' She hoped she'd made a good case and went for the close. 'Evan will go to Houston. He knows people there. His family used to live there before they lived in Austin. He has friends there from his film he did on juvie camp, especially a boy named James Shores. His nickname is Shadey.'

Dezz jabbed his gun against her chest. It was still warm, the heat spreading through the material of her T-shirt. 'If you hadn't let him leave study hall yesterday morning, we'd be in a lot better shape.'

She gently moved the gun away from her. 'You couldn't stop him, either. If you thought before you acted—'

'Be quiet, both of you,' Jargo said. 'All of Carrie's theorizing aside, he may be heading straight to the Bandera police. Gabriel's alive. Let's take him and go.'

They loaded Gabriel in the back of the dented but drivable Malibu, wiping down and abandoning their own car behind a dense motte of live oaks. Gabriel had two bullet wounds, one in the shoulder, one in the upper back, and he was unconscious. Carrie took a medical kit from the car they were leaving behind and tended, as best she could, to his injuries. But there wasn't much she could do other than staunch the bleeding.

'Will he live until we get back to Austin?' Jargo asked.

'If Dezz doesn't kill him,' Carrie said.

Dezz got into the car, jerked the rearview mirror to where he could see Carrie in the back, Gabriel's head in her lap.

'I could kill *you*,' he said again, but now there was just the hurt of the denied child, the tantrum fading into pout.

It was time, she decided, to start playing a new hand. 'You won't,' she said calmly. 'You'd miss me.'

Dezz stared at her and she saw the anger begin to fade in his face. She allowed herself to breathe again.

'Go eat dinner,' Jargo ordered them when they returned to the Austin apartment. 'I need peace and quiet for my talk with Mr Gabriel.'

Carrie did not like the sound of that request, but she had no choice. She and Dezz walked down the street, under the arching shade of the oaks, to a small Tex-Mex restaurant. It was crowded with young, hip attendees from the massive South by Southwest music and film festivals that dominated Austin every mid-March. Her heart was in her throat. Evan had talked about coming to the film festival until just last week, but his mom wouldn't let him skip school and lots of the screenings happened during the day.

Crowded around the tables were young people who reminded her of Evan – talking, laughing, their minds focused on art rather than survival. She looked at the filmmakers and thought, This is who Evan is supposed to be when he grows up. If he grows up. I have to make sure he grows up.

She watched Dezz signal the hostess with two fingers and she followed him to a booth. Carrie excused herself to go to the ladies' room, left him playing with the sugar packets.

The ladies' room was busy and noisy. In the privacy of a stall, Carrie opened a false bottom in her purse. She removed a concealed smartphone, tapped out a brief message, and pressed send. She waited for an answer.

When she was done reading the reply, she blinked away

the tears that threatened her eyes, and washed her face with trembling hands. She came out of the ladies' room half expecting Dezz to have his ear pressed to the door, but the hallway held only a trio of laughing women.

She returned to the booth. Dezz dumped his sixth sugar packet into his iced tea, watching a mound of sweetness filter down past the ice cubes into the tea. She considered him – the high cheekbones, the dyed white hair, the ears that protruded slightly – and instead of being afraid of him, she pitied him. For just one bent moment. Then she remembered him shooting at Evan and disgust filled her heart. She could shoot *him*, right here in the booth. His hands were nowhere near his gun.

Instead she sat down. He had ordered iced tea for her as well.

'My dad, he doesn't mean what he says to me.'

'He hit you.'

Dezz looked at the mound of sugar.

'You're bigger. You can hit him back. Or just leave, Dezz. Go.'

'But he's my dad.' Now he looked up at her. Did his lip tremble, for just a moment? No, she thought. She must have imagined it.

'I know.' She sipped at her tea. The thought of having Jargo as a father raised goose-pimples along her arms, the back of her legs. Don't feel too sorry for Dezz, she thought, because he won't feel sorry for you if you get in his way.

'Do you love Evan?' He asked this in a soft, almost childish whisper, as though he'd spent his day's ration of bravado and bluster.

There was only one answer she could give him. 'No, of course not.'

'Would you tell me if you did?'

'No, but I don't love him.'

'Love is hard.' Dezz poked his straw into his sugar hill, stirred it down to nothing. 'I love my dad and look how he talks to me.' He crumbled a tostada, flicking the fragments across the table, stuck his finger in the salsa, licked it clean, like an ill-mannered child, and she wondered if this was a test to see if she'd dare to correct him. The waitress came and took their orders. Dezz wanted *tres leches* cake first, but Carrie said no, dessert after dinner, and he didn't argue.

'Where did you go to school, Dezz, when you were just being you, not pretending to be someone else?'

He looked at her in surprise, unaccustomed to a personal question. 'Nowhere. Everywhere. He sent me to school in Germany for a while. I liked Germany. Then Switzerland, then New York, and I didn't even know if my dad was alive or dead for three years – he didn't call – then California for two years. Other times he didn't bother with school. I helped him.'

Helped him. The thought of what that meant unnerved her. Jargo taking his own son along on his bloody work, to be his apprentice?

'He taught you to shoot and kill and steal.' She kept her voice lower than the Tejano music drifting from the speakers, than the laughter from the tables. Jargo had left Dezz alone for three years? No Christmases, no birthdays, no calls at all. Her stomach wrenched.

'Sure. I didn't like school, anyway. Too much reading. I liked sports, though.'

She tried to imagine Dezz playing football without kicking the opposing goalie in the face. Or three-on-three basketball, occupying the court with boys whose fathers did not teach them how to disarm an alarm system or slice open a jugular.

'You don't do this often, do you? Just sit and eat with another human being.'

'I eat with Jargo.'

'You call him Dad.'

He sucked a long draw on his sugar-clouded tea. 'He doesn't like it when I call him Dad. I only do it to annoy him.'

She remembered her own father, her clear and unabated love for him. She watched Dezz swirl the tea in his mouth, look up at her, then look back down to his drink in a mix of contempt and shyness. She saw, with a sudden, sad shock, that he believed she was probably the only girl he could talk to, that he could hope for, because she was the only one who knew his truths.

'I'm still mad at you,' he said to his tea glass. Their plates arrived. Dezz forked a chunk of beef enchilada, looped a long string of cheese round his fork, and broke the thread with a flourish. He tested out a smile. It chilled her and sickened her all at once. 'But I'll get over it.'

'I know you will,' she said.

The apartment was quiet and dark. Jargo had rented the two adjoining apartments as well to ensure privacy. He set a small digital voice recorder on the coffee table, between the knives, then poured a glass of whiskey.

'No objections to being recorded, do you, Mr Gabriel? I don't want to trample on your constitutional rights, not the way you did on other people's in years gone by.'

Gabriel's voice was barely a creak, faded from blood loss,

pain, and exhaustion. 'Don't you talk to me about what's moral or decent.'

'You hunted me for a long time, but your license got revoked.' Jargo selected a small knife and a long blade geared for holiday duty. 'This big beauty is designed to cut turkey. Rather appropriate.'

'You're nothing but a traitor.'

Jargo inspected the knife, ran its edge along his palm, making sure that Gabriel could see the glitter of the blade. He came closer to Gabriel. 'Who are you working for these days? CIA, or Donna Casher, or someone else who wants to bring me down?'

Gabriel swallowed. 'You'll kill me regardless if I talk or not.'

'My son didn't leave me much of you to work with, but it's your choice whether the end is fast or slow. I'm a humanitarian.'

'I have nothing to say.'

'I have something to say. You have a family, Gabriel. I checked. A grown daughter, a son-in-law, and grandchildren. I think I might send Dezz to pay them all a visit. He didn't do such a good job shooting you; he needs practice.'

Gabriel's eyes moistened in terror. 'No. No.'

Jargo smiled. Everyone, but him, had a weakness, and that made him feel so much better and secure in his place in the world.

'Then let's chat like the professionals we are so your family gets to enjoy their storybook life. I know you used to work for the CIA, and they kicked you out for being a drunk who accused half the agency of being traitors. Who are you working for now?'

Gabriel took two deep breaths before answering. 'Donna Casher.'

'What exactly were you supposed to do for her?'

'Get fake IDs for her and her kid, get them to her husband, then sneak all three of them out of the country. Protect them.'

'And your payment was what?' Jargo moved closer with the larger knife, brushed its edge along Gabriel's jaw.

'Hundred thousand dollars.'

Jargo lowered the knife. 'I don't believe that hundred thou was the whole payment, Mr Gabriel.'

'Please don't hurt my family. They don't know anything.'

Jargo produced a piece of paper from his jacket, held it up. 'We traced this email from you to Donna Casher. Decode it for me.'

The old training died hard. 'I don't know what it means.'

Jargo waved the knife in front of Gabriel's face. 'You want me to dig the bullets out for you?'

Gabriel shuddered.

'See, Donna Casher turning to an ex-CIA drunk is truly the million-dollar question. Why you? I believe you were willing to take a bigger chance, for more than money. Tell me. For your family's sake.' Jargo leaned down, whispered into the man's devastated ear, 'Buy their safety.'

Gabriel's chest heaved. Jargo restrained himself from cutting the man's throat. He hated tears; he hated to see them. He had been taught, early on, that tears were an unforgivable weakness.

Gabriel found his breath. 'The message meant she was ready to run.'

'Thank you,' Jargo said. 'Running with what?'

'Donna had a list.'

'A list.'

'Of a group of people, inside the CIA ... running illegal,

unauthorized operations. Hiring out assassination and espionage work to a freelance group of spies she called the
Deeps. She had a list of these people, some inside the CIA,
who hired the Deeps – your group of spies.'

'I see.' Jargo could barely breathe.

'She had account information on how the CIA insiders
had paid for your services, like I always suspected.'

'And never proved,' Jargo said. 'Describe the data, please.'

'She said you had clients inside the CIA. Inside the
Pentagon. Inside the FBI. Inside MI5 and MI6 in England.
Inside every intelligence agency in the world. Inside the
Fortune 500. Inside governments, all high-ranking people.
Anytime someone needs a dirty job, forever off the books ...
they come to you.'

'They do,' Jargo said. 'You can see why my clients
wouldn't appreciate you taking their names in vain.' He
brought the knife closer to Gabriel's throat. 'Did Mitchell
Casher know about your arrangement to be his wife's bodyguard?'

'She said he didn't know about her having this client list,
or her wanting to run. He was on an assignment for the
Deeps – for you – and she said we would meet him in
Florida in three days. That was his re-entry point after his
assignment overseas. She wanted me with her when she
talked to him, to convince Mitchell they had no choice but
to run. I was to pose as a CIA liaison, tell him they were
getting immunity and new identities in exchange for the
data. Then they'd run, the whole family, together.'

'Donna made this decision for her husband? No choice for
him?'

'She didn't want to give her husband a choice. She was
burning their every bridge.'

'Where was she running to?'

'I just had to get the Cashers safely to Florida. They would run from there. Anywhere. I don't know. Didn't Donna tell you this before you killed her?'

'My associate Frank killed her. In a rage. Because she would not speak. She was stronger than you, and she had better training.' He ran a finger along the knife, as if trying to decide whether or not to use it. 'And so she summoned Evan home to run.'

'Donna planned to explain to him they had to run – tell him the entire truth: that she worked for your network, she wanted you brought down, that she would give me the information to bring down every one of your clients.'

'Lucky for Evan you arrived.' Jargo brought his face close to Gabriel's. 'This client list and some related files were on Evan's computer. We saw it. We erased it. You're telling me Evan didn't know he had the files?'

'I don't know if Evan knew or not. I'm telling you what his mother knew. He ... he doesn't seem to know anything true about his parents.'

Jargo made his voice a knife. 'Does he know or not?'

'I don't ... think so. He's dumb as a stump.'

'No, Evan's not dumb.' Jargo ran the tip of the blade along Gabriel's chin. 'I don't believe you. Donna cleaned the files off her computer. She sent a backup to Evan's computer. She would need the files to convince Evan of the need for them to vanish. You don't simply just go and run away from your life. So Evan must have seen the files, and taken the precaution of making a copy and hiding it.'

'He doesn't know.'

Jargo put the knife very, very close to Gabriel's eye. The man trembled.

'Are you sure?'

'He knows,' Gabriel gasped. 'He knows. I told him. Please. He knows your name. He knows his mother worked for you.'

'He fought you.'

'Yeah.'

'Beat you. A teenaged boy.'

'I underestimated him, but he has his parents in him. He's born to the shadows.' Gabriel gave off a choked laugh.

'Given your very bad situation right now,' Jargo said, 'I think you'd like for Evan to bring me down.' He lowered the knife, but kept it close to Gabriel's throat.

Gabriel met Jargo's stare. 'You won't live forever.'

'True. Where were you supposed to meet Mitchell in Florida?'

'Donna didn't tell me; she had arranged the tickets for the flights out of Austin, not me, under some of the new names. We would have picked the tickets up at the airport. I assume she wanted me to help convince her husband it was time for their family to vanish, and to accept my help in doing so.'

'And if Mitchell disagreed with her decision to run?'

'Then I was to make sure he couldn't stop them. Not hurt him, but be sure that Donna and her son could get away from him.'

'Where will Evan run? To the CIA?'

'I warned him off the CIA. I didn't want ...'

Jargo stood. 'Selfish man. You wanted the files for yourself. To bring me down. Humiliate the CIA. It would ruin them, you know. Revenge. See where it's gotten you?'

'I've kept my promise.'

'Tell me, do you often respond to any crank who contacts you to help you in your vendetta against the CIA? She must have offered you proof of her credentials, a taste of what was to come.'

Gabriel looked into Jargo's face and said, 'Smithson.'

'What . . . what did you say?'

Gabriel smiled as Jargo went pale. 'I've told you everything I know.'

Jargo struggled to keep his violent emotions from surfacing on his face. How much had Donna told this man? Jargo tried to pretend as if the name Smithson meant nothing to him. 'Presumably you didn't plan on the Cashers flying out of Florida under their own names. I need to know the identities on the documents you created for Evan.'

Gabriel closed his eyes, as though steeling himself for the answer.

Jargo sipped at the whiskey, leaned over close to Gabriel, and spat into his face.

Gabriel spat back.

Jargo wiped the string of saliva from his cheek with the back of his hand. 'You'll give me every name Evan's got documentation for and then we'll go—'

Nowhere. Gabriel whipped his head downward and to the right. Jargo still held the long, silver blade of the knife in his hand, and Gabriel pounded his throat onto the point with one breathless blow.

'No!' Jargo jerked away, letting go of the knife. It wedged in Gabriel's neck. Gabriel collapsed to the floor, eyes clenched shut, and then his breath and his life unfolded out of him.

Jargo slid the knife free. He tested for a pulse; gone.

'You can't know. You can't know.' In a fury, he started kicking the body, the face, the jaw. Bone and teeth snapped under his heel. Blood splattered across the calfskin. His leg

started to get tired, his trousers were ruined, the rage
drained out of him, and he collapsed to the soiled carpet.

Smithson.

How much had Donna told Gabriel or told her son?

'Did you lie to me?' Jargo asked Gabriel's body. 'Do you
know our names?' He couldn't risk it, not at all. He had to
assume the worst.

Evan knew the truth.

He could never let his clients know they were in danger.
That would start a panic. It would destroy his business, his
credibility. His clients could never, ever know such a list
existed. He had to bring Evan down now.

He cleaned the blood from the knife and called Carrie's
cellphone. 'Get back here. We're leaving for Houston.
Immediately.'

No debate now. No discussion. Evan Casher was a dead
boy, and Jargo knew he had the perfect bait for his trap.

SUNDAY MARCH 13

21

Sunday morning, shortly after midnight, Evan finally let himself cry for his murdered mother.

Alone in the cheap Houston motel room, not far from the shadow of the old Astrodome and the distant hum of cars speeding along Loop 610, the lights off and the bed cold from the overused air-conditioner, he lay down, alone, and memories of his mother and father flooded his mind. The tears came then, hot and harsh, and he curled into a ball and let them come.

He hated to cry, but the moorings of his life had been ripped away, and the grief throbbed in his chest like a physical pain. His mother had been gentle, wry, careful as a craftsman about her photos, shy with strangers but cheery and talkative with him and his father. When he was little and would beg to sit in her darkroom and watch her work, she would stand over her photo-developing equipment, a lock of hair dangling in her face, singing little songs under her breath that she composed on the spot to keep him entertained. His father was quiet, too, a reader, a computer geek, a man of few words, but when he spoke, every word mattered. Always supportive, insightful, quick to hug, quick to gently discipline. Evan could not have asked for kinder and better parents. They were quiet and a little close-mouthed, and now that quirk loomed large in his head. Because now it meant more than computerish solitude or artistic introversion. Was it a veil for what lay beyond, their secret world?

He'd believed he knew them, but the burden of a hidden

life, lived just beyond his eyes, was unimaginable to him. A boy of shadows, born to a mother and father of shadows. It wasn't right. Why would they do this?

Ten minutes. Crying over. No more, he told himself. He was done with tears. He washed his face, wiping it dry with the paper-thin, worn towel.

Exhaustion staggered him. He had driven straight into San Antonio, and it wasn't until he got there he thought to change the license plates off the stolen pickup in case the police were looking for him. He'd found a screwdriver in a toolbox in the truck bed, and used it to trade plates with a decrepit-looking station wagon in a neighborhood where it seemed less than likely the police would get a prompt phone call. But he still sweated the entire time, putting the new plates in place, thinking a police car would pull up next to him at any moment. He told himself he had to start thinking like a fugitive. He had to be more careful.

He drove at the speed limit on I-10, heading east, winding through the coastal flatlands and into the humid sprawl of Houston. It was the most driving he'd ever done in his life – he normally only drove himself to school or to the store.

He only stopped for gas, eating Slim Jims and guzzling Cokes, paying with cash when he had to refill the tank. He couldn't stay at a big chain hotel: too many questions, a boy under eighteen, alone, renting a room. They might not rent to him, or they'd call the runaway hotline. He drove off the highway, and found a cheap motel that had few cars in the pocked lot. The clerk seemed to be suspicious that a teenage boy was renting a room, but he didn't ask for ID: Evan's cash was as good as anyone else's, and there were too many vacancies for the night.

Evan locked the door behind him. There was no furniture other than the bed and a worn TV stand, bolted to the floor. The TV brought a fuzzy picture and offered only the local Houston channels.

All gone, the words spoken by one of the killers in the kitchen.

If he was right and his mom had hidden the files inside the music or photos she'd emailed him, then right here in his pocket, on his iPhone, was what everyone hunting him wanted.

So he still had the files that Dezz wanted – still encoded, but not lost. He just needed a way to figure out if the file was somehow hidden in the song. He pressed the song file; it played; it sounded normal, nothing unusual. He searched through the phone's applications; he didn't see any new apps or a file that might have sprung out of the song, hidden until now.

He would need a computer. He didn't have enough cash for one. Tomorrow's problem.

Outside, a woman laughed loudly; a bottle broke on the asphalt.

He dug out the small, locked box he had taken from Gabriel's house. A single wire hanger dangled in the closet; he tried to pick the lock with its bent end, feeling ridiculous. He couldn't force the lock. He walked down to the motel office.

'Do you have a screwdriver I can borrow?' he asked the clerk.

The clerk looked at him with empty eyes. 'Maintenance'll be here tomorrow.'

'Mister, please, I just need a screwdriver for ten minutes.'

'Rental fee is five bucks.'

Evan pulled out a five and gave it to the clerk. He got up, returned with a screwdriver, took the bill. 'You better not be unbolting the television. I'm watching you.'

Customer service, alive and well. Evan headed back to his room.

Evan broke the lock on the fifth blow. Small, paper-wrapped packages spilled out, and Evan hurried back to the grumpy clerk, who didn't look over from his TV basketball game as Evan slid the tool back across the counter.

In his room once more, Evan opened the first package. Inside were passports from New Zealand, held together with a rubber band. He opened the top one; his own face stared back at him. He was David Edward Rendon, his birthplace listed as Auckland. The paper looked and felt appropriately high-grade government authentic; an exit stamp indicated he'd left New Zealand a scant three weeks ago.

He picked up another New Zealand passport from the spill of papers. His mother's picture inside, a false name of Margaret Beatrice Rendon, the paper worn as if it had flown a lot of miles.

A South African passport in the name of Janine Petersen, same last name as his African identity. A Belgian passport for his mother as well, her name now Solange Merteuil. He picked up another Belgian document. His picture again, but with the name of Jean-Marc Merteuil. He opened the second package: three passports for Gabriel, false names from Namibia, Belgium, Costa Rica.

The next package held four bound passports at the bottom of the pile, looped together by a rubber band. He flipped them over, freed them from the band. South Africa, New

Zealand, Belgium, United States. Opened them. And inside each his father's face stared up at him. Four different names: Petersen, Rendon, Merteuil, Smithson.

Odd. Three for him, three for his mother, but four for his dad. Why?

In the final package were credit cards and other identity documentation, tied to his family's new names, but he was afraid to use the cards. What if Jargo could find him if he charged gas or a plane fare or a meal? He needed cash, but he knew if he made an ATM withdrawal from his accounts, the transaction would register in the bank's database, the security tape would capture his image, and the police would know he was in Houston. So what if they know you're in Houston? he thought. You're leaving tomorrow for Florida. But he was still reluctant to go to a bank.

He tucked the passports back into the bag. How many names could he have? How many would he need?

The awful question wormed in past his fatigue: how was Carrie involved in all this?

The thought dried his throat. She had acted upset when he'd stupidly told her he loved her, she couldn't get away from him fast enough. If she was preparing to betray him, why would she care how he felt? His feelings would mean nothing to her. He had known her for a month, and he knew he sounded like a stupid lovesick boy, but he felt he had known her for years. He could not believe Carrie would have any voluntary involvement in this horror.

So who was she really?

He pushed Carrie out of his mind; he had more immediate problems.

He needed money. He needed help.

Shadey. He could call Shadey. Shadey had defended

Evan on CNN, and he was tough and smart and resourceful.

Evan paced the floor, trying to decide. He suspected if the police were serious about finding him, Shadey might be under surveillance, or might have been asked to call the police if Evan contacted him.

But Evan had no one else to ask.

He doused the lights. Played back every moment he had spent with Carrie Lindstrom over the past month, when she had stepped into his life. When he slept, he did not dream of her, but of the noose tightening round his neck as his mother lay dead below his feet.

A harsh buzzing woke him. Forgetting where he was, he first thought it was his old alarm clock and it was time to get up for school, but it was the stolen cellphone from the truck he'd taken in Bandera. Probably the owner, calling to chew him out for stealing the phone and the truck.

It was 4 a.m. on Sunday. He picked up the phone; the display screen didn't reveal a number. Instead the text-message display said, *Answer me, Evan.*

He clicked on the phone. 'Hello?'

'Evan, good morning. How are you?' a voice said. It had a soft Southern drawl.

'Who ... who is this?'

'You can call me Bricklayer.'

'Bricklayer?'

'My real name's a secret, son. It's an unfortunate precaution I have to take.'

'I don't understand.'

'Well, Evan, I'm from the government, and I'm here to help you.'

22

'How did you get this number?' Evan whispered.

Outside was still and quiet, except for the infrequent hum of traffic.

'We have our ways,' Bricklayer said.

'I'm hanging up unless you tell me how you got this number.'

'Simple. We recognized Mr Gabriel from the police description in Austin. We know Mr Gabriel seized you for, well, let's call it his version of protective custody. We know he was in Bandera because of a credit-card charge he made. We know he has a family member with a house that has been occupied, damaged, and abandoned as of yesterday. We know Mr Gabriel is missing. We know a truck with a cellphone in it was stolen from Bandera. You have not been answering your own phone, so we arranged with the owner and the cellphone company to keep the phone activated, so we could talk to you, if you or Mr Gabriel was in possession of the phone. And I see that you are.'

Evan got up and began to pace the room.

'May I speak to Mr Gabriel?' Bricklayer asked.

'He's dead.'

'Oh. That's unfortunate. How did he die?'

'A boy named Dezz shot him.'

A long sigh. 'That's very regrettable. Are you injured?'

'No, I'm fine.'

'Good. Let's proceed. Evan, I bet you're scared and tired and wondering what you ought to do next.'

Evan waited.

'I can help you.'

'I'm listening.' They had found him because of a stolen phone. Could they be tracing the call, reading the connections the phone was making to local cellular towers?

'You and I have a mutual problem: Dezz and his father, Jargo.'

'Two men killed my mother, and Gabriel shot one of them. I think the other man might have been this Jargo guy.'

'Dezz and Jargo will kill you, too, if they get a chance. We don't want you hurt, Evan. I want you to tell me where you're at, and I'm gonna send a couple of men to pick you up, protect you.'

'No.'

'Evan, now, why say no? You're in terrible danger.'

'Why should I trust you?'

'I understand your reluctance to trust me. Truly. Caution is the hallmark of an intelligent mind. But you need to come in under our wing. We can help you.'

'Help me by finding my dad.'

'I don't know where he is, son, but if you come in, we'll move heaven and earth to find him.'

It sounded like an empty promise. 'I don't have the files you all want. They're gone. Jargo destroyed them.' He picked up his phone. Perhaps not. But if he simply gave them the files, they could use them how they wanted, destroy them, and make him vanish. He would only trade them for his father. Nothing else.

Bricklayer paused, as though contemplating unexpected news. 'Jargo won't leave you alone.'

'He can't find me.'

'He can and he will.'

'No. You want what he wants: these files. You'll kill me, too.'

'I most certainly would not.' Bricklayer sounded offended. 'Evan, you're emotionally exhausted. It's understandable, given your horrible ordeal. Let me give you a number, in case we get disconnected. I loathe cellphones. Will you write the number down?'

'Yes.' Bricklayer fed him a number. He didn't recognize the area code.

'Evan, listen to me. Jargo and Dezz are very dangerous. Extremely.'

'You're preaching to the choir.' He risked a guess. 'Are you with the CIA?'

'I loathe acronyms as much as cellphones,' Bricklayer said. 'Evan, we can have substantive talks when you come in. I personally guarantee your safety.'

'You won't even tell me your name.' Evan paced the room. 'I could buy time by talking to the press. Telling them the CIA is offering to help me. Give them this number.'

'You could go public. I suspect, though, that Jargo will kill your father in retaliation.'

Evan swallowed at the words. 'You're saying he has my father.'

'It's most likely. I'm sorry. He'll want to use your father as leverage to get the files. We can work together to get your dad home. Would you meet with me? We can meet in Texas; I assume you're still in the state . . .'

'I'll consider it and call you back.'

'Evan, don't hang up.'

Evan did. He switched off the phone, dropped it on the bed as if it were radioactive. He looked at the phone with panic. He pulled out the battery and the SIM card; he'd remembered from reading a book that a phone could be tracked that way. Was what he read true? He didn't know. If Bricklayer could triangulate on the phone, the government could just bust the door down.

He took a quick shower. He packed his meager belongings: the passports, the stolen cellphone, his own iPhone, the gun with no ammunition.

He couldn't risk that the government could find his location while he'd talked on the phone. They might be here at any minute.

Evan hurried out to the truck downstairs. Down low on his head, he wore a baseball cap that had been in the rear seat of the stolen truck. He dropped the room key off at the front desk and headed out into the predawn dark. Hunger cramped his stomach; sweat slicked his palms. He bought the Sunday *Houston Chronicle* out of a vending machine in front of a decrepit coffee shop.

His face and his father's face were on the cover of the 'Metro/State' section. The paper said his father was also considered missing; no record existed of anyone named Mitchell Casher having flown to Australia from the United States in the past week.

His father going to Australia had been a lie, or he'd traveled under a false name to do his dirty work for Jargo.

No mention or picture of Carrie.

Carrie's here with me, Dezz had claimed in his creepy singsong voice. Evan had not believed him. If Carrie had been kidnapped, it would have been in the papers.

So where was Carrie? Hiding? He ached to talk to her, to hear her calming voice, but he couldn't go near her; he couldn't involve her again.

But he could involve someone else.

23

Of course, Shadey worked part-time at a doughnut shop. The so-not-perfect place for a fugitive to rendezvous, Evan thought with frustration. He'd parked across the street, watching the shop's morning rush swell and dwindle, then swell again. He was afraid to go inside and confront Shadey here; plus, Shadey was working: if he bolted from his shift it would look even more suspicious. He could see Shadey behind the counter, laughing, trying to put on morning cheer, dumping glazed, lemon-filled, and bear claws into paper bags, serving up coffee in big paper cups.

And yes, there was a cop car that came along and stayed at the shop for a bit. Evan considered that clichés were sometimes true. The two policemen left and never glanced over toward the truck across the street, with the boy sitting in it, with the face on the front page of the newspaper.

After another couple of hours, Shadey walked out of the doughnut shop, headed toward a beat-up Toyota, got in, and puttered out of the parking lot. Evan followed him as he headed down Westheimer, toward River Oaks.

He stopped next to Shadey at the first light, waited for Shadey to look over at him. Shadey was a typical Houston driver who didn't mess with glancing into other lanes.

Evan risked a honk.

Shadey looked over, stared as Evan smiled, as he recognized him.

I need to talk to you, Evan mouthed.

Hell no, Shadey mouthed back. He shook his head, blasted through the red in a sudden sharp left turn.

What? Evan wondered. What had happened to the guy who blistered the police on TV, who seemed so ready to defend Evan at any cost?

Evan followed. He flashed his lights once, twice. Shadey made two more turns and drove behind a small barbecue restaurant. Evan followed him.

Shadey was at his window before Evan had shifted into park. 'What do you think you're doing?'

'It's nice to see you, too,' Evan said.

Shadey shook his head. 'I got an FBI agent I'm supposed to call if I see your smiling face.'

'You won't turn me in.'

Shadey swallowed.

'I'm not a suspect. I'm not a fugitive. I'm just ... missing.'

'I don't care about what you're calling yourself. Evan, go.'

'You won't help me? I thought we were friends.'

'Because I let you use me for a stupid student-project film?'

'Because ... because you're a good guy.'

'What a load,' Shadey said.

'You defended me on TV. You defended me like crazy.'

'Yeah, well, it's gotten complicated since then.'

'How? What is it? The FBI?'

'No. Evan, just go and don't ever let me see your face again.'

'Tell me.' And then the horror shifted through his chest. 'Have you been threatened, Shadey?'

'I ...' and he said nothing more.

'Shadey, I'm sorry. Who threatened you?'

Shadey stared ahead, and instead of answering Evan's question he asked his own. 'What kind of help you need?'

'I need ammo for a Beretta.'

'You want me to get you, a minor, *bullets*?'

'And I need cash.'

'Do I look like an ATM?' Shadey lowered his sunglasses so Evan could see his eyes. 'I serve up doughnuts and coffee.'

'I know you can get the ammo, Shadey. You have connections.'

'Connections? Yeah, right. Spare me, man.'

'And I need a computer.'

'Forget your shopping list. Make yourself a movie. Explain it to the world.' Shadey shook his head. 'I'm sorry. No way, no how.'

Evan started the pickup's engine. 'It must have been some threat to scare you. I'm sorry. I'll keep my distance and you won't see me again, till they find my body and report it on the news.' He started to put the truck into reverse and Shadey put his hand on the door. Evan stopped.

'I already got a call. A lady. Said her name was Arwen, like that elf lady in those movies. She said if I saw you, I was to call her, and if I didn't, then they'd kill me. And they'd kill my grandmother. She said we couldn't hide and if I helped you, they'd know. If I went to the police with the threat, they'd know.'

'And you believed them?'

'She read off my grandma's private medical records to me. She knew everything I'd looked at on my computer. She listed off every phone call I've made on my cell.' Shadey stared at him. 'Who are you messing with, Evan? Who can do all that? How do you know they're not watching us right now, through a traffic camera, or tracking both our phones to see if they're ever in the same location?'

Evan felt shaken. 'How did this woman sound?'

'Too-sweet nice.'

'Did she give you a phone number to call?'

'Yeah.'

'Listen to me. They'll kill us both. The people who killed my mom, I think they've got my dad. The only way you're safe is if you help me.'

'I can't risk my grandma's life.'

'Then we don't. You call them. You tell them you saw me and refused to help me and that I left, that I'm heading for Florida.' It was a huge risk, but they would believe that he was going to Florida. 'If you've reported in, they'll leave you alone.'

Shadey stared ahead. 'And maybe then they kill me, for knowing a phone number that could be tracked to them.'

'Phones are easily thrown away. They don't care about you. They care about me.'

Shadey leaned in close to the window. 'All right. You remember where my grandmother's house is, over in the Third Ward, south of Truxillo?'

'Yeah.'

'Meet me there in two hours. My grandma will be out. You ain't there when I arrive, I ain't waiting, and we never saw each other, we never talked, and you never come look for me again.' He got back into his car, waited for Evan to back out, then peeled out of the parking lot.

Evan drove in the opposite direction, looking out for cars that were watching him.

The next theft: a computer.

24

Evan drove until he spotted an independent coffee shop called Caf-Fiend near Bissonnet and Kirby. As a visual-arts student, he'd often study in coffee shops, editing film on his laptop, leaving it at the table because there were always nice folks around and he was just up at the counter getting coffee. He could keep an eye on it, but he'd turned his back on it plenty. Laptop users could be complacent. He thought of the moment he'd met Carrie in the coffee shop close to school, how he'd taken thirty minutes to work up the courage to speak to her, pretending not to notice her, how she'd smiled at him that first time.

Shadey might not show with the money, much less with a computer. He had already stolen a truck that was probably someone's pride and joy; he could steal a computer. Shame welled in him. He needed something, he'd steal it. It would hurt an innocent person to steal, and he still cared about that, but his survival was at stake.

He wondered as he walked into the coffee shop, Who am I becoming?

The boy of shadows, he heard Gabriel's voice ring in his head. Because that awful boy steals whatever he needs. Like trucks, or computers.

He didn't want to be that boy. He put on the sunglasses he had found in the stolen pickup. The shop was busy, nearly every table taken, and there was a steady stream of people buying coffee to go.

A new line of computers stood on a counter running along one wall, Internet-ready. He wouldn't have to steal one – at least not to do half of what he needed. His next serious crime could wait.

He got a large coffee, surveyed the crowd. No one paid him any attention. He was anonymous. He put his back to the room, the sweat dampening his ribs. He opened a browser on one of the computers. He was the only one using the store-provided systems; most people had brought their own.

He went to Google and searched on Joaquin Gabriel. No clear match; there were quite a few men named Joaquin Gabriel in the world. Then he added CIA to the search terms and got a list of links. Headlines from the *Washington Post* and the Associated Press.

'Veteran spy's claims are "delusional", CIA says.' And so on.

Most of the articles were five years old. Evan read them all.

Joaquin Gabriel had been CIA, before the whiskey and paranoia got hold of him. He was charged to identify and run internal operations to lure out CIA personnel who had gone bad – a man known as a 'traitor-baiter'. Gabriel launched a series of increasingly outrageous accusations, condemning CIA colleagues for working with hired killers and thieves on secret, illegal missions. Gabriel accused the wrong people, including a few of the most senior and honored operatives in the Agency, but his claims were hard to swallow given his alcoholism, and complete lack of evidence. He left, abruptly, with a government pension and no comment. He had moved back to his hometown of Dallas and set up a corporate security service.

Why would his mother trust this man – a drunken disgrace – with their lives?

It made no sense. Unless Gabriel had been dead right in theory. A group of powerful people inside the CIA, and in other governments and businesses, were clients of Jargo's.

That's why Mom went to Gabriel. She knew he would believe her; this was the evidence that would vindicate Gabriel, redeem his career, prove his claims.

He had another idea. The names on his father's passports: Petersen, Rendon, Merteuil, Smithson. 'You also don't know anything true about your parents.' Gabriel meant more than the usual unimaginable life of his parents before he was born or their hidden dreams and thoughts, more than regrets of youth or unfulfilled hopes or an ambition never mentioned to him but allowed to die in isolation. Something bad.

Petersen. Rendon. Merteuil. Smithson.

First, he did searches on Jean-Marc Merteuil, the name on one of his fake passports. He found a reference to a Belgian family with that surname, killed five years ago in a Meuse River flood. The dead Merteuils had the same names as those on his family's Belgian passports: Solange, Jean-Marc, Alexandre.

Rendon produced a bunch of results and he specified the search more carefully on the name in his alias: David Edward Rendon. He got a website rallying against drunk-driving in New Zealand and listing a long history of people killed in accidents as meat for the argument for stiffer penalties. A family had been killed in a horrific crash in the Coromandel Mountains, east of Auckland, a few years ago: James Stephen Rendon, Margaret Beatrice Rendon, David Edward Rendon, the three names on the passports.

He searched on the Petersen names. Same story. A family lost in a house fire in Pretoria, South Africa, blamed on smoking in bed.

Dead families hijacked, he and his parents readied to step from the shadows into their identities.

The coffee in his gut rose up like bile.

It was the nature of a good lie to hug the truth. He was Evan Casher. He was supposed to be, in addition, Jean-Marc Merteuil, David Rendon, Erik Petersen. Every name was a lie waiting to be lived by his whole family.

Except the one name that didn't have a match in his mother's or his fake passports: Arthur Smithson.

Searching the name produced only a scattering of links: an Arthur Smithson who was an insurance agent in Sioux Falls, South Dakota; an Arthur Smithson who taught English at a college in California; an Arthur Smithson who had vanished from Washington, DC.

He clicked on the link to a story in the *Washington Post*.

It was a report on unsolved disappearances in the DC area. Arthur Smithson's name was mentioned, as well as several others: runaway teens, vanished children, missing fathers. Links offered the original stories in the *Post* archives. He clicked on the one for Smithson and found a story from sixteen years ago:

SEARCH FOR 'MISSING' FAMILY SUSPENDED
by Federico Moreno, staff reporter

A search for a young Arlington couple and their infant son was called off today, despite a neighbor's insistence that the couple would not simply pull up stakes without saying goodbye. Freelance translator Arthur Smithson, 26, his wife, Julie, 25, and their two-month-old son, Robert, vanished from their Arlington home three weeks ago. A concerned neighbor phoned Arlington police after not seeing Mrs

Smithson and the baby for several days. Police entered the house and found no signs of struggle, but did find that the Smithsons' luggage and clothing appeared to be missing. Both the family cars were in the garage.

'We have no reason to suspect foul play,' Arlington Police Department spokesman Ken Kinnard said. 'We've run into a brick wall. We don't have an explanation as to where they are. Until we receive more information, we have no leads to pursue.'

'The police need to try harder,' said neighbor Bernita Briggs. Mrs Briggs said the young mother treated her as a confidante and gave no indication that the family planned on leaving the area.

'They had money, good jobs,' Mrs Briggs said. 'Julie never said one word about leaving. She was just asking me about what curtains to pick out, what patterns to get for the nursery. They also wouldn't leave without telling me, because Julie always teased me about being a worrywart, and if they just took off and left, I'd be worried sick, and she wouldn't put me through grief. She's a kind young woman.'

Mrs Briggs told police that Smithson was fluent in French, German, and Russian, and that he did translation work for various government branches and academic presses. According to Georgetown University records, Mr Smithson graduated five years ago with a degree in French and Russian. Mrs Smithson worked as a civilian employee of the navy until she became pregnant, at which point she resigned.

The navy did not return calls for this story.

'I wish the police would tell me what they know,' Mrs Briggs said. 'A wonderful family. I pray they're safe and in touch with me soon.'

The archived story offered no picture of the Smithson family, no further links to indicate that there was a follow-up story on them.

Another family dead, like the Merteuils in Belgium, the Petersens in South Africa, and the Rendons in New Zealand. But not dead, vanished.

What had Gabriel said during their wild car ride out of Houston? *I'll tell you who I am, and then I'll tell you who you are.* Evan thought he was crazy. Maybe he wasn't.

He stared at the name of the vanished child: Robert Smithson. It meant nothing to him.

He jumped to a phone-directory website and entered the name Bernita Briggs, searching in Virginia, Maryland, and DC. It spat back a phone number in Alexandria. Did he risk the call on the hot cellphone? Bricklayer would know, no doubt accessing the call log. No, better to wait. It might put her in danger if Bricklayer knew Evan was calling her.

He wrote down Bernita Briggs's phone number. He left, conscious of the barista's eyes on him. He wondered if this was paranoia, settling into his skin and bones, taking up permanent residence in his mind, changing who he was forever.

25

The house stood in the historic Third Ward, on a street of older brick homes, most tidy with pride, others worn and neglected. Evan drove by Shadey's grandmother's house twice, then parked two streets over and walked, the duffel over his shoulder. The cap and shades made him feel like a bandit waiting outside a bank. Every drape in the house lay closed, and he imagined the police waiting, or Jargo handing a suitcase full of cash to Shadey, or Bricklayer and government thugs smiling at him behind the lace. He remembered interviewing Shadey's grandmother, Lawanda, here for his film on reform camp; Lawanda was a kind lady, quiet where Shadey was loud, unwilling to let her grandson wander into trouble without a serious fight. Evan remembered Lawanda was active in her church, and it was Sunday morning, which explained why Shadey had said she wouldn't be home.

Evan waited at the street corner, four houses down.

Shadey was ten minutes late. He came alone, walked up to the front door, not looking at Evan. Evan followed a minute later, opening the front door, not waiting to knock. The inside of the house smelled of coffee, a fading scent left over from breakfast.

'Come back here, Evan,' Shadey called. Evan walked through to the small kitchen. Shadey sat at the table.

'First three months I worked at Doughnut Town, I brought home extras,' he said. 'Me and Grandma got tired of glazed ones pretty damn fast. You get that sugar smell in your nose, you can't hardly get it out.'

Evan said nothing. He glanced around the small, tidy kitchen. He thought, I filmed Shadey; I captured a bit of his life, but not his real life. Not his day-to-day of the high-school dropout who works in a doughnut shop.

'But better dealing doughnuts than dealing other stuff, yeah?' Shadey said. 'Grandma would have leveled me if I hadn't straightened out.'

Evan said nothing.

'I scrounged up green for you, but you get caught, you keep my name out of it.'

'Why are you so mad at me?'

Shadey tented his cheek with his tongue. 'Why do you think I'm mad?'

'I can't tell if you're mad at me or scared of these people who are after me.'

'Both.' He studied Evan. 'You know, once your little movie went out, and I saw it got a million views, I thought, He can do it, I can do it. I wanted to make a movie. Tried writing a script, checked out a book on it from the library, couldn't stitch two scenes together. No head for it.'

'Why didn't you tell me? I would have helped you with your script.'

'Would you? You had your website and your prodigy filmmakers from all over the world. If I'd sent you what I made, you would have laughed at it.'

'Uh, never. I would have helped you.'

'I don't believe that, Evan. You're not the helping type.' Now Shadey gave him a direct stare. 'I let you film my story and you get a million views and you get press and I get nothing, and nothing from you. Barely even a thank-you. You too busy trying to be Spielberg Junior.'

'Shadey, I'm sorry. I had no idea. I do owe you. Thank you. I'm sorry if I never said it before.'

Shadey offered his hand; Evan shook it. 'The whole damn world boils down to you owing another fool something, so it don't matter, because now we're even. If I was mad ... Well, you limited my career options.'

'I don't understand.'

Shadey leaned forward in the quiet of the house. 'After I'd been in your little movie, well, my old friends – the ones who dealt, the ones who stole – they dropped me. Even though I didn't care too much about reform camp, it didn't do much to change my mind about what I was all about, but my friends – who weren't – changed it for me. They didn't want me around. That's why I've stayed out of trouble – not because of reform camp, or Grandma.'

Evan stared.

'Certain times freedom is just painting yourself into a new corner you can't get out of.'

'Then they weren't really your friends. I know that's the kind of thing we hate for adults to say, but it's true ...'

'Don't worry about it. But I didn't like not having control of my own life, and then here comes this lady, calling me, threatening me and my grandmother. Who is anybody to tell me what I can't do, or what friend I can't help? Who are they to tell me who I'm gonna be?' The anger in his voice was a sharp knife.

'They are not going to hurt you or your grandmother, Shadey, I swear it. I won't let them. I can stop them.'

Shadey studied Evan for a long minute, then handed him a case. Evan sat it on the floor and opened it. Cash, a lot of it, all in worn tens and twenties. And four clips that would fit the Beretta.

'Count it. It's about six hundred.'

'I don't need to count it. Thank you.' Evan didn't want to know where he'd gotten the money and the ammo. Maybe from his friends who had shunned him?

'I got a laptop computer, too. It's old and cheap, but you can have it.'

'Thank you, Shadey. Thanks a lot.' Evan blew out a sigh to hide the quaver in his voice. 'I knew I could trust you. I knew you wouldn't let me down.'

'Evan, listen to yourself. I give you money, I give you ammo, that doesn't mean anything. You're not so smart. I want you to wake up and see the world how it is, because you don't know what it is to be in trouble, real trouble. Don't trust unless you must. That's my motto.' Shadey reached out, squeezed Evan's shoulder.

'Thank you.'

'You're welcome.'

'I need to borrow a phone, and I need to use your laptop. Are we safe here for a while?'

Shadey shrugged. 'You're the danger magnet, not me.'

26

Evan sweated through four rings. 'Hello?' A woman's voice, worn, a bit irritated.

'Hello. May I speak to Mrs Briggs?'

'Whatever you're selling, I sure don't want none.'

'I'm not a salesman, ma'am. Please don't hang up – you're the only person who can help me.'

This appeal to elderly ego could not be resisted. 'Who is this?'

'My name is David Rendon.' He decided at the last moment not to use his real name – old people were often news junkies – so he tossed out one of the false-passport identities. 'I'm a reporter for the *Post*.' He tried to make his voice sound older, more gravelly. He thought he just sounded like he'd caught a cold.

She didn't give a reaction to this, so Evan plunged ahead: 'I'm calling to see if you remember the Smithson family.'

Silence for ten long seconds. 'Who did you say you were?'

'A reporter for the *Post*, ma'am. I was doing a search through the archives and saw a story about your neighbors having vanished around sixteen years ago. I couldn't find a follow-up and I was interested to know what happened to them, to you.'

'Will you put my picture in the paper?'

'I bet I can arrange a picture.'

'Well' – Mrs Briggs lowered her voice to a practiced conspiratorial whisper – 'no, the Smithsons never showed up again. I mean, that house was a dream, perfect for a new family, and they just up and walk away. Unbelievable. I'd gotten attached to that baby of theirs, and Julie, too. Arthur was a jerk – didn't like to talk.' Not being chatty was clearly a crime to Mrs Briggs.

'But what happened to their house?'

'Well, they quit paying the mortgage, obviously, and the bank finally resold it through a local realtor.'

He wasn't sure what to ask next. 'Were they a happy family?'

'Julie was so alone. You could see it in her face, in the way she talked. Scared girl like the world had gone up and left her behind. She told me she was pregnant and I remember wondering, Why is there dread in this sweet girl's face? Happiest news you could get and she looked like the whole world crashed down on her.'

'Did she ever tell you why?'

'I considered that she wasn't happy in her marriage to that cold fish. Child might have anchored her down.'

'Did Mrs Smithson ever suggest that she might want to run away, go live under a new name?'

'Good Lord, no.' Mrs Briggs paused. 'Is that what happened?'

He swallowed. 'Did you ever hear them mention the name Casher?'

'Not that I recall.'

Evan had spent his first several years of childhood in New Orleans while his father worked and then completed a master's in computer science at Tulane. When Evan was seven, they moved to Austin. He thought he had been born in New Orleans. 'Did they ever mention New Orleans to you?'

'No. What have you found out about them?'

'I've found pieces that don't quite fit together.' He blew out a sigh. 'You wouldn't happen to be a pack rat, would you, Mrs Briggs?'

She gave a soft, warm laugh. 'The polite term is "collector".'

'Did you keep a photo of the Smithsons? Since you and Julie Smithson were so close.'

Silence again. 'You know, I did, but I gave it to the police.'

'Did you ever get it back?'

'No, they kept it, didn't return it to me. I suppose it might still be in the case file, assuming there is one.'

'You didn't keep another photo?'

'I think I had a photo of them at Christmas that I kept, but I don't know where it would be. They didn't travel at Christmas. No family but each other. They met at an orphanage, you know.'

'An orphanage?'

'Sounds like something from an old novel that they make you read in high school, doesn't it? Oliver Twist marrying Little Nell. I couldn't get to my sister's for Christmas one year because of a snowstorm, so I spent Christmas Eve with the Smithsons. Arthur drank. He didn't want me around. It embarrassed Julie, I could see, but we still had a nice time once Arthur passed out.' She shook her head. 'I just don't understand the pressure people inflict on themselves. It ages them. Me, I never worry.'

An indecisive mother, a drunken father. It didn't sound like his parents. His dad didn't drink at all.

'Mrs Briggs, if you have another photo of the Smithsons, I would be very obliged if I could get it from you.'

'And I would be if you would tell me who you really are. I don't think you're a reporter, Mr Rendon.'

Evan decided to play it straight. Trust her, because he needed the information. 'I'm not. My name is Evan Casher. I'm sorry for the deception.'

'Who are you, then?'

This was a huge risk. He could be wrong, but if he didn't chance it, he was hitting a dead end. 'I think ... maybe ... I'm Robert Smithson.'

'Oh my God. Is this a joke?'

'It's not the name I grew up with, but I found a connection to my parents and the Smithsons.' He paused. 'Do you have web access?'

'I'm old, not old-fashioned.'

'Go to CNN.com, please. Do a search on Evan Casher. I want you to tell me if you recognize any of the pictures.'

'Hold on.' He heard her set down the phone, heard a computer rouse from sleep. She clicked and typed. 'I'm at CNN. C-A-S-H-E-R?'

'Yes, ma'am.'

He heard her clacking on a keyboard. Silence.

'Look for a story about a murder in Austin, Texas,' he said.

'I see it,' Mrs Briggs whispered. 'Oh dear.'

The last time he'd checked out the website, the update included a picture of his mother and of himself on the site. 'Does Donna Casher look like Julie Smithson?'

'Her hair is different. It's been so many years . . . but, yes, I think that is Julie. Oh my God, she's dead.' She sounded as grieved as she would if Julie were still her neighbor.

'Okay.' He steadied his voice. 'Mrs Briggs, I believe my parents were the Smithsons and they got into serious trouble all those years ago and had to take on new identities, hide from their past.'

'Is this you? The picture next to her?'

'Yes, ma'am.'

'You look like your mother.'

He let out a long sigh. 'Thank you, Mrs Briggs.'

'This says you were kidnapped.'

'I was. I'm fine, but I don't want anyone to know where I am right now.'

'I should call the police. Shouldn't I?' Her voice rose.

'Please don't call the police. I have no right to ask it of you, and you should do what you think is right . . . but I don't want anyone to know where I am, or that I know what my family's names used to be. Whoever killed my mom might kill me.'

'Robert.' She sounded as if her heart were breaking. 'This better not be a joke.'

'No, ma'am, it's not. But if Robert was my name, I've never known it.'

'They both loved you very much,' she said, choking back tears.

Evan's face went hot. 'You said they met at an orphanage. Where?'

'West Virginia. Oh dear, I don't remember the town's name.'

'West Virginia.'

'Goinsville,' she said with sudden assurance. 'That's the town. She joked about it, never going back to Goinsville. It was so sad that they were both orphans. I remember thinking that at Christmas, and that they were so happy to have you. Julie said she never wanted you to endure what they did.'

'Thank you, Mrs Briggs. Thank you.'

Now she cried softly. 'Poor Julie.'

'You've been a tremendous help to me, Mrs Briggs.' A terrible reluctance to hang up, to break this fragile link to his past, shook Evan. 'Goodbye.'

'Goodbye.'

He hung up. She might have caller ID. She might have seen the number and be calling the police right now. They might not believe her, but it would be a lead, and it would be followed.

Goinsville, West Virginia. A place to begin.

Smithson. Why would Gabriel prepare a passport with his father's old identity? Possibly that information – of who the Cashers once were – was part of the payment. Possibly it was Gabriel's idea of a joke.

He found Shadey's laptop. He hooked up his phone to the computer, made sure it had all the same music software as his original laptop, and transferred the songs his mother had emailed him late Thursday night.

He searched for newly created files on the laptop, searching by today's date.

None, other than the songs themselves. He went through every folder, opened every file, to see if an unseen program dumped new data, if there was now the list of names that everyone wanted.

Nothing. He didn't have the files. Perhaps since his phone used a different operating system than his laptop, the hidden files didn't make it into the download. Or perhaps they couldn't be extracted again after being downloaded once. It didn't matter.

He had nothing to fight Jargo with now.

Except Bricklayer.

Shadey was watching TV downstairs.

'May I have that number that Arwen lady gave you?' Evan asked.

'You want me to call her?'

'No. *I* want to call her.'

'You can't,' Shadey said. 'She'll know I turned against them.'

'No, she won't,' Evan said. 'Trust me.' Evan put the SIM card and the battery back into the stolen phone and dialed.

Four rings. 'Yes?' A nice-sounding lady, Southern accent, calm.

'Yes,' Evan said. 'Is this Mr Jargo's number?'

'Who's calling?'

He wasn't going to give her enough time to trace the call. He'd seen that about tracing calls on movies before, though he had no idea how long it would take. If she had caller ID, she might be looking up this account right now. 'I'll call back in one minute. Get Jargo on the line.' He hung up, dialed back in one minute.

'Hello.' Now a man's voice. Older. Cultured. Cold like ice against your fingertips.

'This is Evan Casher. Are you Jargo?' Evan forced his voice to be steady.

'Hello, Evan. You're a very resourceful little boy.'

'I'm not a little boy.'

A pause. 'No, I suppose you're not. I always think of you that way, though.' Like he *knew* Evan. 'You got this number how?'

'I stole a friend's phone when he wouldn't help me. I figured he'd been threatened by someone who's looking for me because otherwise, he would have moved heaven and earth to help me and you've scared him into being useless to me. I saw your number in his call log. It was the only one that didn't have a name attached to it.'

'Well, we have much to discuss. Your father is asking for you. He and I are old friends. I've been ... taking care of him.'

Jargo had his dad. Evan sank to the floor. 'I don't believe you.'

'Your mother is dead. Don't you think such a tragedy would make your father surface and run home to you, if he could?'

'My mom is dead because of you.' Now he'd found his voice again.

'I never harmed your mother. That was the work of the CIA.'

'You're lying.'

'I am not lying. Your mother worked for the CIA on an infrequent basis. She stole certain files that would be the CIA's death knell. The CIA will kill you to keep those files secret.'

'I don't care about these files. You killed my mother. Then you sent your son to kill me.'

A pause.

Evan's head started to throb. 'If you have my dad, I want to talk to him.' At these words, Shadey sat on the floor across from him, a scowl of worry on his face.

'I'm not prepared to do that yet, Evan,' Jargo said.

'Why?'

'Because I need an assurance from you that you'll work with us. We came to that house outside of Bandera to help you, Evan, and you shot at us and ran away.'

'Dezz killed a man.' Now Shadey raised an eyebrow at Evan.

'Wrong. Dezz saved you from a man who was using you so he could fight his own war against the CIA. The CIA would use you to get those files back and then get rid of you and your father.'

It fit in with what he had learned about Gabriel – at least, a bit.

'If I give you the files, will you give me my dad? Alive and unharmed.'

He thought he almost heard the barest sigh of relief from Jargo. 'I'm surprised to hear you have the files, Evan.'

The files were real. Here was confirmation. Sweat broke out under his arms, in the small of his back. He had to be very, very careful now.

'Mom made a backup and let me know where they would be.' Wow, he thought. The lie sounded convincing to him.

'Ah. Your mom was a very smart woman. I knew her for a long time, Evan, admired her greatly. I want you to know that because I never, ever could have harmed Donna. I'm not your enemy. We're family, in a way, you and I.'

'No we are not,' Evan said.

'Well, I respect how you've protected yourself thus far. You have much of your parents in you.'

'Shut up. Let's meet.'

'Yes. Tell me where you are and I'll bring you to your father.'

'No, I choose the meeting place. Where is my dad?'

'I'll trust you, Evan. He's in Florida, but I can get him to wherever you are.'

Evan considered. New Orleans was between Florida and Houston, and he knew the city, at least the part around Tulane, where he had spent his early childhood. He remembered his father walking him through the Audubon Zoo, playing catch with him on the green stretches of Audubon Park. He knew the layout. He knew how to get in, get out. And it was very public.

'New Orleans,' Evan said. 'Tomorrow, ten a.m., Audubon Zoo, inside the main plaza. Bring my dad. I'll bring the files. Come alone. No Dezz. I don't like him; I don't trust him; I don't want him near me. I see him and the deal is off.'

'I understand completely. I'll see you then, Evan.'

Evan hung up.

'Meeting him? Are you insane?' Shadey asked.

'Filmmaking lesson number one: show characters in conflict. You remember I interviewed you about why you were at reform camp, sitting next to that counselor who thought you weren't getting anything out of the camp. People in direct opposition, together. Fireworks.'

'But what if he's bringing your dad?'

'He wouldn't let me talk to my dad. He won't stick to the deal. He's trying to convince me that the CIA killed my mother. I'm sure he did.'

'You saw his face.'

'No.'

'Then how are you sure?'

'The voices ... I heard his voice. I'm sure.' Pretty sure, he thought, but not 100 percent sure.

'So what now?' Shadey asked.

'I can't find my dad by running all the time. I've played this by their rules; now I'm playing it by mine. Do you have a camcorder that I can borrow?'

'Yes.' Shadey went and rummaged in a closet, brought out a model from a couple of years ago. Evan looked through its lens. 'These folks stick to shadow. I'm dragging them out into the light.'

'And you gonna do all this by yourself?' Shadey said.

'I am.'

'No, you're not. I'll go with you. They threatened my grandmother, Evan. I'm not letting them walk for that.'

'I'm not guilting you. It's not your fight.'

'Shut up. I'm coming. End of discussion.' Shadey folded his big arms. 'I don't like these people trying to use me.'

'What, only I can use you?'

Shadey risked a smile. 'I'm a little bored, and I don't want to see you get your butt kicked.'

'All right.' Evan picked up the cellphone, punched in the number Bricklayer had given him.

'Bricklayer, good afternoon. It's Evan Casher. Listen carefully because I'll say this once and just once. You want these files, meet me in New Orleans, Audubon Zoo, front plaza, tomorrow, ten a.m.' He clicked off as Bricklayer started to ask questions.

'You're stirring the pot,' Shadey said.

'No, I'm putting it on to boil.'

27

Late Sunday night, Jargo's chartered plane landed at Louis Armstrong International. Jargo hurried Carrie into a suite at a hotel not far from the Louisiana Superdome, off Poydras. Carrie watched a thin Sunday-night tourist crowd ambling toward the French Quarter. Jargo sat on the couch. He had said little en route to New Orleans, which always made Carrie nervous. Dezz had flown alone early Sunday morning to Dallas, planning to break into Joaquin Gabriel's office to find any records of Evan's new passports. He was due to arrive in New Orleans at any minute.

'My son,' Jargo said into the silence.

Carrie kept watching the tourists. 'What about him?'

'He's falling in love with you.'

The announcement was like ice pressing against her skin. She turned to him, stifling the shock in her voice. 'You must be kidding. He barely knows me.'

'He has known who you are for quite some time. He's seen your picture. He's seen video of the meetings you and I have had; he served as my backup to make sure you were never followed to a meeting with me. He feels that he knows you, even if he doesn't.'

'Surveillance is hardly love.' She felt ill.

'Then I should say he feels toward you what he believes love to be, which is a sad mix of possession, anger, longing, and utter awkwardness.'

Now Carrie looked at Jargo. She had been afraid of him for so long, but now she wasn't. 'I wonder whose fault that is.'

He did not bear criticism well and she half expected a slap from him, but instead his voice was quiet. 'I ask only that you not be cruel to Dezz when you reject him.'

'Me cruel to him? He physically attacked me. He threatened to kill me before. He's ...' She searched for the term. 'Crazy' might be appropriate, but it was not a word she could use with Jargo. 'He's got issues.'

'I know I've not given him a normal life. I didn't know how to. I didn't have one. Neither did your dad.' Jargo shrugged, as though his son's difficulties were of no consequence.

Carrie couldn't speak. For Jargo to compare himself to her father ... She felt a tickle of bile in the back of her mouth.

Jargo cleared his throat. He gave her a smile, almost a shy one. 'But you know what a normal life is, Carrie. You could help him.'

'I can't help him until you don't have him stealing and shooting people.'

'That's not the issue,' Jargo said, and Carrie thought, Oh, yes, yes it is. 'Dezz lacks confidence. You could give it to him.'

Her skin prickled. 'How?'

'Pay extra attention to him.'

That was never, ever going to happen, but she simply turned her gaze back to the window.

The hotel phone rang. Jargo didn't look at her; he punched the speakerphone button.

'Good news and bad news. Which you want first?' Arwen said on the speakerphone.

'Bad news,' Jargo said.

'Evan's off the grid,' Arwen said. 'No sign of credit-card use, no police report yet that he's surfaced.'

'He's not stupid,' Carrie said. 'He'll think and move care-fully.'

'Did you pull all stolen-car reports for the five-county area?' Jargo asked.

'Yes. Finally I was able to get it. The most likely candidate is a pickup truck, a one-year-old Ford F-150, stolen from a driveway in Bandera. A note with the keys to a Ducati motorcycle were found on the porch.'

Carrie watched Jargo. 'CIA or FBI trace it to Gabriel, they'll arrive back at that house, start asking questions.'

'I'm not worried,' Jargo said. 'What's of more interest is if they don't trace the Ducati.'

'I don't understand,' Carrie said.

'Sure you do. The Bandera authorities don't trace it, it's because the investigation's been shut down. Because our friends at the FBI and at the CIA don't want the motorcycle traced, don't want the truck theft pursued.'

'Because they're looking for Evan now themselves,' Carrie said in an even tone.

Jargo nodded at her and said, 'So that's the bad news. What's the good?'

'I got a partial decode on the email message that Donna Casher received from Gabriel,' Arwen said. 'He used an English variant of an old plain-language SDECE code aban-doned back in the early 1970s. The name for the code was 1849.' SDECE was French intelligence. Carrie frowned – 1849, the same as the date in Gabriel's email to Donna, telling her what code to use.

'Odd choice,' Jargo said.

'Not really. One assumes Donna contacted Gabriel in a hurry, and they needed a common code base from which they could both easily work.'

'So what's the message say?' Carrie resisted the urge to hold her breath. She didn't look over at Jargo.

'Our interpretation is, *Ready to go on Mar. 8 a.m. Please deliver first half of list upon arrival in FL. Is son coming? Second half when you are overseas. Your husband is your worry.*'

'Thank you, Arwen. Please call me immediately if you get a trace on Evan.' Jargo clicked off the phone.

Carrie studied the tension in Jargo's shoulders, his face. She chose her words carefully. 'The Cashers were to rendezvous in Florida. Where?'

'My people grabbed Mitchell Casher in Miami, returning from a job in Berlin,' Jargo said. 'She must have promised Gabriel the final payoff delivery when the family was overseas and hidden.'

'"Second half." Sounds like two deliveries,' Carrie said. 'What else did she have beside the account files?'

Jargo's face darkened. 'Half the list first, half the list when they were safe.' He looked to Carrie as if he were scared and furious and trying to suppress his rage.

'Jargo, what is this list?'

A knock at the door. Carrie checked the peephole and opened it. Dezz stepped in. He didn't look happy. 'Nothing in Dallas. Gabriel's office is under surveillance.'

'Locals or federal?'

'Locals, but it's got to be at the request of the Agency, probably asked via the Bureau. No other reason,' Dezz said. 'I couldn't get close to see if there was any info on Evan's aliases in his office. They've connected Gabriel with this case.'

Carrie stepped in front of him. 'You didn't answer my question, Jargo. What is this list?'

Jargo didn't look at her. 'Donna Casher stole our client list.'

'I don't believe you, Dad,' Dezz said. 'You wouldn't keep a list.'

'But Donna apparently made one, over the years. She spied on me. A brilliant insurance policy.' Jargo turned to Carrie. 'Either through Gabriel or his mom, Evan knows all about us now. He just promised me the list in exchange for his dad. He knows Dezz is my son. He knows about us, Carrie. He's seen more than the client list. Maybe a list of *us*.'

'So we have to meet him,' Carrie said.

Dezz said, 'Let us take Evan, Dad. You go back to Florida, break out the knives, make Mitchell talk, see if he knows where the client list is.'

Jargo rubbed at his lip. 'But I'm sure Mitchell had no idea Donna betrayed us. He wouldn't have gone on a mission for me if his wife was about to stab me in the back.'

'He could hardly say no to you,' Dezz said.

'He could have easily run from us, and he kept working.'

'You're blinded by affection for Mitchell,' Dezz said. 'It's not like you.'

'I can't afford sentiment. Even when I really wish I could.' Jargo closed his eyes, rubbed his temples.

For the first time Carrie saw a light that wasn't cold and hateful in Jargo's gaze. For the first time since Jargo had told her over a year ago, 'I know who killed your parents, Carrie, and they will kill you, too. But I can hide you. You can keep working for me. I'll take care of you. I'll protect you from the people who want you dead.'

She blinked the memory away.

'Carrie, did Evan ever mention New Orleans to you? They might have told him where to run if he ever got into trouble, or if something ever happened to them.'

'I'm sure they never gave him any kind of escape plan, because he didn't know his parents were agents. If he'd had a hint of the truth, he would have found out long ago. That's who he is.' She shrugged. 'He told me he was born in New Orleans, but he hasn't lived there since he was a child. I assume you know that already.'

Jargo nodded. 'Evan knows you're my son, Dezz.'

'He didn't hear it from me.'

'Perhaps you told him when you were trying to lure him out from under the car.'

Dezz said nothing, but his mouth made a little twist.

'I expect better judgment from you. And you better not lie to me.'

Dezz stood. 'Let me be the one to question him. He can't stand up to a beating. I know his type.'

'You don't harm him unless I order you to harm him.' Jargo gave Dezz a stern glare. 'You will obey orders and curb your emotions.'

Dezz chewed a caramel and stared at the carpet.

'You're in enough trouble as it is,' Jargo said. 'Everything I've asked you to do, you've managed to not do: capture Evan, find out what was in Gabriel's office. Honestly. Your incompetence makes me think I adopted you and simply forgot.' He slapped the candy out of Dezz's mouth. 'What are you, addicted to sugar? Are you five years old?' The brown wedge of caramel landed on the carpet with a glop that Carrie barely heard over the whiplash sting of Jargo's palm against Dezz's cheek.

Carrie couldn't stand Dezz, but she said, 'Stop it.'

A little rope of sugared saliva hung off Dezz's chin and he wiped it silently away.

Jargo stared at Carrie, as though he'd forgotten she was there. She stood her ground, in between him and his silent son. The quiet went from awkward to awful. She decided to shift back to another topic.

'What is Mitchell Casher to you?' Carrie asked Jargo. 'You seem worried about him as much as frustrated with him.'

'I would like for him to contact his son for me, to bring him in. He refuses. He doesn't trust me.'

'Duh. You're holding him prisoner.'

'I'm convinced he wasn't part of Donna's scheme now, but I can't yet convince him of my good intentions toward his son.'

'I wonder why,' Carrie said, 'since you don't plan to honor your deal with Evan.'

'He won't be expecting to see you, Carrie. He'll be expecting to see his dad. You're the element of surprise,' Jargo said. 'I can't let Evan walk away from that meeting. Once we have the list, Evan's simply a risk to us. You know that. He'll talk.'

'The Audubon Zoo is a very public place. Major attraction,' Carrie said. 'Too many people. Too contained. He made a smart choice. You won't be able to grab Evan there, Jargo.'

'Not grab. Kill,' Dezz said.

'Not there you can't,' Carrie said. 'You can't.'

'That's right, I can't. So we'll get him to leave with you. He'll be thrilled to see you,' Jargo said. 'Take him someplace private, where just the two of you can talk. Then you can kill him.'

Carrie didn't look at him.

'That won't be a problem, will it, Carrie?' Jargo said.

'No,' Carrie said. 'No problem.'

MONDAY MARCH 14

28

Evan didn't expect the children.

Monday morning at ten, Evan imagined the Audubon Zoo would be nearly empty, but a good-sized crowd trickled to the gates as the zoo opened. The small parking lot, on the edge of Audubon Park, held a few school buses and three minivans sporting the logo of a retirement community. Then there was the usual spill of tourists, which New Orleans never lacked.

Evan paid his admission to the zoo and hung to the edge of a crowd of school kids who were close to his age, and tried to look like he belonged. He wore his dark glasses and baseball cap. He spotted Shadey, paying in a different line, wearing a Houston Astros ball cap and sunglasses, keeping his distance, walking with a duffel bag slung over his shoulder.

The zoo, Evan noticed, wasn't a place where many people walked alone. Families and couples and herds of students with harried teachers. He circled, keeping his gaze moving across the crowd.

No sign of his father, or Dezz. He had no idea what Jargo looked like. He saw no sign of a squad of guys in dark glasses who might work for Bricklayer, with earpieces and trench coats, but he figured they wouldn't be so obvious.

Evan darted through the swell of the opening-gate crowd. Last night, in the cheap motel rooms he and Shadey had scored off I-10, he had downloaded a map off the Audubon Zoo's website and memorized it. Every way in, every way out. The zoo backed up to the green sprawl of Audubon Park on one side, to an administration building, side roads, and a Mississippi River landing on the other. The map was designed for visitors. He suspected there were private routes for animal handlers and zoo employees that were not shown.

He remembered strolls here with his father, his hand in his dad's, his other hand holding a sticky, melting ice cream. He loved the zoo. He headed in the direction of the main fountain in the plaza, with statues of a mother elephant and her calf cavorting in the spray. He walked a slow, measured pace along the palm-lined brick pathway, glancing behind him, as if he were taking in the sights and were in no hurry. School kids milled around him, a teacher attempting to herd them to his right where the real elephants ambled in the Asian Domain, others eyeing a restaurant to his left, although it was too early for burgers and shakes. He stayed close to the school groups, as if he belonged.

A long, curving bench near the fountain sat empty. School kids and tourist families drifted toward the elephant pen. Most of the early crowd passed him, moving beyond the fountain for the zoo's carousel and the Jaguar Jungle exhibit.

Evan spotted a man walking toward him, eyes locked on him. Tall, a handsome face, hard blue eyes like chips of ice, hair streaked with iron-gray, wearing a dark trench coat. Rain loomed in the skies, but Evan believed the man had something hidden under his coat. That was fine. Evan had his own version of a weapon in his raincoat pocket. Not a gun.

Shadey had the gun, because if either Jargo or Bricklayer grabbed Evan, they'd simply relieve him of the weapon. He had his phone in his pocket, and he would say the files were on it. No argument. No searching. He'd just give it to them, let them worry about decoding it if they could.

He watched. No sign of his father.

'Good morning, Evan,' the man said. Baritone, the same voice he'd heard in his kitchen, heard on the phone.

'Jargo?' Evan had to fight to keep his voice steady.

'Yes.'

'Where's my dad?'

'Where is the list?'

'Wrong. You first. Give me my dad.'

'Your father doesn't really need rescuing, Evan. He's with us, of his own free will. He's worked for me for years, so did your mother.'

'No. You killed my mother.'

'You're confused. I told you, the CIA killed your mother. I would have saved her, given the chance. Please look over to your right.'

Evan did. There was a small playscape, then by the restaurant a patio of tables and chairs for diners. Dezz and Carrie stood at one of the canopied tables, Dezz with his arm looped round Carrie's shoulder. She looked pale. Dezz grinned at Evan.

Evan's heart sank into his gut. No.

Carrie's gaze locked on Evan's.

'But Carrie, she's another matter. My people found her; she got suspicious of my son at your school. She poked where she shouldn't have. The CIA wanted to pick her up. We couldn't leave her for the CIA to kill as well, so Dezz brought her with us.' Jargo made his voice a slow soothe. 'This has all been a terrible, wretched misunderstanding, Evan.'

Evan's mouth went dry.

'Carrie is a true innocent, Evan. I think she's a fine young woman. I don't wish her any harm. I'd like to let her go, and I will, as soon as you give me those files. I know you understand I'm only using her as a guarantee. You and Carrie can talk privately if you like. I will wait for you and then I can take you to your father. He's desperate to see you.'

Evan opened his mouth to speak, but nothing came out. He stared at Carrie. The breeze blew her hair into her face. She shook her head, ever so slightly.

'Yes or no, Evan?'

Evan kept waiting for the government to descend on them. Bricklayer might be lurking nearby, watching the drama play out, seeing who broke the standoff. But he couldn't wait forever.

Evan said, 'Carrie walks out of here, free and clear. She tells that security guard over there she's very sick, needs to go to a hospital. Right now. An ambulance takes her away. When she's safe, she calls me on a number I give her. Then you get my dad on the phone and I talk to him, and then, and only then, do I give you the files.'

'I'm a great believer in compromise, Evan.' Jargo held up a digital voice recorder next to Evan's ear, thumbed it.

'Evan,' his father's voice said. Mitchell Casher sounded tired, sounded desperate. 'The danger you're in is not from Jargo or any of his people. It's from the CIA. You've made a mistake in not trusting Jargo. The CIA killed your mom. Not Jargo. Please cooperate with him.'

Jargo clicked off the voice recorder. 'I've satisfied one of your requirements.'

'I said a phone, not a recording. He could have said all that with a gun pointed at his head. You could have killed him when he was done talking.'

'Do you think your father would lie to you to protect himself? Seriously?'

And he knew that Jargo was telling him the truth, at least about the recording. Evan's head felt dizzy. His father . . . was on Jargo's side.

Was he so sure the voice he'd heard in the kitchen was Jargo's? In the horrifying shock of finding his mother dead . . . had he made a mistake?

'Let me assure you, I would never hurt your dad,' Jargo said in a low voice. 'I don't want to hurt you. You don't want to come with me, fine. You and Carrie can just walk out of here once I have the files.'

'As if I could trust you.'

'That's your call,' Jargo said with a subtle shrug. 'If you want to trust the CIA not to kill you once you're back on the streets, that's your call, too. Give me the list and you and Carrie can walk out of here together if you choose. Start a wonderful life together, although I think the enemies of your parents inside the CIA will keep that wonderful life exceedingly brief. Or you can come with me and I'll take you to your father, and protect you from those murderers.'

'You promised me my father. You can't tell me that he didn't want to come here and see me.'

'Your father's face is all over the news right now. You and he are the most prominent missing people in the country. He wasn't comfortable with traveling, not when the rogues inside the CIA are hunting him as much as they hunted your mother.'

'I don't believe you. We had a deal. You're changing it.'

'The world changes all the time, Evan. Only fools don't change with it.'

'Well, your world just changed. Look over by the elephants,' Evan said.

'I don't have time for games, little boy.'

'I'm not playing one, old man.'

Slowly Jargo made a quick survey of the scattered crowd around the elephant pen, looked back at Evan.

'Thanks for the nice profile shot,' Evan said. 'You're being filmed. On digital, with a high-powered lens that provides me with pristine prints of your face and of Dezz's.'

'I don't believe you.'

'My friends all over the world love to make movies and put them on the Internet for everyone to see. They can get your face on hundreds of websites in a matter of minutes. My face is all over the news, and all they have to do is email it to CNN or certain bloggers or the *New York Times* and your face is right next to mine. You hurt or kill me or Carrie, you're on the evening news. I told you my demands. Let me talk to Carrie. Now.'

Jargo, staring at Evan, beckoned with a single finger and Carrie hurried over to them. Dezz stayed put.

'Evan,' she said, 'hi.'

'No closer,' Jargo told her, raising an arm, keeping her back.

'Are you all right?' Evan asked in a low voice.

She nodded. 'Fine. They didn't hurt me.'

'I'm so sorry,' he said.

She opened her mouth to speak, then shut it.

'She leaves, just as I described,' Evan said.

'You're not very smart,' Jargo said. 'You showed too much of your hand. I would have been willing to let Carrie go once you gave me the files. But film of me? No. I'll need that as well.'

'When she's gone.' Evan narrowed his stare. 'Soon as Carrie's safely away, I'll give you the digital camera and hand you a phone that has the list stored on it. I don't have copies. Understood?'

'No. Give me the list and the digital camera; then she walks. If you've got a camera on us, I certainly am not going to harm you, if that's what you're so wrongly worried about. Then we can all part ways, if you're so determined not to see your dad,' Jargo said.

Carrie broke free from Jargo, closed her arms round Evan, sobbed into his shoulder. He embraced her, smelled the soft peach scent of her hair, kept his stare locked on Jargo.

'Trust me,' Carrie whispered into Evan's ear. Then she pulled a small gun free of her coat and jabbed it under Jargo's chin. 'Tell Dezz to walk away or I shoot you through the neck.'

Jargo's eyes widened in shock.

She pulled Jargo in front of her and Evan, putting the older man between them and Dezz. 'It's okay, Evan. We're getting out of here. He's got a gun in his pocket. Take it.'

'Carrie, what are you doing?'

'Do what I tell you,' Carrie said. Evan did, pulling a gleaming pistol free from Jargo's coat. He risked a look the other way – toward where Shadey actually stood, under the awning at the edge of the food court, with a duffel, one side cut out, the camera resting inside.

Dezz, now hurrying forward, stopped, fifteen feet away from them, staring at the small gun being held against his father's neck. Carrie moved the gun down, pressing into Jargo's back, where it wasn't so visible.

'Back off, Dezz!' Carrie shouted. She lowered her voice to

a whisper. 'Evan, if he comes any closer, shoot him. The chest is easiest to hit.'

Evan, still stunned, nodded.

'Evan, you're making a mistake,' Jargo said. 'I'm the one who can help you, not this lying little nothing.'

Dezz's mouth worked, watching his father, and he ran ten feet to one side, grabbed a young mother pushing a stroller with a fussing toddler. He jabbed a gun into the young woman's throat and yanked her round, putting her between himself and Evan. The young mother's face paled in shock and terror.

'I'll trade you!' Dezz yelled. 'Let my dad go!'

Another woman saw the gun in his hand, shrieked for security, began to run.

Carrie, with a suddenness that surprised Evan, did some sort of weird hybrid kick-shove that knocked out Jargo's legs from underneath him, sending the big man to the ground in a hard sprawl. 'Run, Evan,' she said.

Dezz pushed his hostage away; she grabbed her child and fled. Dezz ran toward Evan and Carrie, pistol out, readying to aim.

Screams erupted around them. Carrie fired past Evan. Dezz ducked behind a bench.

Carrie is shooting a gun, Evan thought, shocked.

Around them, people panicked, stunned for a moment by the oddity of gunfire, then stampeding for cover or for the entrance, teachers herding kids, parents carrying children.

Jargo grabbed at Evan and Evan punched him in the stomach, as hard as he could, and sent him sprawling back over the bench.

A zoo security guard advanced toward them, yelling an order. 'Down on the ground! Now!'

A bullet splintered the palm trunk by the guard's head. Dezz had fired. The guard retreated behind the thick trunk.

Carrie gripped Evan's arm. 'Run, if you want to live and get your dad.'

He ran with her, dodging scrambling tourists, deeper into the zoo. He glanced back. No sign of Shadey; he would blend in with the retreating crowd, escape. Evan had told him to make sure whatever footage he got of Jargo made it to safety, no matter what happened to Evan.

'The entrance,' Evan said. 'It's the other way—'

'I know,' she said, 'but they can cut us off. This way.'

He didn't argue. He was the faster runner and he clutched her arm.

Dezz moved through the fleeing crowd, pursuing fast, gun drawn. People veered away from him in every direction, giving him a clear path. Jargo followed. A man, wearing a Tulane sweatshirt, made a lunge at Dezz, who hit him hard across the face with the pistol. The man went down. Dezz and Jargo didn't slow down; Dezz tossed Jargo a second pistol.

Evan and Carrie ran past the singsong of the zoo's carousel, firing up for its first ride of the day, and onto a tram path where the Swamp Train looped round the zoo. The next section held animals from South America. Evan looked around for an exit sign, or a building where they could hide. They kept running, onto a wooden walkway. It bordered an algae-topped pond for a flock of flamingos on the right and pine-studded land for llamas and guanacos on the left. A family with three kids stood at the walkway's halfway point, admiring the flamingos, snapping photos.

'Over the railing,' Evan said. They couldn't run past the family, who would be caught between Carrie and Evan and their pursuers.

Carrie bolted over the wooden divider, dropped down into the exhibit. A small herd of llamas watched them with disinterest. The ground, groomed to look like Louisiana's best approximation of the pampas, was hard and dusty, and they ran to a dense grove of pines near the exhibit's back perimeter.

'Get the trees between you and them,' Carrie said. They ducked into the short maze of pines. A bullet smacked against a trunk.

'Over the fence,' he said. They climbed in a fast scramble, toppled over the barrier onto an unpaved trail behind the exhibit. The musky smell of wolves in a neighboring exhibit filled their noses. They ran down the service path. Maintenance buildings lined one side, the back of the South American exhibits the other. They tried the doors. Locked.

Through the foliage and the fencing, Evan saw Jargo running past the family on the wooden walkway, spotted Dezz following in their tracks through the South American grounds.

Trying to catch Evan and Carrie between them.

'Keep your head down.' Carrie grabbed the back of his head. 'Security camera up ahead – don't want it to catch your face.'

He obeyed. They ran, eyes to the ground. The service road dead-ended. A glass and stone building to their right held a family of jaguars. Jaguar Jungle was a major attraction of the zoo, a re-creation of a Mayan temple.

They clambered over the padlocked fencing at the dead end, dropped onto a stone visitors' path by the jaguars, who lounged behind thick glass. One yowled at them, baring curved fangs.

Jargo huffed into the Mayan plaza, saw Carrie, fired. A bullet pinged against the Mayan stone carvings. The jaguars raised a ruckus of snarls and snaps.

Carrie and Evan sprinted through dense growth and stone paths, past another faux temple with spider monkeys, past a children's archaeological-dig play area. They stumbled down a creek lined with thick bamboo, hurried back up the other side to the stone path. A few moms and kids ambled along and they stared.

'Crazy guy with a gun!' Carrie yelled. 'Take cover!'

The moms jumped for cover in the bamboo or off the path. Jargo ran past the women, ignoring them.

'Evan!' he yelled. 'I can give you your dad!'

Carrie spun and fired at him. Jargo ducked back into the bamboo. Evan ran past a sign that read NO TRESPASSING. ZOO EMPLOYEES ONLY, Carrie following. It had to lead to a building, he decided, a place they could barricade themselves in – Jargo would then flee to avoid the police, who would be racing into the zoo now.

Evan hit a short fence, they went over it, then rushed up to another short fence, and Evan said, 'Oh, no.'

Alligators. On the other side of the 3-foot divider, on a bank, with a narrow gap of scum-topped water beyond, leading to the zoo's Louisiana Swamp wooden walkway, where visitors walked above the water and admired the reptiles from a safe distance. Three of the gators sunned themselves on the bank. Not five feet from them.

Behind them, a bullet hissed through a silencer. The shot caught Carrie high in the shoulder and she staggered and screamed. On the walkway across the water, a woman screeched for the police. Loudspeakers boomed into life, urging everyone to head calmly for the exits.

'Wrong move, Carrie,' Dezz called from behind a tree. 'Wrongo. Stupid. Disappointingly dense.'

Evan held her with one arm, aimed the gun with the other. To stand there was to die. The gators looked fat and zoo-happy and probably weren't hungry. Please. He hoped. He spotted Dezz peeking round a tree and fired a steady barrage of bullets, forcing Dezz back into the undergrowth, helping Carrie over the fence.

'Dezz . . . hates reptiles,' she said. 'Afraid of them.'

Evan wasn't sure he had a bullet left in the clip. He hurried her past the resting gators. He stumbled over one's tail and it opened its white, razor-ringed mouth in a defensive hiss, but then started a slow waddle away from them.

'Go,' Carrie said. 'Leave me. Get safe.'

'No. Come on.' Dezz would be charging toward them since Evan had quit shooting. He saw Dezz approaching, taking careful aim. Evan's gun clicked on an empty magazine. Evan and Carrie jumped into the green-frothed water. He heard a bullet scream above their heads.

Evan held Carrie's gun above the water, but he couldn't swim, help Carrie, and shoot at the same time. The distance to the wooden walkway seemed like a mile.

People on the walkway scattered, mothers fleeing with children, one man hollering into a cellphone.

Dezz gingerly put a foot over the fence, his gun aimed at the gators, who seemed as uninterested in him as they had been in Evan and Carrie.

Evan kicked forward, pushing Carrie, thinking, Dezz gets a bead on us, it's over.

'Help us!' he hollered up toward the walkway. The cellphone man gestured at Evan to swim to the right.

A log lay between them and the walkway, and with a

sudden, yet ancient horror that spasmed up from his spine, Evan saw it wasn't a log. An alligator, facing away from them, lay barely submerged, ignoring the ruckus behind him.

Evan shoved Carrie to one side, slapped his hand on the water to draw the gator away from her. Carrie paddled toward the walkway. He heard a hiss behind him. One of the gators on the bank opened its mouth again, heckling Dezz, and Dezz gave ground, putting one leg back over the fence, looking scared and furious.

They can move faster in water, Evan thought, logic kicking into his brain. Carrie's bleeding. Does it draw them like a shark?

Carrie reached the wooden supports, the cellphone man offered a hand, another man steadying him, and they hauled Carrie up to the walkway.

Evan kicked away from the track Carrie had cut in the water. The log-gator orbited toward Evan. Evan swam hard, waited for the tug to tear off his leg. His panic felt like a fire in his throat, in his chest. He blundered close to the walkway and put up an arm. The men yanked him up. Six feet behind him, the gator wrenched its mouth open in bravado, then settled and watched him with an ageless gaze. Evan dripped water and scum, and sprawled across the wood. One of the rescuers wrenched Carrie's gun from his grasp.

'Please!' Evan said. 'I need that!'

'Stay down, kid!' Cellphone Man put a heavy hand on Evan's chest, pushed him to the railing. 'I called the police. You stay right here.'

Evan turned toward the bank. Dezz was gone, swallowed back in the bamboo. No sign of Jargo.

'She's shot,' the other man said, shock slowing his voice. 'We got to call an ambulance.'

Evan seized Carrie's hand, shoved Cellphone Man to one side, ran. The man yelled at him to stop. Old swamp-style rocking chairs lined the deck, two older ladies sitting frozen in fright, clutching their purses, as Evan and Carrie ran past. At the end of the walkway stood a gift shop and, just past its door, a railing. They went over the railing; the next walkway led to a wildlife nursery, built to look like a weathered swamp shack with small boats docked in a fronting lagoon. They hurried round the back of the shack. More fencing, covered with ivy, bamboo curtaining a service road beyond.

Evan pushed Carrie up so she could pull herself over. Blood welled from her shoulder and she gasped as she climbed. She tumbled over the ivy, falling headfirst into the blanketing thicket of bamboo beyond the fence. He jumped on the mesh and saw Jargo approaching from his right, Dezz from his left.

'Give it up, Evan,' Jargo called. 'Right now.'

'Stay back or that tape puts your face on the evening news.'

The indecision played on Jargo's face. 'You go, you'll never see your dad again.'

Evan went over the fence. A bullet barked a centimeter from his hand as he let go and fell into the overgrowth.

Carrie grabbed him and they ran, hearing the *pit-pit* of bullets pocking the bamboo curtains. Then the noise stopped. Evan was sure Dezz and his father were only stopping to climb over the fence in pursuit. They ran along a paved road that served as a tram path. Zoo employees headed away from them in a golf cart, hollering into walkie-talkies. Another fence and they stumbled along a stretch of parking lot and grassland on the border of the zoo. He checked behind them. No sign of Dezz or Jargo: they hadn't scaled the fence.

They ran along the edge of the zoo now, hearing the approaching whine of sirens.

'Are you in pain?' he asked. Stupidest question ever asked, he decided.

'I'll make it.' She staggered and puked a bit. He held her. 'Keep moving.' She spat again. 'Are you all right? Did they hit you?'

'No, I'm fine. How did you ...?' Fight and shoot your way out of there? You're sixteen like me. You saved me. He looked at her as if he didn't know her.

'We're getting out of here,' she said.

Beyond the expanse of the parking lot, they could see the whirl of police-car lights near the main entrance.

'Here.' He steadied her. 'I'm getting you to a doctor.'

'No doctor. Evan, you have to do what I say. I've been protecting you since the day we met. I'm sorry I had to lie to you.' Her voice faded to a weak whisper. 'I'm from Bricklayer.'

He stopped in his tracks. 'What do you mean?'

She reached out a hand to him, bloodied from being pressed against her shoulder. 'I've been pretending to work with Jargo, but I've secretly been working for Bricklayer. I ... I was supposed to protect you. I'm sorry.'

'Protect me. For how long?'

She steered him off a path that cut across a swath of deep green. 'Jargo thought I worked for him. He thought I would kill you for him today. But I would never hurt you. Never.'

This wasn't what he'd expected. He hurried her into the truck he'd stolen from Bandera. Sirens rose.

Trust me, she had said. He nearly said, 'I can't leave Shadey,' but if he told her about Shadey and she was leading him into a trap, then Shadey would be caught in Bricklayer's net. He shut his mouth, hoped that Shadey had escaped in the melee.

He eased her over into the passenger seat, looking around frantically for Jargo and Dezz.

She collapsed, blood smearing the seat.

'Bricklayer and I are CIA, Evan,' she said. 'I'm not supposed to tell you, but you need to know.' She gritted her teeth against the pain.

CIA, like Gabriel. The people Jargo and his own father said had killed his mother.

He didn't believe Jargo, and his father shouldn't have, either.

'You're a sixteen-year-old, right? You're not just a really young-looking grown-up?'

She managed a half-cough, half-laugh. 'I'm sixteen.'

'But the CIA doesn't have *kids* working for them.'

'Bricklayer does. Special group. I volunteered ... There they are,' she said as he climbed into the pickup. 'The Land Rover, silver.' Jargo and Dezz, trying to navigate past the New Orleans police vehicles that had responded. Evan didn't see Shadey anywhere in the mass of people milling in the lot. An ambulance stood, lights flashing, but paramedics weren't loading Shadey, or anyone else.

'Hold on.' Evan floored the pickup across the lot, then over the expanse of lawn, headed toward Magazine, the frontage street for the zoo that separated it from Audubon Park.

'Jargo's seen us,' she said. 'You're not trained for evasive driving, Evan.'

'I'm an Austin driver. It's the same thing,' he said, feeling crazy with fear and energy, and he barreled across Magazine, laying on the pickup's horn, bouncing over the curb into the greater expanse of Audubon Park. Think. Think of what they'll try next and be prepared for that. Because you can't make a mistake.

In the rearview he saw the Land Rover narrowly miss hitting another car, then follow him across the grassy yard between the parking lot and Magazine, Jargo pressing on the horn.

Midmorning joggers crossing the green of parkland stared at Evan as he revved the pickup truck along the grass, dodging the oaks. The northern edge of Audubon Park faced out onto busy St Charles Avenue, and the neighboring Loyola and Tulane universities stood on the other side of the avenue. He had forgotten that everyone parallel-parked along the streets here, and this morning cars filled every inch of curb bordering the park. Large concrete cylinders blocked the park's main gate from the street.

No way out.

He veered the car to the left, spotting an opening at St Charles and Walnut, the park's far corner. It was a no-parking zone across from an old estate reborn as a hotel. The pickup lumbered as he spun out onto Walnut and hooked an immediate right onto St Charles.

He started to panic. St Charles was hardly a raceway. Stoplights stood every few blocks; the wide median held two streetcar tracks, with their green tubes lumbering up and down the rails, tourists leaning out to snap photos of the grand homes or of leftover, faded beads still dangling from the street signs from the most recent Mardi Gras. If there wasn't a light, a crossover spanned the median, and cars making turns backed onto the avenue.

But at ten twenty in the morning, traffic wasn't a thick nest. He heard a boom, a thud. The Land Rover exited Audubon Park behind him, navigating an opening on the opposite corner of the park from where he had exited. Shots hit the bumper; the Land Rover powered up close to the back of the pickup.

'He's shooting for the tires.' Carrie shivered, in shock and dripping wet, blood flowering through her shirt.

A light ahead, red. Cars stopping.

Evan swerved the truck into the streetcar median. He nicked a line of crape myrtles and put the truck on the rail tracks to avoid the metal poles that supplied the cars with electricity. He jammed the accelerator to the floor.

From his right, gunfire, a bullet smashing into the rear window. Shards of glass nipped the back of his head.

Carrie said, 'Drive steady, please.'

'Sure!' he yelled back. He zoomed past – no one in the median turn – the intersection with the light, and in his rearview the Land Rover bounded onto the median with him. Accelerated fast.

Ahead, a minivan loitered in the median, waiting for traffic to open up. Two young children in the minivan's windows stared as the pickup truck rocketed toward them, a boy pointing in surprise.

Evan spun back onto St Charles, narrowly missing the minivan, clipping a parked car. A jolt and shattering glass. He could not head farther right – parked cars lined the length of St Charles, and the front yards of many of the homes were fenced or walled in. No clear room to navigate. It was the street or the median. Bad choice versus worse.

Another shot hit the rear of the pickup truck. A line of heavier shrubs lined this stretch of the median. Evan plowed back through them, deciding he was putting fewer lives at risk there than on the street, after he went through another intersection where a car waited in the median to turn onto the westbound side of St Charles.

Then he saw the streetcar coming toward him, occupying the left-side track, and he laid on his horn.

The streetcar driver grabbed at a radio mike and yelled into it. Evan screeched to the left, the streetcar passing between him and Jargo.

Ahead he saw two police cars, lights flashing, sirens blaring.

Evan rumbled right, aiming for the center of the median; another streetcar was approaching and he overshot, revving off the tracks and back onto St Charles, an open intersection. He took a hard right, more to keep from crashing than from strategy, then the next left, and drove down a residential street of neat homes, cars parked on the road. Then another right.

'Turn here, here!' Carrie said.

She pointed at a corner lot, a bright yellow building, antiques in the window, a neon OPEN sign. He saw her idea. The parking and exits were behind the building. He spun into the lot and stopped the car.

Waited.

The Land Rover, its side badly dented, shot past on the street. Evan counted to ten, then twenty. The Land Rover didn't return.

'What now?' Evan didn't recognize his own voice. He could taste the fake-swamp water, and his hands shook.

'Police will be all over St Charles,' she said. 'Can you ... can you get us to the airport? The CIA has an office close to there where we can hide.'

'You need a hospital.'

'No hospital. Our pictures will be on the police wire soon,' she said through gritted teeth.

He gently peeled a torn section of her shirt away from her shoulder. He saw the small but vicious wound in her freckled skin, touched the sticky blood.

'You need a doctor, Carrie, now.'

'Bricklayer will get me help.' She closed her eyes, laid her hand on his. 'You don't have any reason to trust me, but we just saved each other. That means something, doesn't it?'

He didn't know what to say.

She opened her eyes. 'A government plane at the airport can take us to a place we can be safe. Where we can work on getting your dad back from Jargo.'

'What will the CIA do to get my dad back? He's not one of them. He's an enemy to them if he's worked for Jargo.'

'Your father could be our best friend. With his help, your help, we can break Jargo.' She leaned against the door, in pain. 'Certain people in the CIA and Jargo ... have an arrangement. Jargo's selling information to every country, every intelligence service, every extremist group that he can. We're trying to find his client list inside the CIA, get rid of the traitors. They're selling our national secrets to Jargo. I was undercover for the Agency, working for Jargo for the past year.'

'Year,' he whispered. 'Since you were *fifteen*?'

'I had to grow up quick.' And for the first time Carrie sounded unsure, frightened. 'We've never been able to identify any of his people other than Dezz. He has a whole network. Your parents ... worked for him.'

Evan swallowed past the rock in his throat. 'I can't keep pretending they are completely innocent in all this, can I?'

'No one can tell you what to do. I learned that early on.'

'But Jargo knows you've turned on him, and you have me. He'll just kill my father.'

'No. He doesn't want to kill your dad. I don't understand why. Your father is Jargo's weakness. We have to use it against him.'

CIA office at the airport or hospital. He had to choose. Trust the stranger beside him or trust the girl he loved. He started the car, eased out of the lot. No sign of Jargo. Evan drove, finally turning back onto St Charles. He drove through Lee Circle and fed onto the highway. Traffic was light. He steadied his hands.

'So, you knew me before I knew you,' he said.

'Yes.'

'So our relationship was a trick. A lie.'

'You don't understand.'

'No, I don't. I don't understand how you could lie to me.'

'It was to protect you.' Her voice rose in half-hysteria. 'Would you have believed me? If I'd said, "Hey, Evan, even though you're just a kid, both a freelance spy network and the CIA are interested in you. Want to go see a movie?"'

'You answer one question for me.'

'Anything.'

'Did you know they were going to kill my mom?' His voice strained for control.

'No. No, I never knew that, ever.'

'You told him I loved you, didn't you?'

He could see the question jarred her. 'Yes.' She closed her eyes. 'I had to.'

'You must have all had a laugh.'

'No. No, Evan, it was never like that. I was trying to help you.'

'If the CIA wanted to protect us, why didn't they send a team?'

'Bricklayer's group is very small. We're not set up for big operations. We can't reveal our existence to any possible traitors inside the Agency, because they're our targets, along with Jargo. We're not supposed to operate on American soil.'

'Wow, so my family and I, we're really freaking special,' Evan said. 'I don't know why I should believe you now.'

'Because I'm still the same girl you met a month ago. I'm still Carrie.' She spoke after long seconds of silence. 'When you told me you loved me ... I couldn't say anything because I didn't want you hurt. I'm sorry.' She leaned forward, watching the rearview, watching for the police. 'Oh, getting shot *hurts*.'

He made his choice. He followed her directions, stopping at a quiet aviation office near Louis Armstrong International with two cars parked in front.

'Inside. A pilot who works for Bricklayer, to fly us out. Bricklayer's real name is Bedford. There's trust for you. Only three people inside the CIA know his real name.'

He looked at her. He could just run. Leave her. Her colleagues would find her, and he could vanish and never see her again. Never hear another lie from her lips.

He thought of that morning when she'd walked into second period, the new girl. She hadn't glanced at him, but he'd glanced at her. He thought of how beautiful she had been the first time he'd really noticed her, in the coffee shop, frowning at her laptop while she tried to edit a movie. She had simply been lying in wait for him. He thought of the softness of her kisses on his lips, her looking at him as though her heart would burst. Maybe her loving him was a lie, but he loved her.

She was the worst thing that had ever happened to him. She was the best chance to get his father home. And she had saved him now, saved him from certain death.

Evan carried her out of the car and kicked four times on the office door.

29

Keeping a man imprisoned was like buying a tour inside his soul. Jargo had seen men, locked in the cramped confines of his homemade jail, talk to people long dead and gone; cry and sob after days of complete silence; one unfortunate drowned himself in the toilet. Strength was often shallow; confidence was a ploy, bravery a mask.

He already knew Mitchell Casher's soul. It was a soul incapable of betraying anyone he loved. It was a soul that trusted few, but that trust ran deep as gold veining through the earth.

Jargo went inside the room. Mitchell lay on the bed, a heavy steel chain bound round his waist and ankles, long enough to permit him to reach the toilet. Mitchell was unshaven, unwashed, but dignified. The room smelled of the dried-food packets he'd left for Mitchell, since neither he nor Dezz could stay to serve as his jailers.

He stood watching Mitchell, who did not say hello.

'I'm afraid to ask,' Mitchell Casher said.

'I have a difficult question for you,' Jargo said, 'but I really must insist on honesty.'

'I've always been honest with you.' Mitchell's voice was broken, worn with grief for his wife and fear for his son. He sounded like the dead Mr Gabriel. Keeping him in solitary confinement would take months, years, to break him; bad news about his son would shatter him at once, Jargo knew.

'I appreciate your honesty, Mitch. Will Evan fight for you?'

'Fight for me? I don't know what you mean.'

Jargo sat down across from Mitchell Casher. The glow of the light, high above in the ceiling where no prisoner could reach it, was eye-achingly dim. No window graced the room: Jargo had bricked it years ago, after an unfortunate incident involving a shard of glass and the wrist of a stubborn prisoner. But Jargo considered Mitchell not to be missing a view. Outside, the night sky of southern Florida hung heavy with clouds that resembled cancers. 'Evan resisted us. Will he fight for you? Will Evan try and get you back?'

'No.'

'I've been thinking long and hard about Carrie and what she's done. I don't know for sure that she is CIA, but she's taken Evan, probably, to the CIA.'

Mitchell put his head in his hands. 'Then let me go. Let me help you find him. Please, Steven.'

'Find him? You and I can hardly stroll into the CIA's lobby and ask for him back, now can we?'

'They'll kill him.'

'Yes. But not right away,' Jargo lied. You never really forgot how to lie, he thought, the way you never really forgot how to swim, to ride a bicycle, to kill.

'I don't understand.'

This was the conversational equivalent of cutting a diamond. One had to be precise to get the intended effect, and there were no second chances. 'Evan told me he has a list of our clients. He also knows my name, and he knows that Dezz is my son. He has information about us, who we are.'

Mitchell's eyes went wide.

'All our clients, Mitchell. Do you realize what this could do to us? It's one thing if we all have to vanish and start over again. That's almost impossible. But our clients? We could never rebuild if the CIA got that information.' Jargo brought his gaze back to Mitchell's face.

'I swear to you I never knew Donna was betraying us,' Mitchell said in a hoarse voice.

'I know. I know, Mitchell. I know.'

'Then please let me help you.'

'I want to let you go, but you're hardly in fighting shape. You might take off and endanger the only chance I have –' Jargo paused – 'of getting Evan back safely for you.'

'The only chance? Tell me.'

Jargo waited, let Mitchell squirm.

'Evan.' Mitchell put his face in his hands.

'I haven't seen you cry since we were boys.'

'They killed Donna. Imagine your son in their hands.'

'Dezz would never be taken alive. You know how he is.' Jargo didn't look at Mitchell. 'I'm so sorry.' His voice cracked. Jargo closed his hand on Mitchell's arm.

'So let me help you. Please.'

'Evan said he has the client list, Mitchell.'

'I bet he lied ... Donna wouldn't have shared information with him. His finding out about us, it was her worst nightmare.'

'Reality check: the files were on his computer. Donna had clothes packed for him to run. She'd hired a bodyguard to escort them to Florida, to help her convince you to come with them, hired him to create new identities for them. I think Evan knew; she must have prepared him to leave his entire life behind. And he might know what the list is worth.'

'Evan's just a kid ... He wouldn't know how to sell the information. He wouldn't know anyone to contact, and he wouldn't hurt me.'

'You never told him about your background? Not once?'

'Never. I swear he knows nothing.'

You don't know what he knows, and I'm not taking the risk, Jargo thought, but instead he said, 'I'm weighing whether to attempt to get Evan back at all. If he plans on fighting for you, he won't simply hand the files over to the CIA. He'll try and strike a deal. That may give us a window of time to find him, but that's the risk I'm assessing.'

'I don't understand.'

Jargo leaned forward, whispered an inch from Mitchell's face, 'You know I have operatives working for me within the Agency.'

'Yes.'

'And clients within the Agency. Those people are dead if Evan turns over the list.' Jargo put a hand on Mitchell's shoulder. 'My people inside the Agency have every reason to get Evan back for me, for us.'

'They won't hurt him?'

'Not if I tell them to bring him to me alive.' It was so important that Mitchell believe this lie, he thought. 'But either way, we must get Evan and whatever information he has away from the Agency. Alive, so you can be together with him again.'

'Please, Steven, let me help. Let me help you find my son.'

Jargo stood, made his decision. He dug in his pocket and

unlocked the chain, slipped it free of Mitchell. The links made a pool of steel on the hardwood floor.

Mitchell stood. 'Thank you, Steven.'

'Go get showered. I'll cook you dinner.' He gave Mitchell Casher a rough hug. 'How's an omelet sound?'

Mitchell seized him by the throat, shoved him hard against the wall, relieved him of his gun, angled it under his chin. 'An omelet sounds great. But just so you and I are clear. Your agents, they don't hurt or kill my son. Make them understand we need him alive.'

Jargo didn't blink. 'I'm glad that's out of your system. You can let me go now.'

'If they kill my son, I will kill yours.'

'Let go.'

Mitchell released his hold on Jargo; Jargo gently pushed his hand away. 'This is what our enemies want: us at each other's throats.'

Mitchell handed him his gun. 'Evan. Safe. That's non-negotiable. I can control my son once we've got him back.'

'I will do everything I can to bring him home. You realize he'll be the best-kept secret in the Agency. Resources, people will be diverted from their normal work to help hide him and to rally against us. My eyes inside the Agency will be looking for those signs. A well-meaning idiot in the Agency will mass for a secret war against us, and we'll stop them with our own Pearl Harbor.'

'Getting him back will be almost impossible.'

'In a way,' Jargo said, 'I think it might be easy. What we need to do is convince him to come back to us.'

He went downstairs to make the omelet. The curving cypress staircase was full of shadow; he did not like lights burning brightly in the lodge, even with every window carefully sealed and covered. Too much light would glow like a beacon in the vast dark and might attract unwanted attention.

The kitchen in the empty lodge was large, dimly lit. Dezz sat on a stool eating a candy bar, sullen, morose. CNN was on the TV.

'Any details of note?' Jargo asked.

'No. A few people suffered minor injuries in the rush to get out of the zoo. No arrests, no suspects, but no mention of videotape of us.' Dezz chewed his candy. 'Dad, what are we going to do?'

'We'll find them and deal with both of them.'

'Carrie . . .'

'Is a traitor, Dezz. We sheltered her, protected her, and she betrayed us. If only your shot had hit her in the head.'

Dezz looked at the floor.

'Did you miss on purpose, Dezz?'

Dezz glanced up. 'Of course not.'

Jargo stepped close to his son, took his chin in his hands. 'You lost your nerve at a critical moment.'

'I'm sorry, Dad.'

'I need to know I can trust you.'

'I won't freeze up again.'

'I should hope not. I told her I thought you liked her,' Jargo said. 'She laughed at the very idea.' He watched the shock rise and fade in his son's face, replaced by a pale coolness. Button pushed, he thought.

'She's a traitor who needs to die,' Dezz said after a moment.

'That's right, son. That's right.' He pushed Dezz away from him. 'If Evan has the client list and hands it over to the CIA, they won't immediately arrest them – they'll want to be sure. They'll want evidence, more than just a name on a list. So they'll up the surveillance on those targets, but slowly. They can't suddenly commit too many resources to us without incredibly uncomfortable questions being asked.'

'Your point?'

He could share with Dezz what he didn't dare share with Mitchell. 'Very few in the CIA know about us. There is a man, code-named Bricklayer, but I have not been able to determine who he is. Bricklayer is supposed to root out any internal problems in the CIA, problems such as using free-lance assassins, selling secrets, committing unapproved actions, stealing from American corporations. Basically, Bricklayer wants to put us out of business.'

'Bricklayer.'

'Carrie's a resource Bricklayer will have to use. That may be a blessing to us.'

'How?'

'How the CIA uses Carrie will tell us how much they really know about us.' He gathered the makings of an omelet from the fridge. Cooking would calm him. He chopped veg-etables and he thought of a lifetime ago, a child, watching the girl who became Donna Casher standing across a sun-drenched kitchen table from him, cutting vegetables with a calm precision. She had always wanted everything exact, just so. The sun had always caught her hair in a way that transfixed Jargo, and a tinge of sadness and regret touched his heart. He wished, just once, he had told Donna how much he liked her photographs.

'You know, Mitchell and Donna and I, the first job we had together when we went freelance, it was in London. A hit. Really simple – it didn't require all three of us, but there was a sense of power in the three of us doing the kill together. A sense of liberation.'

'Who did the three of you kill?' Dezz asked.

'Victim doesn't matter.'

'It always matters, Dad.'

Jargo ignored him. 'Mitchell and I both did the kill, although my shot hit first. Donna handled logistics.' Jargo cracked eggs in a bowl, stirred in milk, dumped in broccoli and peppers. 'Because it was our first job, we were cutting the bonds of our old life. We were so conscious in making our decisions. Before, we had never been encouraged to think on our own. We were more like human weapons. Point and shoot; don't ask questions. I fingered the bullets I was using for the longest time, like they were the last shackles of a chain that we were all breaking.'

Dezz ate a piece of candy.

'I just traded one set of chains for another, Dezz.'

Dezz knew his father was trying to tell him something important, but he felt impatient, itchy, ready to play a video game to relax. He didn't want to think about what his father had said about Carrie laughing at him. He kept thinking about the bright flower of blood on Carrie's shoulder. He'd hurt her. He wasn't sure how he felt about it. She'd betrayed them; wasn't that enough reason to hate her? She'd betrayed them for Evan. But he'd hurt her, and he felt an odd, unexpected pain in his own chest. Evan. Evan had forced this situation, forced him to hurt Carrie. If it wasn't for Evan, maybe Carrie would look at him. It wasn't like in this secret life she could have many options for boys. Evan was in the way.

He said, 'So how are you getting Evan and Carrie back, or at least shutting them up?'

'Carrie will tell the CIA what she knows, which isn't much. She can't betray enough to hurt us. She can give them descriptions, the apartment in Austin, but not much in terms of usable evidence.'

'Get real,' Dezz said. 'If she's double, she might have information, files ... She could skin you.'

'She had no access.' His father's voice went cold.

'You don't know what she had, Dad.'

Jargo kept his voice low. 'You missed a prime chance to kill them both. Shut up.' He dumped butter in the sizzling skillet, poured in the egg mixture. 'I intend to cover every base, including bases you don't even know are on the field, Dezz.'

The words spilled out of Dezz like a surprise; he had long thought them and never spoken them. 'Leave it, Dad.'

'Leave what?'

'All of it. This ... life. We need to pack and run, set up shop elsewhere. England. Germany. Greece. Let's go to Greece. Anywhere ... Just ... away.'

Jargo stared at him and the words froze in Dezz's throat. 'Are you stupid?'

'No, Dad.'

'I've told you not to call me that. It's sentimental.'

Dezz's voice wavered. 'But let's just run. Let's hide. We can just live someplace and not do this anymore.'

'Don't be weak, Dezz. I'm not dismantling years of work. My chains are still ones of my own choice, Dezz.' The sense of failure dimmed in Jargo. He was ready to roll.

'You're not going to be able to get Evan back.' Dezz was quiet.

Jargo finished cooking the eggs and slid them on a plate. 'Take this plate and a cup of strong coffee up to Mitchell. Be nice: he threatened to kill you a few minutes ago if I don't get Evan back safe and sound.'

Dezz frowned.

'Don't worry,' Jargo said in a low voice. 'Soon Evan will be dead, but Mitchell won't be able to blame us.'

TUESDAY MARCH 15

30

Evan watched the padded walls, and the walls watched back – the small dents in the fabric reminded him of eyes. He imagined cameras lurking behind the fabric. He wondered what dramas they had witnessed in this room. Interrogations. Breakdowns. Death. A faded stain marred the wall, at about the height of a seated man, and he imagined how the stain had got there and why it hadn't been removed. Probably because the CIA – or Bricklayer's group inside the CIA – wanted you to contemplate that stain and what it might suggest.

Two CIA men flew them on the private jet out of New Orleans. Evan told them he would only talk to Bricklayer. They bandaged Carrie's wound, gave her an injection for the pain, left him alone. He made himself hold Carrie's hand while she slept; he kept reminding himself that she'd saved him, even if it wasn't because she loved him. The plane landed in a small clearing in a forest. A private ambulance with NORTH HILL CLINIC written on it, with Virginia license plates, whisked them from the airstrip. A pair of doctors took Carrie away on a gurney, and a thick-necked security guard put Evan in the padded room. He sat and resisted the urge to make faces at the wall, sure cameras watched him. Worried about Carrie, worried about Shadey, worried about his father.

The door opened and a man stuck his head round. 'Would you like to see your friend now?'

It occurred to Evan the man might not even know Carrie's real name. It occurred to him that he might not, either, but he said, 'Thanks,' and followed the man down a brightly lit hallway. The man led him through three doors, and her room wasn't padded; it was a typical hospital room. No windows, the light on the bed eerie and dim, like the glow of the moon in a bad dream. She lay in bed, her shoulder freshly bandaged. A guard stood outside the door.

Carrie slept. Evan watched her and wondered who she really was, in the spaces between flesh and bone. He took her hand, gave it a squeeze. She slept on.

'Hello, Evan,' a voice sounded behind him. 'She'll be right as rain real soon. I'm Bricklayer.'

Evan put her hand down gently and turned toward the man. He was sixtyish, thin, with a sour set to his mouth but warm eyes. He looked like somebody's gentle uncle.

Bricklayer offered Evan his hand. Evan shook it and said, 'I'd rather call you Bedford.'

'That's fine.' Bedford kept his face impassive. 'As long as you don't do it in front of other people. No one here knows my real name.' He stepped past Evan, put a hand on Carrie's forehead in a fatherly fashion, as though checking her for fever. Then he steered Evan into a conference room down the hall, where another guard stood watch. Bedford closed the door behind him and sat down. Evan stayed on his feet.

'Have you eaten, son?'

Evan was never that crazy about people who weren't his parents calling him 'son'. Most of the time it just sounded like a fake kind of endearment. But he didn't argue. 'Yes. They gave me a sandwich. Thank you.'

'I'm here to help you, Evan.'

'So you said the first time we talked.' He decided to test the waters. 'I'd like to leave now.'

'Oh goodness, I think that very unwise.' Bedford tented his hands. 'Mr Jargo and his son and their associates will be hunting for you.' His politeness was formal, like the china Mom only brought out for the holidays.

'My problem, not yours.'

Bedford gestured at the chair. 'Sit for a minute, please.'

Evan sat.

'I understand you grew up in Louisiana and Texas. I'm from Alabama,' Bedford said. 'Mobile. Wonderful town. I miss it terribly the older I get. Southern boys can be stubborn. Let's both not be stubborn.'

'Fine.'

'I'd like for you to tell me what happened since your mother phoned you on Friday morning.'

Evan took a deep breath and gave Bedford a detailed account, but he did not mention Shadey, or Mrs Briggs. He didn't want anyone else in trouble.

'I offer my deepest sympathies on the death of your mother,' Bedford said. 'I think she must have been an extraordinarily brave woman.'

'Thank you.'

'Let me assure you that her funeral arrangements will be taken care of.'

'Thank you, but I'll handle her memorial when I get back to Austin.' He knew he was trying to sound like an adult.

'I'm afraid you truly can't go home again, son.' Like what Gabriel had said. *Your life as you knew it is over . . . Be a boy of shadows.*

'Am I a prisoner?'

'No, but you're a target, and it's my job to keep you alive.'

'I can't help you. I don't have this list he wants. Telling Jargo that I did was simply a bluff to get my dad back.'

'Tell me again exactly what your father said, since he blames us for your mother's death.'

Evan did, repeating his father's plea word for word, as best as he could remember. Bedford took a tin of mints from his pocket, offered Evan one, popped a mint in his own mouth after Evan shook his head. 'Quite a story Jargo's peddling. We didn't kill your mother. He did.'

'I know. I'm not sure why he cares what I think.'

'He just wants to manipulate you.' Bedford chewed his mint. 'You must feel like you've fallen down the rabbit hole.'

'Nothing Wonderland about it.'

'The fact that you survived an attack and a kidnapping is quite impressive. Mr Jargo and his friends, they've stolen your life from you. They put a piece of wire round your mama's throat and squeezed the last breath out of her. How does that make you feel?'

Evan opened his mouth to speak and then shut it. The harshness of the words made him quiet.

'It's the kind of question you ask in your films, and the films you put up on FilmzKool. How did that boy feel about his father's suicide? How did that girl feel when her mother had been out of work for two whole years? I watched several of the FilmzKool movies a couple of months back. I was most impressed. You're a good storyteller, and you recognize good storytelling in others, but just like a reporter with his soul sucked out, you have to ask the dreaded question "How does it make you feel?"'

'You want to know? I hate them. Jargo. Dezz.'

'You have every reason.' Bedford's voice went lower. 'He made your mom and dad lie to you for years. I suspect it wasn't entirely their choice to work for the Deeps, at least for as long as they did.'

'The Deeps.'

'Jargo's name for his network.' Bedford tented his hands again.

'Gabriel said he was a freelance spy.'

'It's true he buys and sells information, between governments, organizations, even companies, as far as we know.'

'I don't understand.'

'This is what we know. There is a man who uses the name Steven Jargo. He has no financial records. He owns no property. He does not travel under his own name, ever. Very few people have seen him more than once. He regularly changes his appearance. He has a young man who works with him, supposedly his son, and the son works under the name of Desmond Germaine, but there is no record of his birth, or his schooling, or him having anything like a normal life that creates a paper trail.'

'Carrie's been working with him.'

'And she's only seen Jargo a few times, never planned. He never sets a meeting with her; he simply arrives at someplace where she is. She never knows to expect him, never when we could grab him, not without putting her life at risk.'

Evan was silent. He was thinking Bedford was willing to put a young girl in extraordinary danger, and he wondered what Bedford was going to ask of him.

'Jargo runs a network of mercenary spies. We don't know if it's less than ten people or if it's a hundred. We suspect, from the times the name Jargo has popped up, that he has clients, buyers for his information and his services, on every continent.' Bedford opened up a laptop. 'I'm about to show a huge amount of trust in you, Evan. Please don't disappoint me.'

Bedford pressed a button and activated a projector cabled to the laptop. The image of a body, sprawled on pavestones, one arm dangling in a turquoise pool. 'This is Valentin Marquez, a high-ranking financial official in Colombia, one that our government was not fond of because he had connections to the major drug cartels, but we couldn't touch him. His body was found dead in his backyard; four of his bodyguards were killed as well. Rumors surfaced that an American State Department official funneled money to a man named Jargo; he put a hit on Marquez. Given the political situation, this would not be an activity we want exposed: American officials illegally diverting taxpayer funds to hired killers.'

Click. Another picture. A prototype blueprint of a soldier wearing a formfitting jumpsuit. 'This is a project the Pentagon has been working on, the next generation of ultra-lightweight body armor for field troops. This blueprint was found in the computer of a senior army official in Beijing by one of our agents, who was attempting to steal data on the latest Chinese missile program. We kidnapped the official, and under duress, he told us he bought the plans from a group he called the Deeps.'

'The Deeps? Jargo's group?'

'We think so. We found an attempt was made to sell the same armor prototype to a Russian military attaché three weeks later. He refused the offer and attempted, instead, to steal the prototype from the seller. The seller killed the man, his wife, and his four children. The wife's aunt, who was visiting, survived by hiding in the attic. She got a glimpse of the killer. Her description matches the description Carrie gave us of Jargo, although his hair was a different color and he wore glasses in Russia. Two months later, a major international arms dealer made a proposal for a body armor that matched these specifications exactly. In short, Jargo works both sides of the fence. He steals from us; he sells to us.'

Evan closed his eyes.

'Those are the closest cases we can tie to Jargo. We have several others where we suspect his involvement but can prove nothing.'

'My parents could not have been involved with a man like that. It just can't be.'

'That's what Carrie thought, I'm sure,' Bedford said. 'Her father worked for Jargo. Jargo killed her mom and dad, or rather, had them killed.'

'What?'

'Her real name is Caroline Leblanc. Her father ran a private security service after a long career in military intelligence. He had come to the Agency and met with me, let me know that Jargo had operatives working in the Agency and people buying his services within the Agency. He came to us because Jargo had forced him to recruit Carrie to work for him. They'd told her she was working for a special division of the CIA that uses teenagers as operatives.'

Evan shook his head, rubbed his temples with his fingertips. Recruited, by Jargo, and lied to by her own father. Was this what his own mother was trying to stop? His recruitment into this dark world?

'I asked him to remain in place, keep working for Jargo, but report to me. Jargo found out, or Carrie's father slipped up. Jargo told her she wasn't actually working for the CIA and tried to convince her that the CIA was responsible for her father's death. She ran away from the aunt who was assigned to be her guardian to work for Jargo, but Carrie came to us soon after – she learned additional details that

convinced her that Jargo was behind her parents' murders.
At tremendous personal risk, Carrie joined us and became
our double agent within the Deeps.'

'You let a sixteen-year-old girl work for you. What is
wrong with you?'

Bedford seemed to weigh his words. 'This man has to be
stopped. He has to be, Evan. It was an incredible opportunity, the closest we've ever gotten to Jargo.'

'You used a kid as a spy, with this dangerous man.'

'No one expects a teenager to be a spy. That was Jargo's
brilliance in recruiting Carrie.'

'Because it's insane to use a kid this way! You could have
grabbed him. You could have stopped him. You could have
hidden Carrie from him so he'd never find her or hurt her
again. You didn't because you want to find his clients; you
want to catch who he works with inside the CIA.' And if
they'd gone ahead and arrested Jargo, would my mom be
alive? he wondered. The thought nearly paralyzed him.
Maybe she would have been arrested, too, but she would be
alive.

'I didn't start it; Jargo did. He recruited her first and then
she came to me, so don't judge me. And, Evan, we need your
help . . . if you're willing to get your father back.'

Evan found his voice after a moment. 'Jargo killed her
folks and then she pretended to work for him.' He tried to
imagine Carrie's ordeal and he couldn't.

'Yes. It was difficult, but she knew it had to be done. Carrie
is our single operative who's gotten close to Jargo, although
she's only seen him face to face less than five times.'

'So who sent her to be my girlfriend, you or Jargo?'

Bedford let the words die on the air. 'It's complicated,
Evan.'

'How? It's either you or Jargo.'

'I asked her to watch out for you. I didn't order her to kiss you, or to care about you. She's not who you thought she was ... but she's still Carrie. Does that make sense?'

Evan wasn't sure. 'Why were you and Jargo interested in me?'

'I, simply because Jargo sent Carrie to watch you.' Bedford cleared his throat. 'He told her he wanted to know what film you were making next.'

The words were like a slap to Evan's face. '*Film?* I don't understand. Wasn't he watching me because of my mother turning against him?'

'That would be the natural assumption, but he wanted Carrie to find out about your film plans. That seems to have been the start of his interest in you, in you beyond being the kid of two people who worked for him.'

Evan felt numb. 'Couldn't he have just wanted me for this network? Like he wanted Carrie?'

'Possibly, but then he'd have gotten your parents to recruit you. You ever hear of a man named John Walker? He was in the navy back in the 1980s. The Soviets recruited him to be a spy. In turn, he recruited his best friend and his own son into becoming spies for the Russians.'

Evan tried to imagine his parents sitting him down for that talk. The picture wouldn't form.

'But ... Jargo never said a word to me about my films. He said I had a list that he needed. He wanted it in exchange for my dad.'

'He told Carrie the list contains his clients – the people in the CIA and elsewhere who hire him to do their dirty work. I don't know why your mother went against Jargo, but she did. We think she contacted Gabriel to extract her and you.

In return, she would have given him Jargo's client list.
Gabriel would have taken the list public, to shame the CIA –
we fired him, because no one believed his stories that we
had freelance spying occurring within the Agency – and to
bring down Jargo.'

'How did Mom get this list?'

'Unknown. Probably she built it over time working for
Jargo, spying on him while spying for him. Waiting to use it
until the time was right for her, and you, and your father, to
run from Jargo.'

Until the time was right. Why now? And why would
Jargo be interested in his film work?

'So Gabriel was telling me the truth. Well, partially.'

'Mr Gabriel let his personal weaknesses and biases cloud
his judgment, both here and after he left the Agency. It's very
sad. I've asked the FBI to move his family to a safe location,
hide them until we bring Jargo down.'

'So ... how long ago did Jargo order Carrie to get involved
with me?'

'A month.'

Evan stood up, paced the room. 'I never thought, never
talked, about making a documentary about spies or the CIA
or intelligence work of any sort. I'm a kid. Why would I
make a movie like that? Why would he tell Carrie to watch
me because of my films?'

'He never gave her a more specific reason,' Bedford said.

'So she's told you about what films I've made or might
make.'

'Yes.'

'So you must have an idea about what sparked Jargo's
interest.'

'Tell me what your planned subjects were.'

'Hasn't Carrie reported all this to you anyway?'

'I'd like to hear it from you, Evan. Tell me everything. This might be the key to locating Jargo. We find him, we get your father back.'

'Won't he just kill my dad? If my mom betrayed him, he'll think my dad did as well.' The thought that something he did now, now that he knew the truth, could be a death sentence for his father was almost too much to bear.

'Carrie tells me Jargo has been rather protective of your father. I'm not sure why.'

'He kills my mom and protects my dad. That's ... insane.'

'There may be a method to his madness. Now tell me about your film projects.'

'I'm not really shooting anything right now; I'm just working on research, on a history of extreme sports. An English girl I met at film camp in New York suggested it to me.'

'Extreme sports?'

'Yeah, skateboarding, snowboarding; it's all mainstream now. We were going to look at particular personalities in the history of the growth of extreme sports. And have it be longer, say forty-eight minutes, long enough for commercial sale to cable. She thought she could get it sold and she wanted to work with me on it. She had told me about a guy in London named Alexander Bast. He was a guy who promoted extreme sports in England. He launched all sorts of extreme sporting events around the world, wrote a book about the movement called *To the Extreme*. Kind of an eccentric character. He got murdered. It was never solved. She thought he would be an interesting framework for the story.'

'Who is this girl?'

'Hadley Khan. A few weeks ago, she sent me clippings about Bast, his murder, his life, just to see if I thought we could craft an interesting film out of it.'

'That's rather unusual, isn't it, for a filmmaker to pitch you a film?' Bedford cupped his hands over his chin, leaned forward on the table. 'Did you tell your parents?'

'No. If she could have gotten it on TV, it would have been huge for me, but . . . I didn't want them to say no.'

'Did Ms Khan say why she wanted you to do this project with her?'

Evan thought, let the silence take hold of the room. 'Well, Bast had lived in Texas before moving to London. She thought we could film both sides of his story, I guess, me in Austin, her in London. She said she thought we could sell it to one of the sports channels if we fleshed it out.' Evan hesitated. 'The idea of selling a film, well, that grabbed me. I thought that would pretty much cap off my portfolio for college, and it would give FilmzKool a huge boost. Hadley said she could put up most of the money, but we'd have to keep it a secret. She didn't want her dad to know and so I didn't tell my parents. But if she decided to run . . . she must have known. She must have been monitoring my emails.'

'And if she was, she might have known if Jargo tried to monitor your email as well. Maybe she shut his monitor feeds down, and that's why he needed Carrie.' Bedford was thoughtful for a moment. 'Did you ever ask Hadley Khan about the information on Bast?'

'No. I told her I'd see if people who knew him in Austin, when he started as a sports promoter, knew anything about him, but no one seemed to remember much about him. I was starting to think it wasn't nearly as interesting a story as Hadley thought it was.'

Bedford got up from his seat, started to pace behind the chair. 'Alexander Bast was a CIA agent,' Bedford said, 'a low-level courier. Not important, but still on our payroll, until the day he died.'

Evan leaned back in the chair. 'Uh, I didn't know that about him.'

'We don't generally advertise,' Bedford said dryly, 'but how interesting that you are making a film about a former CIA agent, and suddenly Jargo is interested in you enough to send a sixteen-year-old girl to pretend to be your girlfriend, and his own son to monitor what you're doing.'

'Bast has been dead for twenty-plus years. If there was a connection to him and Jargo, why would Jargo care now?'

'I don't know, but that has to be part of the reason Jargo was interested in you. Bast was CIA; Jargo has contacts in the CIA. You said Hadley Khan lives in London. Your mother was just there a few weeks ago.'

'She had a photographic assignment for a magazine.'

'Or she had work to do for Jargo.'

Evan decided to broach the subject. 'Jargo said your people killed my mother.'

'We covered that already. He lied, of course.'

'But what you're doing is illegal. Last I heard, the CIA isn't supposed to operate on American soil. Much less use a kid as an agent. Yet here you are.'

'Evan, you're correct. The CIA charter doesn't permit the Agency to conduct clandestine ops on US soil or against citizens.' Bedford shrugged. 'But the Deeps are a very special case. If we bring in the FBI, we hopelessly complicate the situation. We can act and act decisively.'

'"Complicate" means "expose", and that's what you don't want. The fact is, you have active traitors and rogues inside the Agency.'

'I don't want them to know we're on their trail. All our activities will come to light once the bad guys are down. We still have congressional oversight, you know.'

'All I care about is getting my dad back from Jargo.'

'Without the list,' Bedford said, 'we don't have a lot of options.'

'It wasn't hidden in the photos or songs she sent me. I tried to find it.'

'Oh, I believe you. If you knew, you would have given the list to us.' Bedford crossed his legs.

'You said she built the list over time, but that assumes she worked for most of the clients. That's a big assumption.'

'Perhaps.'

'What if she stole it from somewhere? From a central source.'

Bedford tapped his lip. 'Perhaps.'

Evan got up and began to pace the floor. 'So, Jargo gets interested in me because he hears I'm doing a film that threatens him. Somehow, he's worried about me digging into Alexander Bast's murder. That might mean Jargo has a connection to Hadley Khan. He inserts Carrie into my life to watch me. But why does my mother turn against Jargo, after so long?'

'Maybe she learned of Jargo's interest in you. It was probably a protective measure.'

Evan's head spun. His mother set her own death in motion trying to save him from Jargo.

'You get the client list, what do you do with it?'

'The CIA, I hope, has only a few bad apples. I think Jargo

knows most of them. We take them down. Jargo has to be stopped.'

'And you getting a list of Jargo's other clients, that doesn't hurt you, either.'

'Of course not. The British and the French and the Russians want to know about their own loose cannons. But my primary concern is in cleaning our own house. If you might help us figure out where she hid another copy of the list, that would—'

'I told you, I don't have the list,' Evan said. 'So we should steal the list again.'

Bedford raised an eyebrow. 'How?'

'Go backward from when my parents vanished from Washington all those years ago, find another path into Jargo's organization.'

'And what if he's destroyed the list?'

'He still has to have a way of tracking clients, payments made to him, deliveries he does. That information still exists for him to run his business. We have to crack his world.'

'*We?*'

'I want my father back. I can't just sit around a hospital room forever.'

Bedford leaned back. 'And you think you could do it.'

'Yes. If I start getting close to Jargo, he'll try and grab me, or he'll think I'm working with you now and he'll want to grab me to see what you know.'

'Or grab Carrie.'

'No. He nearly killed her. She doesn't go anywhere near him.' Evan shook his head. 'Where were you, by the way, at Audubon Zoo? You sent her alone.'

'Carrie has been an excellent informant, but she had no way to get in touch with us. Jargo watched her constantly.

She didn't have a chance to alert us. We knew he'd taken a charter flight to New Orleans after the fact, but not before. So we just had a team at the airport ... ' His voice drifted off.

'Your people were sticking close to the airport to catch him and extract her. They gave up getting him to help us get out of the city.'

Bedford nodded.

'I can't believe she took the risk for me.'

'She's rather strong-willed.'

'Oh. That's not an act?' Evan said, and permitted himself his first smile in days.

Bedford gave a soft laugh. 'No, that's who she is. She risked everything to save you.'

'I don't want her near Jargo.'

'That's not your choice, though, is it?'

'Get another agent.'

'I can't. Fighting Jargo is not official CIA policy, son, because we don't want to admit he's a problem.' Bedford put the smile back on. 'You're at a secret CIA clinic in rural Virginia. The locals think this is a super-expensive rehab clinic for rich alcoholics. On our books you're listed under a code name, which in the records is a nonexistent Croatian Muslim college student living in DC wanting to trade information on Al Qaeda in Eastern Europe that will, of course, not pan out. Your flight from New Orleans will be logged as me traveling back from a meeting with a journalist from Mexico who had information to share on a drug cartel that is financing terror activities in Chiapas. You see how the game is played? Until we identify who Jargo has in his pocket in the Agency, we dare not tip our hand. We hide every move we make. No one in the Agency can know we're hunting Jargo and the Deeps. According to Agency records,

Carrie is twenty-two years old and she is assigned deep cover to an operation in Ireland that doesn't exist. You don't exist. I sort of exist, but everyone thinks I'm just an accountant who travels a lot checking Agency books.' Bedford smiled again.

'Then let me find the client list. You don't risk anything. I'm not an employee, and I'm the only one who you know can draw Jargo out.'

'You just chastised me for using Carrie because she's a minor. So are you.'

'I take it back. Please. Use me. I'm your best chance to find my dad and get the information you need.'

'No. You're not trained. Jargo and her father at least trained Carrie in how to fight, how to shoot, how to steal. You have no idea what you're heading into.'

'You said you'd use me.'

'For *information*, Evan, not to send you out into the field.'

'I survived the past three days. How much worse could it get?'

'I'm responsible for you now, Evan. No.'

'Look, if I dig back into my parents' past, I'm not in danger. The past is not where Jargo's going to be looking for me. Otherwise I'm just sitting here.'

Bedford didn't answer for a long minute. 'Then you're sitting here.'

'And what about Carrie?'

'It was a flesh wound; she'll be just fine.'

Evan said, 'I don't want her hurt again.'

'She saved you, son. She wants the people who killed her parents to go down, and she's worked this for a year. She's an extraordinary young woman.'

Evan stood up, paced the room. 'I just wish ... you had

been watching my mom instead of me. You had to have checked on me, on my family, when Jargo assigned Carrie to me.'

'We did. Your parents had extremely good legends.'

'Legends?'

'Background stories. There was nothing to make us doubt them, until we went back and found no pictures of them in the high-school yearbooks they supposedly were in.'

'Then why weren't you watching them?'

'We were watching your father, but very carefully. We thought he had the connection to Jargo, as Carrie's father did. These people are extremely good. They'd spot surveillance unless it was perfect.'

'Once again, you didn't want to tip your hand. You left us out in the cold.'

'We didn't know what was happening. We couldn't find it out.'

Evan let the lame excuse pass; there was no point in arguing. What mattered now was finding his father, keeping Carrie safe. 'If my dad wasn't in Australia, like Mom said ...'

'He spent the last week in Europe – Helsinki, Copenhagen, Berlin. We lost him in Berlin last Thursday.'

His father, evading the CIA. It didn't seem possible.

'Either Jargo grabbed him in Germany or he returned to the US without us knowing, and then Jargo nabbed him.'

'If I get the files back, what happens to me and my dad?'

'Your father tells us everything he can about Jargo and his organization in exchange for immunity from prosecution. You and your father get new lives, new identities, courtesy of the Agency.'

'What about Carrie?'

'She gets a new identity and a free college education.'

Of course she would be hidden, as he would.

And that meant they'd never see each other again. He couldn't decide how that made him feel, except that it wasn't good.

'All right,' Evan said quietly. 'I have my phone ... It contained music files and photos my mother sent, I think, but I couldn't decode the files when I downloaded them a second time. And the phone was in my pocket when I jumped in the water in the zoo. It's ruined. I thought if my mom sent me the list, it might be there.'

'Give it to me. We'll try.'

'I have a passport that Gabriel provided. South African. It got wet, too.' Evan pulled it from his shoe. 'I had other passports, but they got left behind in my motel room in New Orleans.' He supposed Shadey took them when he fled.

'Go rest, son. You've done your part in this fight.'

No, Evan thought. No, I've not started fighting at all. But instead he shook Bedford's hand.

31

Carrie was awake when Evan knocked on the door to her room. The guard shut the door behind him, left them alone.

'Hey. How are you feeling?' he asked.

A dinner tray of comfort food sat before her: a bowl of chicken soup laced with thick noodles, a small grilled steak the size of a palm, mashed potatoes, a chocolate shake, a glass of ice water. She'd drunk most of the shake and seemed indifferent to the rest of the food. She loved chocolate. He thought of the mocha lattes he'd bought her at their coffee shop close to school and his face warmed. He wasn't sure how to start this conversation. She had been unconscious much of the time on the fast flight out of New Orleans, and he couldn't talk to her in front of the CIA guys.

'I'm all right.' Her voice was small. In New Orleans she'd sounded like a tough, fierce fighter, and now she sounded the other half of what she was: a teenage girl, sad, on uncertain ground with him.

'You're not hungry?'

'Not really.'

'Bedford said your wound wasn't too bad.'

Color touched her cheeks. 'More gouge than bullethole. It caught the top of my shoulder, missed the bone. It's sore and stiff, but I'm feeling better.'

He sat in the chair next to her bed. 'Thank you, for saving my life.'

'You saved mine. Thanks.'

Awkward silence again. It was hard enough when you were first in love to know what to say at times; conversation could be a minefield. Now Evan felt even worse.

'I just don't know what to believe right now. I don't know who to trust.' He heard Shadey's words in his head: *Don't trust unless you must.* Maybe Carrie had spotted Shadey in the crowd – recognized him from talking about Evan on television or from his clips on FilmzKool – but she still made no mention of him to Bedford. Protecting his friend, showing him, through her silence, that she could be trusted. He didn't dare mention Shadey's name – the room was probably bugged. He just hoped Shadey was safe and lying low.

'Trust yourself,' Carrie said. Now she looked at the tangle of sheet round her waist.

'Not you?'

'I can't tell you what to do. I have no right.'

'Bedford says you'll want to help get my dad back.'

'Yes.'

'At great risk to yourself.'

'Life is nothing but risk.'

'You don't have anything to prove to me.'

'You and your father are the best hope we have of breaking them. It's not a matter of force. It's a matter of subtlety. That's all I want, Jargo broken. And for you to be safe.'

He leaned forward. 'You're free from Jargo now. You don't have to play a role anymore. You don't have to pretend to like me. I'll be fine.'

She stared at him and slowly shook her head. 'Don't sell yourself short, Evan. You're easier to like than you think.'

His face felt hot. 'Why didn't you just tell me the truth?'

'I couldn't put you in that danger. Jargo would have killed you.'

'And you would have lost your chance to take him down.'

'But you're more important to me than Jargo.' She closed her eyes. 'I didn't let myself get close to anyone after my parents died. You were the first.'

He held her hands. 'Bedford says Jargo killed your folks.'

'I don't know who actually pulled the trigger – one of the other Deeps or maybe Jargo himself – but he made sure I thought the CIA was responsible.'

'Tell me about your parents.'

Now she looked up from their tangled fingers and stared at him. 'Why?'

'Because now you and I do have truly a lot in common.'

'I'm sorry, Evan. I'm so sorry.'

'Tell me about your folks.'

She let go of his hands, knotted the sheets with her fingers. 'My mother wasn't involved with the Deeps. She was an advertising copywriter for a small firm that did direct mail. She was pretty and kind and funny – just a really great mom. I was an only child, so I was her everything. She loved me very much. I loved her. Jargo, or whoever, killed her when he killed my father. That's about it.'

'And your dad?'

'He worked for Jargo. I thought he had his own corporate security firm.' She took a sip of water. 'I suspect he mostly did corporate espionage – finding people inside companies willing to sell secrets, or setting up situations where they were forced to sell him information. It was not a nice thing to find out about your dad.'

'Did your mother know?'

'No. She wouldn't have stayed married to him. He lived a life we didn't know about.'

'How long ago did they die?'

'Fourteen months. Jargo decided my father had betrayed him, and he killed them both. It was made to look like a robbery. Jargo stole their wedding rings, my dad's wallet.' She closed her eyes. 'I was already working for Jargo. Through my dad. He recruited me.'

The words felt locked in Evan's throat. 'Why would your father have drawn you into this mess?'

She looked at him with haunted eyes. 'I think he thought if I was doing it too, I couldn't hate him. He told me he worked for the CIA, and that they needed me to help them. He was very convincing.' Her voice went flat with bitterness.

'What kind of work did you do?'

'Low-level stuff. I'd be the go-between from Jargo to other agents or client contacts. I filled dead drops – you know, secret places where you leave documents and the client picks them up. I never even saw Jargo or the client's contact. I never got the location of the dead drop until the last minute, so it was much more difficult for Bricklayer to watch. No one would suspect a teenager of being a courier. I hadn't done a job for Jargo in three months when he ordered me to Austin.'

'You lived on your own?'

'Yes. He had an assistant named Frank, a guy from Denmark. I think Frank is the one who actually ... killed your mom. Frank got me a place to live. He'd pose as my guardian. I'd stay home and read books and just teach myself what I would have learned in school, as much as I could. Frank taught me how to shoot, how to fight hand to hand.'

'Bedford says you came to him to fight Jargo.'

'I never bought the robbery story ... My father was trained to fight; he wouldn't be taken so easily. I was on a job in Mexico City and I went to the embassy. They put me in touch with a CIA official. He got Bedford down fast on a plane. He asked me to stay in place, keep working for Jargo, feed them what information I could. But it was hard. I wanted out. I wanted to shoot Jargo dead. Bedford ordered me not to – we needed to wrap up the whole network, and their clients. I kill them, another Deep simply takes over and we're back to square one.'

'I still don't see why they can't put their hands on this guy.'

'Evan, he's extraordinarily careful, and he's been doing this a long time. Working for him is like doing a never-ending jigsaw puzzle. I'd get my instructions – encoded –

in what would look like an innocent email. Then I'd pick up from a dead drop the materials for the client that another Deep had stolen, go to a second dead drop, often in another city, and leave them. If the CIA picked up whoever picked up the goods, Jargo would know his network was blown, and we wouldn't get any closer. The best the CIA could do was to replace the information I was dropping off with data that was similar but not quite right. He never uses the same email twice, never the same base of operations twice. Everything is cash. He's really, really hard to stop. And when I'm around him, he watches me constantly. I took such a risk calling you in the police car ... He found out and I had to lie to save myself.' Tears threatened her eyes. 'I thought I could do it alone, but I couldn't. I couldn't even save Gabriel. I contacted Bedford when Jargo took him, but they didn't want to risk blowing my cover by saving him.'

He kissed the top of her hands and put her hands back onto the blanket. 'I'm going to find the client list my mom stole. Jargo still has my father. I'm getting him back. Do you know where he is?'

'I think in Florida. Jargo has a safe house there, but I don't know where.'

'Bedford is putting me on the sidelines, but I'm not staying there.'

'Let Bedford hide you, Evan. If your dad can get away from Jargo—'

'No, I can't wait. I can't let my dad down. Bedford already said I won't be able to talk you out of this. Will you help me?'

She nodded, took his hand. 'Yes. And ...'

'What?'

'I know it's hard to trust anyone now, but you can trust Bedford.'

'All right.'

She put her hand on his cheek. 'Lie down here with me.'

'Um, I don't want to hurt your shoulder.'

She gave him a slight smile. 'You're just lying down, ace.'

She scooted over and he stretched out next to her and held her and she fell asleep in a few minutes, her head on his shoulder.

Bedford sat watching a monitor that showed Carrie and Evan lying in the hospital bed, whispering quietly, talking. Love at sixteen, his own little Romeo and Juliet. It was the intensity of it that could frighten, the sureness, the belief that love was a lever to lift the world. He had already lowered the volume; he didn't need to hear what they said. He was a spy, but he did not want to spy on them, not now.

Carrie slept and Evan stared off into space.

I wonder, Bedford thought. I wonder how much you really know, or really suspect, Evan. How much do you really know?

'Sir?' A voice behind him, one of his techs.

'Yes?'

The man shook his head. 'The damaged phone, we can't recover any encoded files from it. Whatever process was used, it did not leave any other files hidden inside the music files when he transferred them to the phone. They also did not leave a copy on the server after Evan downloaded them. I'm very sorry.'

'Thank you,' Bedford said. The tech left, shutting the door behind him, and he watched Carrie sleep, and Evan staring into the air, thinking.

That boy, Bedford thought, is up to something. Maybe I should let him try whatever he wants to try and see where it takes us.

32

Arwen looked at the readouts while sipping decaf and eating a chocolate doughnut. She knew she shouldn't, but stress made her crave carbs. She had hacked into the Federal Aviation Administration database, examining every plane takeoff in Louisiana and Mississippi since Jargo and Dezz had lost Carrie and Evan in New Orleans. Every flight accounted for, recorded, logged, but no flight that led to a place where it should not. Which meant that they hadn't flown; they had driven out of New Orleans, or they could still be in New Orleans.

She had already been through every hospital record she could acquire, stealthily weeding through the databases, and no young woman matching Carrie's description had been admitted to a hospital in that area. She would have to widen the search, cover Texas to Florida.

She sipped her coffee, nibbled at her doughnut. Shame that Carrie was a traitor. She rather liked Carrie, although she had never met her and had only talked with her on the phone a few times. But Carrie and Evan were young and stupid, and sooner or later they'd poke up their heads, via a travel document or a credit activity, and Arwen would see them. Then Jargo would unleash his dogs and end this particular mess.

She had an unusual protocol to follow, designed by Jargo

years ago, in case he feared the network was in danger of exposure. Panic mode. She was to monitor phone lines used only for emergency communications by certain Deeps, to ensure that no one was running. She ran a program that would feed cleaned money into banks around the world. And for some odd reason he added another request last night: she was to track cellular phone-call patterns to and from a small chunk of eastern West Virginia, glean every cellular call made, incoming or outbound, then deliver the data to Jargo.

She wondered, exactly, what conceivable danger could lurk for Jargo on such quiet country roads and fields.

WEDNESDAY MARCH 16

33

Wednesday morning, Evan and Carrie regarded each other's new look over breakfast.

'You don't look like you,' Evan said. Then he thought that was probably the worst thing to say to a girl after a makeover.

Carrie didn't seem to care. 'Welcome to Salon Bricklayer,' she said.

Evan's hair was now colored a rich auburn and cut in a cleaned-up military burr, his blue eyes hidden behind brown contact lenses. He wore dark trousers and a jacket with a white shirt, a shift from his normal colorful clothing. Carrie's hair was now a soft brown and cut short. She wore tinted glasses that made her eyes look brown instead of blue.

'Call me Chameleon Boy,' Evan said.

'Hope and pray that this is the last time you ever have to go through a transformation.'

'You should go and rest,' he told her after breakfast.

'And what are you doing?'

'The same. I need some alone time. My mom.'

'I understand.'

She turned to go back to her room. He watched her go down the hallway and then he stepped outside. He wasn't under guard, he wasn't under arrest, but he was sure he was being watched. This place probably had more cameras than his old film camp.

He walked out onto the cool, morning-damp grass. The old sanitarium was mostly one large house, with a small scattering of outbuildings.

One of them was a garage.

He walked to it. He didn't try to hide, or to sneak, and in the distance he could see a guard strolling along a presumed perimeter. He had nothing to hide. He was just a kid.

Inside the garage were parked four Lincoln Navigators, all black, all with tinted windows. A man in a coverall had the hood of one open, peering inside. He stopped when he saw Evan. It was one of the men who'd flown with them from New Orleans. His name was Frame.

'Hi, Mr Frame,' Evan said.

'Hi. You should be back up in the main house.' Frame's tone was neutral.

'I needed a walk. I've been penned in all last night and today.'

'Well, you should go back to the house.'

'I work on cars with my dad. I've never seen a Navigator. Can I have a quick look before I go back and sit in front of a boring TV for the next ten hours?' He put a hand in his pocket, tried to look sixteen and harmless.

'Sure,' Frame said. He stepped to one side, closer to the front of the hood, and Evan peered down at the engine. Frame leaned in to show him something.

Evan slammed down the hood. Since Evan was leaning in as well, it did not occur to Frame that Evan would slam the hood down on his own head. Which he did not: Frame was 6 inches taller than Evan and the hood cracked down onto his skull; it didn't get close to Evan's.

He grunted and Evan did it again, yanking his own head back, and harder. Then again. Frame went down, bleeding. Evan grabbed a wrench that lay on the edge of the car, but Frame was up again, bigger, and madder now, and he grabbed Evan by the throat.

'What the hell do you think—' and then he jerked, fell, and let Evan go.

Carrie stood behind him, Taser in hand. She thumbed the button again and Frame was lost in an electric delirium.

'Let's go,' she said. 'He'll have a bad headache, but he'll be all right.'

'You're a doctor now, too? I didn't mean to hurt him.'

'You will have hurt him for nothing if we don't get out of here.'

He didn't ask questions; there was no time for that. He fished keys from Frame's pocket and they backed the Navigator out. A guard station was at the end of the road. The kiosk was empty. Carrie used Frame's pass card to lift up the lever and they were through, driving down a road carved from the dense forest.

'We have about five or ten minutes before Frame is missed, I think.' She turned off the car's GPS system. 'There's a tracker here as well, somewhere. Where are we trying to go?'

'Back,' Evan said, 'to the beginning.'

34

An hour later, Evan drove into Goinsville and parked in the town square. Four junk shops angling for antiquers' dollars; an outdoor café with weathered tables, empty under the rain-bottomed clouds; an optometrist's office; a law office; a title office. A normal, anonymous town.

'Goinsville never quite got going,' he said.

'I wonder how long we have until Bedford finds us,' Carrie said.

'He knows we're gone. He could have caught up with us by now. Maybe he's just watching to see where we go, what we do.' Evan gave her a glance. 'Maybe he's testing me.'

She was silent, watching the gray clouds.

He drove a block off the square and parked in front of a small, newer building with GOINSVILLE PUBLIC LIBRARY in metal letters mounted against the brick.

'Shouldn't you kids be in school?' the librarian asked by way of greeting.

'We're home-schooled over in New Paris,' Carrie said, naming the last big town they'd passed, 'but they don't have the newspapers for Goinsville over there.'

The librarian kept her doubting frown in place and Evan said, 'Do most kids cutting school come hang out here?'

She laughed. 'No, they don't. What do you need help finding?'

Evan told the librarian on duty that they were researching county history, of particular families.

The woman – small, dark, pretty – frowned. 'If you're looking for birth certificates, you're out of luck before 1986.'

'Why?'

'County courthouse burned down. All the records went up in smoke with them. Anything from 1986 on, we can do.'

'What about your local newspaper?'

'On microfilm back to the 1940s,' the librarian said. 'We've also got old phone books – in original form, if that helps. What's the family name?'

'Smithson.' First time he could claim the name as his own, first time he had said it aloud in public. Arthur and Julie Smithson. They used to live here, he thought. They grew up here.

'I don't know any Smithsons,' the librarian said.

'My parents grew up in an orphanage here.'

'Goodness. No orphanage here. Closest one would be in Charleston, I'm sure, but I've only lived here for five years.'

She showed them the microfilm machines, told them to ask if they needed any help, and retreated back to her desk.

'The orphanage must be closed,' he said, or Mrs Briggs was mistaken. Or a liar. 'Start with the current phone books, look for any Smithsons. I'll start with the paper. I got to go to the bathroom, though.'

She nodded and he returned to the entry foyer. Next to the restroom was a payphone. He fed it quarters, dialed Shadey's cellphone.

'H'lo?'

'Shadey, it's Evan. I only have a few seconds. Are you okay?'

'Yeah, man. Where are you?'

'I'm fine. I'm with . . . the government.'

'Please be kidding.'

'I'm not. Did you make it back to Houston?'

'Yes. Charged a plane ride back on my Visa. Man, you owe me,' but the earlier bite in his tone, when he and Evan had talked in Houston, was gone. 'You sure you okay?'

'Yes, and I'll see you get your money.'

'Never mind that. It's just now I'm scared, Evan.'

'You should stay out of sight. Maybe you and your grand-mother should go on a trip.'

'My grandma's got a sister in Shreveport. We could go see her for a few days. Normally I beg off from those visits, but if I act like I want to go, Grandma will be happy to head there.'

'Good idea. Did you get Jargo and Dezz on film?'

'Crystal clear. Got Dezz grabbing that little mama, him

shooting and missing that guard, too. That's called attempted murder in Louisiana, I believe.'

'I need you to upload the film to a remote server where I can get it.'

'Sure. Where do you want it?'

Evan gave him the name of a remote-server service he'd used to back up dailies of his films, so he always had an offsite backup in case his computer was stolen or his house burned down.

Shadey repeated the information. 'I'll set up an account under my grandmother's name. Password is "evanowesme".'

'Thanks, Shadey.'

'When are you coming back to Houston?'

'I don't know. Thanks for everything. I'll wire you your money.'

'Man, don't worry about it right now. Watch your back.'

'I will. I got to run, Shadey. Stay safe. I'll call you when I can.'

He walked back to the table and Carrie gave him a smile as he sat down.

'Not much to look for in the phone books, the last twenty years,' she said. 'No Smithsons. I'm already on the newspapers. You start on that set.'

Evan put in the microfilm to search through the town paper. He was conscious of Carrie's closeness, of the smell of soap on her skin, of what it would be like to kiss her and pretend none of this nightmare had happened.

It wouldn't ever be the same between them, he knew. The innocence was gone forever.

'Your parents could have lied to your source,' Carrie said.

'It bothers you I won't tell you the source's name.' He had not told anyone Bernita Briggs's name or how he'd found the information tying his family to the missing Smithsons. Bedford hadn't pressed him, but that wouldn't last, especially since he'd taken off.

'No. You're protecting that person. I'd do the same in your shoes.'

'I want to trust you. I just don't want Bedford to know.'

'You can trust him, Evan.' She went back to her search. She didn't say anything about trusting her.

He started on a set of microfilmed newspapers that began in January 1986. Goinsville news was full of civic events, farm reports, pride in the school's students, and a smattering of news from the wider world beyond. He spun the film reader's wheel past car crashes, births, football reports, a saints' parade of Eagle Scouts and honor roll mentions.

He stopped at February 13, 1986, when the county courthouse burned, read the article. The fire completely consumed the papers in the old courthouse. In the following days, arson rose its head and had also been suspected in the orphanage fire three months before. Investigators were attempting to find a link between the two fires.

'Are you to the end of 1985?' he asked.

'No, halfway through 1983.'

'Go to November 1985. I found it: orphanage fire.'

In a few minutes, she found the newspaper account. The Hope Home for Children sheltered the illegitimate unwanted in Goinsville after the Second World War. The stray seeds of southwest West Virginia that didn't end up at church homes in Charleston or Huntington apparently found root at the Hope Home. It housed both boys and girls. In November 1985, fire erupted in Hope's administrative offices, tearing like wind through the rest of the complex. Four children and two adults died of smoke inhalation. The rest of the children were relocated to other facilities throughout West Virginia, Kentucky, and Ohio.

The Hope Home never reopened. Evan went back to the courthouse-fire story. Most articles written about the orphanage tragedy and the courthouse fire carried the byline of Dealey Todd.

'Let's look him up in the most recent phone book,' Evan said.

Carrie did. 'He's listed.'

'I'll call him and see if he'll talk to us.'

Evan did. 'His wife says he's retired, at home and bored. Let's go.'

35

'Those poor kids,' Dealey Todd said. He hovered near eighty, but he wore the bright, easy smile of a kid. His hair had beaten a long-ago retreat, leaving a trail of freckles mapped across his head. He wore old khakis that needed a wash and a shirt faded with loving wear. His den held a rat's nest of old paperbacks and two TVs, one tuned and muted to CNN, the other tuned to a telenovela, also muted.

'Learning Spanish,' he said.

'Watching pretty girls,' his wife said.

Evan's throat tightened as CNN played. His face had been on CNN repeatedly in the past few days, although other stories, grander tragedies, had now bumped his from the news. But Bedford's disguise seemed to work; Dealey Todd hadn't given him a more curious look than he would have

given any other stranger when Evan introduced himself and
Carrie as Robert Smithson and Caroline Leblanc. Probably
Dealey paid more attention to the telenovela beauties than
he did the newsfeeds.

Mrs Todd was a bustling woman who offered sodas and
promptly vanished into the kitchen to watch yet another television.

Evan decided to play a sympathetic hand. 'We think my
parents came through the Hope Home orphanage, but their
records were destroyed,' said Evan. 'We're trying to locate
any other alternative source of records, and also to learn
more about the home. My parents died last year, and we
want to piece together their early lives.'

'And you two are doing this alone?'

'My parents are with us, at a motel in New Paris. They
just knew that Robert wanted to do this on his own,' Carrie
said.

'Admirable,' Dealey Todd said. 'Interest in your parents.
My own daughter lives over in Huntington and can't be
bothered to phone more than once a month.'

'Dealey,' Mrs Todd called from the kitchen, 'they don't
care about that, honey doll.'

The honey doll made a sour face. 'Okay, the orphanage.'
He shrugged, returned to his smile, sipped at his black
coffee. 'Orphanage got built; then it burned ten years later.
So you might be in for a long, difficult haul to find records.'

Evan shook his head. 'There has to be a source for
records. Who built it? Maybe whatever charity sponsored it
has what I need.'

'Let's see.' Dealey closed his eyes in thought. 'Originally
a nondenominational charity out of Charleston started it up,
but they sold it to ... ' He tapped his bottom lip. 'Let's see.

I want to say a company out of Delaware. You could probably find a record of sale at the county clerk's office, but I
remember they went bankrupt, too, after the fire, and no one
rebuilt the orphanage.'

A bankrupt owner. The files might have been scattered to
the winds. Evan thought for a second and asked, 'How did
the town view the orphanage?'

'Y'know, not that Goinsville isn't a charitable place,
'cause it is, but many folks around here weren't overjoyed
with the orphanage. Kind of a not-in-my-backyard feeling.
Bunch of so-called church ladies were just tight-jawed about
it.'

'Dealey, honey doll, don't exaggerate,' Mrs Todd called
from the kitchen.

'I thought when I retired from the paper, I left editors
behind,' Dealey said.

Silence from the kitchen.

'I'm not exaggerating,' he said to Evan and Carrie. 'People
didn't like in particular that young ladies in trouble could go
to Hope Home and drop their precious loads. You get the
sinners along with the end product.' He stopped suddenly,
the smile now uneasy, remembering that he was speaking of
Evan's parents and grandmothers, and that these were
teenagers.

'Did anyone dislike the place enough to burn it?' Evan
asked.

'Everyone thought it was an accident at first, the wiring,
but six months after the fire, a teenager named Eddie
Childers shot his mama and himself. The police found sou-
venirs from both burn sites – baby socks, a girl's uniform
from the orphanage, family photos from the workers at the
courthouse. All stashed under his bed. I'll never forget that.

I was there when the officers found the stuff. He left a note taking responsibility. He was a wild kid. Sad, very sad.'

'So the records of any children born at the Hope Home were destroyed,' Evan said, 'because *both* the orphanage and the county courthouse were gone, and the owners went bankrupt.'

'Yes, basically,' Dealey said. 'I remember I wrote a few stories about the company that owned the orphanage after it burned . . . because, you know, it brought about twenty or so jobs to the town. People hoped they'd rebuild. Twenty jobs is twenty jobs.'

'Well, we'll look up those stories at the library,' Carrie said.

Evan thought, This is a dead end. And then he thought, That is the point: Goinsville is a dead end. Someone *wanted* it to be the end of the road for anyone who ever came looking for Evan's parents. It can't be. You can't run a business that takes care of kids and have every bit of its history vanish . . .

'Thanks for your time,' Carrie said.

'Twenty jobs,' Evan said suddenly. 'Hey, do you know anyone who worked at the Hope Home that might still be alive?'

Dealey bit his lip in thought.

Mrs Todd emerged from the kitchen. 'Well, Dealey's cousin's wife, Phyllis, worked at the orphanage as a volunteer. Read the kiddies stories every Wednesday, you know. Get 'em interested in books because you know that's the key to success. I remember because Phyllis won a "Volunteer of the Year" award and my mother-in-law nagged at me for weeks to volunteer myself. She might be able to help you, or give you the names of the employees.'

'Does she by any chance still live around here?' Evan asked. 'I could show her pictures of my mom and dad, see if she could remember them.'

'Sure,' Dealey said. 'Phyllis Garner. She lives five streets over.'

'Phyllis is as sharp as a tack,' said Mrs Todd. 'Honey doll, shame it don't run in your family.'

A quick phone call determined that Mrs Garner was home, watching the same soap opera as Mrs Todd. They drove over the five streets with Dealey Todd to an immaculately maintained brick home, shaded by giant oaks. Mrs Garner wore a lavender sweater set, was perfectly coiffed, with a warm and welcoming smile.

Phyllis Garner gestured them to sit on a floral couch.

'I know it's been many years, ma'am.' Evan showed her current photos of his parents. 'Their names were Arthur and Julie Smithson.'

Phyllis Garner studied the photo. 'Smithson. I think I do recall that name. James!' Phyllis called to her grandson, who was puttering around in her garage. 'Come help me a minute.' They vanished down into a basement, leaving Dealey, Evan, and Carrie to talk about the weather and college football, two of Dealey's keen interests.

Phyllis returned fifteen minutes later, dusty but smiling. The grandson carried a box. He set it on the coffee table and left to finish his puttering.

Phyllis sat down between Evan and Carrie, opened the box, and pulled out a yellowing scrapbook. 'Photos of the kids, mementos. They'd draw me a picture and sign it "For Miss Phyllis." One girl always signed it "For Mommy" and told me she needed to practice on me, for the day when she got herself a real mother. It broke my heart. I wanted to bring her home, but my husband wouldn't hear of it. He said we were too old to take on little kids again, and it was the only argument I never won. My heart bled for those children. No one wanted them. That's the worst thing in this world, to be unwanted. I hope you recognize your parents in here.'

She flipped through pages. Phyllis Garner, radiant and beautiful and probably every orphan's dream. Evan wondered if she had been conscious of how the bereft children must have ached for her to slip her hand into theirs and say, 'You're coming home with me.' It might have been less painful if such an angel had kept her distance.

She pointed at a photo of a group of six or seven children. Evan's eyes went to the children first, looking for his father and mother in every face. No, not them. Then he noticed the man standing behind the children.

The man was short, balding, but not completely bald. He wore glasses and a thin, academician's beard, but the shape of the face, the sureness of the stance, were the same. Evan had seen the face several times, in the news clippings Hadley Khan had sent him from London when she proposed the joint film project. The man's smile was tight.

Alexander Bast, London extreme-sports promoter, CIA courier, murder victim.

'That man. Who's he?' Evan asked. He kept his voice steady.

Phyllis Garner flipped the picture over; she had a list of names written in tidy cursive on the back. 'Edward Simms. He owned the company that ran Hope Home. He only came here once that I recall. I asked him to pose with a group of the children. In honor of his visit. My God, he smiled, but you would have thought I scalded him. He acted like the children were dirty. The other ladies found him charming, but I don't have to count scales to know a snake.'

Carrie's hand closed round Evan's arm. Hard. She pointed wordlessly at a tall, thin boy standing near Bast, shock on her face.

'What's the matter, dear?' Phyllis asked.

36

After a long moment, Carrie said, 'Nothing. I thought ... but it was nothing.' She dropped her hand back into her lap.

'Are you all right?' Evan asked.

She nodded. 'I'm fine.'

'This was the last batch of kids that came in before the fire, I believe.' Phyllis Garner laid the open scrapbook on her lap, ran her fingers along the page. 'I remember they were shy at first, and of course they were older kids, not babies. Sad that they hadn't been adopted yet. People wanted babies.'

Carrie pointed at one tall, lanky kid. 'He was in the picture with Mr Simms.' She kept her grip on Evan's arm.

Phyllis prised the picture out of the plastic page cover. 'I wrote their names on the back ... "Richard Allan."' She frowned at Carrie. 'Honey, are you okay? You still look upset.'

'Yes, I'm fine, thank you. You're right, it's sad, these older kids not finding homes.' Carrie's voice was normal again, but Evan could feel the tension in her grip.

'It was just so unfair,' Phyllis said, 'the focus on finding babies. This was an appealing group of kids – nice-looking, bright, clearly well cared for, well spoken. At the orphanage, you'd see kids and all the hope had died in them. Hope that they would not just find families, but have a life beyond low-end jobs. Orphans face such an uphill fight. These kids, they didn't look very broken at all.'

Evan flipped a page. A picture of two girls, a teenage boy standing between them, thick brownish hair, a wide smile on his face, a scattering of freckles across high cheekbones, a tiny gap between his front teeth.

Jargo. His eyes were the same, cold and knowing.

'My God, my God,' Carrie said. It was almost a moan.

Sweat broke out on Evan's back.

'Did you find your dad?' Phyllis asked brightly.

Evan looked down the rest of the page. Two photos down were two kids, a girl, blonde with green eyes, memorably pretty but with a serious cast to her face. A boy was standing with her, holding a football, sweaty from play, light hair askew, grinning, ready to conquer the world.

Mitchell and Donna Casher, young teenagers. Frozen in time, like Jargo.

'May I?' Evan asked.

'Of course,' Phyllis said.

He loosened the picture from the plastic cover, flipped it over. 'Arthur Smithson and Julie Phelps,' written in Phyllis's neat script.

'Smithson,' Phyllis said. 'Oh, that's it! Are they your folks?'

'Yes, ma'am.' His voice was hoarse. He forced himself to smile at her.

'Honey, then you take that picture – it's yours. Oh, I'm so glad I could help.'

Carrie tightened her grip on his hand. 'Phyllis, did any of this last group of kids die in the fire?'

'No, it was younger kids. The older kids all got out.'

'Do you remember where any of these kids went after the fire? Specific other orphanages?' Evan asked.

'No, I'm sorry.' Phyllis leaned back in her chair. 'We were told it was best for us not to stay in touch with them.'

'May we borrow these photos? We can make copies, scan them into a computer, give them back to you before we leave town,' Evan said. 'It would be huge for us.'

'I never did enough for those kids,' Phyllis said. 'I'm glad someone finally cares. Take the pictures, with my blessings.'

After waving goodbye to Phyllis and Dealey, they drove away.

'What?' Evan asked, but half knowing what she was going to say.

'My *father*,' Carrie said, her voice shaking. 'That boy in the picture next to Alexander Bast, he's my dad, Evan. That boy's my dad!'

'Are you sure?'

'Yes. Our parents knew each other, knew Jargo, when they were kids.' She jabbed at one of the photos. 'This Richard Allan ... My dad's name was Craig Leblanc, but this is him. I know it's him. Let's not drive back yet. Let's go get coffee for a minute, please.'

They sat in a corner of a Goinsville diner, the only customers except for an elderly couple in a booth who exchanged laughs and moony smiles as if they were on a third date.

'So what does this mean?' Carrie studied the picture of her father as if he might have the answers. Tears sprang to her eyes. 'Evan, look at him. He looks so young, so innocent.' She wiped the tears away. 'How can this be?'

This evil – Jargo – that had touched their lives went far deeper than Evan had ever imagined. It intertwined his life with Carrie's long before they were born. It frightened him, made the threat against them seem like a shadow always looming over them, both of them unaware that they lived in darkness.

Evan took a steadying breath. Find order in the chaos, he decided. 'Let's walk through it.' He counted the facts on his fingers. 'Our parents and Jargo were at an orphanage together. The home burned down with all its records. The kids get dispersed. Then the county courthouse burns three months later and it's all blamed on a firebug who commits suicide. Alexander Bast, a CIA operative, runs the orphanage under a false name.'

'But why?'

'The answer's in front of us, if we were looking for these kids' pasts. The records. The birth certificates. You could create a false identity very easily, using Goinsville and the orphanage as your place of birth. You can say, "Yes, I was born at the Hope Home. My original birth certificate? Unfortunately destroyed by fire."'

Carrie frowned. 'But the state of West Virginia would have issued them new ones, right? Replaced the records.'

'Yes, but based on information provided by Bast,' Evan said. 'He could have falsified records so that he could claim every orphan living at Hope Home was born at Hope Home. Maybe those kids had different identities before they came to this orphanage, but they come here and they're Richard Allan and Arthur Smithson and Julie Phelps. After the fire, they have new birth certificates in those names, forever, without question. And then you just ask for replacement birth certificates in the names of any of the dozens of kids at Goinsville.'

Carrie nodded. 'A whole pool of new identities.'

Evan took a long sip of coffee. He couldn't tear his eyes away from the photo; his mother had been so beautiful, his father so innocent-looking. 'Go back further. Back to Bast, because he's the trigger. Tell me why a London sports promoter dabbles in a West Virginia orphanage.'

'The answer is, he's not just a London sports promoter,' Carrie said.

'We know he was CIA.'

'But low-level.'

'Or so Bedford says.'

'Bedford's not a liar, Evan, I promise you.'

'Never mind Bedford. This might have been a way for the Agency to create new identities more easily.'

'But they're just kids. Why would kids need new identities?'

'Because ... they were part of the CIA long ago. I'm just theorizing. After all, Bedford's using you and me as agents, in a way.' Boys and girls of shadows, he thought. How long has this been going on?

Her face went pale. 'Wouldn't Bedford know about this if the Deeps were part of the CIA's history?'

'Bedford got the job to track down Jargo only about a year ago. We don't know what he was told.' He grabbed her hands. 'Our folks left their lives, quit being Richard Allan and Julie Phelps and Arthur Smithson and took on new names. Bedford might have been told it's a problem he's inherited, rather than a terrible secret.'

Evan went back to the stack of photos. 'Look here – Jargo with my folks.' He pointed at a picture of a tall, muscular boy standing between Mitchell and Donna Casher, his big arms round the Cashers' necks, smiling a lopsided grin that was more confident than friendly. Mitchell Casher bent a bit toward Jargo's face, as though asking him a question. Donna Casher looked stiff, uncomfortable, but her gaze lingered on Mitchell.

Carrie traced Jargo's face, looked at Mitchell's. 'There's a resemblance with your dad.'

'I don't see it.'

'Their mouths,' she said. 'He and Jargo have the same mouth. Look at their eyes.'

Now he saw the similarity in the curve of the smile. 'They're both just grinning big.' He didn't want to look at the men's eyes – the nearly identical squint. It couldn't be, he thought. It couldn't be.

She inspected the back of the photo. 'It just says, "Artie, John, Julie."'

He flipped over to the other picture of Jargo that Phyllis had shown him. '"John Cobham."'

'Cobham, not Smithson.' She clasped both Evan's hands in hers.

'The photos are faded,' he said in a thin voice. 'It blurs features. Makes everyone look the same.'

She leaned back. 'Forget it. I'm sorry. Back to what you said: whether Bedford knows. He must not. He wouldn't have bothered to send us here.'

'So what are you going to tell him?'

'The truth, Evan. Why not?'

'Because maybe, maybe this is a CIA embarrassment Bedford doesn't know about. Bast brought these kids here, set up names for them, made it hard for anyone to ever trace their records, and he worked for the CIA.' Evan leaned forward. 'Maybe the CIA took these young kids and raised them to become spies and assassins.'

'That's a crazy theory. The CIA would never . . . '

'Use kids? What exactly are you and I doing?'

Carrie didn't answer. She stared out the window.

'Carrie, don't take the CIA's side automatically.' Evan lowered his voice, as though Bedford sat in the next booth. 'I'm not attacking Bedford, but don't tell me what the Agency – or maybe a small group of misguided people in the Agency – might or might not do, or have done so many years ago, because we don't know. Bast was CIA. He brought our parents here, for a reason.'

Carrie held up a hand. 'Let's assume you're right. At some point, this group took on new names and new lives, and they all went to work for Jargo. Why? That's the question.'

'Bast died. Jargo took over.'

'Jargo took over by killing Bast. It has to be.'

'Maybe. At the least, Jargo had a hold on our parents and maybe these other kids, an unbreakable hold. I want to go to London.'

'To find out about Alexander Bast?'

'Yes, and to find Hadley Khan. She knew about the connection between Bast and my parents. It can't be coincidence she suggested him as a subject for my next project.'

'It can't be coincidence, either, that your mom picked now to steal the client list, to run. She knew you'd been approached about Bast.'

'I never told her, never. You were the first person I told.'

'Evan, she knew. You and Hadley emailed each other about Bast. She could have looked on your computer. Or when she met me . . . maybe I reminded her of my dad. Maybe she was afraid you'd be recruited and she just wanted a permanent escape hatch for your family.'

'She spied on me.' He knew it was true. 'My own mother spied on me.'

'I'm so sorry, Evan.'

The photo of Bast, scattered among the pictures of their parents and Jargo a lifetime ago, smiled up at them.

The bell on the diner's door clanged. Evan glanced up. Bedford stood in the doorway, Frame looming behind him, looking murderous.

'Kids, how are the pancakes?' Bedford asked.

Frame drove the car they'd stolen; Evan and Carrie rode back to the compound with Bedford.

Bedford scowled at them. 'How was your fieldtrip?'

'You just wanted to see where we would go,' Evan said.

'I did indeed, Evan. The GPS tracker in the Navigator told me where you were; we turned it back on, remotely. You knew quite a bit more than you were willing to share.' He gave Evan a sideways glance that was either annoyance or begrudging respect; Evan couldn't decide.

'We want to go to London,' Evan said. 'My mother's last travel photo assignment was there, Hadley Khan is there, and Bast died there. Can you get the CIA office in London to get us the complete files on Bast's murder?'

'There is no record in Bast's file about this orphanage,' Bedford said. 'Are you sure it's him in the photo?'

'Yes. Could his record have been edited if someone at the CIA wanted to hide his involvement?'

'Anything is possible.' Bedford's voice sounded tight, as though the rules of engagement had just been rewritten. Evan could see the heightened tension on Carrie's face: *What are we dealing with here?*

'London,' Evan said. 'Can we go? Look, we're just

researching the past. We're not getting into trouble. We find out the truth about Bast, you might get a lead on Jargo. And we're kids: no one will be suspicious of us asking questions.'

'All right,' Bedford said after a long pause. 'If Carrie feels well enough to travel.'

'I'm fine. Tired. I can sleep during the flight,' Carrie said.

Evan wondered if Bedford already planned to say yes, pause or no pause.

'I'll arrange a pickup for you in the London office. I'll talk to our travel coordinator, but I believe you'll have to have a fresh pilot. Change in Washington. And, Carrie, I'll have a doctor check you before you leave for Britain, and another doctor for when you get to London.'

'Thank you.'

Carrie went to rest and Evan stared at the scattered photos. He pretended to be back in his room in Austin, digital tape downloaded onto his computer and him threading his way through hours of images, paring away all the extraneous gunk and talk from the heart of the story he wanted to tell the audience sitting in front of the FilmzKool website, around the world. He had read once that Michelangelo just took away the chunks of marble that didn't belong and found the statue hiding within the mass of stone. His statue was the truth about his parents, the information that would free his father.

So what was the true story under the block of lies?

He felt restless. He got up and walked down the hall to Carrie's room. He gently knocked.

'Come in.'

He stepped inside. Carrie sat by the window, staring ahead of her, hunched as though caught in a chill wind.

Suddenly Evan's heart filled with ... What? He didn't

know. Pity, maybe, sadness, in that neither of them had asked to be born into this disaster. But she had chosen to stay in it. First for her parents, then for Bedford, and now for him.

The weight of what he owed her, as opposed to the confusion and pain from her earlier lies, settled onto his heart. 'What are you thinking of?' he asked.

'Your father,' she said. 'You look like him, in your smile. In those photos, your father had a very innocent smile. I was wondering if he is scared. For himself, for you.'

'Jargo's told him a thousand lies, I'm sure.'

'He only has to tell one really good one.'

'One wasn't good enough to fool you,' Evan said.

She was silent for a long moment. 'I wonder if our parents were ever afraid we would find out the truth and turn away from them.'

'I'm sure they must have been, even when they knew we loved them.'

'But my father recruited me. He pulled me into this world, the same way Jargo did to Dezz. I still don't understand why he did it.' She sounded tired, not angry.

'We don't know he had a choice, Carrie. Or like you said, maybe he hoped if you were involved in the business, you wouldn't reject him.'

'I would have loved him, no matter what. I thought he knew that.'

'I'm sure he did.'

She shook her head. 'Now I just feel he had this whole life I never knew. A whole set of thoughts and worries and fears that he had to keep secret. It's as if I didn't know him at all. Probably that's how you feel about your dad.' *Or me*, he waited for her to say, but she didn't.

He cleared his throat. 'I only know I love the dad that I know, and I have to believe that's the truest part of my father, no matter what else he has done.'

'I know. I feel the same. You would have liked my father, Evan.'

'You must miss him.'

'My God, seeing him in those pictures, so young … it's still getting to me.' She wiped at her eyes. He moved to the arm of her chair, put his arm round her, brushed the tears from her cheek.

'They didn't trust us with the truth,' she said after a moment.

'They were trying to protect us.'

'That was all I wanted to do with you: protect you. I'm sorry I failed.'

'Carrie, you didn't fail me, not once. I know you were in a terrible, terrible position. I know.'

'But you hate me a little. For lying.'

'I don't.'

'If you hate me,' she said, 'I'd understand.'

'I don't hate you.' He needed her. It was a subtle shock. Tragedy forever linked them, the same way his parents and her father were linked. He did not want to be alone.

He kissed her. It was as tentative and shy as a first kiss, a first real kiss, often is. He leaned back to study her, and she closed her eyes and found his mouth with her own, gently, once, twice. A need for tenderness mixed with a need to show her that he loved her.

She broke the kiss, rested her forehead against his. 'Our families lived false lives. I did it for over a year. I don't want to live a lie anymore. You cannot imagine how lonely it is. I don't want you to do it. We can just be us. I love you, Evan.'

There. She said it to him. He kept his eyes closed.

'If we find your dad ... where will you go?' she asked.

'I don't know.'

'Well ... never mind.' He could hear the click of her swallow.

'Come with us.' It was a huge, life-changing offer, but how could he not? He loved her or he didn't. It couldn't be cheap words that he said to make himself, or to make her, feel better. What was she going to do until college? Live under a false name? Would Bedford put her in an orphanage or with foster parents? Bedford wasn't going to take her home with him. She would be alone, in a way he could not imagine. But it was the way she'd been alone for over a year now.

'Come and be with me, then.'

She leaned back from him. 'It's too big a promise to make and for me to ask. We're only sixteen.'

'It's not like you suddenly get smart and mature at eighteen,' he said. 'Do you?'

'I don't want you to pity me. I really do love you,' she said. 'I'll love you no matter what, Evan.'

He wanted to believe. He needed to love; he needed to believe the best in her. He needed to regain what he had lost, in some small measure. The awareness was sudden and bright, a firecracker in his head. He wanted to be alone with her – away from CIA bugs, away from their parents caught as strangers in old photos, away from death and fear.

'I love you, too,' he said quietly.

She settled into his arms and he held her until she slept.

We can just be us.

Yes, he thought. When Jargo pays for what he did to my mother.

As the afternoon faded into evening, and Carrie slept

against his arm, Evan didn't wonder if she was the same girl he loved. He wondered if he was still the same boy she loved.

37

Jargo lay half-awake, half-asleep, waiting for the phone call that would end this nightmare. He was a boy again, sitting in a darkened room, listening to the voice of God ringing in his ears. God was dead, he knew, but the idea of God was not, of a being so powerful he held absolute sway over you, whether you breathed, whether you died. The boy he was then had not slept in three days.

'The challenge,' the voice said, soft, British, quiet, 'is that you must make a failure into an opportunity.'

Jargo the boy – his name had been John then, the name that he liked best – said, 'I don't understand.'

'If you create a situation, and you lose control of it, you must be able to reimagine that situation, turn it to your advantage.'

'So if I fall off a ten-story building . . . I can hardly reimagine that into victory.' Jargo was thirteen and he was starting to question the world he had always known.

'I speak of controllable situations,' the voice said with no trace of impatience. 'You live and breathe; you can manipulate people. You must construct every trap so that if the prey escapes, they do not believe they were in a trap of your making.'

'Why do I care,' Jargo asked, 'what an escaped victim thinks?'

'Stupid, stupid boy,' the voice said. 'You don't see it. The trap still has to be set. You have to remain unknown, no suspicion of you brought to light. I don't really think that you'll ever be ready to lead.'

The phone rang.

Jargo sat up, blinking, the frightened boy in the dark lingering for just a moment, then gone. He groped for the phone, clicked it on.

'I have the cellular records from your little chunk of West Virginia,' Arwen said.

'Okay,' he said.

'They're uploaded to your system,' she said.

'I'll tell you what I'm looking for: calls to the DC metro area.'

'Seventeen,' she said after a moment.

'Get me addresses for all those numbers.'

A pause. 'Three residences, fourteen government offices, mostly congressional offices and Social Security.'

'None to confirmed CIA addresses?'

'None,' she said after a moment, 'but we don't have a complete list of CIA numbers. You know that's impossible.'

'Get me calls from or to all of Virginia and Maryland.'

Another pause. 'Yes. One hundred sixty-seven in the course of the day.'

'Any to Houston?'

'Fifteen.'

'Get me all those addresses, for every call.' His other line rang. 'Hold on a minute.' He answered the other phone. 'Yes?'

'I think they're flying to Britain,' the voice said.

Jargo closed his eyes. Down the hall, he could hear the barest *zoom, zoom* of Dezz's PSP, the quiet of Mitchell's voice. They'd had a long day and accomplished little in trying to devise a way to draw Evan back to them.

But now everything had just changed.

'From where?'

'I suspect from an Agency medical clinic in southwest Virginia. It's called North Hill Clinic. There's a private airstrip close by and the requisition is for that airstrip.'

'They flew there from New Orleans?'

'I don't know. I've only seen the requisition for a plane to go from DC airspace to the UK. Not even sure it's them. A doctor requisitioned for meeting the flight in London. If your former agent is injured ... it could be her. Of course, it could be any Agency boss-type traveling with a medical condition.'

'You said *meet* the plane. Where else has it been?'

'Don't know.'

'You can't find another requisition for today's travel?'

'No, but it must be domestic. A tight lid is kept on domestic data and I'm not cleared for it.'

'What's the ID on the case for the flight to the UK?'

'Also classified, but joint ops with British intelligence. That's all I know.' The voice started getting nervous. 'You better get this under control, Jargo ...'

'It's under control. Hold on.' He got back on the phone with Arwen. 'I want to know if there were any cellular or landline calls to any numbers tied to a North Hill Clinic in Virginia.' He fed her the number.

He heard the hammer of keystrokes. He waited long minutes, listening to fingers dance on a keyboard as she wormed her way into databases. Arwen hummed tunelessly as she worked. 'Yes, just one, if I'm reading the data correctly. Went through a transmitter near Goinsville, West

Virginia, to a number keyed to North Hill Clinic, due east of Roanoke, at two forty-seven this afternoon.'

They had been to Goinsville. These damn kids. A tickle of vomit touched the back of his throat.

Jargo closed his eyes, considered his narrowing options. *You must construct every trap so that if the prey escapes, they do not believe they were in a trap of your making.* The hardest lesson he had ever learned, but the philosophy had kept the Deeps in the shadows, kept them alive, made them rich. He'd racked his brains all night and day today, trying to construct a way to lure Evan out into the open, lure him back into their world to simplify killing him while making Mitchell believe they were rescuing Evan.

But perhaps this wasn't a disaster. Rather, his best chance yet to rid himself of every headache, every threat.

Goinsville. They might have found nothing; what was there to find? Nothing. His life there was a past no one remembered. But they'd found something. London was the next stop in the thread. He could not ignore the possibility that Evan knew far more than his father thought he did.

Certain times called for a slow cut; other times required a final slash across the throat.

It was time to be brutal.

He got back on the other phone. 'I still need your help.'

'What do you want?' the voice asked.

'Want? What a concept, want.' Jargo knew the pain it would cause Mitchell. He wasn't blind to suffering; pain was irrelevant. Jargo would suffer his own setback as well, but he had no choice. 'I want a bomb.'

THURSDAY MARCH 17

38

The London-based CIA field officer – an American woman named Peterson; she didn't offer a first name – picked them up at a private airstrip in Hampshire. Evan guessed she was extremely annoyed to have to play chauffeur to two teenagers. She carried herself with an impatient air; every movement was made with a hurried jerkiness. She wore a dark suit, and her mouth was etched into an unwavering frown. Peterson remained close-mouthed as she hurried them to a car, driving them herself to a safe house in the London neighborhood of St John's Wood. She took her time, circling in roundabout routes, and Evan, who had never been to London, stared out the window at the grand, vast city he'd heard about all his life.

Peterson didn't speak a word to them on the way.

It was early afternoon in London, and they had, to Evan's surprise, left the rain in West Virginia. The sky was clear, the few clouds thin cotton. Peterson shut a wrought-iron gate behind them as they went up the house's front stairs.

Peterson escorted them to tidy, unadorned rooms, with private baths, and they both showered. A doctor, a kind woman in her fifties, inspected Carrie's healing shoulder wound and changed her bandage. Evan and Carrie then followed Peterson into a small dining room where a gray-haired gentleman brewed strong tea and offered Cokes with not enough ice and served a lunch of cold meats, salad, cheese, pickles, and bread. Evan drank down the hot tea and ate the lunch with gratitude.

Peterson sat down, waited until the elderly man had

bustled back into the kitchen. 'This is all damned odd. Being ordered to dig up Scotland Yard files with cobwebs on them. Taking orders from a man with a code name. Playing babysitters to ... teenagers.' She stared at them as though she could hardly believe *teenagers* were sitting in front of her at a CIA safe house.

'My apologies,' Carrie said.

'I have top clearance,' Peterson said, almost peevishly, 'but I live to serve. We didn't have much notice' – her tone held the acid of the long-suffering – 'but here's what we found.'

She handed them the first file, squiring the remaining two close to her chest. 'Alexander Bast was murdered, two shots, one to the head, one to the throat. What makes it interesting is that the bullets came from two different guns.'

'Why would the killer need two weapons?' Carrie said.

'No. Two killers,' Evan said.

Peterson nodded, but not like she wanted to agree with Evan. 'Vengeance killing. To me, it speaks of an emotional component to the killing, each killer wanting to put his imprint on the act. You understand what I'm saying?' As if they didn't speak English.

They both nodded.

She slid them a picture of the sprawled body. 'He was killed in his home sixteen years ago, middle of the night, no sign of a struggle. Entire house wiped down for prints.' Peterson paused. 'He worked for us for ten years before he died.'

'Can you give me more details about his work here?' Carrie asked.

'Well, among Bast's many creative sidelines, he did a lot of extreme-sports promotion. One of his clients got arrested for drug possession. We looked hard at him then – we don't want agents involved with illegal narcotics – but the drug-dealing was just one bad apple. He recruited athletes working in the former Soviet Union countries; he pushed skateboarding and so-called X sports everywhere he could, so he was a valuable contact among the young and wealthy in Russia, and that gave him connections to people in government and business. The amount of travel he did in promoting sports gave him a good cover as a courier.'

Evan studied the picture of Bast, murdered. Bast's eyes were wide in horrified surprise. This man had known Evan's parents, played an unseen role in their lives. 'No suspects?'

'Bast lived a high life, surrounded by the young and the beautiful and the rich. A few husbands were rather unhappy with him. He owed money. He broke business deals. Any number of people might have wanted him out of their lives. Of course, Scotland Yard didn't know about Bast working for the CIA, and we didn't tell them.'

'Rather important information to withhold,' Carrie said.

Peterson's voice took on a peppery tone of disapproval. 'It's not good advertising for recruitment to have your assets murdered.'

Carrie paged through the murder-scene photos. 'The CIA must have suspected Bast was identified as a CIA agent and killed by the Russians or whoever he'd crossed?'

'Naturally, but the murder looked like it coincided with a robbery. Remember, Bast was a low-level asset at best. He never was an original source of valuable information. He was just a very reliable courier and gatherer of contacts. You know, a lot of KGB archives have come to light since the fall of the USSR. There's no record that anyone in Russia ordered him killed.'

'Could we talk to his handler?' Carrie asked.

'Bast's case officer died ten years ago. Brain tumor.'

'The robbery,' Carrie said. 'What was taken? Could the killer have discovered anything that pointed to Bast's connection to the CIA?'

Peterson pushed another file toward them. 'The Agency had an operative sweep Bast's apartment after the murder and after the police had gone through. He found Bast's CIA gear all properly hidden, undiscovered by the police, who of course would have confiscated the stuff.'

'What about his personal effects or his finances?' Evan asked. 'Anything unusual?'

Peterson flipped through the papers. 'Let's see ... a friend, Thomas Khan, supplied information.' She ran a finger down a list. 'Bast had two separate bank accounts. He had a lot of money tied up in his sports promotion ...'

'You said Khan? K-H-A-N?' Evan said. Same last name as Hadley Khan. Here was the connection from Evan to Bast. Carrie shook her head. *Say nothing.*

'Yes. I have a file on Thomas Khan as well.' Peterson fingered the file, pulled out a sheet of paper. 'Mr Khan said Bast kept a fair amount of cash on hand and none of that was found in the house.'

Carrie took the paper and read aloud from the report as she scanned it: 'Born in Pakistan to a prominent family, educated in England. His wife was an Englishwoman, a high-ranking political strategist and university professor who worked on defense initiatives. No trouble with the law. Served as a director on a British foundation that pledged financial support to the Afghani rebels against the Soviet invaders. Worked in international banking for many years, but his real passion is Khan Books, a rare-book emporium on Kensington Church Street, which he's operated for the past thirty years. He retired from banking ten years ago and put his entire focus on the bookstore. Widowed twelve years ago, never remarried. One daughter, Hadley Margaret Khan.'

'I know his daughter,' Evan said. 'Hadley. We went to a film camp in New York together.'

Peterson shrugged; she didn't care. Her phone rang in her pocket; she excused herself with a quick wave of her hand, shutting the door behind her.

Evan made a quick survey of the files. No hint that Bast was also Mr Edward Simms. Bedford had dug last night into incorporation databases and found that the Hope Home in Goinsville had been bought by a company called Simms Charities. The company had incorporated two weeks before it bought Hope Home, sold all its assets after the fire. If the CIA had put Bast up to buying orphanages, though, no sign remained in his official file.

Evan went back to the sheet on Thomas Khan. 'So an international banker and a sports promoter.'

'They might have done business together. It doesn't prove anything,' Carrie said.

'No, it doesn't.' But Evan sensed a thread here; he just didn't know how yet to grab it, follow it. He opened the file on Hadley. It was not a formal CIA file, unlike the one on Thomas Khan, who had had a London station file opened on him when he'd assisted the police in Bast's murder investigation, or on Alexander Bast, who had been a paid operative. It was the little Peterson's people had gleaned after Bedford's hurried request: Hadley's birthdate, schooling, travel in and out of Britain. The school records were not impressive; the success and brilliance of the parents eluded the daughter. Hadley had spent two months in an Edinburgh detox center last summer; she had been home-schooled by a tutor since her release. There was a record that Hadley had bought an airline ticket last Thursday, the day before Evan's mother died, on a flight to Amsterdam, alone, but the CIA had not found any record that she had checked into a hotel in Amsterdam.

The photos of Hadley in the file were culled from her Facebook page; Evan remembered her from film camp, a pretty girl, but her grin a shade too eager, her eyes holding a secret. Hadley always looked like trouble.

'So Hadley Khan urges me to do a film on the murder of Alexander Bast, a friend of her father, which is *not* a detail she mentions to me,' Evan said, 'and then she takes off the day before my mother dies. Hadley never mentioned any connection between Bast and her dad in the material she gave me.'

'That's very odd. It would have simplified your research.' Carrie tapped Hadley's file. 'We know there's a connection between our parents and Bast, and a connection between Bast and Khan. That doesn't mean a direct connection between Thomas Khan and our parents.'

A chill prickled Evan's skin. 'It's no coincidence that Hadley pitched the Bast story. She must have known of my parents' connection to Bast.'

'She approached you, but she didn't tell you everything, so she either copped out or she was stopped from getting in touch with you again.'

'I think she got scared. Hadley had her own agenda. I just don't know what that is.'

They fell silent as Peterson returned. She assembled a sandwich from the cold meats and cheese. 'My source at

New Scotland Yard called. There's been no report filed that Hadley Khan is missing.' She took a jaw-breaking bite of sandwich. 'We've called Hadley's cellphone three times this morning and she's not answering.'

'We'll pay her dad, Thomas, a visit,' Evan said.

'And I suppose you children would like a ride,' Peterson said around a still-full mouth.

'Please,' Evan said, 'ma'am.'

'We don't alert Thomas Khan by barreling in full force,' Peterson said as she parked a block away from Khan Books and displayed a borough resident's parking permit – Evan guessed it had been provided to the CIA by the Brits out of professional courtesy. 'I suggest Evan go in alone. The friend of the daughter, stopping by to say hello.'

'What do you think?' Evan asked Carrie.

'Khan may run,' Carrie said. 'I think I should be ready to follow him.' She pointed at an opposite street corner. 'I can stand there. You can tail him if he comes this way, Ms Peterson.'

Peterson frowned. 'We should have a team set up for surveillance. Bricklayer said nothing about this turning into an active field operation. I would have to alert the Cousins' – using the term British and American intelligence services had for each other – 'we can't start tailing a guy on British soil without approval. Not that I would expect a couple of kids to know the rules.'

Carrie said, 'I just want to be prepared.'

'I'm not entirely comfortable with this,' Peterson said.

'If there's a problem, Bricklayer will deal with it. No heat on you,' Carrie said.

Peterson nodded, and Evan could see that Bricklayer

carried massive weight with this woman. 'All right, then. If Khan bolts, you follow on foot; I'll follow in the car.'

'Watch yourself.' Carrie got out of the car, put on sunglasses, walked down to the corner opposite the bookstore, held a cellphone to her ear as though she were chatting with a friend.

'Be careful,' Peterson said to Evan. 'Do you have any idea what you're doing?'

'No.'

'I shouldn't let you go in alone,' she said, but she made no move to disengage the seat belt. It was a bit like a mom – a not-so-nice mom – dropping off a kid at a new school, Evan thought.

'I'll be careful.' Evan got out of the car, strolled past a mix of antiques shops, high-end eateries, and boutiques. The bell on the door of Khan Books jingled as he went inside. Late afternoon on a weekday, Khan Books's only customers were a French couple exploring a display of Madeleine L'Engle and Scott Westerfeld first editions in an assortment of languages. Evan found himself noting the exit doors, the surveillance cameras posted in the corners of the rooms.

I've changed. I feel like I have to be ready for anything at any time.

A small, wiry man, dapper in a tailored suit, with a shock of chalk-gray hair, came forward. His shoes were polished black ice; an impeccable triangle of blue silk handkerchief peeked from one pocket. 'Good afternoon. May I assist you today?' His voice was quiet but strong.

'Are you Mr Thomas Khan?'

'Yes, I am.'

Evan smiled. He didn't want to be subtle. 'I'm in the market for books on sports.'

'I'll be happy to check. Any specific title?'

'An older one, called *To the Extreme*. I understand the author, Alexander Bast, was a friend of yours.'

Thomas Khan's smile stayed bright. 'Only an acquaintance.'

'I'm a friend of a friend of Mr Bast.'

'Mr Bast died a long time ago, and I barely knew him.' Thomas Khan smiled in good-natured confusion.

Evan decided to gamble, toss another name into the weird ring that joined all these lives together. 'My friend who recommended your store is Mr Jargo.'

Thomas Khan shrugged, quickly. 'One meets so many people. The name does not signify. One moment, please, and I'll consult my files to see if I have the book you want.' He vanished into the back.

This man may have kept a secret for decades, Evan thought; a kid coming in here and tossing around names won't scare him. But then, if you're the first to toss it at him in many years . . . maybe you will rattle him. Evan stayed in place, watching the French couple loiter, the woman leaning slightly on the man as they hunted the shelves.

He waited. Maybe he should have just said he was a friend of Hadley's. He didn't like that Khan was out of his view. Maybe the man was bolting out the back door. Jargo's name might be like acid on skin. Evan stepped behind the counter and went round the corner – cluttered with an antique desk with a computer, a water-cooler, and stacks of books – and went searching for Thomas Khan.

Peterson watched Carrie pretend-chatting on her phone, keeping her gaze near the bookstore entrance. Evan went in. A minute passed; Peterson counted each second. Then she pulled a briefcase from the rear seat of her sedan, got out of the car, and strolled toward the entrance to the bookstore.

She saw Carrie watching her and she lifted her hand in a quick, furtive palm-up signal: *Wait.* Carrie stayed put as Peterson headed for the bookstore.

The maze of offices in the back of the gallery led nowhere.

'Mr Khan?' Evan called in a hushed tone as he went into the bookstore's back. It was empty. Thomas Khan employed no assistants, no secretaries, no junior booksellers in his rabbit hole of a business. Evan heard a slight sound, two sharp *thweets*, maybe an alarm peep announcing a door had opened and closed. Evan found a rear exit door. He pushed it. It opened into a narrow brick alley and he saw Thomas Khan running for the street, glancing back over his shoulder.

'Hey!' Evan ran after him.

Peterson performed best while taking specific orders. She carried out today's instructions with certainty. She stepped inside the bookstore, closed the door behind her, locked the dead bolt above the keyhole. She flipped the fancy hand-written sign over to CLOSED. No one else had left or entered the shop since Evan. She saw Evan stepping into the rear of the shop, quietly calling, 'Mr Khan?'

A couple rummaged for editions on a table. The woman murmured in French to the man, pointing out a volume's price in dismay. Peterson brought out her service pistol and with a hand only slightly shaking, shot them both from behind. *Thweet, thweet*, said the silencer. They collapsed. Ten seconds had passed.

Peterson set down the briefcase. Jargo said there would be a two-minute delay once she set the briefcase's combo lock to the correct detonation sequence: ample time for her to get out, go to the street corner, shoot Carrie in the head, escape in the confusion.

Peterson thumbed the last number of the lock into place. Jargo lied.

39

The explosion tore open the front of Khan Books, flowering into an orange hell, sending glass and flame shooting into Kensington Church Street. Carrie screamed as the force of heat and blast hit her. A car passing in front of the bookstore tumbled and slammed into a restaurant across the street. People fled, several bleeding, others running in blind panic. Two people lay in bloodied rags on the pavement.

Debris rained down on the street, shattered chunks of brick, slicing raindrops of glass, a sooty mist and smoke. She careened backward, into the shelter of the corner of the building, in front of a dress shop, the mannequins indistinct behind the webbed glass.

Evan.

Carrie stumbled to her feet, ran toward the inferno, stopped halfway across the street. Heat slammed against her face. Burning pages settled toward the ground in a fiery snow. One landed on her hair; she slapped at her head, burned her hand.

'Evan!' she screamed. 'Evan!' Only a fierce roar answered her as thousands of books, and the structure of the building, abandoned themselves to flame.

Gone. He was gone. She heard the rising cry of police and

emergency sirens. She ran down the block toward the CIA car. The door was unlocked, the keys still inside. Her mind didn't register, at that moment, how odd it was Peterson would leave the car ready for a rapid departure. She ducked into the car, started the engine.

Shaking, she made a mix of left and right turns, trying to stay on the correct side of the road, avoiding the instant traffic jams, and stopped near Holland Park. She willed her fingers to be still and dialed Bedford. When he answered the phone, at first she could not speak beyond identifying herself.

'Carrie?' he said.

'At Khan's store . . . there was an explosion. Evan. Evan.' He was gone. Evan could not be gone.

'Calm down, Carrie.' Bedford's voice was like steel. 'Calm down. Tell me precisely what happened.'

She hated the hysteria in her voice, but her self-control broke like a rotting dam. Her parents dead, her year of nonstop deceit, worrying that Jargo would discover her at any moment, finding Evan and nearly losing him again . . . She bent over in the car.

'Carrie! Report. Now.'

'Evan . . . went inside Khan's bookstore. Peterson followed him inside a minute later, but she signaled all was well. Then about thirty seconds later, a blast. The entire store is gone. Bombed.' She steadied her voice. 'I need help. Please help me. We need to find Evan. Maybe he's still inside, hurt, but it's all on fire . . .' She stopped. He's gone. He's gone.

'Did you see Evan or Peterson leave?'

'No.'

'Any other exit or entrance?'

This stopped her gasping for a moment. 'I don't know . . . Not on the street I could see.'

'Okay,' Bedford said. 'Assume you're under surveillance. Obviously the Deeps have targeted Khan.'

'Get someone to help me. I need them here now.'

'Carrie, I can't. We can't show our involvement, not with a bombing in London.'

'Evan ...'

'I can be in London in a few hours. I need you to lay low. That's a direct order.'

'Evan's dead, Peterson's dead, and that's just too bad, isn't it? You let him get involved. You wanted him involved because it made this hunt easier for you!'

'Carrie, get a hold of yourself. Right now I want you safe. I want you protected. Pull back. Find a place to hide, a library, a coffee shop, a hotel. You are not authorized to talk to anyone, not even Peterson's superior, until I arrive and debrief you. That's a direct order. I'll call you back when I'm on the ground in the UK.'

'Understood.' The word tasted like blood in her mouth.

'I'm sorry. I know you cared for Evan.'

She couldn't answer him. She wasn't supposed to lose anyone else she loved. He could not be gone.

'Goodbye,' she said.

She hung up. She steadied the tremble that threatened to take over her hands.

She wasn't hiding in a hotel, not yet.

She got out of the BMW. Cars and pedestrians fleeing the blast area choked the streets. She stopped at an office-supplies store near Queen Elizabeth College and asked to borrow their phone book. She found the listing for Thomas Khan.

'Where is this, please?' she asked the clerk, pointing at the address.

'Shepherd's Bush. Not at all far, west of Holland Park.' The clerk gave her a look of friendly concern; the news of the Kensington Church Street blast was all over the television and radio, immediately suspected as a terrorist attack, and Carrie was begrimed and shaken. 'Do you need help, miss?'

'No, thank you.' She wrote down Khan's address. She could break into his house, find if he had any connection to Jargo or to the CIA. It was action. Evan was gone. She could not sit still.

'Are you sure you're all right?' the clerk called as Carrie ran out the door.

No, Carrie thought, I'll never be all right again.

But wait. She stopped herself, stumbling along the sidewalk, the sirens a constant buzz in the air. As soon as the police identified Khan Books as the bombing site, the police and MI5 would be poring over Thomas Khan's house. If the slightest connection pointed back to the CIA – if she was found there and questioned by British authorities – it would be a public-relations disaster for the Agency. She couldn't go to Khan's. Not enough time to search before the police arrived.

Not enough time. Not with Evan. She thought of him in that first moment of talking with him, him buying her coffee, offering to help her fix the trap she'd set for him, her faulty video file. Her first words had been a lie to him, and he had forgiven her. He had told her that he loved her first, but she'd known she loved him days before he said the words.

Carrie leaned against the car. A pall of smoke rose from the direction of Kensington Church Street. She had nowhere to go in London, no one to trust.

Evan. She shouldn't have left him alone. She should have

stayed at arm's length. Her face ached with unshed tears. I'm sorry, sorry for what I've done, Evan. What have I done to you?

Carrie made her decision: run and hide, wait for Bedford's call. She wiped Peterson's car of prints, out of habit taught to her by both Jargo and Bedford, and walked away from it.

She did not see the men following her from across the street, staggered apart by thirty yards, all three closing in on her.

40

Evan caught Thomas Khan's jacket sleeve just as the explosion ripped apart the bookstore. Air rushed forward, blown down the alleyway by heat and force. The blast hammered Evan into Khan, shoved them both off their feet along the brick wall, and they sprawled onto the ground. Dust misted and heated the air.

Evan scrambled to his feet, pulling Khan with him.

'Let me go!' Khan tried to jerk free, but he howled in sharp, sudden pain when Evan pulled on his wrist. It was broken. Without feeling much mercy, Evan tightened his grip and dragged Khan to the street behind the bookstore. Coughing, they stumbled into a mad dash of shoppers, clerks, tourists, and neighborhood residents. A pillar of fire and smoke rose behind them. Khan tried to twist away from Evan's grip, but his wrist was his weakness. Evan manhandled him by the injured wrist and hurried him down the street. He pictured where he had left Peterson and Carrie.

Down a block, then up another two blocks, and they would come up behind Peterson's BMW.

'This way,' Evan said.

'Let me go or I'll scream for help,' Khan said.

'Go ahead – be an idiot. I'm with people who can protect you.'

'You bombed my store!'

Rage seized Evan. He twisted Khan's wrist and the man dropped to his knees in agony. 'You were involved in my mother's death.'

'Your . . . mother?'

'Donna Casher.'

'I don't know any Donna Casher.'

'You're connected to Jargo. You're involved.'

'I don't know any Jargo.'

'Wrong. You just ran when you heard his name.'

Khan tried to pull free.

'Just walk home, Mr Khan.' Evan released Khan's wrist. 'Go on. I'm sure the police will have lots of questions as to why your business was bombed. Get your answers ready. I'll be happy to talk with them, too.'

Khan stayed still, staring at Evan.

'You've got both Jargo and the CIA after you, Mr Khan, but if you help me, you're safe from everyone who could hurt you. Decide.'

Khan looked around, as though help might come from some other direction. Evan shoved Khan against the brick wall of a building. 'Jargo killed my mother. Your daughter wanted me to do a documentary about Alexander Bast and it got back to Jargo, and he panicked and started killing people. He's aiming for you now.'

Khan gave a little headshake of denial.

'Please. I'm a friend of Hadley's. I know her from film camp, and I posted one of her movie projects on my website. Don't you want to protect your daughter, too?'

For a moment Khan looked stricken, as though Hadley's name was a needle in his heart. Then he slowly nodded, cradling his broken wrist to his chest. 'All right. I'll help you.'

Evan hurried the hurt man along the street. They rounded a corner, raced up toward Kensington Church Street where Peterson had parked, fighting against a fleeing crowd.

'Who sent you?' Khan asked. 'You're just a kid.'

'Me, myself, and I,' Evan said.

They reached a block and Evan saw the CIA BMW tear out, backward, Carrie at the wheel.

'Carrie!' Evan yelled. 'Here! Wait!'

But in the chaos of noise, the rush of people and cars, she didn't see or hear him. She spun the car and roared, awkwardly, down the street and out of sight, narrowly avoiding running pedestrians.

Evan groped for his cellphone. Gone. He'd left it in the car with Peterson.

'Listen,' Khan said. 'We have to get off the streets. I have a place where we can hide.' He closed his eyes, rocking against the pain.

Evan considered. Peterson wasn't at the wheel, didn't appear to be in the car. Carrie looked hysterical. Where was the CIA officer? Dead in the street, killed by the blast? Evan looked down the wrecked street but couldn't see in the haze of smoke.

The day, this little research trip, had gone horribly wrong. Maybe it wasn't a good idea to haul Khan back to the CIA

safe house. Evan knew Khan's offer could be a trap. He had
no gun, no weapon, and no choice. He couldn't let Thomas
Khan simply walk away. Evan stayed close to the man,
keeping a firm grip on his arm. Khan no longer appeared
inclined to run. He walked with the frown of a man dread-
ing his next appointment.

As they walked south to Kensington High Street, Khan
said, 'May I hazard a theory?'

'What?'

'You might be a kid, but you came to my bookstore with
the CIA, or maybe MI5. And surprise, you're supposed to be
dead, along with me.'

Evan gave no answer.

'I'll take that as a yes,' said Thomas Khan.

'You're wrong.' No way, Evan thought. No way Carrie
could have been involved if the bomb was meant for him.
She could have killed him at any point in the past few days
if she were against him, and he knew she wasn't. But
Bedford – he didn't want to think the old man had set him
up to die.

Then there was Peterson; maybe she worked for Jargo, or
she was one of Jargo's Agency clients, a shadow who wanted
Jargo protected and the list of clients kept hidden.

Evan said, 'Take me to Hadley.'

Khan shook his head. 'We talk in private. Keep walking.'
Khan ran across the street, Evan still clutching his wrist for
leverage. Khan pointed toward a small bistro. 'We need
transportation. I have a friend who owns that business. He'll
be sympathetic. Wait here.'

Evan tightened the grip on his arm. 'Forget it. I'm coming
with you.'

'No, you're not.' Khan smoothed down his hair,

straightened his suit jacket. 'I need you; you need me. We
have a common enemy. I'm not running off.'

'There's no way I can trust you.'

'You want a sign of my good faith.' He leaned close to
Evan, his jaw touching Evan's, whispering into Evan's ear,
'That was a bomb. It was meant for both of us. Jargo's clearly
after me now. I am a loose end. So are you. We have a
mutual interest.'

He thinks the bomb was planted by Jargo, not the CIA. Or
at least he wants me to think he blames Jargo. 'Why are you
sure it's Jargo?'

'I protected him long enough. But no more. Not now he's
after me and my family. He wants war, he gets war. Wait here.'
He shrugged free and Evan knew he'd have to fight Khan,
here on the street, to keep him close, and it would attract
attention. He watched Khan hurry and vanish into the café.

Evan waited. Panicked Londoners jostled past him, a
hundred people passing him in a matter of minutes, yet he
had never been so alone in his life. He decided that he had
made a huge mistake in letting Khan walk free. But
moments later, Khan drove up to the curb.

'Get in,' he said.

41

Thomas Khan headed southeast on the South Circular
Road. Evan flicked on the radio. The news was full of the
explosion on Kensington Church Street. Three confirmed
dead, a dozen injured, firefighters battling to bring flames
under control.

'Where is Hadley?' Evan said. 'She hasn't answered my emails, before all this started.'

Khan glanced in the mirror. 'I don't know about emailing you, but you'll see her soon enough. I've hidden Hadley from Jargo. I thought my influence with Jargo would protect us both. I was wrong.'

'What happened?' It sounded like Jargo had targeted another family, just like his own.

'Once we're safe.'

Khan exited in Bromley, a large borough of suburban homes and businesses. He navigated a maze of streets and finally steered into a driveway of a good-sized house. The driveway snaked behind the home and he parked where the car couldn't be seen from the street.

'I suspect we don't have long,' Khan said. 'The home belongs to my sister-in-law. She is in a hospice, dying of brain cancer. Soon the authorities will be looking to anyone who knows me for information.'

'Like your friend who owns the coffeehouse. He can tell them you're alive.'

'He won't,' Khan said. 'I smuggled him and his family out of Iraq. I asked for silence; he will be silent. Hurry inside. Our only advantage may be that Jargo will believe us both dead.'

They entered through a back door. It opened into a kitchen. A mineral smell of disinfectant hung in the air. In the den, antique furnishings blended with an eclectic and colorful mix of abstract art. Bookshelves commanded one wall. The room was slightly disordered, a scene out of whack. A table had been pushed away from a chair, a corner of a rug stood, jammed close to a couch. The air smelled of bleach, as though the room had been cleaned. Khan kicked the rug smooth, coughed into his hand, as though embarrassed at the disorder.

'Where's Hadley?'

'She should be here soon.' Khan sat on the couch, clicked on the TV with the remote, found a channel airing live footage of the bombing site. The reporter indicated the destroyed business was owned by an Anglo-Afghani, Thomas Khan. The reporters tossed out theories and speculations as to a reason for the bombing.

'No one's guessing right,' Evan said.

Khan shrugged. 'I'm not going to phone them and correct them.'

Evan went to the kitchen. Hanging along a magnetic strip were a wicked assortment of knives. His hand shook as he picked the largest one and returned to the den. Khan looked up at him.

'Is that for me?' Khan did not act afraid. 'Rather bloodthirsty to be so young.'

'I don't think I want to be unarmed around you, Mr Khan.'

'You won't use that on me, or anyone else. Stabbing is intensely close-range and personal. Nasty. Messy. You feel the person die. A sheltered boy like you doesn't have enough steel in his spine.'

'You're going to help me bring Jargo down.'

'The young never use their ears,' Khan said. 'I said we had a mutual enemy. I can hide for the rest of my life. I don't need to fight Jargo. He thinks I'm dead.'

It was true and Evan sucked in a heavy breath. 'If he's your enemy now, surely you'd rather see him taken down than worry about him ever finding you.'

Khan shrugged. 'The young worry about victory. I prefer

survival.' He tilted his head at Evan. 'I thought you would be far more interested in hearing about your parents than planning an impossible revenge on Jargo.'

Evan took a step forward with the knife. 'You know my mother worked for the Deeps.'

'I only knew her by her code name, but I read the American news on the web. I saw her face on a report after her murder and I knew who she was.'

'You saw her when she was in England several weeks ago.'

'Yes.' His voice was barely a whisper.

'Why was she here?'

'It's freeing to tell you what I always kept secret. I feel like I'm shedding an old skin.' Khan offered a gentle smile. 'She stole data from a senior-level British researcher involved in developing a new Stealth-style fighter. He had classified information on his laptop. You know the sort of man – technically brilliant but hates rules, lax about security. He took his wife for a romantic getaway at a small hotel in Dover. He took the laptop off base with him, which is forbidden, so he could get a bit of work done, and your mother stole copies of the fighter data off his laptop during their stay.'

'So she steals the data and you sell it.'

'No. I provide the technology, the false IDs, the car, whatever she needs to do the job here. I arrange for the money to go into her account. Jargo handles selling the information.'

Money. Khan would have to know where the money came from. The client list, Evan thought. This man had it. He kept his face neutral. 'And who would Jargo sell this data to?'

Khan shrugged. 'Who doesn't need information like that these days? The Russians, who are still afraid of NATO. The Chinese, who still fear the West. India, who wants to take a bigger role on the world stage. Iran. North Korea. But also corporations, here and in America, who want the plans. Because they want to compete or they want to get to market first.' He offered Evan a neat, practiced smile. 'Your mother was very good. You should be proud. She followed me to my office, accessed my laptop, stole some very private files, and I never knew until last week.'

'I can't find pride in her accomplishments right now,' Evan said.

'Now, if we'd wanted the man dead ... well, your father would have been sent. He's quite the able killer.' Khan studied his fingernails. 'Garrote, gun, knife. He even killed a man in Johannesburg once with nothing but his thumbs. Or perhaps that was simply a rumor he started. So much depends on reputation.'

The knife seemed suddenly lighter in Evan's hands. His stomach twisted.

'That's not my dad.'

'You don't know your dad, Evan. Not the real him.'

'You're trying to freak me out.'

Khan made a murmur of sympathy in his throat. 'I know your parents better than you do, yet I never knew their real names. Rather sad, really.'

You're just trying to play me into making a mistake. 'Since we're helping each other, tell me what my mother stole from you.'

Khan's tongue touched his lower lip. 'A list of clients. I didn't realize she had stolen the files until I ran a test on my system last Thursday.'

Thursday, the day before his mother died, the day, perhaps, she decided to run. 'And you warned Jargo?'

'Naturally. He didn't know about the client list. That was

my own insurance in case things ever got ugly between him and me. You see, I have all the other information on the network, too.'

The other information. Khan must have it all – the name of every Deep, every financial account they used, every detail of their operations. No wonder Jargo wanted him dead now. 'I want a copy of every file.'

'Destroyed in the bomb blast, I'm afraid.'

'You have a backup.'

'I must decline.'

Evan stepped forward. 'I'm not giving you an option.' He moved the knife toward Khan's chest.

'It's shaking,' Khan said. 'I don't think you truly have the stomach for—'

Evan jerked forward and brought the point of the knife to Khan's throat. Khan's eyes widened. A globe of blood welled where blade met skin.

'I'm my father's son. The knife's not shaking now, is it?'

Khan raised an eyebrow. 'No, Evan, it's not. But are you going to stab me before my daughter gets here?'

'If you help me, there's a man at the CIA who can protect you from Jargo. Help you and Hadley hide. Give you both a new life. Do you understand?'

Khan gave the slightest of nods. 'Tell me who this man is at the CIA. I hardly plan to turn myself over to one of Jargo's clients.'

He didn't want to give Khan Bedford's name. He decided to stall. 'How much longer until Hadley gets here?'

Khan clenched his eyes shut. 'I don't know. She has to come from Bloomsbury.'

'She pitched me the Alexander Bast film project. Hadley set all this mess in motion. Why did she do that?'

'"How sharper than a serpent's tooth."'

Evan blinked. 'I don't know what that means.'

'It's a quote from Shakespeare. "How sharper than a serpent's tooth it is to have a thankless child."' Khan pressed his fingertips into his temples. 'It is cruel to know a child could hate you so. Did you love your parents, Evan?'

No one had asked him this, ever, not even Detective Durless in Austin, which seemed like a thousand years ago but had been only a few days. 'I do. No past tense about it. Very much.'

'Do you still love them, knowing what they were?'

'Yes. Love isn't love unless it's unconditional.'

'So when you look at your father, you won't see a killer. A cold and capable killer. You'll just see your dear old dad.'

Evan tightened his grip on the knife.

Khan said, 'Ah, the poison of doubt. You don't know what you'll see now when you look into your father's face, how you'll feel. I was clumsy a few months ago. I recruited Hadley to work for me. Jargo needed fresh blood, and the money is very, very good. I thought Hadley would do well.' His voice wavered. 'But I gave Hadley a basic assignment and she barely escaped being caught by French intelligence. She promised me she would do better, but then she decided that she wanted out.'

He'd turned his own daughter into one of Jargo's people, just like Carrie's dad had done to her. Was this part of Jargo's plan to keep this long-term network running: bringing the next generation into his secret, dark world? Dezz first, then Carrie, Hadley, now himself. How many other kids were in danger? How many other parents faced an impossible choice – make their children into their own image or risk losing them forever? The bleach smell of the room seemed heavy as steel in his nostrils. 'You didn't accept her resignation.'

'Jargo told me to make her recruitment work or he would ...'

'He'd kill her.'

Khan was silent for several moments, as though struggling to find his voice. 'She didn't tell me she wanted to quit. This isn't a job you leave alive. In learning how to do my work, Hadley found files on the Deeps – all of them, and their children. She realized that working for Jargo was a lifelong commitment; she wanted out. But if she went to MI5 or the CIA, she knew she would be put into protective custody and my assets would be immediately frozen. She wanted my money first. She wanted Jargo and myself exposed, but not until she could make arrangements to vanish, so she could access my accounts and rob me.' He sounded more tired than angry. 'Such malice in an eighteen-year-old girl. It hurts my heart.'

'So, Jargo has twice the reason to be mad at you. Because of you, Hadley found out about the Deeps, and my mom found out about the clients. Either bit of knowledge could bring him down.'

'Yes. Hadley ... I should have told Jargo she was not suited for this work, but he needs people. And our kids, well, they're perfect. As long as they don't want to betray their parents, see them go to jail for the rest of their lives, or worse. She said I got what I deserved.'

'And just like you used her, she decided to use me.'

Khan gave a thin smile. 'In a way, I was almost proud of her cunning. You were the only child of a Deep involved in the media, with your FilmzKool site. She thought she could befriend you and subtly draw you out to expose the network. Tease you with the murder of Bast, say it was a project you could sell to television. Egg you on to investigate, make you do the dirty work without her putting her own neck in Jargo's noose.'

'But she stopped answering my emails.'

'A fool puts great events in motion and then grows frightened.' Khan raised an eyebrow. 'I'm telling you all – is the knife necessary?'

'Yes. The orphanage in West Virginia. Bast was there. Jargo was there. My parents were there. Why?'

'Bast had a charitable soul.'

'I don't think that was it. Those kids, at least three of them, became the Deeps. Did Bast recruit them for the CIA?'

'I suppose he did.'

'Why orphans?'

'Children without families are so much more pliable,' Khan said. 'They're like wet clay; you can mold them as you see fit.' He gave Evan a mournful look. 'And as Jargo's just learned, it's the children with families that are trouble. The next generation isn't quite as easily controlled as the first.'

'Why did the CIA need them instead of using regular agents?'

'I don't know.' Khan almost smiled, then closed his eyes. He gave a hard sigh, as though confession had lifted a burden from his shoulders.

'Tell me why they needed fresh starts, fresh names, years later. Did they leave the CIA?'

'Bast died and Jargo took command of the network.'

'Jargo killed him.'

Khan nodded.

'Were you CIA?'

'No, but I'd helped support British intelligence ops

overseas. I worked in banking and I helped the British spies clean their payments to informants. I knew the basics. I wanted just a quiet life with my books. Jargo gave me a job that makes a lot more money than selling first editions.'

'Well, Jargo just fired you, Mr Khan.'

'Yes, and now I'll vanish into my retirement.'

I'll. No mention of Hadley. It seemed ... wrong to Evan. Maybe Khan wasn't half the father Evan's was. 'You have to help me bring him down.'

Khan shook his head. 'I admire your nerve, young man. I wish Hadley had become your friend earlier in her life. You might've been a good influence.'

The phone rang. Evan and Khan froze. It rang twice and then stopped.

'No answering machine,' Evan said.

'My sister-in-law hated them.'

The ringing phone bothered Evan. Maybe a wrong call, maybe someone calling for the dying sister-in-law, maybe someone looking here for Khan, maybe Hadley. 'I want my father back. You want Jargo to stop trying to kill you. Do our interests coincide or not?'

'It would be better if we could both just vanish.' Khan swallowed. Sweat beaded his face and he coughed for breath. 'I do want to see a doctor about my wrist.'

'Give me what I need. We can lean on the clients to break Jargo, trace their dealings back to him. He's finished. He can't hurt you or Hadley.'

'It's too dangerous. Better to just vanish.'

'Forget that.'

'I can't think with a knife at my throat. I would like a cigarette.'

Evan saw fear and resignation in the man's face, smelled

the sour tang of sweat on Khan's skin. He'd overstepped. He dropped the knife from Khan's throat.

'Thank you. I appreciate the kindness. May I reach in my pocket for my lighter and my cigarettes?'

'Yes.'

Khan dug out a small, Zippo-style lighter, then kept patting his pocket for his cigarettes. 'I left my pack in the bookstore. I don't suppose you smoke, Evan?'

'Gross, no.'

Khan shrugged. He flipped the lighter in his hand, lit it, snapped it shut, repeated it. He was nervous, Evan could tell. He played with the lighter like it was an ingrained habit.

Evan wondered what kind of adult liked to play with fire. He said, 'Now I want this client list.'

Khan flicked the lighter, closed the metal over the bright flick of flame. 'Ask your mother.'

'Don't be a jerk.'

'You appear to be a bright boy. Do you really think every client won't vanish in an instant once that list is out? Your master back at the CIA won't catch anyone. We've all got escape routes built in if our covers are ever blown. Jargo's people have been doing this for years, long before you were out of nappies.' He considered the lighter. 'I suggest you leave now. I will give you half the money in your mother's account, and I will keep the rest for my silence. It is two million US dollars, Evan. You can vanish into the world instead of a tragically early grave. You will not be able to get your father back. Your dying won't bring back your mother. Two million. Don't be a fool – take the money, get a new life.'

'But . . . ' And then Evan saw it. Escape routes. The phone

ringing only twice. A new life. This was a trap, but not the kind he'd expected.

Khan had all the time in the world sitting here in this house, smiling at him. No dying sister-in-law. No Khan name attached to this house.

'This place is your escape route,' Evan said.

'You cost me my daughter. The accident is your fault. Yours.' Khan flicked the lighter again, holding it sideways, a blast of mist jetting from the lighter's end. Evan threw his jacketed arm across his face. Pepper spray seared his eyes, his throat. He staggered and fell across the Persian rug; he dropped the knife as he put his fists to his eyes in agony. Pain gouged up through his eyeballs, his nose. He screamed and gagged, at the same time.

Khan dashed across the room, knocking a thick book from the shelf, reaching in, drawing a Beretta free, spinning to fire at Evan. The bullet barked into the coffee table by Evan's head. Evan blindly seized the table, brought it up as a shield, charged at Khan, his eyes burning as if he'd had matches poked into them. Two more silenced shots and wood splintered into Evan's stomach and chest, but he rammed the table into Khan, forced the gun downward, drove him back into the oak shelves.

He has only one good hand, Evan thought. You have to beat him.

Pressing and pressing and pressing harder, Evan powered his legs, his arms, the agony in his face fueling him. He flattened the man into the wall, heard Khan's lungs empty, heard him gurgle in pain; the man dropped to the floor, the gun still in his hand.

Evan dumped the table and snatched at the gun, Khan's face and fingers nothing but a blur. But Khan held on to the

Beretta. Evan fell onto the older man. Khan pistoned a knee into Evan's stomach, jabbed bony fingers at his clenched-shut eyes. Evan let go of the gun with one hand and punched, connecting with Khan's nose. The man's face was a haze through his tearing eyes. Evan seized the Beretta again with both hands, fought to turn it toward the cloud of the ceiling. Khan jerked it back, aimed it at Evan's head.

The gun fired.

42

The heat of the bullet passed Evan's ear. He put all his weight and strength into twisting the barrel toward the floor. Khan jerked, trying to wrench the weapon free from Evan's grip, and he fell on top of Evan. The gun sang again.

Khan roared out a short, sharp scream, then went still. Evan yanked the gun free from Khan's hand, staggering, clawing at his eyes.

He retreated to a corner of the room. He could barely see Khan, but he kept the gun trained on him. Evan moaned; the pain in his eyes was blinding.

No movement from Khan. He forced himself back toward the body, touched the throat. Nothing. No pulse.

Khan was dead.

Agony. Evan stumbled into the kitchen, powered on the faucet, splashed handfuls of water on his face. The brown contact lenses Bedford had given him for his disguise washed free. After the tenth handful the agony started to subside. No sound in the house but the water hissing into the sink. He rinsed his swollen eyes again and again, the gun still in his other hand, until the pain lessened. He walked back into the den.

Khan stared up at him from the floor. Evan checked again; the neck, the wrist, the chest were all empty of a heartbeat.

I just killed a man. The thought hit him with the force of a hammer against his brain.

No. Khan pulled the trigger, or fell on it, but he'd died by his own hand.

He should be sick with fear, with horror. A week ago, he would have been paralyzed with shock. Now simple, awful relief flooded him that it was Khan lying dead on the floor and not him.

He went to the bathroom and studied his face in the mirror. His irises were blue again, and his eyes were swollen almost shut. His lip was badly split and bloodied, and his mouth trembled; he made a noise in his throat that he had never heard before.

He sat down on the floor and at some point – hours or minutes later – he opened up the cabinet under the sink and found a fully stocked first-aid kit. Of course there was one here; in this house was everything Khan needed.

This was Khan's escape route.

He had not thought clearly in the chaos of the bomb blast, he was so focused on getting his hands on the man who could unfold the map to his parents' lives.

Khan would not run to a place that would only give him a few hours' sanctuary. He would run for his escape hatch. He'd brought Evan to a place where Khan could hide, clothe himself in a prepared identity, melt into the world. Even better, he would be assumed dead in the bookstore blast.

When Thomas Khan was assumed dead, then no one in the CIA would be looking for him.

It was no small thing to walk away from your life, and if this house was Khan's hidey-hole, his first stop in the journey into a fresh and secret life, he would have resources here to shut down his operations, money and data to cover his tracks and to step into his new identity. But if Jargo *knew* this was where Khan would run – and Jargo might – then Evan didn't have much time at all.

The ringing phone. Maybe it had been Jargo calling for Khan.

Evan might not have much time at all, but he had to risk it. The answers he needed could be inside the house. A boy of shadows couldn't run; he had to find the truth, and it was somewhere here in this house.

Evan checked every window and door to be sure it was locked. He pulled down every window shade, closed every curtain. Two small bedrooms, a study, and a bath upstairs, a master bedroom and bath downstairs, with den, kitchen, dining room. A door off the kitchen led down to a small cellar; Evan ventured down steps, flicked on a light. Empty, except for in the corner, a large, black, zippered bag. A body bag.

Evan eased down the zipper.

Hadley Khan. She had been dead for a few days. Lime powder dusted her delicate face, to minimize the rising odor of decay. A huge bruise marred her temple, like she'd hit her head against something unforgiving. She lay curled tight in the bag.

You cost me my daughter, Khan had said.

Evan stood and walked to the opposite side of the cellar and pressed his forehead against the cool stone and took deep, shuddering breaths. Khan killed his own daughter for betraying him, for betraying the family business.

What would his parents have done to him if he'd stumbled on the truth or threatened to expose them? He could not imagine this. No. Never.

Khan's voice echoed in his ear: *I know your parents better than you do.*

The disarray of the room upstairs, the hardwood floor heavy with the smell of bleach, perhaps to clean up blood, the wound on her temple, and the table knocked out of place.

The accident is your fault.

He hadn't stopped to wonder what accident Khan meant, but now he could guess at the awful, tragic puzzle. This father and daughter had talked, they'd fought about what she'd done in trying to expose Jargo through Evan, and Khan had pushed her against the table. Maybe he hadn't meant to hurt her, but he'd killed her. An accident. Kept her here. Maybe Khan couldn't bear the thought of burying her. Maybe he felt guilty about recruiting her.

Evan closed the body bag. He went upstairs to the den. He dragged Thomas Khan's body down the basement steps, placed him next to his daughter. He went back upstairs, found a folded sheet in a bedroom closet, and covered the Khans with it, a terrible sadness heavy in his chest.

He drank four glasses of cold water, ate four aspirin that he found in the first-aid kit. His eyes hurt; his stomach ached.

He returned to the study and tested the desk and a credenza; both were locked.

Evan went back to the basement and searched Khan's pockets – no keys, but a wallet and a smartphone. He powered it on; a screen appeared, asking for his fingerprint.

He dug Khan's right hand from under the sheet, pressed

the dead man's forefinger against the screen. Denied. He
grabbed Khan's left hand, pressed Khan's left forefinger
against the screen. It accepted the print, opened to show a
normal startup screen. He studied the applications and files.
The smartphone held only a few contacts and phone
numbers: Zurich banks, a listing of London bookstores.
There was an icon for a map application. He opened it. The
last three maps accessed were London; Biloxi, Mississippi;
and Fort Lauderdale, Florida. A notation on the Biloxi map,
showing the location of a charter air service. Biloxi wasn't
that far from New Orleans. Maybe that was where Dezz and
Jargo had fled after the New Orleans disaster.

But nothing that announced, 'X marks the spot where
your father is.'

Except maybe Fort Lauderdale, a specific place in Florida.
And Gabriel had said Evan's mother had claimed that they
would meet his father in Florida. Carrie thought his father
was in Florida.

Carrie. He could try to call her, reach her through the
London CIA office, tell her he was alive. But no. If Jargo's
agents or clients within the CIA thought he was dead ... no
one would be hunting him. The boy of shadows was now
a boy of ashes. And they had known he was in London,
had nearly killed him. Bedford's group had been com-
promised.

He wanted to know Carrie was safe; he wanted to tell her
he was alive, but not now, not until he had his father back.
She wouldn't return to the house Peterson had taken them
to, he believed; if Peterson worked for Jargo, it was too dangerous. She would carefully reunite with Bedford.

Evan opened the password program, studied its settings. He reset the password program to delete Khan's

fingerprint and used his own thumbprint as the passkey. It
might be useful later. He put the smartphone in his pocket.
Standing up, he spotted a toolbox in the corner and took it
upstairs.

He jabbed a screwdriver into the desk lock. He picked
up a hammer and with four solid blows cracked open the
locks on Thomas Khan's desk. In one drawer, he found
papers relating to the ownership of the house. It had been
bought last year by Boroch Investments. Boroch must be a
front for Khan; if there was no obvious connection to Khan,
the police wouldn't come here. Thomas Khan wouldn't
show his face if he could help it in digging his escape
tunnel.

In another desk drawer, he found stationery and
envelopes for Boroch Investments, a passport from New
Zealand, one from Zimbabwe, both in false names with
Thomas Khan's pictures inside. There was a phone, in need
of a charge but working. He dug out the charger from the
back of the drawer and began to power up the phone. He
checked the call log; the list was empty.

The third desk drawer held a metal box, containing
bricks of British pounds and American dollars. Beneath
that an automatic pistol and two clips. He counted the
money. Six thousand British pounds, ten thousand in US
funds. He set the cash on the desk. The side desk drawers
were empty.

He attacked the credenza with a hammer, a screwdriver,
and then a crowbar. Dizziness oozed into his brain, from
lack of eating, from exhaustion, from the pepper spray, but
he knew that he was close, so close to getting what he
needed. So close.

The door cracked under the crowbar. Empty.

No, it couldn't be. Couldn't. Khan would need to still hide and protect the clients now that the list had been stolen, so he would need to access new bank accounts, and he would erase old ones. All that new client data must be stored somewhere. There had to be a computer in this house aside from the smartphone. Unless Khan kept it all in his head. Then Evan was back to zero.

He searched the room. He went through the guest bedrooms – practically bare – and the downstairs bedroom, but he found nothing. The chance to close his hands round Jargo's throat started to turn to smoke.

In the darkened den, he risked a reading light. The bookcase. Khan had hidden his gun behind the volumes.

Evan searched the rest of the bookcase. Nearly every inch was filled with good books, leftovers from Khan's store, but nothing else lay concealed behind the books. He rifled through the kitchen cabinets and pantry. He dumped canisters of salt and flour on the floor. Nothing. A freezer full of frozen dinners, but he ripped them open, dumped them in the sink, hoping a flash drive or CD might be hidden inside. Suddenly he was hungry and he microwaved a frozen chicken-and-noodle dinner, nauseated at eating a dead man's food. He decided to get over it.

He sat on the floor and forced himself to calm down as he ate. The food was tasteless but filling. His stomach settled. The jet lag and the fade of his adrenaline rush swamped him, and he fought the urge to just lie down on the floor and close his eyes, slip into sleep. Maybe there was nothing more to find.

The basement, the one room he hadn't searched. He went down the darkened steps, past the sheeted bodies. The basement was small, square, with a stacked washer-dryer on one side and metal shelving on the other. The shelves held an assortment of junk. More books, boxed. He went through them all. An ancient, boxy television set with a cracked screen. A box of gardening tools, clean of mud, probably never used. A couple of cases of canned soups and vegetables and meats, presumably in case Khan had to hide a fellow operative.

His gaze went back to the TV with its cracked eye. Why would anyone keep a small, broken TV? TVs were cheap now and everything was flat screen. To repair the screen, you might as well buy a new one. Maybe Khan was driven by a sense of waste not, want not. But he had been well-to-do; a broken TV was nothing.

Evan took the elderly TV down from the shelf. He retrieved a screwdriver and unfastened the back.

The television had been stripped of its guts. Hidden inside was a small notebook computer and charger. Evan powered on the laptop; it presented a dialog box prompting him for a password.

He entered, 'Deeps.' Wrong.

He entered, 'Jargo.' Wrong.

He entered, 'Hadley.' Wrong.

The CIA could crack this, but he couldn't. Even if he deduced a password, Khan might have encrypted and passworded the files on the system. He would be a fool not to take that precaution.

Evan stared at the screen. Maybe he should just take the computer and go to Langley, the CIA's headquarters. Turn himself in . . .

. . . and not save his father.

His father's face floated before him in the darkened basement, and he stared at the father-and-daughter bodies of the Khans. If he believed the past few days, his father was a professional killer who had stamped out lives the way others stamped out ants, but that wasn't the father he knew. It could not be; the truth could not be that harsh or that simple. He had to have the data to rescue his father.

Or, he thought, he had to create the illusion that he had the data.

The laptop. He didn't need the data; he just needed *the laptop itself* to barter for his father. It might hold the exact client list his mother had stolen. At the least it was a negotiating point: he could always threaten to turn over the laptop to the CIA unless his father was released.

Because Jargo couldn't know with certainty that the list was, or wasn't, on Khan's machine. Even if this didn't hold the client list, it might hold enough data – financial, logistical, personal – to destroy the Deeps. Maybe this was the very laptop that his mother had stolen the client list from, and here he was, weeks later, following in her footsteps.

He tried the laptop once more. Entered, 'Bast.' Nothing. 'Westvirginia,' because of the orphanage. No.

'Goinsville.' Refused.

He found Khan's car keys on the kitchen counter, stowed the laptop and the money in the car's trunk. He went back inside and put Khan's smartphone, gun, and phone into his jacket pocket. He wanted to sleep, and he wanted to believe that Khan's hiding place could be his hiding place, but it wasn't safe to stay here.

Fort Lauderdale. His mother's mention of Florida to Gabriel. It was his best bet.

He got into the borrowed Jaguar. It was a manual

transmission, but his mom had insisted he learn how to drive one. All his sudden confidence faded when he realized he had never driven a car designed for the left side of the road and, for the first time in days, he really laughed. The laughter nearly went hysterical. This would be an adventure.

Nerves on edge, Evan drove into the darkness. A cold rain began to fall. He had to concentrate entirely on retraining his driving reflexes. He headed slowly, like a rookie driver, back toward London and found a small, inexpensive youth hostel at the edge of the City proper. He paid for a small private room with cash; the clerk, disinterested, didn't ask why a kid was renting a room. He treated himself to a real meal of steak and fries in a small pub, drank a Coke, watched a couple and their grown son laugh over their pints. He was young to be eating his dinner alone and a couple of other patrons kept glancing at him, as if wondering where his family was. The food lost its taste. He paid and went back to the hotel, lay down on the bed.

He turned Thomas Khan's cellphone back on and it chimed that there was a message. He didn't know Khan's voicemail password, but he found a call log, listing a recently missed number.

He opened Khan's smartphone and activated the voice-recorder application. Then he dialed the number on the new call log.

He could not negotiate if they all thought he was dead.

It was answered on the first ring. 'Yes?' He knew the voice, his soft psychotic purr. Dezz.

'Let me speak to Jargo.'

'No one here by that name.'

'Shut up, Dezz. Let me talk to Jargo. Now.'

Three beats of silence. 'Put ourselves back together, have we?'

'Tell your father I have all of Thomas Khan's client list for the Deeps, all of them. I'd like to negotiate a trade for my father.'

'You turned Carrie against us, I think. I'm not going to forgive you for that.' Dezz's voice was ice.

'You say another word to me, freak, and I email the client list to the CIA, to the FBI, to Scotland Yard. And then your dad is as dead as my mom.'

Silence for a long moment. 'You and I will settle one day soon, Evan. Hold on for a minute.'

He imagined Dezz and Jargo seeing Khan's number on a cellphone screen, knowing now about the explosion and weighing if Evan was telling the truth.

'Yes? Evan? You're well?' Jargo, sounding concerned.

'Oh please. You sent in Peterson to kill me, but you missed. Who else do you own?'

'I prefer not to say.'

'I have a proposal for you.'

'Don't you want to know how your father is?'

Evan was silent.

'Your father is worried sick about you. Where are you?'

'Deep in the rabbit hole. And I have Thomas Khan's laptop, from his hiding place in Bromley. With all his files, including the client list.'

A long pause. 'Congratulations. I for one find spread-sheets boring.'

'Give me back my father and I'll give you your laptop, and then we're walking away from each other.' He found strength in his voice. 'I own you, Mr Jargo.'

'And I own you, Mr Casher. I have your dad.'

'I know about Goinsville. I know about Alexander Bast. I know he set up the original Deep network.' All bluff; he wasn't sure how any of this fit together, but he had to pretend that he knew. 'I have Khan's laptop and I'm giving it to you. Not to the police. Not to the press. All I want is my dad. You either take the deal or you don't. I can tear the Deeps apart in five minutes with what I've got.'

'May I speak to Mr Khan?' Jargo asked.

'No, you may not.'

'Is he alive?'

'No.'

'Well, did you kill him or did the CIA?'

'I'm not playing twenty questions with you. Do we have a deal, or do I go to the CIA?'

'Evan, I understand you're upset, but I didn't want Khan dead. I didn't want you dead.' A pause. 'If you've got Internet access, I'd like to show you a tape, to prove my point.'

'A tape.'

'Khan had a digital camera in his business, did a constant feed to a remote server. We take a lot of precautions in our line of work, you understand. I just accessed the server. I can prove to you it was a known CIA operative who set off the blast. Her name was Marcella Peterson. I suspect the CIA saw a way to get rid of you and Khan all at once, nice and neat.'

Evan remembered seeing a set of small cameras mounted in the corners near the bookstore's ceiling. He said what he thought Jargo would expect him to say: 'So what? So I can't trust the CIA. It doesn't mean that I can trust you.'

'Watch the tape,' Jargo said, 'before you make up your mind. I just sent it to Khan's phone. Watch it.'

'Hold on.' He paused the call and opened the phone's email application. After a minute, the attached film clip appeared in the inbox. Evan clicked it, saw himself, from above and to the left, come in and talk to Khan. Khan and then Evan went off screen, and here came Peterson. Flipping the CLOSED sign. Murdering two people in cold calculation. Leaning down to touch her briefcase. Then nothing.

Evan unpaused the phone call. 'I saw what she did.'

'I'm not really into killing my own people,' Jargo said. 'The CIA would be, however. Are you so sure that the not-so-clever Ms Peterson worked for me? I think she worked for exactly who she said she worked for: the CIA.'

'You could have doctored that tape.'

'Evan, please. First Gabriel, now Peterson. Your friend Bricklayer sent you right into that death trap. Kill two birds with one stone, you and Khan. I'm not your enemy, Evan. Far from it. You've fallen in with the wrong crowd, to put it mildly, and I've been trying to save you.'

Bricklayer . . . he knows Bedford's code name. He hated the oily concern that failed to hide the arrogance in Jargo's voice.

'That tape doesn't lie. Now who do you believe?' Jargo asked.

'I want to talk to my dad.' Evan put a calculated quaver of doubt in his voice.

'That's an excellent idea, Evan.'

Silence. And then his father's voice: 'Evan?' He sounded tired, weak, beaten.

Alive. His father was alive. 'Dad. Oh wow, Dad. Are you okay?'

'Yes. I'm all right. I love you, Evan.'

'I love you, too.'

'Evan ... I'm sorry. Your mother. You. I never meant for
you to get dragged into this mess. It was always my worst
nightmare.' Mitchell's voice sounded near tears. 'You don't
understand the whole story.'

He knew Jargo was listening. *Pretend you believe him. It's
the only way Jargo will give you Dad. But not too fast or
Jargo won't buy it.* He had to play his own father. He tried
hard to keep his voice steady. 'No, Dad, I don't understand.'

'What counts is that I can keep you safe, Evan. I need you
to trust Jargo.'

'Dad, even if Jargo didn't kill Mom, he kidnapped you.
How can I trust this guy?'

'Evan, listen carefully to me. Your mother went to the CIA
and the CIA killed her. I don't know why she did it, but she
did, thinking they would hide her, hide you, but they killed
her' – his voice broke, then steadied – 'and now they've
used you to try to draw me and Jargo out.'

'Dad ...'

'Jargo wasn't at our house. It was the CIA. Anything else
you've been told is a lie. Believe your eyes. That CIA agent
in London tried to kill you and she didn't care who else she
had to kill to eliminate you. There's no plainer evidence. I
want you to do what Jargo says. Please.'

'I don't think I can do that, Dad. He killed Mom. Do you
understand that? He killed her!' He gave his father an abbre-
viated account of his arrival at home.

'But you never saw their faces.'

'No ... I never saw their faces.' He let three seconds tick
by, thought, *Make Jargo think you want to believe Dad, that
you want to believe worse than anything, so this horror will
all be over.* 'I saw Mom, and then I freaked, and they put a
bag over my head.'

Mitchell's voice was patient. 'I can tell you it was not Jargo. It wasn't.'

'How can you be sure, Dad?'

'I am. I am absolutely sure they didn't kill your mom.'

Start acting dumb. 'I just heard voices.'

'In the most horrifying moment of your life, you might make a mistake, Evan. Jargo might threaten you to get cooperation, but it's easier than explaining to you. He really wouldn't hurt you. They shot at Carrie at the zoo, not you.'

Not true, but Jargo had fed his father a matched set of lies. He didn't argue the point. Now for confusion. 'But Carrie said—'

'Carrie betrayed your trust. She played you, son. I'm sorry.'

He let the silence build before he spoke. 'You're right.' Forgive me, Carrie, he thought. 'She wasn't honest with me, Dad, not from day one.'

Mitchell cleared his throat. 'Never mind her. All that matters is getting you here with me. Are you safe from the CIA right now?'

'To them, I'm dead.'

'Then bring Jargo the laptop. We'll be together. Jargo will let you and me talk, work out what happens next.'

Evan lowered his voice. 'Say nothing. I have the laptop, but I can't get past its password. I've never seen this client list Jargo wants.' He knew Jargo was drinking in every word.

'It'll all be fine as soon as we're together.'

'Dad ... is it all true? What I found out about you and Mom, about the Deeps? Because I don't understand ...'

'You have been very sheltered, Evan, and you are about to do more harm than good if you expose us. Do what Jargo says. We'll have lots of time, and I can make you understand.'

'Why aren't you Arthur Smithson anymore?'

A pause. 'You don't know what your mother and I did for you. You have no concept of the sacrifices we made. You've never made a difficult choice. You have no idea.' Then Mitchell's words came in a rush, as though his time ran short: 'You remember when I gave you all the Graham Greene novels to read last Christmas, and I told you the most important line in all of them was, "If one loved, one feared"? It's true, one hundred percent true. I was afraid you wouldn't have a good life, and I wanted a good life for you, the best life. You are everything to me. I love you, Evan.'

'I remember. Dad, I love you, too.' No matter what he had done. Evan remembered his father giving him a bunch of Greene novels, but he didn't understand the quote. He had slowly been working his way through them. It didn't matter. What mattered was Dad was alive and he was getting him back.

'Listen closely.' His father's voice was gone, replaced by Dezz's. 'I'm in charge of you now. Where are you?'

'Just tell me where I'm supposed to be to exchange Khan's laptop for my father.'

'Miami, tomorrow morning.'

'I can't get to Miami that fast. Tomorrow night.'

'We'll arrange tickets for you,' Dezz said. 'We don't want the CIA scooping you back up.'

'I'll handle my own travel. I'll call you from Miami. I'm picking the time and place for our exchange.'

'All right.' Dezz gave a laugh. 'Don't run away from me this time. Now that we'll all be like family.' He hung up.

Like family. Evan didn't like the dig in Dezz's tone, and he thought of the faded pictures of the two boys in Goinsville, their similar smiles and squints. Seeing now what he didn't want to see then, the possibility that the connection between his father, a man he loved and admired, and Jargo, a brutal and vicious killer, could be a thread of blood.

Evan had decided to play dumb, to let Jargo think he would blindly rush to save his father, but now he felt dense. Graham Greene quotes that had burned up the precious time talking with his father. Digs from Dezz. It didn't make sense.

Evan sprawled on his bed and stared at Khan's laptop, still hiding its secrets like a willful child.

If he walked this laptop back to Jargo for his father, he'd get his dad back, he hoped, but Jargo would not be stopped. No. Unacceptable. So he had to do both.

Get his father back and bring Jargo down, with no room for error.

He sat and considered the tools at his disposal, the ways tomorrow might play out. He had his own army, of a sort, and now it was time to ask them for help.

If he didn't have the list, but had to convince Jargo he possessed the list, then it was a matter, he decided, of simply being the better storyteller. He needed to outdo a veritable king of lies. His first prop was this uncooperative laptop. It was time to tell the greatest story of his life.

He went to the FilmzKool site. He went to a brief clip of interviews one of the British kids had done. Then he started to type an email message.

Ten minutes later, Evan went downstairs, asked the desk clerk for directions to the café that had been suggested for a meeting. He was too scared to drive the car again, so he got on a bus after studying the map, and headed out into the chilling, cutting rain.

43

'You were very persuasive, Mitchell,' Jargo said. 'I'm proud of you. That was a difficult conversation.'

'I don't want him hurt.' Mitchell Casher closed his eyes.

'None of us want Evan hurt.' Jargo set coffee down in front of Mitchell. 'I hate to criticize, but you should have told him about us long ago.'

Mitchell shook his head. 'No.'

'I told Dezz, as soon as he was old enough to understand. We get to work together. It's very nice to work with your son.'

'I wanted a different life for Evan, the way you wanted a different life for all of us.'

'I applaud the sentiment, but it's misplaced. You didn't trust him, so you put him in greater danger, made it more likely he could be used by our enemies.' Jargo stirred his own coffee. 'You seemed to win his trust back, at least to a degree.'

'I did,' Mitchell said in a hard voice. 'You don't need to doubt him. Your tape convinced him. He's got a false ID; he can get back here.'

'It bothers me he wouldn't let us come fetch him. This could be a CIA trap.'

'Your contacts would tell you if he'd been found.'

'I hope.' Jargo sipped at the coffee, watched Mitchell. 'He seemed to soften toward you, but I'm not convinced.'

'I can persuade my son our best interests are his best interests. You trust me, don't you?'

'Of course I do.' And behind the frown of family concern,

Jargo allowed himself a regretful smile. He left Mitchell alone in his room and went downstairs to the lodge kitchen. He wanted quiet in which to think.

The boy might be lying about having Khan's laptop, but Jargo decided he wasn't. He wanted his father back too badly. He wondered if Dezz would fight so hard for him. He thought not. That was good, because to fight for what could not be won was stupid.

And he loathed stupidity. He'd lightened the world's burden of two idiots today. Khan had gotten too lazy, too complacent, too self-important. Losing Khan as an operative, losing Peterson as a client, were setbacks but not a crippling loss. He could let Arwen take over Khan's duties; her loyalty was unquestioned, and she had no bitter daughters to get underfoot.

Jargo poured a fresh cup of coffee, studied its steam. A boy like Evan couldn't crack the laptop; at least Khan had done one thing right. And Mitchell had, if words were to be believed, snared his own child into a death trap.

He would have one of his Deep agents kill Evan, after he had delivered the client list and Khan's laptop. Without killing Mitchell, of course: from a distance, with a high-powered sniper's rifle. He suspected Mitchell would want to talk to the boy alone. An attack staged on father and son, he decided, and poor Evan just stepped the wrong way and put his young heart in a bullet's path. He liked the approach because it would stoke Mitchell's fury, make him easier to manipulate. Evan dead, Donna dead, that grief could make Mitchell even more productive in the years to come.

But he had to prepare for every eventuality, act as though meeting Evan was a CIA trap, and seal every exit. He picked up a cellphone, made a call.

Jargo then crushed a pill – a sedative – into a glass of orange juice to keep Mitchell calm, and took the doped drink back upstairs. He had a long night ahead of him.

44

Razur was thin, like her sharp-edged namesake. In movies and books, female hackers were always antisocial punk rockers. Razur wasn't. Late at night, she wore an immaculate, fitted gray suit, crimson high heels, and a sky-blue blouse, her blonde hair in a cascade down to her shoulders. She looked more like a young marketing trainee than a criminal. 'Evan?'

'Yes. Razur?'

Razur shook hands with him and sat down at Evan's table, in the far back corner of the café. She tilted her head at Evan, as though inspecting him for coolness.

'You want a coffee?' Evan asked.

'Yeah, black, largest they got.'

The café was grimy and funky, not too busy, a line of computers on one side of the metallic wall, young people web-surfing while downing juices, teas, and coffees. Evan got up and ordered the drink from the barista. He sensed Razur's gaze on him the whole time, deciding whether or not to trust him. Evan came back to the corner table and set a steaming cup in front of Razur.

The hacker took a cautious sip. 'So, you're a friend of the friend who interviewed me for that film clip that got put on your FilmzKool site, *Confessions of a Grrrl Hacker.*'

'Yes.'

Razur's face had been blanked out on the screen, but her words about the ease of slipping into corporate databases had been gripping and frightening.

'And you're being raked over by nasty people.'

'The less you know, the better.' Evan didn't want to get into the details of the Deeps or their entanglement with the CIA.

Razur gave a thin smile. 'But you've gotten their dirty secrets.'

'Yes, on a laptop, but I can't get past the password.'

'I won't, either,' Razur said, 'without the cash.'

Evan handed her a laundry bag from the hotel. Razur peeked inside at the money he'd taken from Khan's house.

'Count it if you want.'

Razur did, fast, under the table, where the bricks of cash wouldn't draw attention. 'Thanks. Sorry I'm not a trusting soul. You got the system?'

'Yes.' Evan brought the laptop out of a shopping bag he'd found in the back of the Jaguar.

'I'm not really into breaking the law; I'm into technical challenges, showing up the jerks who think they're so smart but they aren't. Savvy?'

'Savvy.'

Razur pulled her own sleek laptop out of her bag, revved it up, cabled it to Khan's machine. 'I'll run a program. If the password can be found in a dictionary, we're in.'

She clicked keys. Evan watched as words began to rapid-fire scroll on a screen, faster than he could read them, throwing themselves against the gates of Khan's laptop fortress.

After a few moments, Razur said, 'No joy. We'll try it with alphanumerics thrown in at random and variant misspellings.' Razur slurped at her coffee, watched the slow, solemn rise of a status bar as millions of new combinations attempted to crack open Khan's laptop.

'Hey, do you know much about smartphones?' Evan asked.

'Not my specialty. Low-powered buggers.'

Evan pulled Khan's smartphone out of his pocket, used his thumbprint to open it.

'Biometric security,' Razur said. 'Aren't you posh?' She laughed.

'What are these programs on the phone? I don't recognize them.'

He handed her the phone and Razur studied the small screen. 'My. I'd like to play with these. This one's a cellular interference program – it would emit a signal to jam any cellphone in the room. Should we try?' She grinned mischievously, eyeing the several customers chatting on their phones, then tapped the screen without waiting for Evan's answer.

Within ten seconds everyone was frowning at his or her phone.

'I just broke a law. Third one today.' Razur tapped again and the phone service seemed to return as the customers redialed and started their conversations again.

'And this one' – Razur tapped it open, studied the program with a frown – 'it's like what I'm using on your laptop, but specialized. For keypad alarm systems. Most have only a four-digit password. Patch into the alarm system and it would decipher and activate the code.'

'You mean it would give me the code of an alarm system on the screen so I could enter it?'

'I think that's what it's designed to do. Hmm. This one

copies a storage card or a hard drive, compresses the data so it would fit on this smartphone.'

'You couldn't copy a whole computer hard drive using this, though, could you?'

'No, not this. Too small. But another phone, or a set of files, sure.'

Maybe my mother used an approach like this to steal the client list and the other files from Khan, Evan thought. 'It would be fast?'

'Sure. If you grab other files along with it, no problem. Grab a whole folder, it's faster than searching and grabbing for files. If you can compress it, all the better.' She handed Evan back the smartphone, her eyebrow raised. 'You steal this from the spooks?'

'Spooks?'

'Spies.'

'You don't want to know.'

'I don't,' Razur said.

Evan watched the status bar slowly inching its progress. Please, he thought, crack. Give me the files. But they weren't just files; they were a lifetime's worth of secrets, the financial trails of terrible deceits, the record of lives snuffed out for dirty money. He had one hand to play with Jargo, and it was on these files.

Razur lit a cigarette. 'I could hack a music site while we're waiting. Who's your favorite band?'

Evan shook his head. 'I want your opinion on an idea of mine. If we crack the password, but the files on the laptop are encrypted, would that keep you from copying them to another computer?'

'Possibly. Depends on how they're encrypted.'

'The program to de-encrypt the files has to be on this

laptop, right? I mean, you would need to edit files, so you would have to decrypt them first, make changes, and lock them back up.'

'Yes. If the unlocking program's not on the laptop, it needs to be in a place where it can be downloaded easily. Otherwise it's like a lockbox without a key – worthless. If your bad guy stashed a custom program on a remote server, I'll dig through his cache, if it hasn't been erased, to track it, or I'll have to hack into his service provider.' Razur grinned. 'I detect an evil idea about to take flight.'

'I'm thinking we could decode the files,' Evan said, running a finger along the smooth edge of the laptop, 'and hide a copy, on a server where I could retrieve a copy off the web. Then we encrypt the hard drive of this laptop again, using the same locking software and the original password. I give the bad guys their encrypted laptop, they might believe I never, ever saw the files. It's like returning a locked box to them that they think I never had the key for. So they think I'm no longer a real threat to them.'

Razur nodded. 'I like the way you think.'

'It would be my ace in the hole.'

'No guarantees,' Razur said, 'that I can even break this system open.'

'Then I think I need a Plan B.' Evan toyed with the possibilities. He smiled at Razur. 'I'm going to need a bit more help from you. Of course, I'll pay extra.'

'Sure.'

'Tell me, do you play poker?'

FRIDAY MARCH 18

45

The men caught Evan at Heathrow Airport late Friday afternoon. He made an effort to look like any young tourist. He wore fresh-pressed khakis and a new black sweater, black Puma shoes, and sunglasses provided by Razur. The men let him approach the British Airways counter, buy a round-trip ticket to Miami, paying with cash, even let him glide through security. He used the South African passport he stole from Gabriel a lifetime ago. He was nearly to his gate when the agents came up on both sides of him, said, 'This way, young Mr Casher. Please don't make a fuss,' with cool politeness, and so he didn't. Suddenly walking next to him and in front of and behind him were six British MI5 officers, and they boxed and steered him with grace.

No one around Evan realized he had been plucked into custody.

The agents escorted him into a small, windowless room. It smelled of coffee. Bedford stood at the end of a conference table. Then Evan saw Carrie on the other side of the room.

She rushed to him, embraced him. She murmured, 'Thank God you're all right.'

He gave in to her embrace, being careful of her hurt shoulder.

'I thought you were dead,' she said into his neck. Her words were like hard little hiccups.

'I'm sorry. I tried to stop your car, but you didn't see me. I was too far away. But I knew you were alive. You're okay?'

'Yes. British intelligence had a team following us. They

found me after the blast, took me to a safe house for questioning.'

She pulled back from him, kissed him quickly, put her hand on his cheek. Giddy in her relief.

He shrugged. Bedford came forward, put his hand on Evan's shoulder. 'Evan, we are all tremendously relieved that you're alive and well.'

Another man sat next to Bedford: clipped hair, good suit, a face bland as air. 'Mr Casher, hello. I'm Palmer, MI5.'

'My counterpart, of sorts,' Bedford said. 'Not his real name, you understand.'

'Hello,' Evan said. He ignored Palmer's outstretched hand, shrugged his shoulder out from under Bedford's grip.

'Evan?' Carrie eased him into the chair next to her. 'What's the matter?'

'My problem is with you,' Evan said to Bedford. 'You delivered us into the hands of a murderer.'

Bedford went pale. 'I'm sorry. We've looked at every moment Peterson's spent in the Agency for the past fifteen years and still haven't found her connection to Jargo.'

'I have everything you need to know to bring down Jargo and the Deeps, but before I give it to you, we have to make a deal.'

'A deal.'

'I don't think you can keep me alive, Mr Bedford. You're so worried about showing your face you don't know who to trust. I'm not waiting to be shot by the next Peterson.'

Carrie asked Bedford, 'Could I talk to Evan alone?'

Bedford measured the chill in the room and gave a quick nod. 'Yes. Palmer, let's you and I talk outside, please.' They shut the door behind them.

Carrie took his hand. 'How could you let me believe you

were dead? I've spent the past twenty-four hours going crazy.' She sounded more stunned than mad.

'I am truly sorry, but I didn't know who other than you and Bedford I could trust. Clearly Bedford doesn't know, either. I wasn't going to phone in and walk back into the arms of another Peterson.'

'How did you get information tying Peterson to Jargo?' she said.

'I got resourceful.'

'Will you give it to me?'

'No. If I hand it over, my father is dead. I need your help. I have to get out of here.' Evan spoke in the barest whisper. 'If Jargo gets word that the CIA has picked me up, he'll call off trading me the client list for my dad.'

'You really have the client list.' She sounded stunned.

'Well, thanks. Did you think I wouldn't get them? I got much more than that. I can give him every member of the Deeps network, too.'

She blinked. 'I can't go against Bedford. You're not thinking straight.'

'I can't trust anyone. Jargo not to kill me, Bedford to protect me ... you to love me.'

'I do love you.'

He was suddenly afraid the poker face he'd worn the whole day would crack. He closed both his hands round hers. 'I want to forget everything. I want us to have as normal a life as we can. But that's not going to happen while they have my father. I have to take the fight right to Jargo, and I've got a way to stop him cold, but I need your help. I have to get to Florida. I need you to stay here, out of harm's way.'

'Evan ...'

Bedford opened the door, walked in without waiting to see if their conversation was done. Palmer and one of the MI5 officers followed him into the room, the officer carrying Evan's luggage. He set it down and left, shutting the door behind him.

Carrie mouthed, *He won't let you go.*

'Evan,' Bedford said, 'what do I have to do to regain your trust?'

'It's gone. You've got leaks, and those will get me and my dad and Carrie killed. Now, we can talk about a deal or you can let me go.'

'I don't negotiate with children, Mr Casher,' Palmer said.

'You do today.'

Palmer stared at him. 'Would you open your bag for us, please?'

Evan did, deciding to let them think they were still in charge for another minute. He saw the bag had already been searched. It held only a few clothes that he had bought and a few thousand in American cash. He had left Khan's gun with Razur.

'Your carry-on, please,' Palmer said.

Evan opened up a small briefcase bag. Palmer reached in and pulled out a laptop computer.

'What's this?' Palmer held up the computer.

'A laptop.'

Bedford opened up the laptop, powered it on. 'It's pass-worded.'

'Yeah.'

'Enter the password, please, Evan.'

'I don't know it.'

'You don't know your own password.'

'That's Thomas Khan's computer.'

'How did you get it?'

'Doesn't matter,' Evan said. 'I did what I promised, which is get the information my mother stole, the information that can bring down Jargo.'

The two men were silent.

'Khan is Jargo's moneyman, or was. He's dead.' Evan raised his hands in mock surrender to Palmer. 'It was self-defense: the gun went off while he was trying to take it from me. In case you're prosecuting me, I hope you try me as a minor.'

Palmer said, 'Haven't you been a busy lad.'

Evan turned to Bedford. 'Here's the deal. Let me go get my dad. I guarantee I'll still give you what you need to take down Jargo, but my dad and I, and Carrie, if she wants' – he turned to her, and she nodded – 'we vanish on our own terms.'

Bedford sank into his chair. 'Evan, you know I can't agree to your request.'

'Then I get a lawyer and I talk a mile a minute about CIA officers carrying explosive devices into Kensington book-shops and using children as agents. Your choice.'

'Don't threaten me, son,' Bedford said.

'I have an alternate suggestion,' Carrie said. 'Maybe one that will make you both happy.'

'What?' Bedford turned to her.

'If Evan trades his dad for this laptop, it requires a meeting. That brings Jargo out in the open. I know him – he'll handle this himself.'

'Where is this exchange, Evan?' Bedford asked. 'Since I'm sure you've already arranged a meeting.'

'Miami. Read my ticket, Bricklayer.' He couldn't keep the snark out of his voice.

'I'm not your enemy. I never was,' Bedford said.

'I pick the meeting site,' Evan said to Carrie, 'once I'm in Miami.'

Carrie turned to her boss. 'This meeting pulls Jargo into the light. It's our best chance to stop him.'

'And he'll be lightly guarded. Maybe just Dezz. He won't tell his operatives a word about this if he can avoid it,' Evan said quietly. 'No way his network knows they're on the verge of being exposed. He would face a mass, very fatal defection.'

'You really think, son,' Bedford said, 'that *you're* running the show now.'

'I am. And I don't want my dad put at risk,' Evan said. 'Anything happens to him, you get nothing.'

'I envy your dad, having your loyalty,' Bedford said, 'but your dad's already at risk, because I'm quite sure Jargo has no intention of letting you leave that meeting alive.'

'I have a fallback. We're doing this my way.'

Bedford put his hands flat on the table. 'Would y'all please excuse me and Evan for a moment?'

The others got up and left, Carrie shaking her head. She waited for Palmer to step out, then said to Evan's back, 'If you love me, you'll trust me. It's not a complicated equation. Don't fight us. Let us help you.'

He didn't look at her. She closed the door behind her.

Bedford said, 'This room isn't bugged, and you can speak with complete safety. Just so you know.'

'Palmer's not taping us?'

'No, he's not.' Bedford took a sip of water. 'If you've arranged a trade of this laptop for your father, I assume you've spoken with your dad.'

Evan nodded.

Bedford said, 'Tell me what he said to you, word for word.'
'Why?'

'Because, Evan, I have had my own agent among the Deeps for the past year. No one else in the CIA even knows I had this spy, including Carrie. I don't know his real name. Your father might be my contact, and he might have sent me a message through you. He knows we would be searching for you until we had conclusive evidence that you were dead.'

Evan listened to the silence in the room: his own heart-beat, the hum of the heater fending off the wet cold outside.

'You're lying. You're just trying to get me to cooperate with you.'

'Remember I asked you about what your father said on the tape Jargo played at the zoo. I wasn't so interested in the story Jargo peddled to your father; I was listening for code words, just in case your dad was my guy.'

'No.' Evan's voice rose. 'If Dad was your contact, you would have already known about Goinsville, about the other Deeps, about how to find Jargo and Khan.'

Bedford shook his head. 'The contact approached me. I've never met him. We spoke on the phone; he mailed me cell-phones, to be used once, then destroyed. He was extraordinarily careful. I don't even know how he knew to find me, that I was the one charged with finding the Deeps, but he did. He agreed to work with me on a highly limited basis. I wanted to force his hand to do more – to tell me who he was, to tell me more about the Deeps – but he refused. I didn't even know his location, where he lived. I tried to trace him; he always hid his tracks. He gave me nuggets that proved his good intentions: a warning about an Albanian terrorist cell planning an attack in Paris; the location of a

Pakistani nuclear scientist who wanted to sell secrets to Iran; the hideout of a Peruvian criminal ring. Every bit of evidence he gave me was correct. There was never face-to-face contact. We never paid him for his services. He didn't want a money trail.'

'Why would he help you?'

'My contact said he disagreed with certain missions Jargo assigned him. He thought they were harmful to Western interests. It seemed like he had a complicated relationship with Jargo; he wanted the operations to fail, but he didn't want to hand Jargo over, so he contacted me. I provided him with disinformation to feed back to Jargo's clients.' Bedford shook his head. 'My contact doesn't know where the other Deeps are to be found. The network remains highly separated, with one agent not knowing how to find another agent. But he fed us valuable information about what kind of work Jargo did.' Bedford poured two glasses of water, pushed one toward Evan. 'I had an agreement with my contact – that when it was time to run, he would identify himself to me and I would get him and his family out. Away from Jargo, to safety. It's what your mother wanted for you. I can't help your mother, but I can help you.'

'You could have told me about my dad before.'

'I don't know if your dad is my contact, Evan. And I wasn't going to let anyone know I had a contact close to Jargo unless I had absolutely no other choice. We've reached that point of no return. Tell me whatever your dad said. Word for word, if you can.'

Evan pulled the phone from his pocket, unlocked it with his thumbprint, tapped the voice-recorder application. The conversation with Dezz, then Jargo, then his father, spilled out from the phone, loud and clear. The two men stared at each other while Mitchell Casher's voice filled the small room. When it was done, Bedford closed his eyes.

'Look at me,' Evan said. 'Is he your contact? Is he?'

'Yes.'

A tightness seized Evan's chest. 'If Mom and Dad had just trusted each other ...' He didn't finish the sentence. Mom would have known Dad was helping the CIA. Dad would have known Mom had stolen Jargo's client list as a shield to protect their son.

They could have stopped Jargo without a shot being fired, and Mom would be alive.

'Lies were integral to their lives,' Bedford said. 'I'm so sorry, Evan.'

Silence filled the room until Evan spoke. 'So he's your contact. He's in trouble. What do you do to help him?'

'Did he give you those Graham Greene novels?' Bedford asked.

'What?' The question wasn't what he was expecting. 'Yes, for Christmas.'

'Did he ever mention the "If one loved, one feared" line?' Bedford leaned forward.

'I don't remember it if he did, but Greene is his favorite author, so he always talked about the books with me. The line sounds vaguely familiar, even before he mentioned it to me.'

'The quote is from *The Ministry of Fear.* It's a bitter truth. We always risk when we love. It's also a code phrase I established with your father.' Bedford folded his fingers over his lips.

'Tell me what it means.'

'It means, "Forget me. I can't be rescued."'

Evan felt his poker face crack. 'No. No. Your code doesn't matter now. You have to help him.'

Bedford straightened his stance, with quiet confidence that suggested the battle between them was over. 'Evan, in this business you lose people. It's war. It's sad. I would have liked to have met your dad face to face, to have known him. I believe that I might have even liked him. But he's telling me to walk away. I don't know if he believes Jargo, that the CIA killed your mother. It may not matter what he believes. He expected if the CIA caught you, you'd be brought to me, and I'd ask you about anything unusual that he said. Whatever Jargo is setting up in this meeting is a trap. I can't risk it. My team is too small. We'll have to wait for another chance.'

'You can't abandon him.'

'I can't risk resources to save a dead man. He's warning me off. I'm sure your father wants to keep you from being anywhere near Jargo.' Bedford stood. 'My sympathies. We'll head to Washington instead of Miami. We'll get you in a protection program. The government is extraordinarily grateful for what you've done.'

Evan stayed in his seat.

'I know this is hard for you to hear. You've lost your mother, but, son, you have Carrie.'

'I know.' Evan stared at the warm mahogany of the table-top.

'I give you every assurance we can hide you successfully. We will take care of your college. Maybe, as an adult, you'd like to work for us because you clearly have a talent.'

Evan looked up at Bedford. 'No. We're going to Miami.'

'I'm sorry, Evan, but no. Out of respect for your father—'

'The laptop. Through my film connections, I found a very good hacker. We already removed and hid the client list.

You'll never find them. You try and access the laptop without the right password, it reformats itself. Only I know where Jargo's client list is. And I'm not telling you unless you get my father back.'

'Evan, listen to me—'

'We're done talking.' Evan stood. 'Are we going to Miami or not?'

46

'You're working a scam on me, Evan,' Bedford whispered so he wouldn't be overheard on the CIA jet. They flew miles above the Atlantic, arrowing south toward Florida. Evan sat in the back, Bedford next to him. Carrie sat at a front window. The fourth passenger was Frame, whose head Evan had bashed back in Virginia. He glared at Evan and gave him a crooked smile. Frame, who had seemingly forgiven Carrie for Tasering him even if he hadn't forgiven Evan for outwitting him in the garage, made small talk about the Washington Redskins, apparently his preferred subject. Carrie smiled and nodded and kept glancing at Evan. 'I know a scam when I see it.'

'Excuse me?' Evan asked.

'I don't think you really have the client list, or any other files. You're a responsible kind of kid. If you could take Jargo down in an instant, you would. So you're not telling me everything you know.'

Evan remained silent.

Bedford gave him a half-smile. 'You are a piece of work, young man, blackmailing the CIA.'

'Not the whole Agency. Just you, Bricklayer.'

'Piece of work,' Bedford repeated.

He knew Bedford meant it as a compliment, but he wanted no more of this world. 'I don't think I'm conning you any more than you're conning me.'

Bedford looked hurt. 'I've been totally straight with you about our plan of attack.' Bedford had outlined a simple scheme: get Evan to a safe house where he would call and arrange the meeting; he would take a laptop that looked just like Khan's; Bedford assured him Jargo would never get close enough to it to spot any differences or check a serial number; Evan would suggest an immediate rendezvous at a secluded spot where Bedford and his team would take cover, not giving the Deeps time to set up their own counteroperation; Jargo and Dezz would be taken alive.

'Yes, and your plan sounds thorough,' Evan said. 'Just like Peterson taking us around London was.'

Bedford leaned back. 'Everyone on the team has been vetted. They're clean. Peterson wasn't a team member; she was a decorated field officer who wouldn't ask too many questions.'

'Jargo's worried about his CIA clients being exposed. He eliminated one by getting rid of Peterson.'

'She was one of the most senior CIA officers in Europe,' Bedford said. 'You see the challenge I face, how deep Jargo's reach can be. But I promise you, Evan, I'll honor our deal. I'll bring your dad home. This is the best chance we've ever had to get Jargo. We'll have additional personnel in Florida to help us. I'm finally getting every resource I need.'

Evan glanced toward the front of the plane. Carrie watched him. Frame was reading the *Guardian*'s headlines to her and commiserating about the state of the world.

Evan might not get another chance. He leaned in close enough to Bedford to smell the mints on the man's breath. 'There's a reason Jargo's been able to infiltrate you, and that's because he knows you so well. The Deeps are a CIA problem, aren't they?'

Bedford frowned.

'Spy networks don't spring up out of orphanages. They have to be cultivated. Alexander Bast set up the Deeps for the CIA. You could have agents on American soil who you would never have to acknowledge. A ready-made group of agents you could use for all sorts of clandestine jobs you don't have to explain to Congress, or to anyone. No paper trail of their involvement with the Agency. No record of their training or recruitment. No blame if anything ever went wrong.'

Bedford said, 'I think that's a very mistaken idea.'

'So who set up this network?'

'Alexander Bast, for his own reasons. I suppose he wanted to make money. Freelance spying. Mr Bast was a man ahead of his time.' Bedford stared ahead.

'You'll never, ever admit it was the CIA, will you? I'm wasting breath asking you.'

Bedford smiled.

'You'll kill Jargo, even if you don't need to kill him to save my dad. You don't want him talking about your deals with him, the fact he was pinch-hitting dirty jobs. And you can take over the network, worm your way into every intelligence service and business that hires the Deeps, make the Deeps spy on their own clients for you.'

'You have an evil mind for a young man,' Bedford said.

'I'm right, aren't I?'

'When you and your dad are safe, the Deeps are no longer your concern.'

'They have families like mine, and Carrie's. Kids and spouses who have no idea what they do. You'll hunt them down, won't you? Or use them for your own agenda.'

'Evan, please. Not your concern. Your only worry is getting your dad back. As soon as we have him, the two of you are on a plane to a warm, distant paradise: new names, cash, a fresh start. You needn't worry about anyone else.'

'What about Carrie?'

'Her, too, if she wants to go with you.'

Evan closed his eyes. He did not sleep. He heard Bedford rise from his seat, cough, pour a drink of water, go talk on the jet's phone, presumably to check on arrangements in Miami. Then Evan heard Carrie slide into the leather seat next to him.

'So, you've gotten everything you want.'

'Not quite yet.' He kept his eyes closed.

'The past day has been horrible. I thought you were dead. I thought I had made a mistake, that I had failed to protect you, that you were gone. Like my mom and my dad.'

Evan opened his eyes, tilted his head close to hers. 'I'm sorry.'

'Are you?'

'I trust you,' he said in a low whisper, his mouth a bare inch from hers. 'So you should know I don't have the files yet.'

Her eyes went wide. 'But you told Bedford ...'

'I told Bedford I had the laptop, with the files on it. My hacker did crack the password on the laptop, but all the files are encrypted. My hacker hasn't been able to break the encryption yet. She may not be able to. We could be at a dead end.'

'So the laptop we have ...'

'Isn't Khan's. It's just a new one, the same model, bought this morning in London. It's my decoy, my fake-out. We put a program on it that will appear to reformat the hard drive if anyone attempts to crack the log-in password. My hacker has Khan's laptop back in London, and she's trying her best to unlock the files, but she hasn't yet. So I'm trusting you. Tell Bedford and maybe he'll break his deal with me to hide me and Dad. I'll only give him the real laptop once Dad and I are clear and gone. And I mean gone under our own terms, in identities we've set up. Once we're gone, I don't want Bedford or the Agency to find us. Ever. My family's involvement ends now and forever. So you have to choose, Carrie. If you want to come with me and Dad, you can. I want to be with you. If you don't, if you want to stay with the Agency, that's your choice, but I'm trusting you with this information.'

'What if we can't get your dad back or if Jargo has already killed him?'

'I think my dad is Jargo's weakness. I can't be sure, but . . . ' Evan paused, remembering Jargo's cryptic words the first time they'd spoken on the phone – *We're family, in a way, you and I* – hearing Dezz's taunt – *We'll all be like family* – seeing two boys in a faded photograph who shared similar features. 'I don't think Jargo will kill him.'

'He killed your mother.'

'But Jargo could have killed him when he found out Mom stole the client list, and he didn't. He's kept him alive, fed him a huge lie about the CIA killing Mom. Jargo has some reason to lie to my dad, to make sure my dad never sees him as the enemy.'

'Will you give the CIA Khan's laptop if your hacker can't break it open?'

348 JEFF ABBOTT

'Yes. I still vanish, under my own terms, and I'll arrange for Bedford to get the real laptop. Maybe the CIA can crack the encryption if we can't. I don't want Jargo running free. I want him taken down just as much as you do. If I die today, the hacker turns over the laptop to MI5 in London, with a letter explaining what's hidden on the system.'

She looked at him, then at Bedford.

'I keep wishing we had met in school like regular teenagers,' Evan said, his voice a whisper, 'that we had our dates and got to know each other, without you already knowing everything about me. That we built trust the way everyday people do. I trust you now, but you have to trust me.'

Not a moment's hesitation. 'I do,' she said.

He put his arm round her. She closed her eyes, leaned into his shoulder. He closed his eyes, and this time he slept, heavily. When he woke up, she was asleep, nestled against his shoulder. For a moment the nearness of her broke his heart. Then the plane began its descent toward Florida, toward Fort Lauderdale, toward a fate that had been building since before he or Carrie were born.

What had Gabriel said to him? *Boys your age went to sea, went to war in centuries past.* He was going into the war's last battle.

I'm coming, Dad, and they won't know what hit them.

SATURDAY MARCH 19

47

Florida at midnight. The air hung heavy with damp; the clouds blotted out the stars. The CIA jet shuttled to a remote hangar at the Fort Lauderdale Airport, and two cars – a black Lincoln Navigator and a Lincoln Town Car – waited for the passengers. A woman and a man, dressed in dark suits, stood by the cars. The man held a travel bag. The woman stepped forward as they approached.

'I'm McNee, out of the Mexico City office. This is Pierce, who just flew in from HQ.' She handed Frame their credentials. 'Who's Bricklayer?'

'I am.' Bedford didn't introduce the others.

'Sir, you have several calls to return ... regarding the bombing in London yesterday. If you take the Navigator, you can talk privately.' She gave 'privately' the subtlest stress.

Frame nodded at Carrie and Evan. 'The kids can ride in the Town Car with McNee and Pierce.'

Evan said, 'I'd like to keep hold of the goods, if you don't mind.'

'Fine,' Bedford said.

'Where are we headed?' Evan asked.

'A safe house in Miami Springs, courtesy of the FBI. We told them we had a Cuban intel agent willing to defect,' McNee said.

'Then you'll make your phone call,' Bedford said.

McNee gave Evan a kind smile. 'I promise you, kids, when we get to the house, you'll get a good meal. I like to cook. Hope you like grilled chicken and potato salad.' She popped open the trunk and Carrie and Evan put their luggage inside. Evan kept the decoy laptop clutched against his chest, as though it were the dearest object in the world to him, and McNee held the back door open for them. Pierce, the other CIA operative, tossed a bag into the trunk and got in the front seat.

They slid onto the cool leather of the back seat. McNee shut the door, got in the driver's seat, and started up the car. 'We'll shake any shadows first.' She powered up the dividing window between the front and rear seats so that Carrie and Evan could talk in private. Evan glanced back; Bedford was in the passenger seat of the Navigator behind them, already talking on a phone. Next to him was Frame, at the wheel.

Evan stared out at the night. The air felt as warm as a kiss. Billboards, palm trees, and speeding vehicles flashed by. The two cars made a long series of turns and backtracks round the airport, stopping and checking and ensuring no one followed, and then McNee headed onto I-95 South. Even after midnight it was a busy highway.

They rode in silence for a while, Evan watching the night.

'You shouldn't go to the rendezvous point.' Carrie broke the quiet.

'I'm the bait.'

'No, your call is the bait. I don't want you near Jargo. You can't imagine ... what he would do to you if he catches you.'

'Or to you.'

'He'd give me to Dezz,' Carrie said. 'I'd rather die.'

'I'm going, end of story.' Evan read the signs. I-195W to Miami Airport. McNee inched over into the right lane. But then she wheeled over fast, taking the I-195 East exit toward Miami Beach.

He looked through the rearview window; Bedford's Navigator swerved round two cars, horns blaring, staying with them, narrowly avoiding a pickup truck.

'What's wrong?' Evan said.

McNee flashed a look in the rearview mirror, gave a shrug. She pointed at the wire in her ear, as if to suggest she'd been radioed new instructions.

Pierce – the CIA guy in the front seat – unhooked his ear-piece, fidgeted with a frown. Then he slammed backward into the passenger door and slumped down. McNee raced round a truck, putting distance between her and the Navigator.

Pierce wasn't breathing. Evan could see the blood seeping from a wound in his chest.

McNee stuck the silencer-capped gun in the drink-holder.

Evan kicked at the reinforced divider as McNee swerved across more lanes of traffic. It didn't budge. 'She's kidnapping us,' he told Carrie.

Evan stared through the back windshield. Bedford's Navigator vroomed up next to them, a black Mercedes in fast pursuit behind him. Bullets pinged against the driver's side of the Town Car as McNee tore away from Bedford's Navigator. Bedford, from his passenger window, shot at McNee. Flashes, the Mercedes firing at Bedford. But beyond the Mercedes, Evan spotted another car, a BMW, revving up next to the Navigator.

McNee cranked it to ninety, heading for Miami Beach. The towers of downtown Miami glittered beneath the clouds.

Carrie kicked at the divider; the glass was bulletproof and her heels slammed ineffectively against the faintly green material.

Evan tested the locks. They'd been stripped; the controls didn't work. He kicked at the window. It was reinforced.

Bedford's Navigator accelerated close to the Town Car, like a lion chasing down a gazelle. The Mercedes roared on the Navigator's other side in pursuit. Bullet fire from the Mercedes peppered the side of the Navigator's windows.

Evan slid back the cover on the sunroof, framing a gleam of the moon as it slid between two heavy clouds. He thumbed the control. The sunroof stayed still. He kicked again. The glass didn't budge.

'We have to get out,' Carrie said. The Mercedes nicked the Navigator, sparks flying up between the cars like a fountain of light. Gunfire erupted from the Mercedes and the side windows in the Navigator shattered.

Evan saw Bedford return fire from the front passenger side of the Navigator. The Mercedes answered with a burst of bullets and Bedford collapsed, half out the Navigator's window, a smear of blood along the door and the front window.

Bedford. Gone.

McNee's voice crackled to life on the intercom: 'Stay still and you won't get hurt.'

There has to be a way out. Not the windows, not the roof. The seats. Evan remembered a news report he'd seen about a trend in recent models, to make back seats more easily removable to accommodate the constant American hunger for trunk room. *Please, God, don't let the Agency have modified everything or we're in a death trap.* He dug his fingers into the seat and pulled. It gave a centimeter. He yanked again.

He glanced over his shoulder: McNee's eyes burned into his in the rearview, watching him, but she couldn't reach him any easier than he could reach her. He heaved again at the seat and now he saw the Navigator veer behind them, its side crunched, Bedford's limp body dangling over the shattered glass. The Mercedes approached to attack the driver's side.

Frame wasn't surrendering. He wasn't abandoning them.

Around them, other late-night Miami Beach traffic sped and spun out of their way, cars steering to the shoulder, drivers reacting in alarm and shock to the war waging in the lanes. With bay on both sides, the highway offered no place to exit until Alton Road and the residential neighborhood edging South Beach.

She has to slow for the exit, our chance to get out. Evan eased the seat back, exposing the dark of the trunk.

'Go!' Carrie shouted.

Evan wriggled through into the pitch-black. He swept his arm in the darkness ahead of him, looking for the thin wire and handle that would release the trunk door from inside. Assuming there still was one. Maybe the CIA or McNee had removed it.

Bullets dinged above his head, hitting the trunk's top.

The Town Car careened to the right, then again to the left. Evan lay wedged in the narrow opening, and the charging rocked him back and forth. He twisted, pulling himself through the tight gap, pushing their small luggage out of the way. Carrie pushed his feet and he popped through the leather canal into the full dark of the trunk. She pushed the laptop bag into the trunk after him.

Evan found and jerked the release cord.

The trunk popped up and the wind of traveling at 90 miles an hour boomed in his ears. The night lay vacant of stars, the clouds low and heavy over the city like smoke, and the Navigator drove up close to the bumper, ten feet from him, Frame's face a white smear behind the dazzle of the lights.

McNee urged more from the engine, the speed surging past 100 miles an hour as she barreled onto the South Alton Road exit, blasted through a green light, blaring on her horn, cars screeching as drivers slammed brakes to avoid crashing into the Town Car.

The Mercedes charged close and a man leaned out of the passenger side, gun leveled at Evan. Dezz. Grinning, hair ghost-white in the moonlight. Gesturing him back into the trunk.

Evan hunched down, reached back into the rear seat, groped for Carrie's hand. Nothing.

'Come on!' he yelled to her.

The Mercedes rammed the Navigator again and a second burst of gunfire flared. The Navigator flew over the median through a gap in the palms and flipped. Bedford's body flew from the wreck and tumbled along the asphalt. The Navigator slid on its side in a shower of sparks, nose-diving into a darkened storefront, metal and glass splintering and shattering.

The Mercedes retreated to the right, then revved forward, coming up close behind the Lincoln. Dezz leaned out the passenger side, fired into the trunk hatch. The bullet hit above Evan, ricocheted into the night. Warning shot; he didn't doubt Dezz could put a bullet through his throat.

Evan fumbled in Pierce's travel bag, which he'd tossed into the trunk. Did he have another gun with him? Please.

His fingers closed on metal just as the Mercedes tried to ram the trunk.

Evan slammed a clip home, raised the gun, thumbed off the safety, and fired.

Missed. He was no pro. He fired again and the bullet popped into the Mercedes's hood. The Mercedes backed off twenty feet. He didn't know the pistol's range, but he wasn't about to waste another bullet. And too many people around; he could kill an innocent bystander.

McNee lay on the horn, driving with insane abandon, powering down Alton Road, through the maze of beautiful people in their beautiful cars. She would kill people; he couldn't stop her.

But he could shoot out the tires.

The idea occurred to him with almost eerie calm. Before she killed innocent people, before she got back on a highway. It was the only way he could take command of the situation.

Evan leaned out again, aimed the gun at the tire below him. He wondered if the tire's exploding would kill him, if the car would somersault into the night sky and kiss the unforgiving concrete. In the car, Carrie might survive. He wouldn't have a prayer.

He held the gun steady and the Lincoln slowed.

Dezz sees me and he radios McNee, Evan thought. It's like having a gun to her head.

He fired.

The tire detonated. The car's swerve threw him back into the trunk. The Town Car spun into the oncoming lane; a banner for Lincoln Road passed above his head. Then the car slammed hard into the corner of a building.

The passenger window shattered on impact. Seconds

later, Carrie scrambled out, feet first, hitting the concrete in a tight roll, her arm out of the sling, and the Mercedes skidded to a stop twenty feet from her, crashing into a Lexus.

She held the decoy laptop in her good hand, raised it like a trophy. She glanced back at Evan, as if to be sure he was all right.

And then she ran, away from both cars, into the snarl of traffic.

Dezz and Jargo came out of the Mercedes and fired at her. Evan took aim, but two people got out of the Lexus, between him and Dezz, and he stopped, afraid of hitting them.

Dezz fired once at him, pinging the trunk lid, and Evan ducked down. People on the street, in front of the cafés, fled and screamed. He risked a look.

Dezz and Jargo ignored him: they saw Carrie had the laptop. Carrie bolted toward the western end of the street; she hurtled into the parting crowd, into traffic, and the two men followed her.

They vanished round a corner.

Evan heard a police siren approach, the spill of blues and reds racing along the scorching path they'd taken. He grabbed the laptop bag and jumped out of the trunk. McNee's door was open; she ran hard in the opposite direction, her gun out, aiming at anyone who tried to stop her.

The BMW – that had been behind the Mercedes on the highway – headed straight for him, braked. The window slid down. 'Evan!'

His father behind the wheel, dressed in a dark coat, a bandage on his face.

'Dad!'

'Get in! Now!'

'Carrie! We have to help Carrie!'

'Evan! Now!'

Clutching the laptop bag, Evan got in. This was not what he had expected; he thought Jargo had his father locked in a room, tied to a chair.

'Here.' Mitchell Casher pulled away from the Mercedes, tore along the sidewalk, steered off the chaos on Alton, took a side road, then another.

'Dad.' He grabbed his father's arm, thrilled his father was all right, half needing to convince himself that his father was really there.

'Are you hurt?'

'No, I'm fine. Carrie—'

'Carrie is no longer your concern.'

'Dad, Jargo will kill her if he catches her.' Evan stared at his father, this stranger.

Mitchell took a street that fed back onto Alton, two blocks away from the chaotic mess of the crash, then went onto 41 and cruised up to the speed limit on the stretch of road that cut through the bay. On the left, giant cruise ships shimmered with light. On the right, mansions crowded a spit of land, yachts parked on the water.

'Carrie. Dad, we have to go back.'

'No. She's not your concern anymore. She's CIA.'

'Dad, Jargo killed Mom. *He* killed her.'

'No. Bedford's people did, and we've taken care of them. Now I can take care of you. You're safe.'

This couldn't be. His dad believed Jargo. 'And Jargo just let you go.'

'He made sure I had nothing to do with your mother stealing the client list and running to Gabriel.'

'You were CIA, too. Bedford told me. *If one loved, one feared.* I know the code.'

Mitchell kept his eyes on the road. 'The CIA killed your mother, and I didn't want Bedford coming for me. All that matters now is that you're alive.'

'No. We have to be sure Carrie got away from them. Dad, please.'

'The only person I work for now, Evan, is myself. The only job I have is to keep you safe, where none of these people can ever find us again. You have to do exactly what I say now, Evan. We're getting out of the country.'

'Not without Carrie.'

'Your mother and I made enormous sacrifices for you. You have to make one now. We can't go back.'

'Carrie's not a sacrifice I'm willing to make, Dad. Call Jargo. See if they got her.'

His father drove the BMW past the emergency vehicles racing toward Miami Beach, eased them back onto I-95 North. 'Where are we going, Dad?' Evan still had the Beretta in his lap, and he imagined the unimaginable: pointing the gun at his father.

'Not a word, Evan. Say nothing.' His father tapped at his phone. 'Steve, can you talk?' Mitchell listened. 'Evan ran into the crowd. I'm still looking for him. I'll call you back in twenty.' He didn't look at Evan. 'They have Carrie. They carjacked a ride. They escaped from South Beach, but he has Khan's laptop.'

'The laptop she had is a decoy,' Evan said. 'Call him back and tell him I'll trade the files for her safety.'

'No. This is over. We're getting out. I did what you asked.'

'Dad, stop and call them back.'

'No, Evan. We're talking, just you and me. Right now.'

48

His father drove Evan to a house in Miramar. The homes were small, with metal awnings, painted from a palette of sky: sunrise pinks, cloudless blues, light eggshell the shade of a full moon. Fifties Florida. Stumpy palmettos lined the road. A neighborhood of retirees and renters, where people came and went without attracting attention. The perfect place for his father to hide.

Mitchell Casher steered into the driveway and doused the lights.

'I'm not abandoning Carrie.'

'She ran. She abandoned you.'

'No, she drew them away from me. She knew the laptop was empty; she knew they'd follow her. Because I can still bring down Jargo.'

'You put a lot of faith in a girl who lied to you.'

'And you put no faith in Mom,' Evan said. 'She wasn't leaving you. She wasn't running without you. She was coming to Florida to *get* you.'

Mitchell's mouth worked. 'Let's go inside.'

As soon as they stepped in the door, Mitchell closed his arms round Evan. He leaned into his father's embrace and hugged him back. Mitchell kissed his hair.

Evan broke down. 'I . . . I saw Mom . . . I saw her dead . . .'

'I know, I know. I am so sorry.'

He didn't break the embrace with his dad. 'How could you have done this? How could you?'

'You must be hungry. I'll make us omelets, or pancakes.' Dad was always the weekend cook, and Evan sat at the island counter while his dad chopped and mixed. Saturday breakfast was their confessional. Donna always lounged in bed and drank coffee, left the kitchen to her guys and stayed out of earshot.

He thought of that kitchen, his mother's strangled face, him hanging from the rafters at the end of a rope, dying, stretching his feet toward the counter where his father made pancakes before the hail of bullets cut him free.

'I can't eat.' He stepped away from his father. 'You're really not much of a captive, are you?'

'Be happy I'm free.'

'I am, but I feel like I've been played for a fool. I risked my life ... so many times in the past week, trying to save you ...'

'Jargo only agreed to let me talk to you this way today. Just today.'

'He made it sound like he would kill you.'

'He wouldn't have. He's my brother.'

Evan's stomach twisted. It was the truth of a fear that had lurked in the back of his mind since he'd seen the photos from Goinsville. It explained his father's belief in Jargo, his torn allegiance. He looked in his father's much-loved face for echoes of Jargo's scowl, Jargo's cold stare.

'Your brother is a vicious murderer. He tried to kill me, Dad. More than once. In our home, at Gabriel's, in New Orleans, in London, and just now.'

Dad poured them both glasses of ice water. 'Let me ask you a few questions.'

This was worse than being interrogated with a gun at your head. Because this was reality given an awful twist. Acting normal, talking normal, when nothing was normal.

'Do you know where the files your mother stole are?'

'No. Dezz and Jargo erased them, so I went to the source.'

'Khan. What did you actually take from him?'

'Plenty.'

'That's not an answer.'

Evan knocked the water glass out of his father's hand. It shattered on the floor, sprayed cubes and liquid across the carpet. 'I don't even know you. I came here to rescue you, and you want to grill me. Dad, we need to go out, get in the car, and get Carrie. Then we run. Forever. Jargo killed Mom. She wanted to protect me from this life, and you know it.'

'Just tell me exactly what evidence you have against my brother.'

A horrible thought occurred to him. 'You told Bricklayer to stay away. You didn't want to be rescued. If you couldn't get me back ... you want to stay with these people. You really do believe Jargo, not me.'

'Evan.' Mitchell looked at his son as though his heart were an open wound. 'It doesn't matter now. We can both go, both hide. I know how. We never have to worry again.'

'You answer me, Dad. You were Arthur Smithson. Mom was Julie Phelps. Why did you have to vanish?'

'None of that matters now. It won't make a difference.'

Evan gripped his father's arm. 'You can't keep any more secrets from me.'

'You won't understand.' Mitchell bent as though in physical pain.

'I love you. You know that is true. Nothing you can say will make me not love you.' Evan put his arm round his father. 'We can't run. We can't let Jargo win. He killed Mom; he'll kill Carrie. Doesn't that matter?' Evan's voice rose. 'You don't even act like you miss Mom.'

Mitchell stepped back in shock, grief twisting his face.

'My heart is broken, Evan. Your mother was my world. If I lost you as well . . . '

The cellphone in Evan's pocket vibrated. Evan opened it. 'Yes?'

His father stared at him, looking as if he wanted to reach for the cellphone, but he didn't.

Razur had provided Evan with the phone, and only Razur had the number.

'They really should name a computer after me,' Razur said, 'or an entire programming language, because I am made of awesome.'

'You did it.'

'I decoded the files. Nail-biter of a job. The files even had passwords against them when decoded. One file was triple-locked, so it must be the grand prize. It's just a list of names and pictures. It's called "Cradle".'

Probably a code name for the client list. That would be the file most carefully guarded. 'How can you get it to me?'

'I'm uploading copies to your remote-server account. You can download the files and the encryption software all at once. Can I delete the originals or trash the laptop?'

'No. I may need them. But I would suggest you hide them someplace very safe.'

'And here I was all tempted to mount that laptop on my wall, like a tiger I'd brought down.' Razur was laughing with her triumph.

'Thank you,' Evan said. 'Enjoy the money.'

'I shall.'

'You just saved lives.'

'That's a bonus, then,' Razur said.

'Drop out of sight for a while.'

'I'm going on holiday, but you know how to reach me.'

Razur hung up and Evan erased the number from his call log. Time to decide if he could trust his dad.

'Is there a computer and Internet access in this house?'

'Who was that?'

'Never mind. Tell me.'

Mitchell licked at his lips. 'Yes. In the back bedroom.'

Evan went to the bedroom, found a PC connected to broadband. He fired up the computer, accessed the remote-server account Shadey had set up for him when he'd called him in Goinsville. 'Where will Jargo take Carrie?'

'To a safe house for questioning.'

'Call them. Tell them to let her go or Jargo's client list is on the front page of the *New York Times* tomorrow morning.'

'If you hurt him, he'll just go underground and he'll hunt us.'

'Is it that you're afraid of him or that he's your brother?'

'Both,' Mitchell said. 'But listen to me. You release that list, we'll be hunted by far more than the Deeps. Intelligence services, criminal rings around the world, will put bounties on our heads.'

'Stop with the global guilt trip, Dad. You got us into this; I am getting us out of it.' Evan tapped on the keyboard, downloaded Razur's uploads.

'Evan, stop.'

'No, Dad, I won't. You'll have to stop me. You'll have to pull me away from this computer and you'll have to punch me to keep me down. You'll have to beat me senseless. I did not come all this way to stop.'

Mitchell stayed where he stood.

Evan opened the first of the many uploads Razur put on the server. Account numbers, a good three dozen, in various

Swiss and Cayman banks. He clicked open a folder called 'Logistics'; a file inside, one of many, held the requirements for his mother's last assignment in Britain. A third held arrangements to meet with the Israeli spy service and hand them a Palestinian fighter who had reneged on a deal to provide information to Jargo. A report on how to steal secrets from the French manufacturer of fighter jets, and a price in the millions for those secrets. And so on. Every document a page in the diary of a secret world.

A document that listed clients. For all the fear and death it had caused, the file was a simple spreadsheet. A few names at the CIA – including Peterson's – at the FBI, at Mossad, at both Britain's MI6 and MI5, at Russia's SVR, at the Chinese Guoanbu, at the German and French and South African intelligence agencies, the Japanese, both the Koreas. Fortune 500 companies, military commanders, high-ranking government officials in Washington, London, Paris, Nairobi, Rome, Moscow, Tokyo, and more.

'My God,' his father said behind him.

Evan clicked back to the folder file for logistics. He opened a subfolder named 'Travel.' He read the last three entries. A chill rose on his skin.

'Dad, how did Jargo grab you when you came back to the States?'

'I flew into Miami on Wednesday night. He called me back from my job early. He said there was a problem, he had to hide me. They took me to the safe house and they locked me up.'

'Wednesday. Then what?'

'He went to Washington to get a lead on Donna's contact at the CIA.'

'No, he went to Austin.' He pointed at a listing in the

logistics file. 'Khan arranged for a charter flight for him from Miami to Austin on Thursday. He went to see Mom. That's what triggered her to run Friday morning. Maybe she spotted him watching her.'

His father stared at the screen.

Evan clicked down to another spreadsheet. 'UK Operations.' Money funneled into an account in Switzerland, from one to another. 'Dad, look. This transfer, with the notification of a purchase of explosives. Who is Dundee?'

His father had found his voice again. 'An agent's code name.'

'Paid the day I arrived in London and Jargo tried to bomb me. Dundee is probably the bomb-maker. Your brother paid to kill me.'

Mitchell sank to the floor in shock, still staring at the computer.

The final document – titled 'Cradle' – sat alone at the window's bottom. Evan clicked it open as his father grabbed his hand and said, 'Don't, son, please, don't.'

49

Too late. Evan opened 'Cradle.' It held old photos – of children. Sixteen children. One of his father, with his wide smile. His mother was a blonde wisp of a child, high-cheekboned, her hair twisted in a garish, girlish braid. Jargo at seven already had the flat, cold eyes of a killer. A sweet-faced girl looked like a childish version of the driver McNee. Names lay underneath each photo. He stared at his parents and Jargo. And Carrie's father.

Arthur Smithson. Julie Phelps. John Cobham. Richard
Allan.

'Those were your real names,' Evan said. 'What happened
to your parents?'

'They all died. We never knew them.'

'Where were you born?'

His dad didn't answer. Instead he asked, 'Did you download the encryption software?'

'Yes.'

His father leaned over and clicked buttons. Dropped the
'Cradle' document on it again and the file reopened.

Not the CIA. Not an independent organization that
Alexander Bast had started and Jargo had hijacked. New
names lay beneath each schoolchild photo.

His mother. Julija Ivanovna Kuzhkina.

His father. Piotr Borisovich Matarov.

Jargo. Nikolai Borisovich Matarov.

'No,' Evan said.

'We were a great, great secret,' his father said behind him,
in tears. 'The seeds of the next wave of Russian intelligence.
The gulags were full of women, political dissidents, who
were not allowed to keep their children. Our fathers were
either other dissidents or prison guards who impregnated
the women. Our mothers got to see us – once a month, for
an hour – until we were two and then never got to see us
again. Most of the children ended up in labor or re-educa-
tion camps. Alexander Bast went through the camps. He
found the female prisoners with the highest IQs – giving
them legitimate tests, because the Soviets claimed dissidents were mentally damaged and had low IQs – and he
tested their two-year-olds, and then he took a group of us
away.'

'Bast was CIA.'

'And KGB. He was a double agent. His loyalty was to the USSR. He played the CIA for fools.'

Evan touched the screen, the photo of his mother. 'He transformed you into little Americans.'

'In Ukraine, the Soviets built a replica of an American town. Called it Clifton. Bast had another complex near it. We had the best English and French teachers; we spoke it like natives. We were even taught to mimic accents: Southern, New Englander, New Jersey.' Mitchell cleared his throat. 'We had American textbooks, although our instructors were quick to point out Western falsehoods in favor of Soviet truth. From an early age we were taught tradecraft. How to fight, if needed. How to kill. How to lie. How to spy. How to live a completely double life. We grew up in constant training, programmed for success, for fearlessness, to be the best.'

How to be boys and girls of shadows. Evan put his arm round his father.

'At the time, Soviet intelligence was in disarray,' Mitchell said. 'The FBI and the CIA kept rolling up and shutting down Soviet operations and agents in the States, because so many of the American-born agents had ties to the Communist Party before the Second World War. And if you were a Soviet diplomat, the FBI and CIA knew you were also likely KGB – it tied the spies' hands, constantly. The illegals – spies living under deep cover, under false names – were more successful, or at least Bast sold the upper management of KGB on this idea. Very few knew of the program. It was identified under a training program called Cradle on budgetary documents and reports, and given an extremely low profile. No one could know. The investment that would have been lost was too much, much more than training an adult agent.'

'Then Bast brought you to the orphanage in West Virginia.'

'He bought it, set us up in our new names and identities ...'

'And then promptly destroyed the orphanage and the courthouse, giving you a fallback position if your identity papers were ever questioned. And a source for new identities when needed.'

Mitchell nodded.

'To grow up and be spies.' Evan pictured his parents as children, drilled, trained, groomed for a life of suspicion and deceit. In the photos they looked as if they just wanted to go outside and play.

Mitchell nodded again. 'To be sleeper agents. But we were to attend college – our scholarships paid from an orphans' fund run by a company that was a front for Bast – and then he, as a longtime trusted CIA operative, would smooth the road for recruitment.'

'Into the CIA.'

'Yes. Or land us jobs in defense, energy, aviation ... wherever would be useful. We were to be flexible. To focus on operations. To wait for opportunities. To serve when summoned.'

'And as the Smithsons, you got a job as a translator for military intelligence, Mom worked for the navy. You were perfectly placed. Why did you become Mitchell Casher?'

'For you.' Now his father seemed to draw strength from the moment. He stood before Evan, his hands folded in front of his waist like a penitent, his eyes moist with tears, his voice strong, not trembling.

'I don't understand, Dad.'

'We saw what America was. Freedom. Opportunity. Honesty. For all its warts, its many problems, America was our home. We wanted to raise our children here, Evan, without fear. Without worry that we would be caught and killed or summoned back to Russia, where our parents had been in jail and we'd never been given a choice in our lives. Did you know at Clifton, we had to be taught how to make choices, how to deal with real independence?' Mitchell shook his head. 'We had freedom; we had interesting work; we had food in our stomachs and no lines to stand in. We knew we had been lied to, completely lied to.'

Evan put his arm round his father once more.

'The only thing that shielded us from the KGB was Bast. He was our sole handler, our sole contact. We were not listed in official KGB files. We were not acknowledged. The KGB command never knew I existed, otherwise those fools in the KGB – more like a black hole than a bureaucracy – would have gotten impossibly greedy, asked us for the moon and stars and destroyed us all by giving us impossible jobs. And then the Soviet Union fell.'

'What did you do? You didn't go home?'

'Russia wasn't home to us, anyway. And in a strange way, we were like Bast's children.' Mitchell closed his eyes. 'We were not supposed to be in contact with each other, but we were. My brother saw an opportunity. We would finally be real Americans. We'd be capitalists about our work.'

'So the Deeps killed Bast. Two shots from two different guns, Jargo and another Deep.'

'Me,' Mitchell said in a soft voice. 'Jargo and your mother and I went to London, shot him. Jargo first, then me. It was like killing my own father, but I did what I had to do. I knew we would have children someday. We weren't taking the chance of you ever having to be shipped back to Russia with us.' Mitchell swallowed. 'We killed him and the few we could reach in Russia who knew about Cradle. It was less than ten men at that point. That file of us as children, it looks like a scanned paper I saw once of all of us, back in Russia. It belonged to Bast.'

'And Khan kept it, for insurance, in case you all betrayed him the way Jargo did Bast,' Evan said.

'I think you're right. We created the evidence and fed it to one of Bast's KGB handlers that he had been murdered by the CIA, his fictional agents eliminated by the CIA. We all vanished from the lives we had lived.'

'But once the Soviet Union fell ... you could have stepped forward.'

'We could hardly step forward and say, "Hey, we're here under false pretenses. Can we stay? We've been breaking laws for years." We could have been deported, or put in prison.'

'So you went freelance.'

'We worked for anyone. We stole from the Israelis for the Syrians. We kidnapped old Germans in Argentina for the Israelis. We stole from German scientists and sold to KGB agents who never knew we were once their colleagues. Corporate espionage because it's fast and lucrative.' Mitchell ran his hand along his face. 'Espionage is illegal in every country. There is no clemency. Even ex-KGBers that are working as consultants now in the US, they had not done what we had. They had not committed murder. They had not lived under false names. They had not sold their services to the highest bidder.'

'And this noble work was done for my sake. Why didn't you just not spy at all?'

'We had been trained. The money was good. We wanted good lives for all our children. For you. For Carrie. We didn't want you to never have choices. We didn't want to take you away from everything you had ever known. We' – here Mitchell's voice broke, that of a boy torn from a mother's arms – 'we didn't want you to be taken from us. We wanted to be alive and free.'

The shock of his statement made Evan's bones feel like water. 'This isn't freedom, Dad. You haven't been able to do what you wanted. Be what you wanted. You just traded one cage for another.'

'Don't judge me.'

Evan stood. 'I'm not staying in the cage you built for yourself.'

Mitchell shook Evan's shoulders. 'It wasn't a cage. Your mother got to be a photographer. I got to work with computers. Our choices. And you got to grow up free, not afraid, not with us rotting in a prison, just like our mothers.' Mitchell's mouth contorted in fury and grief; rage fired his eyes.

'Dad . . .'

'You don't know the evil you were saved from, Evan. I don't mean the evil of murder. I mean the evil of oppression. Of your soul suffocating. Of constant fear.'

'I know you think you did the right thing for me.'

'There's no think about it. I did. Your mother and I did!'

'Yes, Dad.' Evan drew his father into a long embrace, and Mitchell Casher shuddered. 'It's okay. I will always love you.'

His father hugged back, fiercely.

'You did the right thing at the time,' Evan said, 'but this life killed Mom, and it has nearly killed me and you both.

Please. We have a chance to end it. We can go anywhere else. I'll dig ditches. I'll learn a new language. I just want what's left of my family to stay together.'

Mitchell sank down in the chair in front of the computer and put his face in his hands. Then he sat up, quickly, as though he'd assumed an unnatural posture.

He has to be ready all the time. Every moment that he's awake. Then Evan realized he had moved to that same edge of life in just a week. He went to the computer, studied the faces of the lost children. He took Khan's smartphone from his pocket, wirelessly moved all the client names and agent names from the files on the computer to the smartphone.

'What are you doing?' Mitchell said.

'Insurance.' Evan erased the downloaded files from the PC, erased the browser history so it wouldn't point back at the remote server. He shut down the laptop and closed the lid. He could re-download the files from the Internet again. If he lived.

'The files paint a target on our backs. You should destroy them,' Mitchell said. Evan wondered which face his father wore now: the protective dad, the frightened agent, the resolute killer. Evan's skin went cold with shock and with fear.

'I'm afraid of you,' he said.

Piotr Matarov, Arthur Smithson, Mitchell Casher, looked up at him.

Evan walked out of the bedroom. In the small breakfast nook, his father's raincoat lay over the back of a chair. Evan dug around in it, pulled out a satellite phone, clicked it on, paged through the few numbers listed. One for J. He carried the phone back to his father.

'You did what you did to have your life. I have to stop Jargo to have mine.'

'No. I won't let you.'

'Dad, I cannot let him kill Carrie, and I cannot let him get away with killing Mom. He gets stopped in his tracks. Now. You can either help me or not. But before you walk away, I need you to make this phone call.' Evan put his hand on his father's arm. 'Call. Find out if Carrie's all right. You haven't seen me. I got away.'

Mitchell studied his son's face, then clicked the buttons on the phone. 'Steven.' A pause. 'Yes.' Another pause. 'No, he got away from me. He has a friend or two in Miami. I might try them.' A pause. 'Don't kill her. She might know where Evan would go. Or if I find him, she could be useful in bringing him in. We still need to know how large Bricklayer's group is.' Mitchell spoke with a soldier's brisk tone: weighing options, offering countermoves, speaking like a man comfortable in shadows. 'All right.' He clicked off. 'They're at the safe house, our final stop on our escape route. She's still alive. He's . . . questioning her. He wants the password to the laptop.'

What had she said in the car? *He'd give me to Dezz. I'd rather die.*

'She doesn't know the password. That computer's empty, anyway.' Except for my fallback, my poker bluff for Jargo, if he ever cracks it.

'I bought her time,' Mitchell said, 'but it won't be pleasant for her. He already thinks of her as a traitor.'

'Where is she?'

Mitchell shook his head. 'You can't save her.'

'I can, if you help me. Just tell me where Jargo has her.'

'No. We're running, just you and me. Never mind Carrie. You and me.'

'I will not leave her, Dad.'

'I'm sorry. You're going nowhere near him.'

'I will not leave her. You can try and force me to go with you, but at some point, Dad, you fall asleep and I just head back here. I am not leaving her.' He was scared in a way he'd never been scared before, because his father could stop him. He knew it. He couldn't fight his dad. 'You made the tough choices, Dad, for me, because you loved me, but I'm not leaving Carrie. Tell me where she is. If you don't want to go, it's your choice.'

His father shook his head. 'You don't know what you're doing.'

'I absolutely do. Your choice.'

Mitchell closed his eyes.

50

It will end tonight, Evan thought. One way or another, all the years – the whole life – of lies and deceit end. Either for my family or for Jargo.

Mitchell drove north to 75 West – nicknamed Alligator Alley. As they headed west, the night cleared and the adrenaline surged into Evan's flesh and bones. They listened to a news station out of Miami; McNee was dead, shot by a police officer as she tried to flee the scene in Miami Beach.

'Jargo won't kill Carrie right away. They'll want to know everything that the CIA knows – they'll take their time. Jargo can't afford to let the CIA work another mole into the network.'

'Will Jargo torture her?' *Torture*. It wasn't a verb you wanted within a mile of the girl you loved.

'I don't know. He'll do whatever it takes to get her to talk.'
The answer sounded flat in the dark space between them.
'You cannot dwell on Carrie, Evan. If you go in thinking
about Carrie ... or your mother, you'll die. You must focus
on the moment at hand. Nothing more.'

'We need a plan.'

'This isn't my forte, Evan – rescue operations. We're not
a SWAT team.'

'You kill people, right? Consider it a hit. On Dezz and
Jargo.'

'I don't usually have an untrained person to protect,
either.'

'This is my fight as much as yours.'

'Son, this is how this goes.' Mitchell cleared his throat. 'I
go in alone. You'll stay hidden outside. They'll expect me to
return here, if I can't find you. I'll say you're still missing.
No report that the police have found you. I'll tell them that
I've heard the news report that McNee is dead, but that I
heard on the police band that she's alive but captured. Since
Jargo stole a civilian car, he won't have heard any police-
band reports.'

'We hope.'

'We hope. They'll know if McNee is alive, the FBI and
CIA will bring extraordinary pressure to bear on her. We
need to run.' Mitchell glanced at his son. 'That movement
creates an opportunity of weakness. They will want to shut
down everything in the house before they go.'

'The decoy laptop, they'll take that with them?'

'Yes, unless they've already broken it with an unlock
program.'

'They won't have,' Evan said.

'What did you put on the decoy?'

'Let's just say I learned a few tricks from all the kids' movies on FilmzKool. You have to be overly dramatic to get attention for your work these days. I'm gonna get dramatic on Jargo.'

'When they come out of the lodge, Jargo will be walking alone; Dezz probably will have Carrie in cuffs. Both will be armed and ready. I'll drop back and get them both in my kill zone. I will shoot Dezz first, because he will have the gun on Carrie, then Steven.' His voice wavered at the thought of shooting his own brother.

'Don't hesitate, Dad. He killed Mom. I promise you it's true.'

'Yes, I know he did. I know. Do you think knowing makes it any easier? He's still my brother.'

'What if they want to kill Carrie before leaving? The Everglades – you could make a body vanish forever.'

'Then,' Mitchell said, 'I'll lie and say I want to kill Carrie myself, but slow. For turning you against me.'

The cool calculation of his father's voice made Evan shudder. 'I don't think it's right you go in alone. You don't have to fight my fight.'

'The only way this will work is if they believe you and I are *not* together and have not been together.'

'All right, Dad. Can I ask you a question?'

'Yes.'

'Did you love Mom?'

'Evan, my God. Yes, with all my heart.'

'I wondered if maybe the marriage was arranged, to give you cover.'

'No, no, son. I loved her like crazy. My brother, he was in love with her, too. It was the only time I beat him in any-thing, when Donna chose me instead of him.'

The night was dark and vast. Evan had never seen the Everglades before and it was both empty and full, all at once. Empty of the human touch other than the highway, filled by a plain of dirt, water, and grass that throbbed with life. Mitchell headed south down Highway 29, on the edge of the Big Cypress National Preserve. No lights of a town or business, just the curve of the road heading into black.

In the darkness by the side of the road, his father stopped the car.

'Hide in the trunk. Break the trunk light so it won't shine.'

A jolt of panic hit his chest. So much unplanned, so much to do to try to prepare, but no time.

'The driveway goes around to the back of the lodge, where there's a large porch. I'll park with the trunk aimed away from the lodge. You'll see a gray brick building toward the back of the property. It's a garage and houses the generator. Run as fast as you can for it. Stay behind it until I come for you. If we come out and I miss a shot, you should have a clear line at Dezz or my brother.'

'Dad, I love you.' Evan took his father's hand in the darkness.

'I know. I love you, too. Go get in the trunk.'

51

Inside the trunk – for the second time in a night, and he hoped for the last in his life – Evan felt the BMW come to a stop. He heard his father get out of the car. No call of greeting broke the still quiet, and he heard his father climb porch stairs, then a door open. Then he heard a murmur of cautious hellos, his dad's voice sounding actor-pitch perfect in its weariness and fear, and finally the door shut.

He eased the trunk open, rolled out the back. The night air was cool and moist, but his palms were drenched in sweat. He held the Beretta that Frame had given him a few hours ago. No spill of lights glowed in the night to show him his way. He lay flat for a moment on the concrete, waiting for a door to fly open, shots to fire.

Nothing.

He ran, keeping the cars between him and the lodge's back porch.

Blackness. He didn't have a flashlight; his dad said not to risk using one. He ran into the pitch-dark and hoped that he wouldn't trip and plunge into wet or a hole or a stack of trash cans that would set off a din. He stumbled against the garage, eased round its corner. Evan stayed still. Every rustle sounded like a snake or a gator – he did not want to see alligators again – slithering closer.

He thought he heard a click: probably an alarm system, reactivating after his dad was inside. He stayed still as stone, the sweat oozing down his ribs, his breath sounding huge in the silence. He had a gun. He had Khan's smartphone, with its fancy alarm-deactivator software, which he had no idea how to use. Now he needed patience.

Alone, in the quiet dark, he didn't feel so brave. He felt like an everyday boy again. Not the boy of shadows. Not a boy raised by two master spies. Just a scared kid who wanted his mom alive again and wanted his dad and his girlfriend safe.

Five minutes. Ten minutes. No blast of shots from his father's gun. No creak of footfall on the back porch. He peeked past the corner of the garage, past his father's parked car, up to the lodge. Only the sound of his breath, of the ocean of life around him.

Then he heard the slightest crush of a heel on tall grass. Fifteen feet away. He froze.

'I ... see ... you,' a voice called in singsong. Dezz. 'Sitting so still ...'

A bullet smacked into the brick wall ten feet to his right. Evan lurched backward. Another shot hit the corner, well above his head. Shards of brick pelted his face.

Terror thumping his heart, Evan pointed the gun in the direction of the shots. He'd seen a moment of flash, but he was shaken and he hesitated.

'I see you sitting on your butt, pointing a gun, pretending that you're tough. You're not even close,' Dezz said. 'Put the gun down. Come inside. Or I'll march back inside and I'll shoot your father in the spine. He won't die; it'll be worse than death, because when we roll out, we'll just dump his paralyzed self in the swamp and let nature take its course. The choice is yours. It's over, Evan. You decide how nasty it gets for your dad and little girlfriend.'

Evan dropped the gun. The clouds parted for a moment and he saw, in the dim moonlight, Dezz hurrying toward him, gun stretched out. Then a savage kick hammered him into the wall. Brick cut the back of his head.

Dezz drove the heel of his boot into Evan's cheek.

'You think you can beat us,' Dezz said, bending to retrieve Evan's gun from the grass. 'You can't, cousin' – he made the word sound foul – 'and you never should have tried.'

52

'I hear an idiot pissing his pants.' Dezz pushed Evan up the back-porch steps, his gun nestled at the back of Evan's head.

His skull throbbed, and his face ached. He kept his hands up.

Dezz grabbed his arm, shoved him through a doorway. Evan tried to stop, but he splayed out on the tile floor.

Dezz flicked on lights. He trained his gun – the same one he'd smashed Evan in the face with – on Evan.

Dezz pulled the goggles free from his face and tossed them on the counter. 'Night-vision, with an infrared illuminator. Nowhere you can hide from me. Not that it matters anymore. You are quite the fearsome opponent. It's like watching a Special Forces bloopers tape.' Dezz clicked on a light, and now, close to him, Evan saw a twisted, altered version of himself: the same high cheekbones and slash of mouth, the same slim build, but Dezz's face wore a harsh thinness.

Dezz jerked Evan to his feet and locked the gun on his head.

'Please run. Please cry. Please give me a reason to hurt you.'

Evan blinked against the bright lights. The lodge opened up into a broad foyer. Dim lights shone, but none of the glow slipped past the boarded-up windows. The furnishings of a lobby had been stripped clean, except for a wagon-wheel chandelier that hung from the ceiling. It had the air of an expensive building trying to look rustic, aimed at the eco-tourist or hunting crowd.

'I'm surprised you came out looking for me,' Evan said, 'since you're so scared of gators.'

Dezz drove a hard punch into Evan's stomach, ramming him against the wall. He collapsed, fought to stay conscious. Dezz grabbed Evan's throat, pulled him back to his feet.

'You're' – he slammed Evan's head against the wall – 'a' – slammed it again – 'nothing,' Dezz said, finishing with another head pound. 'A wannabe filmmaker. That counts for zero in the real world. You thought you were smarter than me and you're just so unbelievably dumb.' Dezz opened a piece of caramel, chewed the candy, shoved the wrapper into Evan's mouth.

Evan spat the wrapper out. Blood trickled down the back of his neck. 'I talk with Jargo, not you.'

He heard a scream. Carrie. Screaming in fear.

Dezz laughed. He prodded Evan with the gun. 'Reunion time. Get up there.'

He pushed Evan up the curving grand staircase. 'I bet you scream, too. I bet you cry first, then you wet yourself, then you scream your throat raw. When I'm done with you, I'll have to take notes so I don't forget.' The staircase led to a wide hallway with four doors, all but one shut. Boards covered the window at the end of the hall. Dezz pushed Evan into a room.

The room had once been a conference space, where people sat with open three-ring binders full of corporate presentations, fought off meeting fatigue, watched droning talks about sales projections, and probably all wished they were out fishing or hunting in the Everglades instead of deciphering a pie chart. They would have drunk coffee or ice water or sodas cold from a bowl filled with ice, muffin tray in the middle.

Now the table and the drinks were gone, and Jargo stood, holding a red-stained knife and a pair of pliers. He stared at Evan with a cold, fierce hatred, then stepped aside so Evan could see.

His father lay on the floor. Pain fogged Mitchell's eyes; blood seeped through his shirt where he'd been stabbed. Next to him was Carrie. Her right arm was thrown over her head, handcuffed to a steel hoop in the floor, installed where carpet had been pulled away.

Mitchell's face crumpled when he saw his son.

Jargo rushed forward and slammed his fist into Evan's face. 'You little punk!' he yelled.

Evan hit the floor. He heard Dezz giggle, heard him step aside, make room for his father.

Jargo kicked Evan hard, in the spine. 'I kicked a man to death once.' Jargo kicked Evan in the neck. 'I kicked Gabriel until he couldn't draw breath.'

'Don't smash in his face yet,' Dezz said. 'I want him to see everything we do to his dad. That'll be cool.'

Evan said, past the blood in his mouth, past the agony in his neck, 'I came here to make a deal with you.'

Jargo kicked him again, in the stomach. 'A deal. I don't care about any deal. Give me the files, Evan. Now.'

'All right then,' Evan whimpered. 'Please stop kicking me so I can . . . tell you.'

'Get him up,' Jargo said, tucking the knife back into his pocket. Dezz yanked Evan to his feet.

'Steve, don't hurt him,' Mitchell said. 'I'll do whatever you want. Just let him go, please.'

Jargo glared back at his brother. 'You traitor, you nothing, don't you beg me.'

'What I'm offering,' Evan said with a calm assurance that

surprised him, 'is a deal that lets you stay alive.' He looked past Jargo's shoulder at Carrie; her eyes opened. She looked exhausted but relatively unhurt.

'Well, this I can't wait to hear,' Jargo said, a trace of cold amusement in his voice.

'We could have brought the police. We didn't,' Evan said. 'We want to settle this, just between the four of us.'

'Give me the files. Right. Now.' Jargo raised his gun. 'Or I take you outside and I shoot out both knees and I start kicking the flesh off your bones.'

'Don't you even want to hear my offer?' Evan asked. 'I think you do.'

53

For a moment Jargo's face wavered behind the gun-sight.

'Because if you kill me, there is no deal. No files for you,' Evan said. 'No more Deeps. I didn't come to kill you. I came to deal.'

'Then why'd your father come in alone?'

'His idea, not mine. He's overprotective. I'm sure you're the same way with Dezz, Uncle Steve.'

Jargo smiled.

'Or should I just call you Uncle Nikolai?'

The smile faded.

'You're running out of time,' Evan said. 'You want the files on Khan's laptop, I can give them to you.' Evan stepped round the gun. He knelt by his father. 'I told you this wouldn't work, Dad. We're doing it my way.'

Mitchell nodded, stunned.

Evan looked up at Jargo and it was hard to keep the hate out of his eyes. 'You stabbed him. Your own brother.'

'Mitchell didn't tell us you were outside, though, if that's what you're wondering.'

'I don't doubt him,' Evan said. 'I'm sure I can trust him completely, the same way you can trust Dezz.'

'What is that supposed to mean?' Dezz said.

Evan's gaze met Carrie's. His back was to Dezz and Jargo, and he mouthed, *It's okay.*

She closed her eyes.

'I can give you the files now,' Evan said.

Jargo put the gun back to his head.

'But not if you shoot me.' He couldn't believe how steady his voice was. He was afraid, more afraid than he had ever been, but somehow he had moved past the dazzling glare of his fear. Into shadow. He was the boy of shadows.

Evan leaned down to the decoy laptop's keyboard. The laptop was powered on, a prompt screen awaiting the password.

Evan leaned down, typed the password, and stepped back.

'There you go,' Evan said.

The laptop digested the password; the prompt screen disappeared; a video application started automatically; a film file loaded into the application and ran.

'What is this?' Jargo said.

'Watch,' Evan said.

The film opened with the Audubon Zoo on last Monday morning, the sky gray with the promise of rain. The camera zooming in close on Evan's face, then Jargo's. Jargo in full profile, talking rapidly, his cool starting to break.

Then Evan's voice began to speak on the film. 'That angry

man in the picture is Steven Jargo. You've been doing business with him for a long time. You've hired him to kill
people you don't like, steal secrets you don't have, do your
dirtiest, most secret jobs. You may not have seen his face
before – he hides behind other people – but here he is. Take
a good look.'

On the screen, Jargo's face turned toward Shadey's hidden
camera. Angry, almost frightened, vulnerable.

'Mr Jargo's operations have been ruined. He lost a list that
had the name of every client who used his freelance spy
network. Officials in every major intelligence agency, government leaders, high-ranking executives. If you have
received this emailed message, your name is on this list.'

Jargo made a noise in his throat.

Then the scene fell apart into gunfire, Evan punching Jargo,
Evan and Carrie fleeing into the depths of the zoo, Jargo pulling himself up from the ground, he and Dezz giving chase.

'Why am I alerting you to this problem?' Evan's voice
resumed. 'Because we value your business, your loyalty to
Mr Jargo's network. But every organization needs to grow to
meet new challenges. Our time for change is now. I understand this may make you uneasy about conducting
additional business with us.'

Dezz said, 'You rotten little creep.'

'Please, have no fear,' Evan's voice said. 'There is no need
for you to order your intelligence services to kill Mr Jargo.
We are his associates, we have taken command of his
network, and the situation is now under control. You will be
contacted in the near future by a new representative of our
company regarding your future business with us. Thank you
for your attention.'

The screen faded as the crowd in the zoo continued to

run past Shadey's station. Then the film started again. Evan let it play, let it work under their skin.

Jargo stood frozen, a man whose world had vanished. Dezz grabbed Evan's throat.

'Do you think ... for a moment ... I'm going to let you blackmail us?' Dezz half screamed.

'Back down,' Evan said. 'I'm not done laying out the deal for you.'

'Let him go. Let him talk,' Jargo said in a cracked voice.

Dezz didn't listen. He tightened his grip on Evan's throat. 'No. You're not taking my dad's work away from him. You're not.'

'Let him go, Dezz,' Jargo repeated.

Evan could hardly breathe. He felt Dezz's fingers tighten on his throat, lifting him up off the floor.

'I said let him go!' Jargo yelled, and as the blackness crept into Evan's vision, he fell to the floor. He opened his eyes, saw Dezz sprawled next to him, blood coming from his mouth.

'When I give you an order,' Jargo said, 'obey it. Evan, finish what you're saying. Dezz, if you interrupt him again, I will hurt you badly.'

Evan clambered to his feet. Dezz's face began its slow swelling of a bruise; he looked confused, even frightened.

Evan gasped for air. 'Your clients are powerful people who don't want their dirty laundry aired. Maybe they'll work with me and Dad, maybe not. They have reason to stick with the Deeps. We can hurt them, they can hurt us, but if we all hold our noses, they get what they want and we'll make a lot of money.'

'*We'll?*' Jargo said.

'Yes,' Evan said. 'My dad and I are taking over the Deeps.'

54

The only sound in the room was the looping video and the whisper of Evan's recorded voice. Mitchell and Carrie stared at Evan; Dezz looked ready to murder; Jargo's mouth worked as though struggling to form words.

'That still cool with you, Dad?' Evan called. 'You want Jargo in or not?'

Mitchell found his voice. 'I don't want my brother dead, but, no, he can't stay in command.' Playing along with Evan, stepping into his son's charade.

'Very well, Dad.' Evan gave Jargo a smile, the hardest gesture he'd ever made. 'I'm not cutting you entirely out of the family business. I mean, if you want to retire, it's your choice.' He pulled Khan's smartphone out of his jacket pocket. 'I took this from Thomas Khan. A copy of that film we're all enjoying is also sitting on a computer, preset to email in less than ten minutes. To every client. And to every Deep, those kids you were raised with, who you trained with to be spies here in America. I know you've killed at least two of them – my mom and Carrie's dad. That leaves twelve who don't know what a murdering traitor you are. They'll find out in ten minutes.'

'So I just hand over the reins to you?' Jargo said.

Dezz bounced on the soles of his feet. 'No, Dad, no.'

'Yes, you do. Sound familiar? You pulled a similar stunt on Alexander Bast so many years ago, but I'm not killing you.' Not yet, he thought. He gripped the smartphone, willed his hand not to shake. 'I can stop the email program from scaring your whole network and every client of yours.

Only *I* have the key. You kill me, you hurt my dad or Carrie, the files go, and you're history. You're burnt to a crisp. The Deeps will hunt you. The clients will hunt you. And when they find you, *you'll* be the one kicked to death.'

'Dad,' Dezz said in a strained voice, 'he's lying. Don't listen to him.'

'I had a hacker break all of Khan's files open for me,' Evan said. 'I know your name, Uncle Nikolai. I know who you are and who pays you. It's done for you. Over.'

'He's lying!' Dezz screamed.

'Shut your mouth!' Jargo screamed back. He backhanded Dezz; the boy fell to the ground, blood dripping from his mouth. And for the first time, ever, Evan felt sorry for his cousin. What chance had Dezz ever had, with Jargo as a father?

'Am I lying? I have Khan's laptop. I have his files, his smartphone, and that film footage.' Evan narrowed his stare. 'You messed with the wrong kid.'

'It's all a bluff,' Dezz said from the floor. Still trying to win over his father. His reddened face sweated; he grimaced, showing small, white teeth.

Evan kept his gaze on Jargo, unlocked the smartphone with his thumbprint. He tapped open a file on the phone's screen, held it out for Jargo to read. A long list of names, clients. He clicked to the next screen. A list of the Deeps.

'Do I look,' Evan said, 'like I'm a boy who bluffs?'

The glow of the smartphone's screen played along Jargo's face. He read the names; Evan could see the names reflected in his eyes. Jargo blinked. 'What ... do I have to do to get you to not send the email?'

'Put your guns on the floor. Unlock my father and Carrie. Leave. Immediately. Just go.'

Dezz got to his feet, his gun still in his hand. 'No!'

'Kill me and it goes,' Evan said. 'Decide.'

'You could still send the email,' Jargo said.

'You'll just have to trust me,' Evan said. 'Dad still wants to run the Deeps, I won't destroy his business.' The lie didn't trip on his tongue. He held out his hand. 'Your gun.'

Jargo said, 'Mitchell, for God's sake . . . you know I never would have hurt you. I gave you the life you wanted, the life we dreamed about. I cannot believe you would turn on me.'

'You just stabbed him a minute ago,' Evan said.

Jargo took an unsteady step. 'You're doing this because you think I killed your mom. I didn't. *I* did not.' A stress on the *I*. 'I just wanted to find out what she had taken, why she had taken it. I . . . ' He shuddered, uncertain in his sudden weakness.

'Shut up and give me your gun. Eight minutes.'

Jargo handed him the gun.

'Unlock Carrie. Unlock my dad.'

'Do what he says,' Jargo said to Dezz.

'No way, no way, no way!' Dezz's voice morphed to a high shriek. 'It's a lie. He's just telling us a story. It's like he's made up a movie. It's what he does! Why can't you see it?'

Jargo slapped Dezz back to the floor. 'If you'd been half as smart as him . . . if you'd been half as inventive as him . . . you'd be worthy of being my son.'

'Dad, please.' Dezz sounded caught between rage and tears.

'I told you not to call me that.'

Evan aimed the gun at Jargo. 'Seven minutes. You want to get down the road, I imagine.' He just wanted them gone, his father safe, Carrie safe. The police could pick them up on Alligator Alley, whether they fled back to Miami or headed northwest to Tampa.

Jargo grabbed the keys from the tabletop and knelt by Mitchell. Mitchell pushed himself away from the wall, in pain.

Dezz closed the laptop, cut off the reel of video, and swung the gun toward Evan. 'I am as smart as Evan, Dad. He's bluffing.'

'Are you going to risk that I'm lying?' Evan said. 'You're running out of time.'

'Dezz, shut up.' Jargo clicked loose the cuff that held Mitchell to the iron bar and glared at his son. 'If not for your lack of self-control . . .'

'Quit blaming me,' Dezz whispered.

Mitchell climbed to his feet, one side of the handcuff still on his wrist, an open steel circle dangling at the end of its chain. He stared at his brother. Anger, hate, hurt, a kaleidoscope of emotions built over the years of deception, played across his face.

Evan saw it, keeping his gun trained on Dezz, thinking, Dad, just let them go. We've got the upper hand. Play it out, they're gone, and we're fine . . .

'You killed my Donna,' Mitchell said to Jargo. His mouth sounded as if it were full of gravel. 'You flew to Austin and killed her.'

Then he swung the heavy cuff.

The open circle of steel caught Jargo in the face, sliced through skin, hooked hard into his cheek. Jargo screamed. Mitchell yanked the cuff and tore his brother's face open.

Dezz swung his gun toward them, but Mitchell spun with a kick and caught Dezz's arm. The bullet blasted into the cypress flooring.

Evan jumped forward. His hands closed on the gun, trying to lever its aim toward the ceiling, away from his father and Carrie. Dezz wrestled with him; the gun's aim swung wildly, around the entire room, as the boys fought.

Boom. And then another.

The first bullet caught Jargo in the back of the head as he staggered, his hooked face chained to his brother's wrist. The second hit flesh with a wet pop as the two brothers collapsed together.

Evan and Dezz both screamed in horror as their fathers fell to the floor.

Evan, filled only with thoughts for his dad, crawled to the two men. Jargo was dead, the back of his head a wet mess, unseeing eyes bulged in disbelief.

Mitchell looked at his son. He moaned and closed his eyes. A circle of bullet gouged the middle of his shirt. Blood began to spread across the dark cotton.

'Evan!' Carrie's voice cut through the haze of shock. She pulled hard at the cuff that bound her to the floor. 'Dezz!'

Evan turned. Dezz still held the gun, in his wavering hands, staring in shock at his father's body.

'Dezz, give me the gun.'

Dezz shook his head and Evan thought, That's it. He'll just shoot us all. I can't stop him before he kills one of us.

But then Dezz made a strange, sad noise in his throat. And put the warm pistol up against his head.

55

For one awful moment Evan thought, Let him do it. Then shock and shame welled up in him. 'Dezz! Don't! Don't!'

'Why not?' Dezz's voice was thin, frail. 'I just killed my dad. My dad. My fault.'

'Not your fault. No. Listen to me. Don't do this to yourself.'

'It's what you want.' Dezz's voice shattered, like a glass against concrete. 'Me dead. Debt settled. Your mother avenged.'

'No. Not what I want,' Evan said. 'Put the gun down.'

'Dezz, listen to Evan, please,' Carrie said.

'I shot my dad!' and Dezz gave out a scream of such anguish it sounded torn from the deepest recesses of his heart.

'I know,' Evan said. Every word he thought of saying felt inadequate. But he knew if he said nothing, Dezz would pull the trigger. 'I know what it is to lose a parent. Worst feeling ever. But listen, hurting yourself isn't the answer . . . '

'You won. You took it all from him, from me, Evan.'

'Give me the gun.' Evan took a step forward. He could hear the wet gurgle of his father, fighting for life. I have to get him to a hospital, but I can't let Dezz kill himself.

'Don't kill yourself over a man who beat you, Dezz,' Carrie said. 'You're free of him now. Let us help you. Please.'

'He . . . he . . . '

Carrie kept her voice calm. 'None of us have to do what our parents did. None of us. It can all end now. We can have normal lives, Dezz.'

'Normal? Me? How am I supposed to be normal now?' Dezz screamed.

'He was your dad. You loved him. I know. It was an accident, Dezz.' Evan held out his hand for the gun. 'But this wouldn't be an accident. Don't.'

'I ... I ...' Tears welled up in Dezz's face. 'I don't have anything to live for, Evan. You took it all away from me.'

For a moment the gun wavered. Evan launched himself at the bigger boy. His hand caught the edge of the gun. The two boys staggered, fighting for it, just as their fathers had fought a minute ago. The gun caught between them and Evan powered Dezz backward, trying to get him away from his father and from Carrie.

The stairwell loomed.

'Stop it, Dezz. It all has to end!' Evan yelled. And as the two boys fell down the hardwood stairs, the gun, caught between them, spoke a final time.

SEVEN DAYS LATER

56

'You have a decision to make,' the man said.

Evan stood on the wet sand, watching the tide dance around his feet. Carrie stood on the porch of the rental house, arms crossed, watching them. Mitchell Casher stood next to his son, his arm still bound in a sling. Evan could see his father's bandages under the shirt's thin material.

'Your father agrees with me, Evan.' The man was the new Bricklayer, Bedford's replacement. 'My proposal is simple. The film you made to bluff Jargo actually has a wonderful idea sewn up in it: taking over the Deeps network. It's brilliant in its simplicity.'

'I only made the video to scare Jargo if he caught me,' Evan said. 'I don't want anything to do with this.'

'Well, Evan, your father could face serious charges. As could you, and Carrie. Not to mention your ... cousin.' He glanced at Dezz, sitting at a distance in the sand, looking out at the ocean, his arm still in a cast. For a moment Dezz's glance met Evan's. The gaze was thoughtful. Dezz didn't smile, but he had smiled last night, over dinner, for the barest of seconds.

Cousins. It was technically true. They were family, even if they felt like complete strangers. But Evan wasn't sure they could ever be friends.

Dezz went back to looking at the horizon.

'This was supposed to be over. We're supposed to be free of the past now,' Evan said. 'Are you telling me you're going to send my father and Dezz to prison if we don't cooperate?'

'You could help us take over the Deeps,' Bricklayer said. 'We can feed their clients – at least the unfriendly ones – whatever information we want.'

'Or blackmail them into doing your bidding,' Evan said. 'But you can't do that without the client list.'

'And you will give us that list, Evan.' The new Bricklayer lacked Bedford's charm; he spoke, instead, with a quiet arrogance. 'We've made a sizable investment in you and your odd little family.' Because he was a bureaucrat, he started naming the favors of the Agency: 'Set you up here in Hawaii; cleared your names so that you are no longer wanted by the Austin police; hired a private tutor for the three of you; provided funerals for your mom and Jargo; paid a large sum of money to your friend Shadey for the help he gave you. We've given you your life back.'

The life Evan had had was gone, but he said, 'I appreciate all you've done.' He didn't want to talk to this new Bricklayer – this thin shadow of the decent man Bedford had been – anymore. Bricklayer smiled at Evan, pretending that he wasn't using guilt to shame him into stepping back into being the boy of shadows.

Evan stared out at the water. He counted to ten. 'Let me think about it.'

'There is no thinking, Evan. I have operatives who can be here within minutes to arrest your father. I'm tired of being Mr Nice. Give me the client list.'

'Evan, do what you think is best,' his father said.

'I'm not going to let you go to prison, but we have to get out of this life, Dad.'

'Maybe we have to earn our way out,' his father said.

Evan glanced at him. 'What do you mean? I never wanted to be in this life.'

'But you are now, for better or worse. And I'm sorry for that.'

Bricklayer still stood on the beach, glancing out at the white of the waves, turning his gaze back to them, waiting for an answer.

Carrie walked down from the porch. Dezz got up from the edge of the surf, dusting the sand from his backside with his good hand. Evan walked a distance from Bricklayer and waited until his father, Carrie, and Dezz stood by him, silent, quiet.

'We're done paying for the sins of our parents,' Evan said.

They stared at him, glanced at each other.

'But I'm making a different choice than my mom made,' Evan said, 'when she had to choose how to use the client list. She used it as a shield. I'm using it as a battering ram.'

His father shook his head. 'How? They'll never leave us alone.'

'We take over the Deeps, but we do it in a way for good. We take down the bad guys, the clients, the people like Peterson, one by one. We clean up your mess, so you don't go to prison, and the other kids of the Deeps don't have to go through what we went through,' Evan said. 'This new Bricklayer . . .'

'Jerk,' Dezz said under his breath.

'This new jerk doesn't run our lives. We do,' Evan said. 'We keep him from using the clients for his own purposes. We pretend to work for him, but if he wants to use the clients for bad, we stop him, too, without him or the CIA knowing it. And when all the clients are taken down, we're done. This is how we get out of this life, Dad. This is how we get back to normal. Me and Dezz and Carrie, we all agree on it.'

Mitchell stared at the three teenagers. 'Are you sure?'

'Yes. It's the only way to put the past behind us forever. You'll be in charge, but we make sure the job is done right. After all, no one will suspect us, will they?'

'I won't agree to putting you three in danger like this,' Mitchell said. 'I'd rather go to prison.'

'If you don't agree to serve as our boss, our leader, then Bricklayer will. Do you think he'll be so careful about our safety?' Carrie said. 'You have to agree, or they'll get us all a new guardian.'

'All right,' Mitchell said after a moment.

Evan took a deep breath. His old life was gone. His new life was uncertain: working for his father's freedom; working for a future with Carrie – could he even think the word 'future' with her; working with a dangerous, unstable boy who had once been his mortal enemy and was now, oddly, family. He felt like his parents must have felt years ago, deciding to live in shadow, deciding to live in secret, to protect him.

He walked toward Bricklayer, now standing in the shade of a dense growth of palm trees.

'I have a proposal,' he said to Bricklayer, 'one you can't refuse.'

And as he walked from the heat of the sun-blasted beach into the cool dark of the palms, Evan Casher went from the boy in sunlight back to being the boy of shadows.

ACKNOWLEDGMENTS

This book is fiction. That means it's made up, entirely a product of my imagination, is conjured out of thin air, and bears no reality to the actual world or any person or organization in it.

I owe great thanks to Peter Ginsberg, Mitch Hoffman, Carole Baron, Brian Tart, Kara Welsh, Susan Schwartz, Erika Kahn, and Genny Ostertag for their enthusiasm and support for the book in its original edition.

In particular for the *Panic: Ultimate Edition* version of this novel for teens, I would like to thank David Shelley, Samantha Smith, Daniel Mallory, Shirley Stewart, Katherine Agar, and a special thanks to my youthful writing assistants, Charles Abbott and Michael Groth.

For their help in researching and completing this novel, I thank many people:

My sister-in-law, Vicki Deutsch, my brother-in-law, Michael Deutsch, and my niece, Savannah; . Phil Hunt, MD, Charlyne Cooper; my in-laws, Rebecca and Malcolm Fox.

Roberto Aguilar, DVM, senior veterinarian, and Sarah Burnette, public-relations director, at the Audubon Zoo in New Orleans, Louisiana, kindly gave me a detailed behind-the-scenes tour of the zoo. Dr Bob and Sarah answered even my clumsiest questions with grace and humor. The Audubon Zoo is one of the jewels of the South, and I encourage you to visit it the next time you're in New Orleans.

Jennifer Wolf-Corrigan, Martha Ware, Joanna Dear, Jo Shakespeare-Peters, and Sarah von Schmidt provided welcome opinions regarding the London settings.

Marcy Garriott, director of *Split Decision* and president of the Austin Film Society, patiently answered my questions about the craft and practice of filmmaking.

Christine Wiltz was a generous guide to New Orleans. Elaine Viets kindly drove me around Miami and Fort Lauderdale. Jonathon King pointed me to the perfect location for the Everglades scenes. They are all terrific writers, buy their books.

As always, my deepest appreciation goes to my wife, Leslie, and my sons, Charles and William, for their encouragement and support.